Praise for Leann Sweeney's Yellow Rose Mysteries

"As Texas as a Dr Pepper–swigging armadillo at the Alamo. A rip-roaring read!"
—Carolyn Hart, author of *Death of the Party*

"*Shoot from the Lip* is full of emotions! Anger, sadness, fear, happiness, laughter, joy, and tears . . . they are all there, and you will feel them along with the characters in this book!" —Amanda Shafer, Armchair Interviews

"I adore this series." —Roundtable Reviews

"A welcome new voice in mystery fiction."
—Jeff Abbott, bestselling author of *Panic*

"A dandy debut . . . will leave mystery fans eager to read more about Abby Rose."
—Bill Crider, author of *A Mammoth Murder*

"*Pick Your Poison* goes down sweet."
—Rick Riordan, Edgar® Award–winning author of *The Sea of Monsters*

"A witty, down-home Texas mystery . . . [a] fine tale."
—*Midwest Book Review*

PUSHING UP BLUEBONNETS

A YELLOW ROSE MYSTERY

Leann Sweeney

AN OBSIDIAN MYSTERY

OBSIDIAN
Published by New American Library, a division of
Penguin Group (USA) Inc., 375 Hudson Street,
New York, New York 10014, USA
Penguin Group (Canada), 90 Eglinton Avenue East, Suite 700, Toronto,
Ontario M4P 2Y3, Canada (a division of Pearson Penguin Canada Inc.)
Penguin Books Ltd., 80 Strand, London WC2R 0RL, England
Penguin Ireland, 25 St. Stephen's Green, Dublin 2,
Ireland (a division of Penguin Books Ltd.)
Penguin Group (Australia), 250 Camberwell Road, Camberwell, Victoria 3124,
Australia (a division of Pearson Australia Group Pty. Ltd.)
Penguin Books India Pvt. Ltd., 11 Community Centre, Panchsheel Park,
New Delhi - 110 017, India
Penguin Group (NZ), 67 Apollo Drive, Rosedale, North Shore 0632,
New Zealand (a division of Pearson New Zealand Ltd.)
Penguin Books (South Africa) (Pty.) Ltd., 24 Sturdee Avenue,
Rosebank, Johannesburg 2196, South Africa

Penguin Books Ltd., Registered Offices:
80 Strand, London WC2R 0RL, England

First published by Obsidian, an imprint of New American Library,
a division of Penguin Group (USA) Inc.

First Printing, January 2008
10 9 8 7 6 5 4 3 2 1

Copyright © Leann Sweeney, 2008
All rights reserved

The Edgar® name is a registered service mark of the Mystery Writers of
America, Inc.

OBSIDIAN and logo are trademarks of Penguin Group (USA) Inc.

Printed in the United States of America

DEDICATION

This book is for my wonderful writing group: Amy, Bob, Charlie, Heather, Kay, and Laura, as well as for surrogate members Susie and Isabella. Thank you for being who you are individually and for what we have as a group. I am forever grateful.

ACKNOWLEDGMENTS

I would like to thank my husband, Mike, for supporting me through this part of my life called a writing career. The challenges have been many, but he is always there for me. My writing group is amazing and I never could have written this book without their insights and encouragement. A huge thank-you also goes to Officer Sheri Rowe of the HPD Crime Scene Unit and Bart Nabors, HPD Homicide investigator. Every question I posed was answered thoroughly and completely. I learned so much. Also, a special thank-you to Sue Klein for sharing her knowledge of Glenwood Cemetery. I also owe much gratitude to my wonderful agent, Carol Mann, and to Will Sherlin, as well as Hilary Dowling and my fabulous editor, Claire Zion.

1

My daddy used to say there's news and then there's sit-down news. When I received the call from a police officer named Cooper Boyd asking me to help him identify a car-wreck victim, I was thankful to be already seated in the big leather chair in my home office.

"Oh my God," I said. "Is it Kate? Or Jeff? Or—"

"Ma'am, the victim is female. Who is Kate and when did you see her or speak to her last?"

My heart was racing now. "Kate Rose is my twin sister. She has dark brown hair and brown eyes. She works in the Texas Medical Center and I talked to her before she—oh God. What happened?"

"Take a deep breath. The victim has blond hair and the incident occurred in Montgomery County last night. Obviously this woman is not your sister."

"That's good. That's so good." Now that my thoughts were no longer focused on worst-case scenarios, I noticed Boyd's voice sounded like he'd gargled with axle grease this morning.

"This wasn't exactly an accident," he said. "I've come here to Houston from Pineview, where I'm the police chief. The victim was life-flighted to Ben Taub General around midnight. She's in a coma."

"Will she pull through?" My pulse slowed a little, but the coffee I'd just finished was still sloshing around after being stirred by panic.

"Doctors aren't saying much," he answered.

"You said Pineview? I've never heard of it."

"Small town, northwest Montgomery County. You

know anyone up that way? A client? A relative? A friend?"

The word *client* caught my attention. "You must know more about me than my name. Why do you think I can help you identify this person?"

"The victim had your business card in her possession, ma'am. Yellow Rose Investigations, right? And adoption reunion is your specialty?"

"Yes," I said.

"See, her having your card is one of the two things we know about her."

"And the other?" I asked.

"Someone wanted her dead."

I closed my eyes and pictured a young woman tangled in the wreckage of an automobile. It didn't help the swirling in my gut. "And she had *my* card?"

"Yes, Ms. Rose."

"Okay, I'm worried she might be one of my former clients, even though I'm pretty sure I've never done a search for anyone up that way. But she could have just moved there or—"

"Listen, I need your help now," he said. "This young woman probably has relatives who should know she's in critical condition. Think you could meet me in the hospital lobby?"

"I—yes. Sure. Which hospital did you say?"

"Ben Taub."

At least she was in good hands. Ben Taub has one of the best trauma centers in the country. "I can be there in fifteen minutes. How will I know you?"

"I'm in uniform. Brown and gold." He disconnected without a good-bye.

Since it was August and hotter than hell's door handle, I was dressed in shorts and a tank top. I decided that wasn't suitable hospital attire and hurried upstairs with my calico cat, Diva, on my heels. I quickly changed into lightweight cropped pants, a sleeveless cotton blouse and summer clogs.

"What the heck do you think this whole identify-the-coma-patient thing is about?" I asked Diva as I applied lipstick. No time for any other makeup to cover my usual crop of summer freckles, the ones that had appeared despite the gallon of sunscreen I'd gone through since May.

Diva answered my question with several insightful meows. Too bad the cat whisperer wasn't around to interpret her answer.

As I stepped outside and went through the back gate to the driveway, I wondered if I'd even had a letter from anyone from Pineview. I sure couldn't remember, but then there were times when I couldn't even remember the Alamo.

Using the remote on my key chain, I turned off the car alarm on my new silver Camry. I'd had a super-duper special-order car alarm installed that beeped a reminder to engage it whenever I parked. No one got near my car without that thing making enough noise to embarrass thunder. I'd had a little trouble on a case last year with a very bad man sticking GPS devices under my bumper every time I wasn't looking. That would *never* happen again.

Five for Fighting's latest CD started playing once I started the ignition. "The Riddle" was currently my favorite song. The drive took only ten minutes and that meant I had five minutes to find a parking place in the Medical Center complex—a definite challenge. But since it was nearly noon, most of the morning clinic appointments were over and I located a spot pretty fast. Then I walked the long path to the hospital.

The air-conditioning made the small, stark lobby almost as cold as my ex-husband's heart. I quickly spotted Cooper Boyd thanks to his brown uniform. He looked to be in his midforties with dark, gloomy eyes. He'd be a pretty darn good-looking guy without the gloom. I approached him and we shook hands.

"Abby Rose," I said.

"Thank you for coming." Boyd reached into his pocket and pulled out a folded sheet of paper and handed it to me. "This is a copy of what we found under the woman's front seat. We sent the actual card for fingerprinting."

My business card, all right—front and back. Someone had scrawled the words "adoption searcher" and "Do this today" on the back. The card appeared smudged and wrinkled, and this condition made the copy a poor one.

I looked up at Boyd, who must have been at least six feet tall. "I could use more details," I said. "Maybe I did have contact with this person in the last few years. Otherwise, how did she get my card?"

"For one thing, a passenger could have dropped it, but speculation is a waste of time at this point. What kind of details do you need?" His drawl had to be East Texas. Very pronounced.

"You're sure this was a murder attempt?" I asked.

From the look on his face, I wished I would have eaten those words before they'd tumbled out. I'd just questioned a lawman's conclusions. You don't do that. Jeff, my boyfriend, is HPD Homicide and I know better.

Boyd's right jaw muscle tensed. "Yes, ma'am, I'm certain. Even the assailant didn't much mind if we figured that out. Now, can we go upstairs and have a look at the victim? Then you can be on your way."

"I am so sorry. I didn't mean to question your assessment. My daddy always said I had a tongue like a bell clapper."

He smiled briefly and I breathed an inward sigh of relief. Conflict with strangers is not my favorite pastime.

"No offense taken," he said.

"Please call me Abby, by the way."

"And I'd prefer Cooper." We began the short walk to the elevators. "*Chief* seems like a title I don't deserve. Like I should be a genius and God knows I'm not. I've only been doing this job for a year."

"What did you do before?" We entered an empty elevator and Cooper punched the button for the fourth floor.

"FBI. But not anymore."

I wonder why, I thought. "And now you work in a small town," I said.

"Very small." He crossed his hands in front of him and stared up at the indicator lights.

Once we hit the fourth floor and walked out of the elevator, he said, "This young woman was found on a county road, her car wrapped around a tree. Didn't take a mechanic to figure out her air bags had been removed. That's why she suffered the head injury."

I felt a small shiver unrelated to the AC. "And she had my card, but no purse and no insurance information?"

"That's right. They could have been stolen from the wreck immediately after she crashed or maybe she never had them with her in the first place."

"What about the vehicle identification number? Couldn't you track the car ownership that way?" I asked.

"Deliberately destroyed. Even the confidential VIN had been sanded down."

"There's more than one?"

"On this model, there were three—dash, door and the confidential one. Newer models than what she was driving also have VINs etched into the windshield. That's tough to tamper with, but I didn't get lucky there."

"And her thumbprint didn't come up when you ran it by DPS?"

He glanced my way, studying me with what I thought might be amusement. "I'm used to asking the questions, not answering them. We didn't get a match or I wouldn't be here."

"Duh. I knew that." Why couldn't I stop putting my mouth in motion before my mind was in gear?

We followed the signs to the neuro ICU and I explained to Cooper how I work, that many people contact me and that most of them can do their own searching with only a few pointers from the "tip sheets" I send out on how to locate lost relatives. I always send my card when I answer inquiries.

"Because I get far more letters than I could ever handle in person, I take on the more difficult cases—even though I'd be glad to work every case if I had a clone or two. It's sort of a mission for me."

"A mission, huh? I wondered why someone as rich as you—I do my homework, by the way—ran a PI business."

He obviously knew Daddy left my sister and me buckets of money and a successful software company. *What else does he know?* I wondered. That our own adoption had been illegal, that discovering this changed my life forever and led me down an unusual path as an adoption PI?

"Anyway," he went on, "that means you don't see many clients in person." He sounded disappointed.

"I do as many cases as I can. And that could mean your mystery woman *was* one of my clients. Or related to one of my clients. Or a friend of a friend. Believe me, I meet plenty of relatives during the reunions."

"Good. There's still hope you can ID her, then. Let me warn you, she's banged up—her face is swollen. I hope you might recognize her anyway because finding out who attempted to kill her is pretty difficult when I don't know who she is."

"Tell me the truth, Cooper. Is she . . . going to die?"

"Don't know. They're keeping her knocked out to let her brain calm down. Swelling, they say." He stared straight ahead, his jaw tight again. "She had her whole life ahead of her and who knows what she'll face if she ever wakes up?"

"Any possibility she did this to herself? Maybe she was depressed."

"Females usually take pills or slice their veins open. And she wouldn't need to cut the brake line to drive into a live oak. Did I tell you the brake line was cut? Anyway, she could speed up to a hundred and slam right into that tree on her own if she wanted to die."

I nodded my agreement, noting his tone had hardened. We walked in silence until we reached the waiting area for the neuro ICU, which was across the hall from the forbidding doors that would allow us in. Boyd told me to have a seat and he'd arrange for us to visit her.

When he came back to get me, he said, "We've got five minutes."

We were admitted into the ICU and Boyd led me to the mystery woman's room. She was covered with a white thermal blanket and was so tiny she seemed lost in the small space crowded with medical machinery, all of the equipment either beeping or blinking. An IV dripped slowly into tubing that fed her bruised arm. But that wasn't all that was bruised.

Her thick dark lashes rested against the purple crescents under her eyes. She had a battered forehead, a split lip and stitches above the largest lump on her forehead. Any skin not bruised was as pale as the sheets.

"Heck fire," I whispered. I blinked several times, wondering how anyone would recognize this young woman, even someone who knew her. Seemed a miracle to me that she wasn't already pushing up bluebonnets.

I'd stopped a few feet into the room, but Boyd urged me toward the bed with a gentle hand on my back. "Get closer. Try to picture her without all the damage."

"Kinda hard, Cooper, but I'll give it a try."

When I came up beside her, I tilted my head, hoping to get a feel for a profile, maybe. That helped a little. Then I squinted, mentally thinning her face. That seemed to work, too. I could envision the person who might lie beneath the injuries. A sweet face, late teens, early twenties maybe.

"Sorry. I don't think I know her," I finally said.

"You're not sure, though?" Boyd said.

"Like you said, her face is pretty messed up. Maybe I could come back in a few days? Have another look?"

This wasn't what Boyd wanted to hear. "See, I don't know if *I* can come back. There's only four officers in Pineview."

"I can come by myself." I smiled and tried to sound encouraging. "I sincerely want to help. If I could have that copy of my card, I'll enhance it on my PC. I get plenty of letters and maybe I could match the handwriting."

He pulled the paper from his pocket and handed it to me. "Anything's worth a try, I guess." But *glum* was the only word to describe Cooper Boyd.

"Can I buy you lunch? The cafeteria in the basement here isn't half bad."

"I don't think—"

"Come on." I tugged his arm, anxious to escape the sleeping Jane Doe. I felt helpless seeing her so still, so banged up and with no family to hold her hand. I understood why Boyd was bummed out. "You need a decent meal before you head back to Pineview."

We took the elevator down, both of us silent. I was thinking how I'd hate to be comatose with no one there to cheer me on, sing to me or talk to me and make me want to fight for my life. Maybe that's what Cooper Boyd was thinking, too.

Once in the cafeteria I chose the comfort of macaroni and cheese—with a salad to cancel out the fat and carbs.

Boyd had a sandwich piled high with turkey and lettuce on whole-grain bread with no mayo. I should introduce him to Kate. Maybe they could share a soy smoothie or a black-bean burger. I glanced at Boyd's ring finger, making sure I hadn't seen a wedding band. Yup. My brain had registered correctly. Not that Kate needed to date another older man. She'd been there, done that, and it had been a disaster. And besides, she'd apparently given up dating altogether thanks to him. Every woman I know has had some jerk mess with her head, but this particular male mistake had taken a big toll.

"You prefer small-town police work over the FBI?" I asked. I needed to slow down on the mac and cheese. I was upset after what I'd seen upstairs and emotional eating always seems to add twice as many inches to my thighs. Which means twice as long a workout to remove those inches.

"They're very different. The FBI was my dream job and I learned a lot. But that's over now."

There was a story here, one he wasn't about to share with a stranger. This was a scarred man and I sure did wonder why.

2

A half hour later, I returned to my home in the West University area, anxious to scan the poor copy of my card so I could enhance and enlarge the writing, but unfortunately my aunt Caroline's Cadillac pulled into my driveway right behind me. Great. What did *she* want?

But she got right to the point. "We need to talk about your sister, Abigail," she said as she got out of her car. Then she marched past me and opened the back gate. "You need to keep this gate locked. I hope you haven't left the house unlocked, too."

I silently counted to ten and smiled. "Nice you could drop by."

I unlocked the back door, which prompted, "At least you have *some* sense" from my aunt. We walked through the mudroom and into the kitchen.

"Where have you been, by the way?" She dropped her latest Prada handbag on the oak kitchen table. "I drove by at least five times."

"Out on business, if that's okay with you." It wasn't really business. I had no client, but she didn't need to know that.

"Oh. You mean snooping around and getting yourself in trouble again. I wondered if you'd perhaps met Katherine for lunch."

"Sorry, no. And 'snooping around,' as you call it, happens to be my job. Can I get you something to drink?" I was getting better at letting her remarks pass without too much sarcasm. Besides, I was wondering if she was sick. I'd noticed that sweat had beaded along her snowy hairline, which was puzzling. She'd been in her very air-conditioned luxury car, after all.

Aunt Caroline sat in one of the kitchen chairs. "Water, please. Lime if you have it."

"I do. It's Corona season and Jeff likes lime in his beer."

As I cut up a lime, Aunt Caroline said, "He's still hanging around, is he? How's he coping with the sister—the one who's, well, *you know*."

"The one who has Down syndrome? Doris is a delight. Matter of fact, she and Jeff are coming for dinner tonight." I plopped lime wedges into two glasses of ice water and brought them to the table.

"You're cooking? My word, the earth has tilted a bit more on its axis." She gulped greedily at the water.

I lifted my chin. "Yes, I am cooking. I *do* know how." Actually we were ordering pizza and watching one of Doris's favorite DVDs, *Finding Nemo*. Movies and pizza had become our Friday night ritual. Jeff didn't make it half the time because of his job, but Doris's caretaker, Loreen, would sometimes join us.

"You *should* know how to cook," Aunt Caroline said. "Chef Ramone cost us a pretty penny for those lessons. But as I recall, he said you'd rather play with the food than learn the basics of preparation."

"I was twelve, Aunt Caroline. I still played with my G.I. Joes, too. I wasn't the only one in the family who enjoyed boy toys."

Damn. Sarcastic relapse. I hate when that happens.

Aunt Caroline's face became infused with color. She'd given up face-lifts for injections from her dermatologist—all kinds of procedures to smooth the wrinkles she'd earned after seventy-plus years on earth. But they only made her look like a doll with a plastic face and I was surprised there was actually a blood supply to the surface.

"How rude, Abigail," she said. "You know my dalliances ended a long time ago."

"Try about two years ago. Anyway, you came to talk about Kate?"

"Yes. I went over to her house last night and found her in her pajamas. She'd been reading a book. It was only eight o'clock and she looked exhausted and, well, depressed. I am very concerned about her. A thirty-one-year-old woman should not be holed up like a nun."

I had to agree with my aunt. I was worried, too. But the last thing Kate needed was Aunt Caroline sticking her nose in this. "Give her time to heal," I said.

"She's had enough time. It's been ten months since that horrible man fooled her into believing he cared for her. She's refused every date I've tried to set up for her—close to forty of them. Now it's your turn. Do you know anyone suitable? He has to have money, of course. We don't want someone taking advantage of her. You two are blessed with wealth, but it does make you vulnerable to predators, so—"

"I am not setting her up with anyone. She'll move forward when she's ready." I *so* wanted to believe that, but I honestly wasn't sure. My sister had changed—her smile now not as spontaneous, her dark eyes lacking the spark I'd once thought would always be there.

"But don't you see, Abigail? Katherine needs—"

"Aunt Caroline," I interrupted. I had to get her off this subject. "Remember when you helped me organize files a while back?"

Her eyes brightened. "Do you need help again? Silly question. Of course you do. Your organizational skills are . . . well, anyway. I'd be glad to assist."

"It's not filing, actually." Finding out who was lying in that hospital bed was more important than allowing Aunt Caroline to meddle in Kate's business through me.

"I'm very good with any office task." She stood and rubbed her hands together. "Let's get started."

I took a deep breath and removed the folded paper from my pants pocket. "Hope you're wearing those bifocal contact lenses. You'll need good eyes for this job."

I explained about the unidentified woman and how I hoped I could match the handwriting on the card to some letter I might have received from a prospective client.

"Since you didn't recognize her when you saw her," Aunt Caroline said, "this could be a waste of time."

"You don't have to help if—"

"Are you being facetious? I can't think of a better way to waste time than solving a mystery like this. Wait until I tell the girls at the club."

I had to smile. The "girls" ranged in age from seventy to ninety. "Let's get started, then."

I hadn't spent more than two hours alone with my aunt in years—mostly because being with her is like wearing shoes that hurt—but we had a focus other than my life or Kate's, so I hoped I could tolerate her.

I'd printed a thousand business cards when I started up my agency, and gave the first hundred to Angel Molina, my mentor, who had a PI business of his own. He sent me my first few cases and still called me when he had a potential client for me. I'd handed out dozens of cards when I was meeting clients or investigating someone's past. And I'd also sent them attached to every letter I answered along with my tip sheets. Only about two hundred cards remained. That meant I could have as many as six hundred letters in the file boxes in my office.

Matching a snippet of handwriting on a business card to the writing in one of those letters seemed about as likely to happen as a pig laying eggs, especially since half were probably printed on a computer and bore only signatures. But I'd promised Cooper Boyd I'd do what I could to help identify his mystery woman.

I went to my office and scanned and enhanced the xeroxed card, and printed out one copy for Aunt Caroline and one for me. Then I took two file boxes with my saved correspondence into the kitchen.

"Get comfortable. This will take some time," I said.

But she'd already brought in a throw cushion from the living room and tucked it between her back and the chair.

She maintained slow-paced but intense interest in those letters and I asked her to speed up more than once. This wasn't story time at the library, though some of those letters did read like Shakespearean tragedies. Adoption is usually a wonderful thing and some of my cases have produced reunions that turned out to be dreams come true. But not everyone gets what they expect when they search for secrets in their past.

In the three hours that followed, Aunt Caroline and

I compared that small sample of handwriting over and over. I kept glancing her way wondering if this task was making her fatigued. Her doctored skin held up, but her shoulders slumped and she had to use lens solution several times. Plus she drank enough water to float the battleship *Texas* and that meant a hundred trips to the bathroom.

"This seems like an exercise in futility," I finally said. I was getting even more worried about her. We were almost done and Jeff and I could finish this tonight after Doris went to bed. Yes, there was a much-anticipated sleepover planned. Besides, I didn't want Aunt Caroline asking me when I would need to start "cooking" for the expected company.

"We're not quitting now, Abigail. It's only four o'clock. We can get the rest done in the next hour."

"But—"

"I have twelve letters in my 'maybe pile.' How many in yours?" she said.

"Only six."

"Let's plow through the rest and then revisit those remaining letters," she said.

There was no arguing with Aunt Caroline—not ever. But even *I* was getting tired. "How about chocolate to get us through this, then?"

She tilted her head and squirted more lens solution in her eyes. "Chocolate sounds wonderful."

Two Ghirardelli dark bars later, Aunt Caroline and I were revived. She was downright giddy with energy.

We started in again and I could understand why fingerprint experts used to be able to spot a matching print just by looking at it. It's because they'd compared that print over and over with hundreds of samples.

The same thing happened to me when I picked up my second letter after our chocolate fix. I let out a "Yes, ma'am," and stood up with my arms raised, like a football fan whose team had scored the winning touchdown as the clock ran down.

"You found it?" Aunt Caroline said. "Let me see."

She started to grab for the letter, but I stepped away from her outstretched hand. "There could be fingerprints on this. Chief Boyd might be able to match them to the mystery woman." I walked to the kitchen drawer where I keep the Ziploc bags. Using my thumb and index finger, I carefully put the letter in a bag and walked back to the table.

"I'll read it to you," I said.

But this time, she was able to snatch the bagged letter before I could blink. She should consider pickpocket school, I decided.

She read:

Dear Ms. Rose,

I learned about you from a Houston TV morning show. I am adopted and would like to find my birth family. If you could help me, I would very much appreciate it. Please let me know what you charge and use the enclosed stamped envelope for your answer.

Yours truly,
JoLynn Richter

"May I please have that back? I need to call Chief Boyd."

But Aunt Caroline was squinting, her gaze traveling between the letter and the copy of my business card. Then she leaned back. "I think this is the same handwriting."

I wanted to say, "Um, yeah, 'cause it's as plain as the hand on the end of your arm," but I did appreciate her help and instead said, "Glad you agree. Now, I've got to phone Chief Boyd and then start dinner. Can I get you anything before you go?"

Aunt Caroline started to rise and I could tell she was a little hurt that I seemed to be kicking her out—which I sort of was.

But when her eyes rolled back and she crumbled to the floor, I quickly realized her expression had nothing to do with hurt feelings.

3

Terrified, I hurried over and knelt beside my aunt, fearing she'd had a heart attack. That's how my daddy—her brother—had died. Just keeled over and never took another breath. But when my shaking hand felt for a pulse, I discovered her heart was pumping hard and steady.

Resting a hand on her cheek, I said her name, then got close to her face to make sure she was breathing. She smelled like she'd been chewing Juicy Fruit gum all day and that's when I knew what was wrong. I *do* occasionally read my *Prevention* magazines—Kate had given me a subscription as a Christmas gift.

I leaned back on my heels and whispered, "You're a diabetic, Aunt Caroline."

She was starting to come around and I wasn't about to let her run this rodeo. I pulled my cell from my pocket and called 911 before she fully opened her eyes. By the time the paramedics took her away, she was still almost as quiet as a sparrow in a hawk's nest, not hollering for them to leave her alone like I would have expected. She didn't even seem to know where she was. That meant she was definitely sick and I was definitely feeling guilty about that giant chocolate bar she'd eaten right before she passed out.

I'd given this information to the paramedics, mentioned the fatigue and the hundred drinks of water and told them I'd be at Methodist Hospital as soon as I made some phone calls. No "cooking" tonight. Heck, now I even felt guilty about lying to Aunt Caroline about that.

I called Kate first—she's a psychologist and was still

at her office in the Medical Center. I told her what happened. She was upset, wondering immediately why she hadn't picked up on the symptoms. She had a client who was diabetic, after all. I decided we both needed to shelve the guilt trip and said I'd meet her at Methodist Hospital. Jeff was next on my call list, but he wasn't available, as usual, so I left a message. I was about to call Loreen, Doris's caretaker, when someone knocked on the door. I checked the security monitor and saw Loreen and Doris standing on the stoop holding hands.

I opened the door and they stepped in out of the heat. After Doris gave me a big hug, she hurried off to find Diva. Meanwhile, I told Loreen what had happened.

I said, "I have to go to the hospital, but if you could please stay here with Doris, order pizza and—"

"I'm so sorry, Abby, but I can't. You know that guy I was telling you about? The one I met at the post office?"

"Yes—Wyatt, right?"

"He's taking me out dancing tonight. That's why I brought Doris a little early. I need time to go home and get ready." She smiled, unable to hide her excitement. "Any other time, but—"

"Oh, I understand. That's great about Wyatt." I was happy for Loreen. Though she'd had a rough life as a street kid, she was a quality human being who loved Doris as much as we did. But why did the first date since I'd known Loreen have to be tonight?

"I'm leaving," Loreen called, jingling her car keys.

Doris came pounding from the direction of the kitchen, Diva clutched to her chest. When she arrived back in the foyer, she dropped the cat and wrapped her arms around Loreen, squeezing her as hard as she'd probably squeezed Diva.

The cat was wise enough to race up the stairs while Doris wasn't looking.

After Loreen left, I said, "Aunt Caroline—you remember her, right?"

Doris pouted. "The lady with the white hair. She doesn't like me."

"Who couldn't like you?" I smiled and placed my palm on Doris's cheek. "Anyway," I went on, "Aunt

Caroline's very sick in the hospital. Think maybe you and I could visit her?"

Doris's chubby cheek grew warm under my fingers. "Do I have to? Because when Linda went to the hospital, she never came back. I don't want us to never come back, Abby."

Linda had been the caretaker in Seattle, the one whose death precipitated the move that brought Doris to Houston. I said, "You and I aren't sick. We'll just be visiting."

She shook her head, crossed her arms over her chest. "Uh-uh. I don't want to. You said we'd watch Nemo and Dory. Dory's name is almost like mine and I like her a lot more than I like visiting places."

I'd learned that though Doris was sweet and genuine most of the time, she could also be as willful as a two-year-old. Kate would simply have to go to the hospital alone until Jeff arrived to stay with his sister.

After I ordered a pepperoni pizza and Cinnamon Stix, and Doris started the *Finding Nemo* DVD, I stepped out of the living room and called Kate to explain the situation.

"No problem, Abby. They won't let me see Aunt Caroline anyway. She's having all kinds of tests."

"You're at Methodist already?" I said.

"It's not like I had far to go," she answered.

Duh. Kate probably walked to the hospital. "Sorry, I'm not firing on all cylinders after the day I've had. I promise I'll be there as soon as I can."

"I know you will," she said, and hung up.

I closed my phone and shook my head. She sounded sad. And probably not only because of Aunt Caroline's illness. Kate's clients depended on her for answers and wisdom, and my guess was that she was putting up a good front, but that she knew it was a front—and that made her feel like a fraud. I know how her mind works.

"When's Jeffy coming?" Doris called.

I went back to the living room and sat on the chenille sofa. Doris was lying on the floor, belly down, chin supported by her fists. She paused the DVD and rolled onto her back and sat up.

"I'm not sure," I said.

"When Jeffy gets here, you stay. We can do a puzzle."

"Sorry, sweetie. I have to see my aunt. She's sick."

Doris's lower lip quivered and a big, fat tear rolled down one cheek. "Abby, I don't want you to die."

I sat next to her on the floor. This time Doris received the hug rather than giving one out. "I won't die. I promise."

She pulled away and I grabbed a tissue box from a corner table and offered it to her.

She blew her nose. "I miss Mom and Dad and Linda."

"I know. I miss my daddy, too."

"You loved your daddy, huh? You talk about him a lot."

I willed back tears. "I sure did love him."

"He taught you good stuff. He taught you to shoot. Jeffy won't let me touch his gun. Will you teach me to shoot, Abby?"

I tried not to look horrified. "No, Doris. Jeff wouldn't want that and neither do I."

"But why? Then I can help you and Jeffy because Loreen says your jobs are scary."

"We won't leave you, Doris. I promise."

She smiled. "You promise?"

"I swear."

That seemed to satisfy her and she returned to her movie. Jeff didn't arrive until the third replay of *Finding Nemo*, which I was ready to retitle *Finding Jeffy*. I'd called him several times without luck—even tried Travis Center, where Homicide Division is housed on the sixth floor, but the officer I spoke with said he was out in the field.

Finally I heard his key in the back door and Doris and I went to meet him in the kitchen. Time for Doris to dole out another bear hug.

He said, "How are my two best girls?" He was chewing Big Red and that meant he probably hadn't had the best day on the job.

"We're—"

But Doris interrupted me. "The mean lady with the white hair is gonna die and Abby's sad."

"No one is going to die, Doris." My patience was running thin. Doris had clung to me all night, unable to completely let go of her fear despite our talk. It seemed like every five minutes she paused the DVD to get my reassurance that I wouldn't leave her.

Jeff ran a hand through his short blond hair and took the Big Red pack from his pocket. But when he saw Doris eyeing the gum, he returned it without taking out a stick. He had recently spent a small fortune on dental work for his sister. Unfortunately the late Linda had allowed Doris to drink Coke and eat candy all day.

"Doris, let Abby explain, okay?" he said.

"Okay. We saved pizza for you," she said before turning abruptly and returning to her movie.

"Why didn't you call me back?" I said.

Jeff reached in his pants pocket and took out his cell. "Dead. Won't recharge. Won't do anything. I used a department phone all day. I should have called and given you the number. Now, what is Doris talking about?"

"Aunt Caroline collapsed. She's at Methodist and I promised Kate I'd join her as soon as you came." I explained what happened and how Loreen couldn't stay tonight.

"Wow. Sorry, hon." He pulled me to him. "We're working a complicated case and I couldn't leave the scene."

I stood on tiptoe and kissed him. "You're forgiven. But I really have to go. Last time I checked in with Kate, Aunt Caroline was finishing up her tests and being admitted. She should be in her hospital room by now."

"Then get going." Jeff opened the trash compactor and spit out his gum before opening the pizza box.

I whispered, "Doris is pretty freaked out. She thinks if I go visit Aunt Caroline, I'll never leave the hospital alive."

"Thanks for the heads-up. I'll deal with her."

I grabbed my keys from the hook by the door and brushed his lips with mine before I left. I didn't say good-bye to Doris. She and I would both be better off without further discussion concerning the danger of hospitals.

Fifteen minutes later, I was looking for a parking spot

close to Methodist. I realized I'd been on a similar hunt in the Medical Center earlier today—at Cooper Boyd's request. "Cooper. Oh no." I thunked my forehead with my palm before maneuvering into an angled spot on about the hundredth floor of the garage. I'd forgotten to call him with the JoLynn Richter information. I waited until I was off the elevator and walking toward the hospital before I dialed his number from the business card he'd given me.

He answered before the phone rang even once. "Yes." One word as intense as the man himself.

"Sorry I didn't call earlier, but we had an emergency and then I had to—"

"You got something?" he said. I could hear music in the background.

Blues, maybe? That would be about right. "I have a phone number and you'll probably want to get a professional handwriting expert to check this letter I matched to the scrawl on the card."

"Like we got a dozen graphologists around here. What's the name and address?" He cleared his throat. Maybe he had that gravel voice because of a cold or something.

"JoLynn Richter, but I must have sent her the card and my tip sheets without recording her address—she sent a self-addressed envelope. Once I send the card, folks usually call me, so I don't keep track of addresses."

A long silence followed. "Richter? You're sure?"

"If I'm not, there isn't a white tooth in Hollywood," I said.

"I'll be damned."

4

"Do you know JoLynn Richter?" I said. If so, why hadn't he recognized her in the hospital?

"I'm familiar with the family name, but I've never heard of her. Listen, I have to get out to the Richter place, see if they have a relative who's missing. Thanks."

He hung up, leaving me staring at the phone and thinking I might never hear from him again. That bothered me. I felt connected to JoLynn Richter since she'd once asked for my help, and I wanted to know more about why she'd written to me. *Not your case, Abby,* a voice in my head said. But it *seemed* to be my case, even though no one had hired me. I wanted—no, *needed*—to know why someone had wanted her dead.

I rode the elevator up to Aunt Caroline's floor, switching my thoughts to her. She was asleep when I walked in—it was past ten p.m.—and Kate was curled up in an armchair reading a magazine. She looked up and put a finger to her lips.

I tiptoed over to the bed. Aunt Caroline had on her own lavender nightgown. Five containers of various skin creams sat on the bedside table and her hospital pillow was encased in pink satin. Aunt Caroline must have kept Kate busy running back and forth to her house for things she simply *had* to have—which meant she was in better shape than when she'd left my house in an ambulance.

Kate stood and motioned toward the door.

Once we were in the hallway, she whispered, "Her blood sugar has dropped to around three hundred, thanks to the insulin. She is a diabetic."

"That's what I figured. Three hundred is still high,

right? During my last physical, mine was about ninety and the doc said that's normal."

"Considering it was over five hundred when she got here, I'd say she's made plenty of progress," Kate said.

I gasped. "No way."

Kate shushed me. "Keep your voice down. Patients are sleeping."

But one of them wasn't sleeping anymore, because Aunt Caroline called, "Abigail? Is that you?"

We both reentered her room.

I said, "Sorry I couldn't get here earlier, but—"

"Katherine took good care of me." She smiled at Kate as if to say at least one of her nieces cared.

"Since she's taken the first shift," I said, "I'll stay with you tonight."

"That's ridiculous. If you think I'm dying, you're sorely mistaken, Abigail. Both of you will go home and let me alone to bother the nurses all night. That's what they get paid for."

I said, "But Aunt Caroline, I—"

"Before you go, Abby, I need to know if you called the police with that girl's name. She needs to be identified in a timely manner."

"Of course I called." Maybe not in a timely manner, but I didn't share that piece of information.

"Have her people arrived, then? And if so, do they have any idea who might have done this to her?"

Kate rescued me by saying, "You and Abby can catch up on—what's the woman's name?"

"JoLynn Richter," I answered.

"Tomorrow," Kate said firmly.

"You sure you don't want me to stay?" I said to my aunt.

"No. Both of you need your sleep. Especially Abigail, since she has a new case to solve."

Funny how "snooping" now seemed acceptable, probably because she'd helped me all afternoon. "This *isn't* my case," I said. But I was protesting too emphatically.

"Abigail, if your daddy were here, he'd say you must think I don't have as much sense as God gave a sack of flour. This surely *is* your case." She offered her best semblance of a smile, considering her cosmetic limitations.

I hated when she was right. "If the chief asks, I'll be more than happy to help."

"Don't I know that," Aunt Caroline said. "Now, go home and leave me to harass the night staff."

So we left and once we were in the elevator, Kate said, "Is she right? Do you have a new case?"

"You know Aunt Caroline. If the truth isn't available, she makes up her own version." But like my aunt, Kate can read me like a label on a can of soup at Whole Foods Market—her home away from home.

"She *is* right," Kate said. "I'd like to be involved, if that's okay. I thought I'd be better off not consulting on your cases, since you've proven to be far braver than me. But I've missed the work. Dangerous or not, I want things back the way they were." Kate smiled and I saw the first real light in her eyes in almost a year.

"Good, because I always need your help. But be warned, I'm prying into a situation without an invitation. Ought to be interesting." I went on to tell her about Cooper's phone call and what I'd discovered with Aunt Caroline's help.

"Abby, they'd be foolish not to want you working on this."

I put my arm around Kate and squeezed her to me. "Thanks." We stepped off the elevator and I said, "What about Aunt Caroline? From what little she said, she's not exactly understanding how serious her diagnosis is."

"She thinks if she cuts out chocolate and Mocha Frappuccinos, problem solved."

"I feel sorry for the dietitian who gets to teach her about her new diet and the nurse who gets to show her how to give herself an insulin shot. She'll be on insulin, right?"

"The doctor thinks she can go on oral medicine once she's stable. Now, when can I see JoLynn? That convention I went to in Atlanta had a few sessions on therapy with head-injury patients. I'm no expert, but I did pick up a few things."

"She's in a coma, Kate. I don't think she's ready for psychotherapeutic rehab."

"Just anxious to get started. I'd like to see what kind of shape she's in."

"Not pretty. You have anything planned for this weekend?" I asked.

"Oh, sure. A speed-dating session," Kate said sarcastically. "In other words, nothing besides laundry and taking care of Aunt Caroline."

"And you're sure you want to help?" I said.

"I'm ready as long as we don't have any role reversals—like you shrink my head while I find some dark alley where I can teach a bad guy a lesson with a Lady Smith and Wesson."

"It's just called a Lady Smith."

"Whatever. A gun is a gun and I don't like them," she said.

"There's a news flash. I'll meet you here tomorrow morning. We'll see Aunt Caroline first, then head over to Ben Taub."

"Sounds good," she said.

I pulled her to me and we hugged. "Thanks for doing ditzy-aunt duty."

"No problem. Are you parked in the garage next to the hospital?" she asked.

"Yeah, up in a hole in the ozone."

"I'm in my contract spot way in the other direction. Good night, Abby."

I found my way back to where I'd parked. The night was sticky hot and seemed to amplify the smells in the garage—the vomit, the discarded remnants of fast food, the oil leaks. No security around, or none that I'd noticed. I'm not usually bothered by being out late alone, but I felt jittery tonight. It had to do with JoLynn, of course. There are so many easier ways to murder someone than to mess with a car. Her killer wanted to make sure she knew there was nothing she could do since her brakes were gone; wanted her to know a terror like she'd probably never known before. This seemed like a rage crime to me. I've always had nightmares about dying in a car wreck, which is probably why this bothered me so much, why evil seemed to linger in the dank air. I felt relieved when I climbed behind the wheel and locked my doors.

I arrived back home to find Jeff asleep in the recliner. Doris must have gone upstairs to one of the two guest rooms, because she was nowhere to be seen. I walked quietly past him toward my office, thinking I'd see what I could discover about the Richter family before my hospital visit tomorrow.

But I wasn't halfway across the living room when I heard Jeff's sleepy voice. "How's your aunt, hon?"

I turned to him and smiled. "As feisty as ever and probably in denial she's diabetic. But she does look a whole lot better than when she left here on a stretcher. She was all confused then and it scared me."

"Diabetic, huh? How will that affect her lunches and dinners at the club? The few times we've gone there to eat with her she always has at least three glasses of wine and something chocolate for dessert."

"I have no idea how she'll manage. I only know I don't want to see her carted away by paramedics again."

Jeff got up. "How about wine for us? We're not diabetic—at least not yet."

"Sounds good to me," I answered.

We walked into the kitchen and while Jeff took an unopened bottle of chardonnay from the fridge, I gathered the letters that I'd left on the kitchen table and dumped them back into the file box without bothering to put them back in their correct folders. Maybe Aunt Caroline would take on that thankless task when she felt better.

As Jeff poured our wine, he said, "What were you doing with those files?"

"That's an interesting story," I said.

He walked over and handed me my glass, then picked up Cooper Boyd's copy of my business card. "Have anything to do with this?"

"Yes, Sergeant Kline, super detective." I reached for the manila envelope where I'd put JoLynn's letter, and then handed it to him. "Also has to do with this."

After he'd read the letter through its plastic protection, he looked at me quizzically. "I'm missing something. Want to share?"

"Most certainly." I took his hand and led him to the sofa.

We settled in, my legs draped over his lap, and I told him the whole story.

"Sounds like an interesting case," he said when I'd finished.

"No one's actually hired me, but—"

"You don't need to explain. You do what you have to do and no one had better get in your way. Now, put down that glass and come closer. I have a few things to share that have nothing to do with our jobs."

I crawled into Jeff's lap, ready to forget the stress of the 911 call I'd had to make earlier today.

5

The next morning, Jeff woke early and took Doris home while I went to my office computer to do a little research before Kate and I visited both hospitals. But searching for the name JoLynn Richter gave me no results in any database, not even the DMV. Either she was driving without a license or she was from out of state.

Then I tried to find a Pineview newspaper online to see if they'd run an article on the accident, but nothing there, either. A small piece had appeared in the *Houston Chronicle* yesterday morning reporting that an unidentified woman had been life-flighted to Houston after a crash in north Montgomery County, but that was it. I had one more option—a search for any other Richters in Montgomery County, hopefully leading me to information on the family Cooper had referred to.

Finally I was in business, and Diva must have sensed this because she jumped down from her perch on the windowsill and into my lap. I stroked her, excited by all the hits related to the Richters. Now I understood a little better why Cooper had reacted to the name the way he had. They seemed to be *the* prominent family in the area, even though they didn't live right in Pineview. Elliott Richter, a widower, owned a ranch about ten miles north of town. His daughter, Katarina, had died at age twenty and I immediately checked for obituaries on Richter's wife and daughter. I learned they were both buried in Glenwood Cemetery right here in Houston—a very famous old graveyard dating back to the nineteenth century. Then I found something that really caught my attention—an article from a Montgomery County newspaper with the title "Mysterious Katarina Richter Succumbs to Cancer."

Mysterious how? I wondered as I printed out what I'd found.

The mystery turned out to be a two-year disappearance right after the girl graduated from high school—which at first had been considered a kidnapping. Weeks of searching had turned up nothing and no ransom request was ever received. Then, Katarina returned two years later, unharmed and refusing to talk about her absence. The sadness the community had expressed at losing one of their own had turned to speculation—not very nice speculation, either. The locals decided she'd become a street person in Houston, a crack addict, a stripper or a wanderer trying to find herself in Europe or Africa. Indeed, plenty of Pineview folks voiced their opinions for the reporter, all of those opinions apparently not supported by any facts, as far as I could tell. My daddy always said gossip travels over grapevines that are sour and right now I totally agreed with him.

Since Katarina was buried here in Houston, I figured Glenwood might be the resting place of generations of Richters. Wouldn't hurt to pay a visit to their family plot. Katarina had been only twenty when she died, and I'd learned in my short career as a PI that the younger people were when they died, the more words on their tombstones.

The article mentioned Elliott Richter's son, Matthew, born six years after Katarina—which would make him around thirty-three now. His recent wedding had been written up in the *Chronicle* and was probably a lavish affair, since the reception site was the Four Seasons Hotel. Matthew's wife, Piper, was a Baylor grad, just like her new husband. I loved how much information they gave away on the wedding pages—names of friends and relatives, where the bride and groom went to school, where they planned to honeymoon and live. I printed out the article. Never hurts to be prepared, even if this wasn't officially my case.

Matthew and Piper, I read, would be working for Richter Oil and Gas in executive positions when they returned from their honeymoon in Tahiti. Since the wedding had been several months ago, they were probably home and doing their jobs.

Richter Oil and Gas? I thought. *Never heard of them.* I Googled the company and discovered it was a very healthy business with new prospects in West Texas as well as down near Corpus.

But where did JoLynn fit into this family? I'd found absolutely nothing on the Internet about her. Was she a cousin? Was she Katarina's daughter? If so, why had she written to me saying she was adopted? She might not be a blood relative. Maybe Elliott Richter adopted her. She had signed her letter "JoLynn Richter," which made me believe that was the case. Was she a substitute for the daughter he'd lost? But this was speculation on my part. I really knew next to nothing yet. I needed more.

I glanced at my watch. Only eight thirty. I had time to check out that graveyard before meeting Kate at the hospital. I remembered the Glenwood Cemetery from a Halloween graveyard tour I'd taken as a teenager—an outing Daddy encouraged because he said it would teach me about Houston's deliciously scandalous history. Kate had refused to go with me. She considered the whole idea "gross." But I had a blast, especially since I met the geeky but very cute guy named Andre who would become my boyfriend for the next two months. Did I learn much about Houston? I did remember Howard Hughes was buried in Glenwood and that there were all these creepy angels all over the place, their concrete skins scarred by lime deposits and mildew. It was an upscale cemetery in the Heights section—upscale considering that we'd visited some graveyards that had been no more than overgrown fields.

Figuring the mosquitoes would be out in droves this morning, I put on nylon cargo pants and a long-sleeve T-shirt. Traffic was its usual nightmare, but no one seemed interested in visiting a cemetery on a Saturday morning. Everyone was probably headed for the beach in Galveston or the mall. I parked my car and, hoping to check out the directory, walked to the Victorian cottage that formerly housed the caretaker. I soon discovered it would be quite a trek to the Richter plot.

As I wound my way around tombstones and crypts, I

was mindful of all the statues of cherubs and huge angels surrounding me, some of them missing arms or hands thanks to vandals or accidents or simply time—and all of them more damaged by the elements than I recalled. They still gave me the creeps, even in the intense morning sunshine, sadness seeping from them and lingering in the humid air. Despite the heat, I shivered. Even the brilliantly colored mounds of fresh flowers lying on several graves couldn't effectively oppose the gloom.

The Richter plot was maybe twenty feet square and enclosed by a low wrought-iron fence, which I stepped over. I counted ten graves. A few of the tombstones were simple and lay flat—early deaths dating back to the 1920s. Several markers were upright, but the ones for the people I had come to see—mother and daughter— were far more elaborate. Elliott Richter's wife's site was marked by a black granite tombstone with etched flowers on the beveled upper borders. The lettering was elegant and flowing and below the name *Richter* were the words:

> *Mary, beloved wife of Elliott, mother of Katarina and Matthew, a star in the darkest night, an angel who brought joy to all who knew her.*

Katarina's white marble marker was arched on the top with a weeping angel clinging to the tombstone. The brown, dry remnants of a bouquet of flowers lay at the base. Her etched name and birth and death dates curved along the upper part of the tombstone and were followed by several lines about the daughter who had died so young.

> *Beloved Katarina. Taken to sit beside the Lord, taken from the secretive world, taken from the pain of life, and when taken, to our hearts a knife.*

I swallowed, reread the words. Graveyard poetry isn't all that good—and damn depressing. I turned and walked away, glancing at the other tombstones before stepping back over the fence. They were older markers with nothing more than names and dates. While I hurried to my car, several grackles squawked at me as if to admonish me for trespassing. And I did feel like an intruder.

I'd almost made it to my car when I heard the buzz of a Weed Eater. I walked around a border of hedges and saw a groundskeeper working away at overgrown grass along a fence. He had earplugs in and wore a wide-brimmed hat, khaki pants and a matching shirt.

I didn't want to startle him, since he couldn't hear me, so I took a wide path around him until I was in his line of vision. I smiled and offered a small wave.

He turned off the Weed Eater and pulled out the earplugs. He had to be in his sixties, his skin darkened by years in the sun. White stubble sprouted along his chin and on his cheeks. He said, "There's a directory in the cottage near the front if you're looking for someone in particular." He gestured that way and started to put the earplugs back in.

"That's not what I need," I said quickly before he could start up the noisy equipment again. "Can I ask you a few questions?"

"I'm no tour guide and I ain't got time to teach you about this place, if that's what you want."

Grumpy old guy, I thought. But the temperature was already approaching ninety and he probably wanted to get this job done before the heat sizzled him like a sausage on the grill. "Just a few questions, I promise." I removed a business card, walked over and handed it to him. "I'm a private detective and I'm working on a case."

"Cemetery's a funny place to be huntin' up private-eye stuff. Ain't many folks to talk to here—unless you fancy yourself some kind of ghost whisperer."

I laughed and this seemed to crack his stoic facade because he smiled.

"No, sir," I said. "I don't believe in ghosts."

"I'm glad for that. All kinds of weird people trample through here who do. What you want to know?"

"Does anyone visit the Richter plot? I saw flowers on one of the graves."

"Richter plot, huh? Those flowers are from the girl. Pretty thing. Started coming here a year ago. She visits every week on Friday—Katarina Richter's grave—but she was a no-show yesterday. None of them other Richters come regular except the mister. He's here 'bout once a month and a'course always on Katarina's birthday."

"The mister?" I asked.

"Mr. Elliott. Always slips me a hundred, tells me to take care of his Katarina. And I do spend extra time keeping her grave tended to."

Elliott Richter, huh? "This girl who visits. Do you know her name?"

The man shook his head no. "Never talked to me. Seemed afraid, if I read her right."

"Small? Blond hair?" I asked, considering whether Katarina could indeed be JoLynn's mother.

"Yeah. She send you here?"

"In a way," I answered. "Thank you so much, Mr. . . . ?"

"Sam. Everyone calls me Sam."

I pulled a twenty from my purse and handed it to him. He smiled and nodded, then plugged his ears and went back to work.

I drove a little too fast on the way to Methodist, the poem on the tombstone replaying in my brain. By the time I arrived outside Aunt Caroline's hospital room, I'd managed to quit silently repeating those words and was now wondering about these weekly visits to the grave. Had to have been JoLynn unless there were more petite blond Richters in the family.

Kate met me at Aunt Caroline's door and kept me out with a raised palm. I looked past Kate into the room and saw a striking young woman with silky black hair deep in conversation with our aunt.

Kate looked me up and down. "It's supposed to reach a hundred degrees today. Why are you wearing—"

"I'll tell you later. What's up?"

She took my arm and led me out into the hall. "That's Nancy Song, the dietitian. The doctor's releasing Aunt Caroline today. She'll be on oral medicine and a diet that doesn't sound all that strict. But she will have to test her blood sugar every day and I think that might be a problem."

"Why?" I asked. "She knows she's diabetic and that's what diabetics have to do."

"Not so simple when you're in denial," Kate said. "Sticking herself with a sharp object and keeping a record of her sugar levels means she has to accept reality."

I nodded. "And accepting a reality she hasn't created herself will be challenge."

"You get the picture."

"Can we hire someone to stick her finger? At least for now?" I asked.

Kate grinned. "Do you really want to put someone through that kind of torture?"

Nancy Song came though the door then and said to Kate, "There you are."

"Sorry. I wanted to fill in my sister. How did that go?"

"She's an interesting woman," Nancy Song said. "Intelligent but perhaps a little strong-willed."

"You mean as stubborn as a rusty pump," I answered.

Song smiled. "Texas has such an interesting language. She will learn and accept eventually. But be prepared for a few bumps in the road."

"Oh, we're used to those," I answered.

Song handed Kate a stack of diet plans. "These will help. I gave your aunt the same ones. After the nurse trains her for blood sugar testing, the doctor will probably release her. I urged her to attend the hospital's diabetic support group as well and she told me she would think about it."

"Great." How I wished they'd keep her one more day. But I should be glad Aunt Caroline had rebounded quickly. Once Nancy Song left us, I turned to Kate. "Guess we'll have to wait on the doctor. Want to slip over to Ben Taub and pay JoLynn Richter that visit? You should see her. It's awful what someone tried to do to her."

"I do want to go, but let's clear it with General Caroline."

Aunt Caroline was more than happy for us to leave. She wanted to shower and put on her makeup before the doctor arrived. On our fifteen-minute walk to Ben Taub, Kate told me Aunt Caroline seemed quite taken with her new endocrinologist.

"What is he? About thirty?" I asked as we stopped at a corner.

"More like forty, but age has never mattered to Aunt Caroline when it comes to flirting."

During our walk—a far easier option than changing parking spots—I filled Kate in on what I had learned about the Richter family and how I had nothing on Jo-Lynn. When we entered the lobby, I was grateful the place was as cold as a knothole in the North Pole because I was sweating bullets.

"Why don't you know anything about JoLynn?" she asked. "You're the queen of finding out anything on anybody."

"Not this time. And that's very strange. If I can find baptismal records on someone born in the seventies—which I've done before—why can't I find anything on her?"

As we entered the elevator, Kate said, "Sorry, but I kind of like that. Apparently Big Internet Brother hasn't been watching *everyone*."

We rode in silence and then visited the restroom so I could run a comb through my sweat-dampened hair. Turned out I didn't have a comb, but Kate is always prepared.

"I like this cinnamon color. You should stick with it." She was watching me try to make her comb work a miracle—a miracle that wasn't about to happen.

When she saw my frustration, she tousled my crown. "Go with the natural look." Then she handed me a lipstick—Mocha Pink. "This will help, too."

The lipstick did make me look more normal, especially since my flushed cheeks were less pronounced thanks to the AC. I no longer felt like I'd just emerged from a rain forest tour. We then walked down the corridor to the neuro ICU. Two men sat in the waiting area. One was a Montgomery County sheriff's deputy and the other a young man in his twenties.

The deputy must be here for JoLynn, too. I smiled at him, but he didn't react. I stopped a nurse assistant about to enter the ICU and said, "We'd like to visit JoLynn Richter for a few minutes. I'm working with Chief

Boyd on her case." Not completely true, but how would she know?

The woman thumbed at the deputy. "Ask him." She then entered the unit without another word.

Kate and I turned and walked over to the deputy, who had picked up a *People* magazine and was paging through it.

"Hi," I said as I approached with Kate on my heels. "I was the one who identified Miss Richter and I'm working with Chief Boyd on this case. I'm a private investigator." I handed him a card.

His name badge read DEPUTY WELLS and though I was the one talking, his gaze was on Kate as he stood.

The man was built, not to mention hot. And tall enough I'd need a stepladder to look him in the eye. He said, "Funny, Coop didn't mention you when he asked for county help to protect JoLynn Richter. I'm Greg Wells, by the way. Who's your friend?" He smiled down at Kate.

I could almost feel the heat of Kate's blush. "Dr. Kate Rose. I've had a little experience with head-trauma victims and am here to evaluate her."

Nice little twisting of the truth, I thought. Kate might be getting back to her old self after all.

"I think Miss Richter has a bunch of doctors already." The deputy looked back and forth between us. "I take it you two are related?"

"Sisters. And I'm not a medical doctor," she answered. "I'm a clinical psychologist."

"Last time I looked in her room, the girl was in a damn coma. How do you work with sleeping people?"

"That's not why we've come, Deputy Wells," I said. "My sister—"

"Excuse me," said the other guy who'd been sitting in the waiting room. He was now standing behind Kate. "I couldn't help but overhear. JoLynn is my cousin."

Wells looked at him, obviously surprised. "Why didn't you say something?"

"I had no idea you were here for JoLynn," he answered. "The police think she's still in danger, then?"

"We're taking precautions," he replied.

Compared to Wells, the new guy was so skinny he could lie under a clothesline and not get a sunburn. Not bad looking, though. Baby face, hazel eyes dotted with gold, and plenty of highlighted hair—unlike Wells, whose receding hairline reminded me of low tide. The cousin's designer polo shirt was coral, his khakis were unwrinkled and he smelled very metrosexually nice.

"What's your name?" Wells asked him.

"Scott Morton. My mother is Uncle Elliott's sister. I promised my uncle I'd stay here until he could get free." He looked at me. "Uncle Elliott never mentioned any investigator to me, either."

"Chief Boyd probably didn't have a chance to tell anyone," I said quickly.

Wells smiled. "Why don't we clear this up? I'll call up Coop and ask him about all three of you."

6

My stomach fluttered as Wells made the call. Oh, what a tangled web and all that crap. But after Wells told him who was waiting in line to see JoLynn, he listened for a second before handing the phone to me. "He wants to talk to you."

"Why are you at the hospital, Abby?" Cooper asked. Seriously, the guy ought to get his obviously stressed vocal cords checked.

"Can't help myself," I answered. "I'm a sucker for anyone who's written to me for help."

"Pro bono?" he said.

"If that's what I need to do, yes," I answered.

"I called a friend at HPD and he says you're smart and know your way around a whodunit. I have to admit I could use someone like you."

"Why, Cooper Boyd. I'll bet you're not afraid to ask for directions, either."

He laughed and said, "I'm not sure how visiting a comatose woman can help solve an attempted murder, though."

I told him how Kate and I work together, that she'd had training in the psychological aspects of brain injury and wanted to evaluate JoLynn for herself.

"I'm up for anything, so go for it," he said. "I'll tell Wells you're good to visit. He tells me Scotty is there, too."

"Um . . . yes. But you sound amused." I fought the urge to look over at Scott Morton.

"Nerdy kid but nice. He came with the bail money for Matthew, Richter's son, one time last year. I've been told Matt used to be a regular visitor to our local facility—local facility meaning jail. Drinking and public lewdness—which translates to pissing on the main street in Pineview. Anyway, his father sent him to rehab. He sobered up and got married."

"I see. Interesting," I said.

"Scott standing right there, huh?"

"You got it."

"Take him in there with you. If by chance her condition has an effect on him, I'd like a report on his reaction. Hell, I'd like a report on *anyone's* reaction. Richter was cold as stone when I told him about JoLynn. 'Course, I've met him a few times at town events and that's the way he always seems."

"Should I hand you back to the deputy?"

"Yes. And thanks, Abby."

"No problem." I gave Wells the phone and looked at Scott and Kate. "We can go in, but I'm guessing only if and when the staff gives the okay."

That okay didn't come for a half hour and then we were told we had five minutes max.

Kate went straight to JoLynn's bedside, but Scott hung back, as pallid as if he'd had a visit from Dracula on the way in here.

"My God," he whispered.

JoLynn's bruises were changing to the icky stage—all blotchy with yellow and brown beginning to taint the purple and black.

"Pretty nasty, huh?" I said quietly.

"Who would do that to her? She's the sweetest person on earth," he said.

I gauged his reaction as Boyd had asked me to do and the words *authentic shock* came to mind. But that didn't mean he hadn't engineered the murder attempt—it meant only that he hadn't realized the human toll taken after a person experiences a powerful impact with a large immovable object.

"How are you two related again?" I asked.

"She's my cousin."

"You two grow up together?" I probed.

"No. She's only been back with us for about a year."

"I don't understand," I said.

"I'll leave the explanations to Uncle Elliott. What matters is that she recovers." He walked over to Kate's side and picked up JoLynn's hand.

I followed, looked at my sister. "What do you think?" I asked.

"She responded to painful stimuli when I pinched her arm. Moaned a little when I whispered in her ear. She's not in a deep coma."

"That's good news, right?" Scott said.

"As I said in the waiting room," Kate replied, "I'm not a medical doctor. You should talk to her physician."

"I did," Scott said. "He said I'm not next of kin and he's waiting for Uncle Elliott to arrive to report on her condition."

"And when do you expect Uncle Elliott?" I asked.

"I thought he'd already be here. We're the only two who—" He pursed his lips, looked down at his shiny loafers. "He'll be here soon."

Family issues? I wondered. According to what I'd already learned, there was plenty of family. "You certainly got here quickly," I said with a smile, hoping he'd open up a little more.

"I didn't want her to be alone. I wish they'd let me sit with her so I can be here when she wakes up, but the answer to that request was an emphatic no. But she *will* wake up." His lips tightened but not before I saw them quiver.

Scott seemed like a supersensitive guy. But maybe his concern was an act.

A nurse opened the door, interrupting my thoughts. "Your time is up," she said softly.

He squeezed JoLynn's hand before letting go and I noticed her forehead crease ever so slightly. Seconds later the three of us rejoined Deputy Wells in the waiting room.

Wells looked at Scott. "You need some Dramamine, kid? 'Cause you look like you're about to toss your lunch."

"I'm fine." Scott seemed distracted, lost in his thoughts.

Wells addressed Kate then. "You work a miracle in there, Doc? She tell you what happened?"

"Sorry to disappoint you," Kate answered.

No matter how hot this guy might be, he'd never get out of the batter's box, much less to first base, with my sister. You do not make fun of Kate's job—unless you're me. I'm the only one she takes a ribbing from on that front.

"Come on, Abby. We need to get back to Aunt Caroline," Kate said. "Nice to meet you two."

She started toward the corridor and I followed. "Listen, I think Scott could be a help. Can you call me when Aunt Caroline's ready to be released and I'll head back to Methodist then?"

"Sure. But I need to get out of here. I don't like that deputy one bit."

"Gee. Who would have known?" I said.

Her fair skin colored again. "That obvious, huh?"

"He liked what he saw and was trying to be funny. You're gorgeous, after all. Men notice and that's normal."

She blinked several times and I could tell she was fighting tears. Kate needed to get over her last romantic debacle—and soon.

"I'll call." She turned, walked quickly toward the elevator and nearly slammed right into a man with steel gray hair who was coming at her at about the same swift pace.

He then rushed by me and said, "Have you got that doctor's pager number, Scott?"

Uncle Elliott, I presumed.

"I saw her. She's hurt bad." Scott's eyes filled.

Jeez. First Kate, now him.

Wells stood and offered his hand to the new arrival. "Greg Wells. Montgomery County Sheriff's Department."

"Elliott Richter. I can't thank you enough for being here to protect my granddaughter. I'm arranging for security and private nurses to start as soon as possible."

Granddaughter, huh? So she was probably Katarina's child. I noticed Scott had his cell phone out, probably to page the doctor, but before you could say *Verizon*, a scrubs-clad medical person came out of the ICU and noticed the phone. "No cell phones," she said sternly, then hurried down the corridor.

Scott snapped the phone shut. "I'll go to the lobby, make the page and wait for Dr. Vickers to answer." He still looked taken aback by seeing JoLynn and probably needed a break from this place.

"Thank you," Richter said.

Meanwhile, I'd been quietly inching closer to Richter and now said, "Abby Rose. I was the one who—"

"Yes," he said, looking a little surprised. "Chief Boyd told me you discovered it was our JoLynn. Thank you so much, Ms. Rose. But why are you here?" He was a handsome, distinguished man and I was betting his woven blue shirt cost as much as my entire wardrobe.

"Please, call me Abby. And I'm here because, well, after I saw JoLynn, I couldn't get her out of my head. I'm a PI specializing in adoption searches and she wrote to me last year asking for help."

Richter looked bewildered by this information. "She wrote to you?" he said.

"Yes. I recognized her handwriting from something she scribbled on my business card—the card found in her car. What is her adoption situation, by the way? She didn't elaborate in her letter."

He ignored my question, saying, "Chief Boyd merely said you were an investigator who helped him. Anyway, I thank you for everything you've done and for your continued interest, but I think we can take care of Jo-Lynn now." Richter turned back to Deputy Wells.

I was being dismissed. But maybe not because this guy was an arrogant SOB. Nope. I've learned to read people pretty well since I started investigating, and I'd seen fear in Richter's intelligent blue eyes before he'd turned away.

I cleared my throat. "Um, Chief Boyd asked for my help and I've agreed. He's stretched pretty thin up there in Pineview."

"I can hire someone, since you seem to specialize. I already have people lined up, so one more person won't be difficult to find."

"Who will you hire? Will they care as much as my sister and I do?" I said.

"Now I'm confused," he said.

"My sister, Kate, is a psychologist and she evaluates my clients. She could be a big help when your granddaughter wakes up—and from what Kate said after visiting JoLynn a few minutes ago, she's not in a very deep coma. She'll probably need psychological support to deal with the emotional and physical trauma when she regains consciousness, wouldn't you say?"

Richter didn't speak for a few seconds. Then he smiled. "You're a good businesswoman, Abby. You've played to my weakness. I want the best money can buy for JoLynn, of course, but you can't put a price tag on commitment and caring. Perhaps we could talk later."

I handed him my card, deciding he needed time to check me out for himself. "I'm sure you want to visit JoLynn now. Call me." I nodded at Wells. "Nice to meet you."

Then I walked back to Methodist so Kate and I could take Aunt Caroline home. I'd rather have visited a little longer with Elliott Richter—for the distraction and for the mystery. I wondered if he had any ideas about who tried to kill his granddaughter—and perhaps even more important, did he know *why* someone would want her dead?

7

I arrived home around two p.m. with my patience in shreds, partly due to Aunt Caroline's nonstop whining on the way back to her house and partly because my stomach had been growling for the past hour. We'd finally left my aunt in the capable hands of her best friend, Martha, after we purged Aunt Caroline's refrigerator of all the ice cream, syrups and sugared drinks. We hadn't found so much as a stalk of celery during the cleanfest. Kate had agreed to do the grocery shopping, which meant she would arrive back at Aunt Caroline's with all things green and yellow. Thank God I wouldn't be there to hear my aunt's rebel yell—a sound similar to what I let loose with after I've slammed my fingers in the car door.

Diva was sitting by the answering machine when I came in the back way, tail swishing as if to say, "Where the hell have you been? People are calling and talking on this thing and you know how that annoys me."

I scratched her under her chin. "I must have food before all else, Diva."

She walked along the granite countertop and met me at the refrigerator. Guess she was hungry, too. I ate from a bowl of grapes while I found a half can of Fancy Feast and one slice of leftover pizza. After Diva was served, I ate cold pizza while listening to the single message.

"Abby, this is Scott Morton. Chief Boyd gave me your number and I was hoping to slip out and pay you a visit. My uncle hasn't told you the whole story about JoLynn. Text messaging me with directions to your office would work best."

Hmm. Interesting. One little mystery on top of another.
I loved it.

Forty-five minutes and half a bag of Cheetos later, I
saw Scott Morton on my security monitor screen. I let
him in and we went to the living room, since the office
was, well, more than messy.

After he had a Dr Pepper in hand, I took the recliner
and he sat adjacent to me on the sofa. He said, "First,
I wanted you to know that Uncle Elliott has people
checking up on you already."

"Figured as much," I answered.

"It's not that he's sly or mean-spirited or anything.
He's simply careful."

"Probably a very smart man," I said.

"True, but I think he's wasting time when you and
Chief Boyd could be working on finding out who did
this to JoLynn. This person might try again, right?"

"I don't see how. Sheriff's deputies, private security
and private nurses would be hard to get by."

Scott chewed a thumbnail. "You're right. I worry,
that's all. Anyway, you should know the story. Because
wherever she was before she came to our family might
have something to do with what happened to her and
what might happen next."

"She was adopted?" I said.

"You know that already?"

"I figured as much. Go on." I leaned back in the over-
stuffed chair.

"My mother is quite a bit younger than her brother—
that's Uncle Elliott. Anyway, he had a daughter—Katarina.
I was five or six when she died. She had cancer, but
before that, she'd left home for a couple years. I don't
know why. Uncle Elliott never talks about it—in fact no
one talks about much of anything important from the
past in our family. But she came back and was already
pretty sick by then."

"She was about eighteen when she left?"

He stared at me, confused, then finally said, "You
already knew?"

"I do my research, but tell me about this absence. Is
that when JoLynn came into the world?"

He slowly smiled. "Yeah. Katarina gave her up for

adoption before she returned to the ranch. JoLynn told me when she first arrived about a year ago that she'd hired some detective agency in Houston and they located us for her. I've never seen Uncle Elliott so happy. You'd have thought he'd gotten Katarina back."

"Did you know about the baby she gave up before JoLynn arrived?"

"Like I said, we don't talk about the past. Uncle Elliott may have known, but I won't be the one to ask him. I'm hoping you will, though."

"Why?"

"Because I don't want him to shut me out if I bring up the subject. I'm afraid that's what he'd do. I've seen it happen in the family more than once. See, he needs me right now, even if he doesn't realize it."

"Needs your support?"

Scott nodded. "He won't get any from the rest of the family."

"That helps me understand the situation better. How long ago did you say JoLynn arrived at the ranch?" My brain had revved into high gear. The girl told Scott she'd used an agency to find Elliott Richter. What agency? The Texas Adoption Registry? Could be. And if she was looking for her birth family, why did she sign her letter to me using the Richter last name?

"She's been living with Uncle Elliott a little more than a year now. In the big house. The rest of us have houses on Uncle Elliott's property, but she stays with him."

Thinking about what life would be like if Aunt Caroline lived down the street, I shuddered. "This agency. Did JoLynn tell you anything about it? Like how they found Mr. Richter?"

He rubbed the stubble along his jawline. "Not how they found him, but I do remember the agency had a funny name—not the detective's name like you'd expect. What the hell was it?"

"Texas Adoption Registry?" I offered.

"No. Something-Something Investigations. Sorry, I just can't—"

"Yellow Rose Investigations?" I said.

Scott pointed at me. "That's it. You do know your stuff, Abby."

I tried hard not to look surprised. "Research is invaluable," I said. Obviously he hadn't seen one of the business cards I'd been handing out like Halloween candy the past two days. I decided not to tell him that *I* was Yellow Rose Investigations—why, I wasn't sure. Maybe because he seemed so stressed-out. His uncle had known the name of my agency, that's for sure, but probably because Cooper told him. Had JoLynn told Scott the same things she'd told Richter? If not, that could explain Richter's surprised expression when I mentioned adoption.

I said, "You seem to care very much about JoLynn, despite her being a part of your family for such a short time."

He grinned. "She's incredible." Then his smile faded. "She's got to pull through this." He rolled the Dr Pepper can between his hands and stared at the floor.

"Did she talk about her adoptive family at all?" I asked.

Scott tightened his lips and shook his head. "Nope. Not to me anyway. Maybe she confided in Uncle Elliott or someone else in the family."

"Guess it's time you listed what family you're talking about," I said.

"Sure. There's Matt and Piper. Matt is Uncle Elliott's son. He and Katarina were six years apart. He married Piper a few months ago. They work for the company just like we all do."

"What do you do?" I asked.

"Petroleum engineer."

I smiled. "Smart guy, huh?" The minute I'd asked about the rest of the family, I'd seen him tense up, but this question seemed to relax him. Comfortable territory, I assumed.

"Not all *that* smart," he said with an embarrassed laugh. "I've only been out of school for two years and have a lot to learn. Anyway, there's also my mom and my stepfather."

"Their names?" I reached over the end table and opened its drawer. I took out the pad and pencil I always keep there.

"Adele and Leopold Hunt. Also, my half sister, Simone, and my mom's ex-husband, Ian—he's Simone's dad."

"What about your biological father?" I said.

Scott again focused on the Oriental carpet. "He died when I was a baby."

"Sorry," I said quietly. Perhaps this was why he had such a strong bond with JoLynn—they'd both lost a biological parent. But why was an ex-husband still considered family? Because of Simone?

Scott must have read my mind because he said, "You're probably wondering why Ian's still around despite the divorce. It's because he's a damn genius. A geologist from England. Richter Oil and Gas couldn't function without him."

"How's that situation working? Does he keep his distance aside from the job?"

"Oh, that would make things too easy," Scott said. "Not that I don't like Ian, because he's an okay guy. Weird, but okay. Uncle Elliott, however, includes him in everything and when Ian and my mom are in the same room, shrapnel flies the entire time. Especially when Ian brings the latest girlfriend with him to dinner or parties."

"I see." Ah, families. Some of them walk around forever in misery up to their armpits. "Tell me more about Mr. Richter and JoLynn. This agency directed her to him and then what happened?"

"What do you mean?"

"Come on, Scott. She must have told you *something* about her past aside from how she found her grandfather." Time to push this guy a little. I could tell he was holding back.

"Okay, I did ask her once, but she only told me that her past was painful, not something she wanted to discuss. She said life is about the present, not the past. She's learned to live in the moment and she does. She's so . . . different than the rest of us. She's *happy*."

I thought about this for a second. Happy, maybe, but she'd sure made someone very angry.

8

I awoke Monday morning feeling anxious and irritable. The long hot weekend had dragged on without a call from Elliott Richter all day Sunday. I wondered if he'd learned something about me he didn't like, something that made him decide to exclude me from the investigation into JoLynn's attempted murder. Seems I had a bruised ego; I had thought that Richter would know I could save the day. But good work seldom comes from someone with a swelled head, and I needed to get over it. I rolled out of bed and Diva followed me to the bathroom. I thought about how humility never applied to her. Cats are exempt from humility.

After a steamy shower that normally would have revived me, I realized I was still tired. Jeff had been called at four o'clock Sunday morning to help out the night shift with a triple homicide and asked me to go to his place and stay with Doris. I hadn't caught up on my sleep yet. This drill was becoming routine—me getting up in the middle of the night to care for Doris. I told him I might install a fire pole from my bedroom to the first floor and have my clothes ready in the foyer, maybe even buy myself a little fire engine. He liked the idea of a pole in my bedroom, but not the kind I was referring to.

If we lived together, things would be easier as far as Jeff's emergencies, but Doris's arrival last year had halted any ideas of us moving in together. With Doris in the mix now, making a home together before we got to know what the added challenges were might spoil what Jeff and I had. Neither of us wanted that to happen. We decided we could wait.

I was on my second cup of Stellar Brew coffee when the phone call from Richter came. He got right to the point.

"You come highly recommended, Abby. Nothing but good reports from your former boss, Mr. Molina, your lawyer friend Mark, and several of your more publicized clients."

"Why did you have to bother my ex-clients?" I asked, knowing I sounded annoyed, and hoping he knew it. Those people needed to be left alone.

"Because that's how I do things. Check every source. I'd like you to drive up to my place, the Magnolia Ranch. We can discuss how you'll be involved in the investigation."

My clients usually come to me, but I wanted to see the ranch anyway, maybe even take a look at the spot where JoLynn had her wreck. I got directions and hung up.

It was supposed to reach ninety-eight degrees today, so I chose a T-shirt and summer-weight khakis for my visit. Pineview is north of Houston and west of the two largest cities in Montgomery County. One of them, The Woodlands, is filled with folks who have enough money to use an imported anesthetic rather than a *local* anesthetic when they visit the cosmetic surgeon. West of the interstate that runs through the county, the landscape is a far cry from the cement and glass and endless looping freeways that make up Houston. There are pines, hardwoods and rolling hills. The toll roads helped make the trip less than two hours, but I spent the last part of the journey on a narrow country road leading to the Richter place. I drove under a sign that said THE MAGNOLIA RANCH as my Camry bounced over the cattle guard and through an open iron gate.

I drove down a paved lane lined by giant gnarled magnolias, their huge white blooms browned and dried by the August sun but still possessing their own special kind of beauty. I rolled down the window, but their sweet fragrance had faded like their flowers. I came to a sprawling one-story stone house and whispered, "Wow" as I drove along the curving drive. This was about twice as big as my old digs in River Oaks—and that house had checked in at around five thousand square feet. A pristine red barn with THE MAGNOLIA RANCH painted on one of the arching outside walls had my attention—so much, in fact, that I didn't notice the rider on horseback come up behind me. When I parked, Elliott Richter halted his giant dapple mount alongside my car.

"Howdy, Mr. Richter," I said as I got out of the Camry. Seemed like a good word to use here.

"No *howdy*s. I'm a Longhorn." He pointed to the silver University of Texas logo attached to the band of his cream-colored ten-gallon hat. He'd just gotten off a horse, yet his jeans were still creased and his burnt-orange cotton shirt looked fresh from the dry cleaner.

"Oops," I said with a smile. "My late daddy went to Texas A&M, so I hope we can get along." Texas A&M and U.T. are notorious rivals and the A&M Aggie students are known for saying "Howdy" to every person they pass on campus.

"I forgive your daddy," Richter said, "but only because he's passed on. I hear they do let a few Aggies into heaven." A stableman seemed to appear from nowhere to gather the horse's reins. "I've taken the day off and arranged lunch on the porch, if that suits you, Abby."

"I'm as hungry as a moth on nylon, so lead the way." But the porch? I was already sweating despite only a minute without air-conditioning.

I shouldn't have worried. The "porch" turned out to be a large and elegant glassed-in room with beautiful Mexican tile flooring and six swirling ceiling fans. I looked out on the gently sloping green lawn and the brilliant, lush gardens, thinking I could live in a place like this. My former River Oaks property, though probably as pricey as this, had led down to a bayou and didn't offer this kind of view.

I was given a choice of what to have for lunch by the aproned chef whom Richter called Otto, more food than I could possibly eat in a week—bratwurst, sauerkraut, German potato salad and thick slices of homemade rye bread. I could have also feasted on sandwiches piled high with roast beef or ham with slices of cheddar, but sausage is a rare treat when you have a health nut for a sister. If Kate ever saw a German sausage in my fridge, she'd get bent out of shape. I finished off my meal with a salad of summer fruits drenched in some kind of delicious liqueur—Cointreau maybe?

Our conversation during the meal remained purely social—mostly questions about my current life as a PI, my daddy and his business, questions that I was sure Richter already knew the answers to. But this soft-spoken, impeccable man with every gray hair in place was very good at drawing me out. I talked on and on about Daddy, Jeff and Doris, Kate and Aunt Caroline. After I speared the last piece of gold pineapple—Richter had finished his meal long before I did—his demeanor changed. Time for business.

A pretty, young dark-haired woman who introduced herself as Estelle cleared our dishes. She wore so much makeup that I wanted to tell her to wash her face, help her realize she'd be even more beautiful without all the lipstick and eyeliner. And the dark brown hair drew attention away from her flawless skin. But who am I to give advice on hair color? Ask Kate. I have ruined my hair so many times I might be in the running for worst swatch picker ever.

After Estelle was gone, Richter said, "Here's what I'd like you to do. Although one or more of my relatives might well be capable of this murder attempt on JoLynn, I think it's wise we explore her past. I know nothing of her adoptive background, for example—who she lived with or for how long."

I tried not to look too surprised. He'd checked me out thoroughly, so why hadn't he investigated someone he'd invited to live with him, someone he now admitted was adopted, before she showed up here? Something wasn't right. "She didn't tell you anything about her past?"

"None of that mattered at the time." I started to speak, but he held up a hand. "If I researched JoLynn's life as I did yours—as if she were a prospective hire—that information would find its way into the hands of one or more of the vultures who call themselves my family—and it *would* find its way, believe me. I feared they might chase her off. You see, she was like one of my magnolia blossoms, hearty but prone to bruising if handled too roughly. She was part of Katarina and I wasn't about to let them ruin something very special."

"You know *nothing* about her past aside from the fact that Katarina was her mother?" I said.

"From the moment I met JoLynn, I knew she belonged here and that was enough for me. She had Katarina's eyes, Katarina's soft-spoken ways." He raised his chin and rested his elbows on the round glass table, leaned forward and whispered, "And if one of the people I support with homes and jobs and a secure future had anything to do with harming her, I will *kill* that person."

"But—"

He sat back in his cushioned wrought-iron chair. "You see why I need your help? That's not exactly something I could say to Chief Boyd."

I stood, shook my head. "That's not something you can tell *me*, either." I didn't bother to hide my anger. "I'm sorry, but you'll have to hire another detective for this job if you expect me to—"

"Good for you. That's what I hoped you'd say." He stood as well, his smile broad.

I wasn't amused. "What's that supposed to mean?"

"You're as ethical as everyone has told me and you've shown as much with a vigor I admire. I'll admit I was concerned when I discovered you're wealthy. I wondered if you gather people's secrets for some perverse reason other than altruism."

"*What?*" I felt my face forming what Kate calls the "Are you nuts?" expression. Richter must have a screw loose in his thinker assembly.

"You don't know my family," he said, obviously recognizing that look. "They love to gossip and some of what they say about other people, well, it's less than pleasant. They play with secrets like children play with toys. I had to know if you might be even a little bit like them."

"You judge the rest of the world by the way they act? No sir, this is not the job for me." I turned and started to walk away, thinking he should take a good look at himself if he wanted to know how his relatives got that way.

"I'm sorry I offended you," he called after me. "I need your help, Abby. And I promise you, I could never murder anyone. I truly regret that remark."

I stopped, took a deep breath. This had to be the strangest case I'd ever considered taking on. But Richter reminded me of my daddy in a way. Older money in this family, yes, but both men had that same attitude of invincibility and confidence that comes from having enough power and cash to think you can get anything you want. Daddy and I went a few rounds on living the privileged life. I didn't like his "events" and the business meetings and the parties and I sure as hell hated playing dress-up. I got rid of the big house with the greenhouse, tennis courts and pool when I decided to take on my first independent venture—creating Yellow Rose Investigations. Dealing with someone like Richter might be a good reminder of why I do what I do and might also be a way to make a little peace with my past and my father's flaws.

I faced Richter again. "You're a man who wants control. But I can't work with you pulling my strings. Is that clear?"

"Very. JoLynn *needs* a bulldog to take charge of this investigation."

"Hold on. Chief Boyd is in charge and he will require everyone's cooperation. As for my role, there will be a few ground rules."

"Certainly. In my business dealings I would never agree to be bound by your rules, but this is not business. This is personal."

Personal enough for him to forgo his usual background check on JoLynn last year, something I found very difficult to understand or even believe. Yet now he wanted me to do what he might have already done himself.

I returned to the table and sat, waiting in silence while

another servant, an older woman with clear eyes and a stocky build, asked if we wanted anything more to eat or drink.

Richter looked at me questioningly and I shook my head no.

"*Danke*, no, Eva," Richter said.

She said, "*Bitte,*" and left us alone.

"Your ground rules?" Richter asked.

"Give me access to anything connected to JoLynn. I'll need to search her room and interview you and your family, ask any questions I decide are important. And I want to know about Katarina and why you think JoLynn is your granddaughter despite no concrete evidence aside from the lies JoLynn told you and Scott."

"Lies? Scott? I'm confused."

"JoLynn told him that she'd hired Yellow Rose Investigations to find you. You've already discovered that *I* am Yellow Rose Investigations."

Confusion was turning to what almost looked like panic. "She told Scott she *hired* you?"

I nodded. "And I know that's not true, though she did have my card and did write me a letter."

His eyes narrowed and his brow furrowed. "All right, here is what she told me. She said an adoption registry informed her about me. A registry that Katarina had provided information to before she passed on. According to JoLynn, the people she went to for information at this agency said Katarina informed them she was dying and wanted to give up her baby. If one day JoLynn came looking for her birth parents, which she did, Katarina wanted her daughter to know she gave her up because her daughter deserved a normal, happy family with two loving parents. That's definitely something Katarina would do, so I never questioned this story."

I sat back. Was *this* the truth? JoLynn went through the registry? Why did she tell Scott something different, then? And why write me that letter about wanting to find her birth parents? Richter was looking at me expectantly and I said, "Why didn't she stick with one story?"

Richter stiffened. "I'm sure she had a good reason to lie to Scott, though he is the most rational and trustworthy of the bunch. I did tell her to be careful what she said to family members."

I said, "There is a Texas Adoption Registry and guess what? I inform folks all about it in those tip sheets I send out—and I sent one to her. Here's the problem. They might have told her Katarina was deceased, but if *you* never registered with them, they would *never* have given JoLynn your name. Reunions must be requested by both parties when you skip court petitions and go through them."

"I certainly didn't register," Richter said, "but every bureaucracy has its cracks. There are ways she could have learned about me through them."

"Does the fact that she may have lied twice about her search for her birth family tell you something?"

"Obviously she was afraid to tell the truth. Someone harmed her for a reason and that's what you need to focus on. *Not* on her missteps," Richter said. The more I'd pressed him, the redder his neck had become.

I leaned toward him and in a quiet voice said, "I'll bet you're used to folks kowtowing to you. For the record, I focus on what I consider important to getting at the truth, and the truth may not be what you're ready to hear." That was my short version of the "You can't handle the truth" speech because I feared this was the case.

Richter closed his eyes and calmed himself before speaking. "I have handled many difficult events in my life, the death of my wife and Katarina being the worst, of course. I apologize if I sounded arrogant. I'm simply remembering JoLynn in that hospital bed and I'm sick at heart to think someone would do that to her. If this murder attempt is connected to her past, I need to know—so I can continue to protect her after she gets well and comes home. Name your fee. I'll pay whatever you wish."

After I quoted him the highest price I'd ever charged anyone—ten thousand dollars, which would go toward my dream of building the most fabulous user-friendly group home for folks like Doris—I said, "Let me get to work. Her bedroom?"

9

When I'd first arrived, I hadn't fully taken in the grandeur of the Richter home, but grand was everywhere. Pillars of dark wood separated the living areas from the hall that led to the back of the house. These were double living areas separated by the longest dining table I'd seen outside a wedding reception. Vases sat on little shelves; paintings that probably cost a small fortune hung on the walls; thick Oriental rugs protected polished oak flooring. As we headed back toward the way I'd come in, I glanced at rustic leather furniture and end tables with fresh flowers in the less formal living area. Up ahead to my right, brocade and satin upholstered chairs faced a grand piano. Richter led me to another hallway off the foyer.

We'd had no shortage of expensive art and antiques in our home while I was growing up, but this place was more well dressed than you'd expect a "ranch" to be. We turned left and seemed to travel for minutes, passing closed door after closed door. What was behind all of them? Bedrooms? Studies? Offices? Maybe a media center or a billiards room? Finally we reached JoLynn's room and Richter produced a ring of keys from his pocket and used one to open her door.

Locked? Hmmm. Who is he keeping out?

He caught my expression and said, "I only added the lock this weekend. I didn't want the others snooping around in her things."

"The others? You mean your family?"

"That's right." Richter widened the door. "This is it."

I expected more expensive decor, but the room,

though large by non-master-bedroom standards, seemed, well, *plain*. The linens on the four-poster were beige. The two mahogany dressers had no photos on top. Two brown upholstered wing chairs with a small round table between them sat in front of a window that looked out on a fenced-in garden and fountain. I felt like I'd walked into an upscale hotel room—pleasant but impersonal.

Just then Eva appeared in the doorway. "Herr Richter? The policeman is here. He's asking for you." She had a thick German accent that hadn't come through when she'd spoken so few words earlier.

"Did he say what he wanted?" Richter said impatiently, never taking his eyes off me as I walked into the middle of the bedroom. I was taking in every corner, hoping to see something—anything—that might give me a hint of JoLynn's personality.

Eva said, "He says nothing except that he wants to speak with you, *mein Herr*."

"Go ahead. I'd prefer to work alone anyway, Mr. Richter," I said.

"I'm not sure—"

"My ground rules, remember?"

Richter turned on his heel and left with Eva.

I sighed and closed my eyes, the tension leaving my body. I hadn't realized how strongly his presence affected me. I kinda liked the guy who'd been charming and intelligent at lunch, but the intensity when he spoke about JoLynn seemed, well, *scary*. This little room search would be a welcome distraction. Maybe Kate could help me make sense of Richter when we talked this over later.

Since nothing in plain sight struck me as informative, I hit the nightstand and found a Bible with a gold-tasseled bookmark in the drawer. I opened to the marked page. Ecclesiastes, the fourth chapter. Not the chapter about how everything has a time and a season, but rather the one about how wealth cannot bring happiness, how you need a friend to help you up when you fall. We'd done Ecclesiastes in my adolescent Bible study and if I remembered right, these passages were about oppression and friendlessness. Her saving this particular page could be telling me something about JoLynn, or it could simply be the spot she'd stuck the thin gold ribbon attached to the Bible.

I moved on and found a half dozen pairs of shorts and T-shirts and some simple cotton underwear in one dresser. The drawers below the television armoire were filled with jeans, lightweight sweaters and pajamas. No trendy clothes like you'd expect from someone her age— not even in the nearly barren closet. Two black dresses, a few pairs of shoes, a pair of slacks and a shirt still in their dry-cleaner bags—that was about it. Her wardrobe pretty much resembled mine.

But then I went into the adjoining bathroom. The ledge of the corner whirlpool tub looked like a candle and bath-salts store. JoLynn apparently liked some luxury in her life, after all. I picked up one candle and sniffed. Vanilla. A jar of bath salts was brown sugar and, again, vanilla. And there was a coconut-vanilla foot scrub. Loofahs, bath pillows and a basket of French-milled soaps sat on the tub's marble seat. *Nice and inviting,* I thought. This was someone who took relaxation seriously.

The sink and vanity revealed a minimum of makeup— higher-end department store brands. Nothing you could buy at Walgreens. I knelt and opened a cabinet beneath the sink. Shampoos, a hair dryer and a curling iron. Again, everyday stuff. I was about to close up the cabinet and leave when I spotted a grocery-style plastic bag in one dark corner.

I sat on the floor and opened the bag. Here was the drugstore makeup, the cheap moisturizer and three-dollar shampoo. Interesting. And three boxes of wash-in hair color. Black, chestnut and ash-blond. What was this about? My first thought was that she could grab this little escape kit, change her looks and disappear.

But before I could think of any other explanation, I heard voices in the bedroom and then Richter called my name.

I emerged from the bathroom after returning the bag to where I'd found it.

Cooper Boyd said, "Hi, Abby. Good to see you again." His melancholy smile and raspy voice were more welcoming than anything offered by Elliott Richter once the topic had changed to JoLynn.

"Chief Boyd has something to tell you," Richter said. "But can we talk in the great room? I find it rather uncomfortable in here."

"Uncomfortable without JoLynn, you mean?" I swore I was gonna get more out of this guy than perfect manners and a possessive attitude when it came to his granddaughter.

"Y-yes," he stammered. "I suppose there is a certain emptiness in the room that I find prickly."

As we followed Richter back down the hall, I decided I got at least some of what I was hoping for. He was flustered by the question, but *prickly*? I don't think I'd ever heard anyone use that word other than when describing a walk through a dewberry patch.

We went to the less-formal living area closer to the back of the house, the one with a giant stone fireplace, a distressed-leather sofa and matching club chairs. I took one of the chairs facing the sofa; Cooper sat across from me. This forced Richter to take the other chair.

Estelle appeared without Richter summoning her. All this hovering, kind of creeped me out—and she must have been hovering, since I didn't see Richter press any magic button or ring any bells to summon her. She asked what we wanted to drink and Boyd asked for iced tea. I declined and Richter spoke a German word. Not being up on my foreign languages, I didn't understand.

Once the drinks arrived—turned out the German word was the brand name of a beer—Richter said, "I'd like you to tell Abby everything you've told me. I've hired her to look into JoLynn's adoption. I fear someone from JoLynn's past has committed this crime against her and since I know nothing about her family or acquaintances prior to her arrival here, it's wise to find out about them."

"I agree," Cooper said. "Now, here's what I've—"

"One more thing." Richter stood and started pacing in front of us. "If by the grace of God JoLynn awakens soon, I ask that you do not discuss anything either of you have learned once you are in her presence."

Cooper pressed his lips together, looking pissed off.
Then he took a long, slow drink of tea before carefully
setting the glass on the end table next to him. "With all
respect, Mr. Richter, when that girl wakes up, I *will* be
interviewing her about anything and everything. A good
lawman doesn't make promises like what you're asking."

Even though this disagreement didn't exactly involve
me, I felt my shoulders and neck muscles tense. Cooper
definitely had his back up and that voice made him
sound meaner than he was.

Meanwhile, Richter's expression reminded me of
someone who'd taken a slug of sour milk, and he might
actually have felt that way because he grabbed up his
beer from the end table and drank, perhaps to wash
away the distaste of being challenged by yet another
person today.

Richter finally said, "You're saying I can't be in the
room?"

Cooper cocked his head. "Why do you need to be,
sir?"

"B-because she's . . . fragile. She was that way when
she came to me and this horror will only make her more
vulnerable. I won't have you upsetting her."

"Well, guess what? You're making me think there's
something you need to convey to this girl before she
answers my questions. Is that a possibility?" Cooper's
smile was long gone and his East Texas twang had grown
stronger with each exchange.

"What's that supposed to mean?" Richter shot back.
"Because if you think I had anything to do with JoLynn
getting hurt, you'd better check your facts. I would never
harm that girl. *Never.*" Richter's face was florid with
anger.

His emotional escalation seemed to please Cooper for
some reason, because his half smile had returned. "I'm
short on facts, Mr. Richter," he said. "I need plenty
more. It's my job to find out who did this and why. Not
your job, not even Abby's job, though I do appreciate
her help. We on the same page?"

Richter had finished off the beer and set the bottle
back down. He appeared more composed. "Certainly.
Now, if you would inform Abby about the automobile

and show her the driver's license, that might be useful information in her research of JoLynn's past."

"Sure." Cooper looked at me and now that he'd won the top-dog contest, he was relaxed, too. I realized he had generous laugh lines that had to have been created during another time in his life. He looked younger when he smiled, maybe forty tops.

"What have you got?" I asked.

"It's more what I haven't got—but that tells me something. The inspection sticker and registration sticker? Both fake. Good ones, I'll admit. No record of insurance that I could find."

"What about the plates?" I asked.

"Never used on any automobile registered in Texas," Cooper said. "I imagine someone's got an illegal source for plates, too."

Richter was standing in front of the fireplace, arms folded and looking concerned. "I once asked JoLynn about that car—in fact, I offered to buy her something more accessorized than that cheap compact. But she refused, said it was the first brand-new car she'd ever bought. So I asked about helping her with insurance, since she would have to change her county of residence, but she said she'd take care of it. I'm certain any fraud was the work of the charlatan who sold her the car in the first place."

Cooper tried to hide his "You've got to be kidding me" expression, but I caught it. He said, "No matter what the explanation, I have an untraceable car, so I can't check on Miss Richter's activities or acquaintances prior to her arrival here. We have to go down a different road—with Abby's help." He looked to Richter. "You got that birth certificate we talked about?"

"Yes," he answered. "Would you follow me?"

I started to get up, but Cooper spread his arms along the sofa back. "We'll wait here. Damn comfortable furniture you got, sir."

I eased back down in the chair.

Richter hesitated, then finally said, "Fine. I'll get it." He headed toward the long hallway with all its mysterious closed doors.

Cooper removed a driver's license from his uniform

shirt pocket and held it up. "JoLynn left her purse when she took off that night. The address is this ranch, so I'm betting the license is fake, too. My guess? Richter will probably come up with an explanation that clears JoLynn of any wrongdoing."

"Are you saying there's a possibility JoLynn isn't related to Richter?" I said.

"Can't say for sure, yet," he answered. "Richter says she arrived here with that birth certificate, that Katarina's name was typed in the mother slot. Father *unknown*, which is damn convenient."

"Forged or not, that birth certificate might be enough for me to learn if JoLynn lied about being the granddaughter. I've come across plenty of fake certificates in the last few years and almost every forger screws up something."

"Being former FBI, I'm more familiar with counterfeit money than counterfeit birth certificates," he said.

But when Elliott Richter returned, he looked confused and troubled . . . and had no document or envelope in his hands.

"Sh-she gave it to me to put in the wall safe. That was over a year ago."

Even if I had barbed wire for brains, I could figure this one out. "Let me guess," I said. "It's gone."

10

If I'd thought the disappearance of the birth certificate combined with the fake registration and inspection stickers would open Richter's eyes, make him at least a little suspicious of JoLynn, I was wrong. He simply refused to believe she had anything to with the certificate's disappearance.

"One of *them* took it," he'd said. "They don't want her around."

"One of them?" Cooper said as we stood in a room off Richter's office where the safe was located.

"The precious little family. The ones who'll peck on me like carrion when I'm feeble and senile."

"I see," Cooper answered, checking out the safe's digital lock.

Meanwhile, I said, "Did you give anyone else your entry code?"

I was afraid he'd say JoLynn, but he simply shook his head, looking bewildered.

Along with the wall safe, there were shelves filled with reams of paper, a large shredder, an IBM copier and a backup server for the computer. And an additional door besides the one we'd come through. Maybe some of the rooms were connected, or maybe Richter had an adjoining spot to store his gold bricks.

Cooper was still examining the safe's keypad. "No tool marks or other signs this was tampered with, but if you have the right high-tech gadget, you're in. There's also the tried-and-true method of someone standing over your shoulder and watching you punch in the numbers."

"No one did that," Richter said, his bluster back.

"Maybe you wrote down the code somewhere?" I said quickly, not wanting them to start flapping at each other again.

"My attorney has the numbers in a sealed envelope—in case anything should happen to me."

"And he'd be in big trouble if he shared that code, wouldn't he?" Cooper said.

"He would be dismissed, yes," Richter said.

Richter's eyes kept moving left, then right, then left. *Bet he's trying to think who could have possibly figured out that code.* "Memory is a strange friend," I said. "Little betrayals all the time. Maybe if you sleep on it, you'll figure out how someone could have gotten those numbers." But I was certain that if Richter came up with a name, it wouldn't be JoLynn's. Kate always tells me denial is the most powerful defense mechanism there is and this guy was using it like he'd just won the Blind-Spot Lottery. I couldn't understand why he was so hell-bent on believing JoLynn.

Cooper said, "I've got to get back to the shack we call a police station in tiny little Pineview. Either of you get anything, call my cell."

Richter led the three of us to the foyer and Cooper took off after promising to keep this case his top priority.

I turned to Richter. "I'd like to interview the rest of the family. Can that be arranged?"

"With work schedules, daytime is out. Would you find a dinner meeting acceptable? Here? Tomorrow evening?"

"I'd prefer to speak to each one alone."

"Certainly. If they're in my house, they'll cooperate. If you came to the office or went to their homes, I can't promise you their cooperation. You're free to use the library for your interviews."

"I'll need to bring my sister with me. She's in on most of my initial interviews and from what you've said about your family, I might need her. She's a psychologist."

Richter ran a hand through his hair and smiled for the first time since lunch. "Maybe she can cure the whole crew, make them forget about my money and concentrate on their own lives."

"Let me call her, see if she's free."

I opened my phone and hit her speed dial. Kate answered, saying she was hurrying into a session but would be available tomorrow evening. Richter and I settled on a six o'clock dinnertime and then I left for Houston.

First I drove by the crash site—Richter had given me directions. JoLynn had slammed into a live oak near the bottom of a hill and without brakes, only a miracle would have saved her. The two-hour drive stretched to three thanks to an accident, and when I passed a mangled car, I couldn't help thinking again about what Jo-Lynn must have felt as she tried to avoid that gigantic tree.

Once the traffic cleared, I headed straight to Jeff's place so I could have supper with him, Doris and Loreen. I let myself in with my key and found Doris watching an educational DVD on her Learning Laptop. Doris had never been to school prior to coming to live with Jeff and had lots of catching up to do. Besides Loreen, who was wonderful, we'd also found her a great tutor. We already knew Doris was high functioning, but it seemed like she picked up something new every day.

When she saw me, she set down her computer and jumped up from her big floor pillow. She wanted her hug. How could you not love someone whose affection was so genuine? And I had come to love Doris very much.

Loreen was in the kitchen of Jeff's spacious new condo. She had a "life list" now, one of those daytime-TV ideas she'd known nothing about when she'd been working as a prostitute at age sixteen. That list included learning how to cook and she was making as much progress as Doris was with her goals.

My arm around Doris, we walked to the breakfast bar that separated the living area from the kitchen, and sat down.

"What's on the menu tonight?" I asked Loreen.

"Grilled chicken, herbed rice and an arugula salad with toasted almonds. Jeff called, by the way. He won't be home for hours."

"What else is new?" My nose was busy sniffing out another wonderful something beneath the aroma of herbs. "Is that bread I smell?"

"Almost homemade." Loreen brightened. "I bought a bread machine—they're cheaper than I thought."

"What kind are you baking?" I hoped it wasn't something with fifty grains. Kate makes her own bread sometimes, but it's about as heavy as an anvil.

"Potato bread. Probably too many simple carbs, but it sounded good."

"Simple carbs?" I said. "Sounds like Food Channel talk."

"Yum. Potatoes," said Doris. "Mashed potatoes with butter."

"Butter's not good for you, Doris," Loreen said, her expression that of a good mother. "Besides, the potatoes are in the bread."

Doris scrunched up her nose in confusion and glanced at the machine. "Potatoes are big. How do you fit them in there?"

Loreen smiled. "They're mashed at the place they make the bread mix, so you *are* getting potatoes the way you like them."

I smiled, too. Loreen was so good for Doris and vice versa.

We sat down to eat about twenty minutes later and the meal was scrumptious. Loreen limited Doris to two slices of the "mashed-potato bread" by saying that we had to save enough for Jeff. Same for the chicken and brown rice. Doris would always have a weight issue, but Loreen was determined to keep Doris as healthy as possible.

The salad was delicious, however, and Loreen had no problem with Doris finishing that off. When Jeff's sister had come to live with him, most vegetables had been met with a vigorous shake of the head, but those days were over.

After the three of us cleaned up the dishes, I told Loreen I'd stay with Doris until Jeff came home. Loreen's protests to the contrary didn't last long and soon she was on her way.

Doris and I did a jigsaw puzzle until she tired of it and asked to go to her room. "Can I watch TV, Abby?"

"Would Loreen let you?" I asked.

"I can watch one hour if I do the homework. Five spelling words. Bird. B-I-R-D. Cat. C-A-T. Dog. D-O-

G. Fish. F-I-S-H. Rat. R-A-T." She grinned like a mule eating cockleburs.

"Good job," I said. "Don't go watching any of those gory shows with the bodies. You'll get nightmares, remember?"

"I remember. I'll watch TV Land, okay?"

"Good choice. I'm proud of you." These sounded like Kate's words coming from my mouth, but my sister had been right when she advised me to give Doris plenty of praise. The tantrums Doris used to throw were history.

Another hug and she was off to her room. When I peeked in a half hour later, she was sound asleep, so I turned off her small television.

I made coffee and now that Doris was down for the count, I took my mug into Jeff's office and booted up his computer. Without the birth certificate, my job had become a lot tougher.

I sipped my coffee while the computer screen populated, then clicked on the browser icon. The Internet is scary when it comes to all matters illegal. While doing a search for a case, I've sometimes found advice on how to con people out of their savings, bomb buildings and buy assault rifles. But I'd never looked into how you could completely obliterate the identity of a car. I ran a search just for my own education and discovered this kind of crime seemed to be more prevalent in the United Kingdom—but that was a Google search. After logging on to one of my private-eye databases, I discovered forgery didn't involve only checks, birth certificates and wills, and counterfeit didn't apply only to money. If people needed documentation for something they owned or had perhaps stolen—especially expensive jewelry and cars—someone could manufacture the right paperwork for a price.

Okay, now what? JoLynn had a life before showing up at the Magnolia Ranch last year. Could she have been reported as a missing person by someone? But after an hour of searching—there are thousands of missing-persons' pictures on the Net—I gave up, my eyes blurry from gazing at photo after photo.

I checked my watch and saw it was nearly ten o'clock.

Still not too late to make a call. I wandered back into the living room, found my purse and took out my cell. I located the phone entry for Penny Flannery.

I'd met Penny, a Children's Protective Services case-worker, after she called and asked me to help an adolescent foster kid who wanted to meet his biological father. The man had been AWOL from the kid's life for about fourteen years. Unfortunately that case didn't turn out well. I discovered the father was in Huntsville State Prison on an armed-robbery conviction. The young man decided he didn't want that reunion after all.

But Penny and I had become friends and I'd told her to relay to Health and Human Services that I would be willing to take cases pro bono in the future.

I punched CALL and Penny answered on the fourth ring, sounding out of breath.

"It's Abby. Did I catch you at a bad time?"

"No way," Penny said with a laugh. "I was running around in circles trying to find the damn phone. What can I do you for?"

"I need help with a case and I realize you can't search adoption files, but this particular person appeared in a man's life with his family name on her birth certificate. She told him she'd been adopted as a baby and was his biological granddaughter. In fact, the man's daughter's name was on that certificate."

"But that doesn't make sense if she was adopted. They put the *adopted* parents' names on the certificate, not the biological mother's name. Unless this woman went to court, had her adoption file opened and re-claimed her original birth certificate, that is."

"Exactly. If she didn't petition the court for her records, could she have been in foster care and not an adoption case?" I said.

"For sure. We don't change their names—we keep their original birth certificates until they're officially adopted."

"Okay, you've given me a glimmer of hope here. How confidential are foster-care records?" I asked.

"The records are pretty private unless there's a good reason to reveal a child's identity," Penny said.

"This girl—her name is JoLynn Richter, by the way—is too old for foster care now, so does that change anything as far as the confidentiality?"

"Maybe. Get to the point, Abby."

I told her the situation and how I wasn't sure we had correctly identified the woman in that coma. With the fake ID and the birth certificate conveniently missing, I definitely smelled a scam. Or, at the very least, a girl who was protecting her past.

Penny said, "This sounds like a special circumstance. I'll run the name, check with my supervisor and get back to you."

"Would a picture help?" I certainly could use one myself and felt stupid I hadn't asked Richter to provide a photo today. Maybe he could e-mail me one.

"I only need to run the name. Her picture will be in her file if she was in foster care."

"You'll call me when you know something?"

"Sure, Abby. Should be tomorrow."

We hung up and I logged off Jeff's computer. This was a start, but for some reason, I felt less than hopeful, something that never happens to me early in a case. Heck, I'm usually so optimistic, I expect to bring home a bird from a wild-goose chase. JoLynn obviously went to plenty of trouble to hide her past. The birth certificate could have been the original and she was ashamed of being a foster child. I could only hope it was as simple as that.

When I heard Jeff's key in the lock, my mood brightened.

We embraced in the living room and he murmured, "You are the best thing I've seen all day."

I pulled away and smiled. "I look better than a corpse? Gee, I'm flattered."

"Shut up, smart aleck." He drew me back and his hands gently lifted my face to his, his fingers in my hair.

Oh, yes, let the undressing begin.

An hour later, Jeff sat at the breakfast bar eating left-over chicken and rice. I'd pulled a stool to the end of the bar so I could see more than his profile.

My hands were supporting my chin as I admired him. "I think you should always eat wearing only boxers. Shirtless suits you."

"Tell me that again in about twenty years and I might smile. As for you, I get a total kick out of your hair all messed up like it always gets after we make love."

I laughed. "I can do messy hair for a lifetime. Now, I hate to change the subject, but you wanna hear about my case?"

"Sure."

I told him about my meeting with Richter, the forgeries, the missing birth certificate. "This might be my toughest job yet. Richter's got his head in the sand when it comes to JoLynn."

"Maybe he's playing you," Jeff said. "Are you sure he was as heartbroken and confused as he seemed?"

"Playing me? Why would he do that?"

Jeff finished the last grain of rice, reached over the bar to the kitchen counter and grabbed a napkin from the wicker basket. "Maybe he hopes you'll find out things about JoLynn he can use to discredit her and get her out of his life." He wiped his mouth.

"No way, Jeff. He loves that girl. Besides, Cooper found out plenty of information to open that particular door and Richter never walked through. But there's something else going on, something I can't put my finger on."

"You'll figure it out like you always do, hon. How's about we go back to bed and continue this conversation there?"

"Conversation? I don't think that's what you have in mind."

Jeff just grinned and we walked back down the hall to the bedroom, arm in arm, my head on his shoulder.

11

I left Jeff's place right after Loreen arrived early Tuesday morning to begin her day with Doris. Diva snubbed me when I came in through my back door. She always has what I call her "kitty buffet"—three dishes of her favorite dry foods and a water feeder that could be used to quench a desert. Didn't matter. I'd left her overnight and she didn't like that one bit. She ran off to a hiding place as soon as she saw me, but she *had* been waiting in the kitchen for my arrival and that made me smile.

Penny called not long after I arrived home, and I was glad I didn't have to wait around all day to hear her say, "Though I cannot tell you who *was* in foster care in Texas, I certainly can tell you who was not. No one named JoLynn Richter came through our system in the last two decades."

I sighed, thanked Penny for her help and hung up. Maybe JoLynn had been placed in foster care in another state or maybe she really had been adopted. But then how did she get her original birth certificate if it wasn't fake like everything else? There was no way to find out. I made a pot of strong coffee and went to my office. Stopping only for a few snack breaks, I spent the rest of the day again searching missing-persons databases, which apparently made Diva forgive and forget. She made good use of my lap for hours.

I'd called Richter and left a message with Eva for him to call me. I needed a picture of JoLynn for comparison with those I was searching through on the Web. I began a file, saving any missing person's profile and photo that could possibly be JoLynn's—tedious swivel-chair detective work and the part of the job I swear I'm allergic to.

Richter didn't get back to me until almost three o'clock and said he had only a family photo from last Christmas, the one time she'd agreed to be photographed. He said he'd been in Houston this morning to visit Jo-Lynn and could have brought it then but would give me a copy when Kate and I came for dinner.

An hour later, dressed in black slacks, a lacy white tank and the platinum and diamond necklace Jeff gave me for my birthday, I drove to Kate's house. She, too, lived in West University, so that was the short part of the trip. Then we were off to the Magnolia Ranch. I filled her in on yesterday's visit there and told her the plan to interview each family member alone.

When we finally reached our destination and I drove down the winding driveway to the house, I said, "Hope you have your shrink brain in gear, Kate. The way Richter talks, you're gonna need all your skills tonight."

Eva answered the door dressed in a white uniform, her gray hair pulled back so tight she looked like she'd had a face-lift. She even had a starched little maid's cap set back on her crown. After looking me up and down, unsmiling, she appraised Kate—who had chosen a red sundress with a wide patent leather belt. That's when Eva's expression softened. Kate's beauty can make anyone smile and she has *style* while I have *clothes*.

"Come in, please," Eva said.

Without a word, Eva led us through the house to the porch, where several people were drinking wine. A large glass bowl sat on a high round table and was half-filled with ice and mounded with peeled shrimp. No one was partaking. There was still plenty of daylight left and Otto, the cook who had served us yesterday, was working away at a stainless barbecue grill and prep center just outside the porch. That setup would take up my entire backyard.

Kate and I stood in the doorway with no one acknowledging our presence. Then, before I made a fool of myself by standing among these rude people and shouting, "Hi,

I'm Abby and this is Kate. We're not invisible," Scott Morton came in behind us and saved me from myself.

"Abby and Kate. I'm so glad you're helping us," he said.

Heads turned. Disdainful looks came our way. The porch, with its spinning fans and glassed-in elegance, seemed to grow chilly enough to freeze the balls off a billiards table.

"Come and meet my parents," Scott said. But I could tell the hostile atmosphere made him nervous and fidgety.

Kate whispered, "This ought to be fun."

"Yeah," I answered through the side of my mouth. "Fun as chasing armadillos."

Scott introduced his parents to Kate and me as "Mom and Leo." "Kate, this is my mother. She's Uncle Elliott's sister. That reminds me. Maybe someone needs to tell him you two are here." He made a hasty exit—and I felt like following him.

His mother switched her wineglass from right hand to left and extended her diamond-loaded fingers. "Adele Hunt. This is my husband, Leopold."

I squeezed her hand, but got nothing in return. She then greeted Kate with the same flipperesque shake. Leopold was more enthusiastic, maybe because Kate's cleavage had his full attention. Adele was obviously younger than her brother, Elliott, but Leopold was at least sixty.

Adele wagged a finger between Kate and me. "Which of you will be the interrogator?" Her bloodred lips formed a smile that said "I hope you know who you're dealing with."

"We'll probably both have questions," I said.

"I see. A double-your-fun twin killing." She sipped her white wine, her eyebrows raised knowingly at me.

Twin killing? She knew we were twins? What exactly had Elliott Richter told his family? My life history? Probably. And he'd no doubt researched Kate as soon as he knew she would be coming this evening.

Kate said, "Are you concerned about meeting with us, Mrs. Hunt?"

"Adele only worries about the stock market," Leopold said. "People never intimidate her."

"And Leopold only worries about the level of Glenlivet in the bottle he keeps in his office," Adele countered, again with her nasty smile.

I nodded at Adele. "Can't wait to talk to you after dinner." Then I took Kate's elbow. "Guess we'd better introduce ourselves to the rest of these folks."

My eye caught a woman who I assumed was Piper, Richter's new daughter-in-law. She was fashionably, or rather *sickly*, thin, her arm around the waist of a broad-shouldered man with a very fine butt. I assumed this was Matthew, Richter's son. They were talking with a tall man standing beside a wildly overdressed woman in her twenties. I mean, I'm all for free expression, but she was wearing a spangled blue gown better suited to a Las Vegas show.

I took a deep breath and pulled Kate along with me. Their little circle parted a tad when we approached them. We introduced ourselves and learned the tall man was Ian McFarland, Adele's second husband—his emphasis definitely on *second* in his charming British accent. His companion was not the daughter he shared with Adele, the one Scott told me about, but rather a young woman named Cinnamon. Mental note. Do not name any future offspring after spices.

Matthew and Piper offered the same cool reaction we'd received from Adele, but Ian and his "date" actually seemed happy to see us.

Ian looked at us and said, "You've no drinks, do you? How atrocious." Then the fair-haired Ian yelled, "Eva, you slacker. Where are you when we need you most?"

But Estelle appeared, also dressed in a white uniform. At least she'd toned down the makeup. Eva didn't make an appearance. Maybe the word *slacker* had sent her running to the kitchen to spit in Ian's salad. Estelle quickly brought Kate and me glasses of white wine.

Meanwhile, I glanced over at Adele and saw her appraising Cinnamon with disgust, but when she spotted me looking at her, she put a hand on her husband's arm and drew close to him. Oh yeah, this was gonna be some show tonight.

Piper looked healthier up close, her highlighted shoulder-length hair tucked behind her ears and secured with turquoise-studded barrettes. They matched the low-slung silver and turquoise belt she wore over a pale yellow sleeveless dress. Matthew was muscular, with the same blue eyes as his father.

"This Poirot-like visit with you sounds like such fun, Abby," Ian said. "You and your sister work as a team, I assume?"

"At times," Kate answered.

Ian focused on her, his gaze admiring. "And what might you do at other times, Kate?"

Cinnamon nudged Ian's side with her elbow. "Sugar, would you get me some of that shrimp no one else seems to want?"

His eyes still on Kate, Ian said, "Certainly, sweetheart." He walked toward the ice-filled bowl.

Piper and Matthew had stepped a few feet away and were practically feeling each other up. His hand rested on her nearly invisible butt and she had drawn close enough to breathe in his exhaled CO_2. She might pass out if they stayed that way too long.

"You two live around here?" Cinnamon adjusted the built-in bra on her gown, which practically thrust her breasts right out of her sequined bodice. She didn't seem to care.

But before we could engage in small talk, Scott reappeared with Richter at his side. All previous surliness in the room evaporated and white-tooth smiles shone on the family's golden-egg man. Richter took charge at once, insisting we all enjoy the shrimp and the wine and the beautiful summer evening for the next few minutes. Dinner would be ready in fifteen.

I headed for that bowl of shrimp like I had to get there before this roomful of sharks consumed everything including me.

12

After a fabulous dinner, Kate and I were escorted by Richter to the library at the end of that long corridor with all the closed doors. A huge bay window with cushioned seating was flanked by loaded shelves. Someone had set up an old writing desk in the center of the room and I let out a sigh at the comfort of having at least a thousand books surround us. We each took a mahogany armchair with upholstered tapestry seats and readied our notebooks for the first test. And it sure felt like a test. A test like the SATs. A test that would require focus and every one of my brain cells working.

That's why I'd cut off the wine after a taste of the wonderful Syrah served with our grilled steak, mushrooms in Marsala and skewered vegetables. I decided during the salad phase of the meal that Richter had not exaggerated about his family. By the end of dinner, I was sure Cinnamon was the only sane person besides Scott. She'd fended off barbs left and right—less-than-subtle remarks about her dress, her thick Texas accent and even her dark roots. That last one came from—who else?—Adele, who had hair so red I was certain her hairdresser's fingers were permanently stained.

Kate hardly said a word and made sure she chose a spot at the dinner table as far from Ian and Leopold as possible. I couldn't be sure this was the usual male behavior in the Richter house—to gawk at someone as lovely as Kate—but I suspected it was.

"What is wrong with these people?" Kate asked after Richter left us alone to await our first interview. "No one mentioned JoLynn or asked how she was doing. Not even Scott."

"Maybe Richter told them to keep their mouths shut about her until we talked to each of them alone. His wishes are their commands, if you didn't notice."

"Even a gecko crawling up the window would have noticed that dynamic, Abby. It's all the other stuff going on that set my head spinning."

"Dynamics," I said. "Yup, plenty of dynamics—which is only a few letters different than dynamite."

There was a rap on the door. Then Elliott Richter entered with a young woman in tow. "Simone, please cooperate with these ladies," he said. "Your mother was telling me you're wanting a new lens for your camera, and I can make that happen if you help sort out what happened to JoLynn." Richter faced us. "This is my sister Adele's daughter. If she gives you any trouble, let me know."

Simone plopped on the chair across from us. She had a camera bag with her and clutched it tightly in her lap. Skintight denim capris hugged her legs, and she wore an off-shoulder peasant blouse. Her pale makeup was so much lighter than her bronze shoulders and arms, she reminded me of a mime. She kept her focus on her camera case.

In a quiet tone Kate said, "We missed you at dinner."

"Someone missed me? That would be a first," Simone said. "Anyway, eating here is bad for the digestion. Sorta makes you want to puke."

"You're talking about the family hostility?" Kate said.

Simone lifted her head, met Kate's gaze. "I take it you're the shrink."

Kate nodded.

Simone slid down in the chair, her legs crossed at the ankles. "This isn't about what goes on here. This is about JoLynn. Ask away."

"What can you tell us about her?" I said.

"All sweet on the surface, but might be an act," she answered.

"Really? How do you know?" I said.

Simone started twisting a strand of her parti-color

hair—a mix of reds, purples and browns. "She won't talk to any of us except to smile and say hello and good-bye. Her room looks like a convent closet. But obviously someone didn't like her because she's lying in a hospital half dead."

"Maybe it wasn't JoLynn that this somebody didn't like. Maybe she learned something while living here that made her a target," I suggested.

"You mean she found out something about us?" Simone laughed. "Ooooh. Something evil lurks in the hearts of the Richter clan. Something besides self-serving arrogance."

Kate said, "You sound like a very bright girl. Insightful. Are you in college?"

"I start at U.T. the end of the month," she said. "Some stupid freshman orientation. I know how to get around. Why do I need an orientation?"

Kate ignored the attitude. "You like photography. Do you plan to do something with that?"

"If Mom and Uncle Elliott will get off my case, yes. *Everybody* has to work for the company. Well, not this girl."

Even though she still sounded insolent, Kate was getting her to open up. Yup, Kate was good at that, so I shelved my impatience and let her continue.

"Sounds like you know a lot about your family. You mentioned they're self-serving. Who's the best at that?"

"That's easy. Big daddy, of course. Dear Uncle Elliott. When the rest of us weren't worshipping him enough, he found someone else to kneel at his feet. Little Jo-Lynn, bless her heart."

"And how does that make you feel?" Kate asked.

"Oh, no. We're not heading down that road. I have my own shrink, thank you very much."

"We can change the subject." I tried to sound as pleasant as my sister. With this girl, I found that difficult. "But you're young enough that you haven't worked for your uncle yet?"

"No. I work for my *father*—that's Ian McFarland by the way," Simone said.

"And Mr. McFarland works for Richter Oil and Gas?" I said.

"Yes, but I have nothing to do with those freaks. My father is a brilliant man. There's more to his life than consulting with Uncle Elliott. He does research. He writes papers." She wasn't looking at us again but rather examining a nail bitten to the quick.

"You live with your father, then?" Kate asked.

"Don't I wish? But what does that have to do with JoLynn? No, wait. I'll answer myself. Absolutely nothing."

"You're angry, Simone," Kate said. "Is JoLynn the reason? Because you understand that she's badly hurt, that she might die."

Simone blinked several times. "Are you trying to see if I flinch? If I care?"

If she wanted to convince me that she didn't, she wasn't succeeding. Concern had crossed her face, even though she was trying hard to hide it.

I said, "Did she talk to you about her life before she came here?"

"We *weren't* best buds," Simone said.

"Your uncle mentioned a lens for your camera," Kate said. "I'm guessing you'd like to be able to buy your own equipment."

I was wondering about this abrupt change in direction, but when I saw Simone's reaction to the question, I understood. Her fingers with their chewed-down nails fiddled with the camera-case strap and her face softened so much she looked like a different girl.

"Yes, but I'm not very good yet," Simone said. "I couldn't make a living at this."

"Is that where you were tonight? Taking pictures?" Kate said.

"Summer sunsets are awesome," she said. "And they teach you a lot about lighting and angles because you have to make adjustments if you want to get a shot that really captures all the hues. There's so much to learn about shooting directly into light."

"And so you missed dinner," I said.

"Yeah. Is there anything else? Because I don't know anything about JoLynn. We hardly spoke."

Why didn't I believe her? "She never seemed scared? Worried?" I said.

Simone stood. "Who would notice something like that in this place?"

I'd clearly pushed her buttons again because she turned and strode out of the room.

After the door slammed shut, I said, "You, my dear Simone, *would* notice something like that."

"And that's why she wanted out of here," Kate said.

"What's with all the anger?" I said.

"Maybe she felt overshadowed or threatened by Jo-Lynn, though you'd never get her to admit it in this setting with all those *self-serving others* hanging around the house."

Before I could respond, someone rapped on the door. The smiling Ian came in carrying a quarter-filled brandy snifter and greeted us both by kissing our hands. He sat in his daughter's vacated chair.

"Simone give you a bit of hell, did she?" he said.

"Why do you say that?" Kate asked.

"She left the house in rather a hurry. Emotional girl, but I do love her very much."

"I believe she decided we were invading her privacy," I said.

"There is no privacy in this family, something she has yet to fully understand. I fear they'll run her off one of these days, just as they did Katarina."

"Who are *they*?" I said.

Ian glanced around the room. "This is a much more pleasant setting after that god-awful, tense dinner, though I feel like I've walked into an episode of *MI-5* on the BBC. Rather like domestic surveillance being conducted in person by you two lovely ladies. You think JoLynn's little mishap could be terrorism?" Amusement twinkled in his eyes.

"Interesting you should change the subject and interesting you should jump to that conclusion," I said.

"Oh, we're all somber, are we? Guess I should put on my serious face. How can I be of help?"

"How long have you worked for Elliott Richter?" I said.

"Let me see," McFarland said. "Katarina was ten and Matthew was four, so that would mean twenty-nine years. Elliott and I have made a great team. But the poor chap's endured far too much tragedy. Awful luck."

"And how well did you know JoLynn?" I asked.

"Hardly had any contact with the girl. Bit of a shrinking violet compared to the rest of the family. But Elliott was smitten, that's for certain."

Kate leaned forward, her arms folded in front of her on the desk. "Smitten in what way?"

Ian pointed a long, well-manicured finger at Kate. "You're the psychiatrist?"

"Psychologist," she corrected.

"Too bad. I was hoping you might help me out with a bit of Ambien. I always have trouble sleeping after a visit here."

"You didn't answer my question," Kate said.

"If you're considering incest on the part of Elliott—which is where I believe mental-health experts love to go first—I'm afraid it wasn't like that. Adoration. Blind paternal love. That's what I'm speaking of."

"What did Richter say or do to make you come to that conclusion?" I asked.

"What didn't he say? 'JoLynn is sweet, so much like her mother.' 'JoLynn thinks she might want to help children in Africa.' 'JoLynn is thinking about college, but she never finished high school.' 'JoLynn refused the BMW I wanted to buy her, can you imagine that? None of you would have refused.' Meanwhile, his other drooling heirs were out on the job while JoLynn was home admiring the swimming pool—or perhaps the swimming pool attendant? Quite an attractive young woman, our JoLynn. Looked very much like Katarina."

"You believe Mr. Richter made sure she stayed away from the others? That he did this intentionally?" I said.

Ian cocked his head. "Ah, you're quite brilliant, aren't you, Abby? Yes. Good summary, my dear."

I ignored the smiling sarcasm, the attentive expression and the body language that indicated he'd like to talk more about me and less about JoLynn. "You're saying you were never alone with her? Never got to ask her about her past?"

Ian threw back the last of his brandy or whatever had

been in his glass. "Not on your life. She was treated like a precious gem Elliott needed to keep in a glassed-in case. Though he never gave warning, one knew better than to get too close."

"You're very insightful, Mr. McFarland," Kate said.

"Please call me Ian." The charming blues focused on Kate now.

"Simone is your daughter with Adele, correct?" she went on.

"We're back to my daughter, are we? I suppose she's raised suspicion, perhaps due to the surliness I'm sure you were forced to endure. Let me be clear that Simone, though prone to fits of temper, would never harm anyone. Adele, however, is quite another story. You might want to focus your efforts there."

"You mentioned Katarina earlier. How well did you know her?" I asked.

"Quite a shining light in the world, Katarina was. A tragedy she had to wither away like that. They've made great progress with cancer in the twenty or so years since she's been gone. Though I was never privy to what kind of cancer she had, she surely would have lived longer had she been born years later."

Kate said, "Do you know why Katarina ran off for those two years?"

He laughed, an openmouthed loud laugh, at that. Too much wine, maybe?

"You've got to be kidding," he said. "You've met Elliott. Katarina was being smothered, of course. We all knew she had to do something. Her running away came as no surprise to Adele or me—one of the few things we ever agreed upon when we were married, by the way."

"How did you know she was being smothered?" Kate placed her elbow on the table and rested her chin on her fist.

"Elliott, as I said earlier, acted with Katarina rather like he's been behaving with JoLynn. Possessive. Adoring. And toward the end, after Katarina returned from God knows where, he kept the details very hush-hush—that is, if he knew any details. Like where she'd been. The cancer. I mean, we were all shocked when we learned she was dying."

I recalled the words on Katarina's tombstone. *Taken from the secretive world, taken from the pain of life.* That memorial to Richter's daughter certainly jibed with what Ian was saying and made me believe that Richter might not have known where his daughter had run off to.

"Is there anything else I can offer?" Ian asked, glancing at his watch.

I wondered if his time matched the ticking clock on the fireplace mantel that had begun to distract and annoy me. Hard to believe it was already past nine p.m. "Not now," I said, trying to assimilate everything I'd heard so far. Which was more accurate? JoLynn the sneak or JoLynn the gem under glass? Maybe both, I thought.

He stood, bowed at the waist and in a mocking tone said, "I am your servant."

After the door closed, Kate said, "He's not telling all he knows."

"What makes you say that?" I said.

"Body language. Eye shifts. All very subtle but still there," she said.

"Good thing you were paying better attention than I was." I glanced at what looked like an antique mantel clock, resisting the urge to throw my notebook at it. "Is that damn clock bothering you as much as it is me?" I said.

But before Kate could answer, a knock sounded and Eva stuck her head in the door. Her ridiculous little hat was gone, thank goodness. You cannot take someone seriously when they're wearing a doily on their head.

She said, "Herr Richter thought you might require a break and some refreshments. Coffee? Tea? A brandy? Water? Whatever you wish."

"Coffee for me." I looked at Kate.

"If you have green tea, that would be wonderful," she said.

Eva nodded and closed the door.

While Kate left to find a powder room, I stood and stretched, then walked around, glancing at the books, resisting the urge to tamper with the clock. It had one of those pendulums that matched its loud *tick-tick-tick* and was probably wound with a key at the back. Worth plenty, I'd bet. I then focused on the books and noted Richter had a variety of titles, everything from Shakespeare to a collection of first-edition Nero Wolfe mysteries by Stout.

Since Kate had left the door open, I was startled when Richter spoke. He had stepped into the room without a sound.

"This is JoLynn's favorite room," he said. "She would sit in the window seat and read for hours. She told me she never finished high school and yet I caught her reading Chaucer one day and Poe another time. A very bright girl, but perhaps I told you that before."

"No, you didn't," I said. "I think you've been too worried about whether she'll pull through to offer me much information. How was she this morning?"

"Peaceful. As if she wasn't in as much pain as she has been in the last few days. They'll gradually bring her out of the coma soon, I'm told."

I smiled. "That's good news."

"Yes. I'm optimistic." He reached into his suit jacket and pulled out a photograph. "You wanted a picture of JoLynn, but this is the best I can do."

I took it from him and found her immediately. She and her grandfather were the only ones smiling. "She's . . . beautiful." I continued to stare at her face and felt anger building in my gut. The person in that hospital bed hardly looked like this person. Who could have done this to her?

Just then, Estelle arrived with a tray of cups and steaming pots. Richter stepped aside and said he would give us ten minutes until he sent in Adele. He left the room with a nod and an almost pleasant smile.

Estelle said, "Anything else?"

How could we need anything more? There was not only a pot of coffee for me and Kate's green tea but biscotti, cookies and a bowl of Andes chocolate mints.

"This is beautiful, Estelle. Do you eat all this wonderful food, too? Because I might just have to get a job here if that's the case."

"I don't think you want a job here." She smiled and then was gone.

She's probably right, I thought. *Bet she sees the worst*

of everyone. I poured coffee and was dropping a mint into my cup just as Kate came back.

"What's that?" she asked.

As if she didn't know. "My own special energy drink."

She raised an eyebrow but made no comment as she poured from the small teapot. Her tea smelled wonderful—a touch of citrus, maybe?

I slid the photo over to her. "Check out JoLynn."

Kate's eyes widened and I heard her intake of breath. "My God, she looks so different than . . . what we saw. Really lovely."

I held up a biscotto for Kate. "How's about we leave that photo right on the table?"

She refused the biscotto—her loss, since they tasted homemade. She sipped her tea and sat deep in thought while I ate two of those crispy critters, along with three cookies. Then I added another mint to my second cup of coffee.

Adele arrived minutes later, and with her came a blast of cold air. "Pardon my saying so, but this is probably the most *ridiculous* thing my brother has ever subjected us to. And who chose what order we'd be interrogated?" She'd seated herself in front of us. She wore a blue silk blouse with see-through cap sleeves and tiny pleats from collar to hem, this with a black crepe skirt.

But her shoes were what had caught my eye earlier. The same bright blue as her blouse. I'd never bought shoes that cost hundreds of dollars just to match a blouse. But Aunt Caroline had. Maybe there was a nice person under the facade Adele presented just as with my aunt.

Kate was saying that Adele's brother, Elliott, decided who would be interviewed in what order.

"I assumed as much," Adele said. "Get on with this so Leopold and I can leave. We'd like to be home before ten." She then caught a glimpse of the photo on the desk and quickly looked away.

"What can you tell us about JoLynn? Did she share anything about her past with you?" I said.

"She never told me anything, but I can tell you where she came from. Some trailer park or other low-rent housing. Her clothes had to be from the sale pile at Wal-

Mart. Cheap earrings, Payless shoes and makeup from CVS pharmacy. And she continued to wear those atrocious outfits. Dollar flip-flops by the pool. Blue jean short shorts when we barbecued. Did she think she came here to audition for *Li'l Abner*?"

"You're very observant," Kate said with more warmth and sincerity than I could have mustered.

Adele actually smiled, the first one I'd seen her allow since we arrived. "You can tell a considerable amount about a person from how they present themselves. And she presented herself as white trash."

"Could you tell anything from her accent? Her grammar? We'd like to figure out where she lived before arriving here," Kate said.

Thank God my sister was taking over. That damn clock coupled with a woman who made Aunt Caroline seem downright charming was about to drive me insane.

"Hmmm," Adele said. "She was Texan, I believe. Plenty of *y'all*s in her vocabulary. I must admit she seemed almost intelligent, however."

Finally something positive, I thought. "How did you know?" I asked.

"Books. She knew about books. Young people rarely read literary anything, but when Elliott gathered us all for my birthday, JoLynn and Simone discussed Edith Wharton over dinner, if you can imagine that. Simone has had the best possible education, but this girl? I was surprised, to say the least. But other than that, JoLynn seemed like, well, the word *hick* comes to mind."

Adele knew more about JoLynn than I'd thought she would. I said, "Did she ever seem nervous or concerned for her safety?"

"No," she said curtly. "She was being protected by my brother. That's what this is all about, you know. He failed her. He failed and he can't stand to fail. About time he had a lesson in fallibility."

"You're pleased JoLynn was injured?" I blurted. I blamed the blurting on the clock. Even if I could shut the thing off, I'd probably still hear it. Hell, I might not even get any sleep tonight because it would still be ticking away in my brain.

Adele squared her shoulders, color rising up her

throat. "If you tell my brother that's what you've dis-
cerned from this *stupid* little interview, I promise you,
you'll regret it. I have nothing more to say."

And she didn't, because she got up and left.

"Like mother, like daughter," I said after she was
gone.

"Abby, you could have kept that last observation
about JoLynn to yourself. I'm guessing Adele knows
more than all the others we've talked to put together."

"I screwed up and I'm sorry. But that clock is making
me slap-assed crazy."

"You mean the one on the mantel? Or the big grandfather clock by the door?" Kate said.

I stood and walked over to the fireplace, pointing at
my enemy. "This thing. Can't you hear it?"

"No. You have superpowers now?" Kate said with
a laugh.

Enough was enough. I gently moved the clock to get
at the controls in the back, fearing I might break something. But I shouldn't have worried. It was plenty sturdy.
A small lever turned the whole thing off. There. Noise
gone. But when I went to slide the clock back into place,
a folded piece of paper that had been taped to the bottom dislodged.

13

I turned to Kate and held up the folded paper. "Funny place to save something," I said.

Kate offered her disapproving-mother stare. "Maybe the clock was unstable and what you've removed was making it work correctly."

"There is nothing *correct* about that clock and the damn thing's lucky I didn't bring in the Lady Smith and put it out of its misery." I started to unfold the paper because I could tell there was printing on it, but someone knocked on the door, so I stuck it in my pocket. After I called, "Come on in," Leopold Hunt entered the room.

"Thanks for waiting around so long," I told him as I sat back down.

"No problem." Hunt sat opposite us. "Elliott's pretty upset about this whole thing with JoLynn. I'll do anything I can to help."

Hunt reminded me of our computer company's CEO. He was trim, had expertly dyed hair with just enough gray to look distinguished and wore a striped silk tie now loosened. His suit jacket had been left behind somewhere.

"What's your opinion of JoLynn?" I asked.

That seemed to throw the guy off, which was what I'd hoped. "Opinion? You think I had an opinion, Miss Rose?"

"It's Abby. Your observations? Is that a better question?"

"Well, let me think how best to describe her. Pretty.

Intelligent. Cheerful, for the most part. I—I don't know what else to say."

Kate said, "Cheerful for the most part. Did you see her when she wasn't so happy?"

"We all have our days. It was nothing really." He laughed nervously.

"Are you worried about talking to us?" I said. "Because Mr. Richter wants us to find out anything and everything we can to assist the police in investigating this murder attempt."

With the mention of Richter, he started talking rapidly. "Sh-she was in here, in the library, one day. I came in to grab a book we needed for a business meeting Elliott had arranged here at the house. He sometimes does that. Anyway, she was sitting over there." He pointed at the window seat. "You can't exactly ignore someone when they're crying, so I asked her what was wrong."

"And her answer?" Kate asked.

"She said nothing was wrong, she just needed a cry. But she was wedged into the corner. She had a book clutched to her chest and—take this with a grain of salt because I know little if anything about women's emotions—she seemed extremely sad."

"When was this?" I asked.

"Maybe two months ago."

"You have no idea why she was sad?" I said.

"I couldn't even offer a guess, but she looked so lost . . . like a small, scared child."

I leaned forward. "You didn't ask her anything else?"

He squirmed, avoided my stare. "I don't recall. But I offered her my handkerchief and she refused."

"She give you any explanation?" I said.

"She asked me not to tell her grandfather. But I never would have done that anyway. Elliott and I have a business relationship and weeping relatives aren't the kind of thing we discuss. It's not like I knew the girl more than to say hello. The whole episode was very awkward—for both of us."

"Ah, awkward," I said. "Kind of like this little talk right now?"

"To be honest, yes. I have no idea what you expect from us," he said.

"You seem like a smart guy," I said. "We want to know what JoLynn shared about her past and who might have wanted to kill her. And since no one has given us any possible suspects, I guess we'll have to continue to concentrate our efforts on all of you." I smiled.

"That's ridiculous. None of us would have hurt her."

Kate said, "Who do you include in that *us*?"

Hunt seemed relieved to interact with my kinder, gentler sister. "Anyone in the family. Adele and me, for sure. Certainly neither Scott nor Simone. Simone is my stepdaughter and since she didn't show up—"

"Actually, she did show up," I said.

"Really? How was she?" he asked.

I was surprised by his reaction. He seemed genuinely concerned. "Pissed off," I answered.

The wrinkles on his forehead deepened. Definitely worried, but why? Of course all these people knew things they weren't saying, and Hunt was no different, but he might be a weak link in the chain of the unspoken.

He pressed his lips together and shook his head. "Let me apologize for Simone. She's—anyway, I'm sorry."

"Don't worry about causing *me* any discomfort. See, I even had the roof of my mouth tattooed, so I can take whatever she or any one of you wants to dish out," I said.

Hunt's eyes widened. Guess he believed me about the tattoo.

"Abby's kidding," Kate said.

But Hunt didn't seem to hear her. *Still dwelling on his stepdaughter?* I wondered.

"Were there other times you and JoLynn interacted?" Kate asked. "Anything else you noticed about her mood or demeanor?"

"As I said before, I don't usually pick up on those things."

"But your stepdaughter is able to get your attention?" she said.

He hesitated, seemed to be considering how to respond. "Since you've met Simone, you must realize she gets most people's attention. As for JoLynn, she was a pleasant person who could discuss books. World affairs were another story. She didn't have much to add to those conversations. Aside from Elliott, Scott seemed the closest person to JoLynn. Have you talked to him?"

"We have," I said. "But you know what, Mr. Hunt? I sense you know more about this girl than you're saying."

His face reddened. "I do not."

I leaned even closer. "Was there talk in your family about how big her slice of the pie might be now that Elliott Richter has welcomed her into the family?"

Hunt still wouldn't make eye contact. "This line of questioning . . . is, well—"

"All I need is a simple yes or no."

He finally looked at me. "No. We don't discuss money."

"Ah. So Mr. Richter keeps you guessing about your wife's inheritance," I said. "No wonder you people are all as tense as terriers watching a rat hole. Thanks for your time."

He stood and nodded, his jaw tight after that remark, one I wished I could take back. Making nice with these folks might be a better approach, but my patience had been used up.

"Good evening, ladies." Hunt offered a polite smile and left the room.

Kate said, "Why were you so hard on him?"

"Because I'm frustrated. Everyone's holding back. Leopold's probably Adele's puppet, but he has a weakness: his stepdaughter."

"You're right about that. And you can assume anything related to JoLynn, even that crying episode, was duly reported to Adele."

Another knock on the door and Matthew stuck his head in the room. "Would you mind if my wife and I came in together?"

I glanced at Kate. "Your call, Doc."

"That would be fine, Mr. Richter." She smiled at him, probably hoping to show me how to get on the right side of folks.

He widened the door and he and Piper came in hand in hand. Since we had not spoken to these two at all, even at dinner, I had no clue what to expect.

Matthew hurried to bring over another chair to face us and waited until his wife sat down before he took his seat. He said, "Before you start asking questions, you should know that Piper has been so busy in the last year with the whole wedding thing that she hardly knows JoLynn."

I looked at the bride. "But you've had several months since the wedding, right?"

Piper's thin face colored. "I have my own circle of friends and besides, she didn't seem to show any interest in getting to know me."

Indeed, the world obviously revolved around Piper. I said, "No one seems to have taken time to get to know JoLynn." I shifted to Matthew. "Tell me you're different."

"Different how?" He was deflecting the question, maybe hoping to figure out what we wanted from him.

"Did you welcome her into the family?" I said.

"Certainly. But we were busy planning a wedding around the time she showed up. Besides, I had to adjust to becoming her uncle. I knew next to nothing about my sister, Katarina—we were so many years apart. I only knew she was some kind of saint. The way my father reacted to JoLynn's arrival? Well, it was as if my sister had risen from the dead."

Now we were getting somewhere. "Katarina was his favorite?"

"What does Matthew's childhood have to do with this?" Piper gripped her husband's hand tighter.

I wanted to come back with something a lawyer might say, like "It goes to motive, ma'am," but Kate saved me by addressing Piper.

"You're the newest member of the family. What's your take on JoLynn's relationship to everyone?"

"My father-in-law kept her as isolated from the rest of us as possible," she said. "He's a very complex man whom we all adore. But sometimes we simply do not understand him."

"Why do you think he kept her *isolated*?" I said. This wasn't the first time we'd heard this tonight.

But Matthew cut in before his wife could respond. "Ask my father. That's about him and JoLynn, *not us*."

"Sorry if we've upset you, Matthew," Kate said in her soothing therapist tone.

"He's not upset," Piper said. "Matt is the calmest person I know."

"Okay," I said. "So you *don't* think your father is playing favorites again?"

"You're here to find out who harmed JoLynn, right?" Matthew said.

"In part," I said, "but my real job—"

"If you're implying I tried to kill JoLynn so I could have Dad all to myself, that's plain stupid. If you haven't noticed, I'm a grown man, not an adolescent."

I nodded. "And no one in *this* family could be accused of adolescent behavior."

"I don't appreciate your attitude," he said.

"And neither do I," the Piper piped in.

"Let me give this to you straight," I said. "Chief Boyd is investigating a *murder* attempt on someone who lived in this house. I'm here because your father wants to find out exactly what happened and why. JoLynn could have mentioned things in passing to family members that might help me get to the bottom of this. I'm merely trying to gather information tonight, not to accuse anyone of anything. But the bunch of you make me feel like I'm riding circles around a swamp. What's in that swamp, Matthew?"

"I have no idea what you're talking about." He studied his diamond-encrusted watch.

"Right. Guess I'll have to tell your father none of you were much help."

He looked up quickly. "I don't know anything about JoLynn. What I do know is that my father is an idiot. And you can tell him I said that."

"An idiot when it came to JoLynn?" Kate asked.

"Yes." Matthew Richter rested back in the chair and sighed in frustration. "He's a meticulous man. He does extensive background checks on everyone he hires, but he lets *her* take over his life without even knowing her last known address."

"How do you know he *didn't* research her past?" I asked.

"Because if he had, he would have discovered what I did. That she doesn't seem to have existed before she showed up here. Does that tell you something?"

Piper's eyes were wide when she turned to her husband. "I thought we weren't going to talk about that, baby."

Finally *something*. I said, "Did you hire someone to check her out?"

"I was worried about my father, that's all," he said.

"I take it that's a yes?"

He drew a deep breath and said, "Okay, yes. Are you happy? Can we leave now?"

"Who did you hire?" I said.

"That's none of your business," Piper said.

But I could tell Matthew's wheels were turning. He knew I reported to the man with the money.

"I hired an investigator named Rocco Green. He told me there was no record of any driver's license for Jo-Lynn Richter and no vehicle was ever registered in her name. I wasn't sure what to do after learning that," he said.

"Did you tell your father?" Kate asked.

"Yes," he answered. "He said I should stay out of his business. Obviously he didn't care because that was six months ago and she's still here. Or . . . *was* here."

And you're hoping she won't come back, I thought. "Did this detective learn anything else during his background check?"

"No. He said I'd need her Social Security number if I really wanted to find out about her, and well, I couldn't give him that."

His eyes drifted away from mine and Piper wasn't looking at me, either.

"Because you couldn't *find* her Social Security number?" But I knew the answer. The tips of his ears were bright red and Piper had taken a keen interest in her fingernails.

"You're making a lot of insinuations," Piper said, still not making eye contact.

"You searched her room, right?" I said to Matthew. Then I looked at Piper. "And maybe you helped."

Matt's flush deepened and Piper smoothed a strand of hair away from her face.

"No need to say more," I said. "You've both been a *big* help."

*   *   *

Kate and I left Magnolia Ranch for Houston after ten p.m.—which was late for Kate, but she wasn't complaining. She seemed more like her old self than I'd seen in months. I told Elliott Richter I'd use what information I'd gotten from the family to help research JoLynn's past. He'd pressed me for specifics, but I said I needed to sort through what we'd learned first. He hadn't been exactly forthcoming with me about JoLynn from what Matthew said, and before I reported on those interviews, I wanted to calm down, maybe understand why.

"That was an interesting evening," Kate said once we reached the main highway. "Why do you think Richter didn't tell you what Matthew learned?"

"I don't know. Maybe he wanted me to find out for myself—he is paying me a lot of money, after all. But oh boy, Aunt Caroline would have loved every minute of tonight." I steadied the steering wheel with my left hand and reached into my right pocket. "By the way, I forgot to turn that clock back on. But let's see what's written on this." I handed over the folded paper.

Kate turned on the map light. "Could be some old note that came with the clock. Who knows? Maybe we'll end up on *Antiques Roadshow* showing off something Washington wrote to Jefferson."

"You watch *Antiques Roadshow*?" I said.

"Well, yeah. Lately."

"Dreamer," I said. "There's nothing old about that paper. Looked brand-new to me."

"You're right," Kate said. "This is a Xerox copy of a newspaper article. The print is small and all I can make out is the headline. 'Mysterious Katarina Richter Succumbs to Cancer.' "

I nearly swerved off the road. "You're kidding. That's the same article I found online. The one that talks about Katarina's disappearance and how at first they thought she'd been kidnapped. Do me a favor? There's a plastic grocery bag in the backseat. Could you put that paper in there? Cooper Boyd has JoLynn's prints and I'd like to see if she handled this paper."

"You think *she* put it under the clock?" Kate said.

"I have no idea. Could be something Richter saved. But JoLynn spent time in that library, according to both

Leopold Hunt and Richter himself. If this article meant something to her and if she had a clue that people were searching through her things—which of course they were—she might have hidden it."

"What does the article say?" Kate asked.

For the rest of the trip home, I filled her in on my Internet research into the Richters, Katarina and missing persons. Then we discussed the bigger picture the Richter family had presented—their lack of concern about JoLynn's welfare, the threat she represented and, beneath it all, what I had felt and Kate confirmed: smoldering hostility.

14

Diva and I lay in bed past our usual time to get up on Wednesday morning. While she purred next to me, I thought about the case. Each family member offered me something different to consider.

Matthew's discovery that JoLynn's license was a fake made me wonder why no one in the family came right out and said JoLynn might be faking other things—like why she made her entrance into their lives. So what made Elliott Richter so trusting? Did he need the closeness and affection their relationship seemed to provide? Something that simple might be the answer.

As I stroked Diva, she turned on her back and stretched out, her purrs almost as loud as that dumb clock last night. Now in possession of a photo of JoLynn, I could return to my missing-persons Internet search with a better idea of what she looked like. Though she was using an invalid driver's license, she did have a name, though perhaps not *JoLynn Richter*. The birth certificate could have been fake, too. But maybe her story wasn't. Maybe JoLynn was put up for adoption— but never found a home as a child. I reached for my phone on the bedside table. *Penny Flannery, here I come with more questions.*

I got Penny's voice mail and left a message for her to call me when she was free. She didn't phone back until after I'd done forty minutes on my new elliptical trainer. I bought the contraption after deciding to give up running in Houston's summer heat. It was just too draining, not to mention very bad for the skin. I have nice skin, one of my decent features, and was discovering that ugly red bumps erupted after every outdoor run.

While I'd exercised, Diva watched me huff and sweat with great interest and seemed to be smiling slyly and maybe thinking, *When will she figure out she's not getting anywhere?* I just finished and was about ready to shower when Penny called back.

"Same problem case?" she asked.

"Yup. Question: You put up pictures of foster kids on a Web site, right?"

"Sure. First names and case numbers only," she answered.

"And I'll bet like all things on the Internet, those pictures are available for eternity, even if they've been removed from the site."

"I—I guess so. I'm sure someone has those files on their computer, maybe in Austin, maybe in Houston." She paused. "And that's what you want me to do? Find an old photo array that might have your girl's face?"

"Can you do that for me?" I asked.

"I can, but I don't know how long it will take."

"I know you're busy and I'm sorry, but—"

"This is no problem, Abby. You've done so much for the foster kids, we'll help any way we can. I don't have any dealings with our Web site people, that's all. But I promise I will find someone in the know as soon as I can. What years are we looking at?"

"If she was in the system, she would have aged out about five years ago max."

"To be safe, I'll get as many files as I can," she said.

"Great. In the meantime, I'll keep checking missing-persons databases. I have a photograph now, which will help. You're the best, Penny. I owe you."

"You don't owe me anything," she said.

An hour later, fresh from the shower, I sat down at my computer with my coffee and a day-old bagel that turned out to be as hard as a frozen turtle shell. I gave up after two attempts to bite into it and concentrated on the work instead.

I tried the HPD missing-persons site first and discovered there were very few photos. It seemed to be geared more to giving information on whom to contact to file a missing-person's report. I sat back. Maybe Jeff could make this chore a whole lot easier.

I picked up the phone again and punched his speed dial number. Lucky for me, he actually answered with, "Hey, you. You're the kind of distraction I can use."

"Because you're dealing with something gruesome right now?"

"About as gruesome as it gets. Court. I'm outside and don't plan to go in until the last possible minute."

"You don't care if you're sweating like a penguin on the equator when you have to testify?"

"Couldn't care less. What do you need, hon?"

"A little help. I've already made one swipe at missing-persons databases on the Internet and it's a little overwhelming. Do you know anyone in the missing-persons division who could help me?"

Jeff laughed. "You gotta be kidding. Do you know how many people are reported missing in Houston in a year?"

"I have no idea."

"Try seven thousand. And with only nine investigators to handle the load."

"Shut *up*. I had no idea. Guess I need to handle this myself."

"That would be wise," he said. "How's your aunt, by the way?"

"Shoot. I need to call her. I've gotten so wrapped up in this case, I've been ignoring my obligation to be nice to her while she tells me how the cow ate the cabbage."

Jeff laughed again. "I was thinking about asking Loreen to stay late tonight with Doris so you and I can spend some alone time. That sound good?"

I smiled. "Sounds better than good. Now I'm the one who'll be distracted all day. I'll see you later, then."

"Bye, hon." He disconnected.

I sighed. Alone time. And he would arrange it. God, I loved that guy.

I got busy on my computer, the conversation with Jeff making me feel upbeat and the recent picture of JoLynn making me feel a tiny bit more optimistic about my chances of finding out if anyone reported her missing.

But my optimism was about used up by two that afternoon. The bagel had been replaced by a ham sandwich I didn't even remember making, the coffee by two Dr Peppers. I was beginning to believe way too many people in this country had been kidnapped, been run off by their families or died without anyone finding their bodies. The saddest part was that many of the faces I kept seeing were of missing children. Most of them were probably parental abductions, but that didn't make me feel any better. Those kids were lost to someone who loved them dearly, someone who probably waited every day for a phone call that might never come.

Some of the databases allowed me to narrow my search; some of them didn't. I checked all the bigger sites in Texas first, but I couldn't exclude any state in the Union. Though JoLynn sounded like she was from Texas, according to Adele, that didn't mean JoLynn hadn't moved around and been reported missing from someplace other than here.

I took a Snickers from my desk drawer stash, opened the wrapper and enjoyed a taste of comfort as I pulled up what had to be my hundredth missing-persons site, an obscure one put together by a Houston group called "Friends of the Lost." *Sounds like a cult,* I thought. *No wonder it didn't come up right away.* Thank goodness the site was blessedly easy to navigate and allowed me to narrow the search by entering fields like age, ethnicity and hair color.

I'd just loaded JoLynn's data when the phone rang. I picked up and said hello, my eyes on the newest rows of faces.

"It's Penny. Sorry it took me so long, but it was a struggle finding out who takes care of our archived pictures. I'm sending you an e-mail now with a zip file. All the Web photos of adoptable foster kids from 1995 to 2005."

But I didn't reply, instead focusing hard on the current photo display.

"Abby? You there?"

My heart quickened as I honed in on one grainy picture. I blinked a few times and found my voice. "Sorry, Penny. Thank you so much. Anytime you need my help, you know where to find me."

"Damn right I do. Good luck." She hung up.

I fumbled to find the recharging stand for the receiver, unwilling to take my eyes off the screen. I held the photo Elliott Richter had given me next to the unfocused face on the monitor.

The computer copy was poor quality and another woman had obviously been cropped out of the picture. I could see a shoulder and a dark-skinned feminine hand holding fast to the blonde's upper arm. The blonde *had* to be JoLynn. Same jawline, same tilt of the head. But though I believed I had finally found her, the caption under the picture did *not* say "JoLynn Richter."

This young woman's name was Elizabeth Dugan. She disappeared from Houston over a year ago and was listed as "missing from home." Her height, weight and gender matched what I knew, but there was little else. Maybe I was wrong—maybe this wasn't JoLynn.

I sat back and squinted at the photo and still found the similarities too close to be ignored. Though some of the pictures had case numbers and police contacts listed beneath them, this particular picture gave only an e-mail address.

I jotted it down but decided to try something else first. I typed "Elizabeth Dugan" into Google and the only promising hit led me to a missing-persons message board. The same e-mail address was attached to a message that read,

> No one seems to think Elizabeth is really missing, especially since her husband reported to the police that she left on her own after an argument. She wouldn't do that without talking to me. She is 5 feet 4 inches, 105 pounds, blond hair and blue eyes, twenty years old. You can see her picture on the Friends of the Lost Web site. E-mail me if you have any information. My name is Roberta Messing.

A husband? A different name? A friend or relative who was worried about her? Would this be a break in the case that might also break Elliott Richter's heart? I sent out an e-mail to Roberta Messing with trembling fingers.

15

I waited at my desk fifteen minutes for a return e-mail from Roberta Messing, but like my daddy always told me, I was never burdened with patience. When I started in on my fingernails rather than adding more chocolate calories, I knew I couldn't sit around hoping to see a pop-up on the monitor informing me of new mail.

I plugged Messing's name into Switchboard.com and found not only her phone number but her business and personal information as well. If people only knew what the Internet had on them.

Roberta was a veterinarian in a practice with two others at Oakdale Veterinary Hospital. I snatched up the phone and punched in the numbers.

But Fran, the energetic receptionist, said the doctor was with one of her favorite furry friends and couldn't be disturbed.

"Listen, Fran," I said, "I think Dr. Messing would want to talk to me. Just say the name Elizabeth Dugan."

"But—"

"You have an intercom or something, I'm sure. Whisper the name if you're afraid of freaking out a Great Dane in the middle of a rabies shot. You'll get your boss's attention."

I heard a big sigh before she reluctantly put me on hold. I looked at my watch, wondering how long it would take Roberta Messing to pick up the phone.

Thirty seconds later I heard a click and a breathless, "Elizabeth? Is that you?" Her low, soft voice was filled with urgency.

"Sorry, Dr. Messing, no. My name is Abby Rose and

I'm a private investigator. I think I may have found Elizabeth, however."

"Where is she? Why isn't she calling me instead of a—a private investigator? Is that because something's wrong? Please don't tell me she's—"

"She's injured. In a coma," I said quickly.

"A *coma*? Is that where she's been? In a coma for the last year?"

"It's been less than a week," I said. "She was in a serious wreck."

"Oh, no. God, no. Wh-who was driving?"

"She was. No passengers," I said.

"Will she be okay . . . or does she have some kind of brain damage?"

"The doctors are optimistic. They're keeping her in a medical coma because of the head injury."

"Did she go through the windshield or—"

"All I know is her car hit a tree," I said.

"This is unbelievable. Thank goodness you found me. Who hired you? Did that jerk of a husband finally decide to do something about her disappearance?"

Jerk of a husband? Uh-oh. "I think we need to talk in person."

A short silence, then Messing said, "I'm totally booked all afternoon. This is our late office-hours day. But you could come here. I have a little time between patients. Would that work?"

"Works fine for me."

The feline-entrance waiting room at Oakdale Veterinary Hospital was filled with cats growling, howling or cowering in pet carriers. Cats know what they like and what they don't. I'm sure they believe thermometers up their butts are unnecessary intrusions that cannot be assuaged by the stale, dried-out cat treat offered at the conclusion of this particular humiliation. Yup, all of them knew what was coming.

The receptionist sat in a circular office that could access both waiting rooms—the dogs were on the other side of the building. I introduced myself and this time I didn't get put off.

"Dr. Messing wants you to go right back, Ms. Rose.

I'll show you the way." She hit a button and a door opened to my right.

I went through and a young woman met me in a hallway. She wore scrubs covered with brightly colored cats and dogs playfully chasing one another. My Diva would consider this place anything but playful.

I was led to a small and very messy office. At least the doc had the perfect name.

"I'll go get Dr. Messing." The girl hurried off.

The only chair not piled with documents or boxes was behind the vet's desk, so I stood and looked at the framed graduation certificate hanging crookedly on the wall—she'd gone to A&M—and took in the computer with its jungle-birds screen saver and the complete and utter disarray emphasized by scattered papers on the desk, granola bar wrappers everywhere and the wilting jumbo-size paper cup of some soft drink from a convenience store. It had completely dampened and smeared whatever document it sat on.

I smiled. Here was a woman after my own heart. But then I started when I felt something brush my leg. I looked down and saw what had to be the oldest, mangiest dog in the universe. He or she had one lower tooth that no longer fit in its mouth and was looking up at me expectantly with round cloudy eyes mostly obscured by floppy hair.

I knelt and the small gray dog's tail began to thump against the wastebasket. I held out my hand for sniffing and a warm pink tongue greeted me instead. Maybe the sniffer didn't work anymore.

"I see Buttons has introduced himself," a woman behind me said.

I stood and wiped my hand on my shorts before offering it out. "Abby Rose. I take it you're Dr. Messing?" She was thirtyish, black and makeup free, her long hair braided and beaded. I wondered if she was the woman who'd been cut out of the picture on the Web site.

We shook and then Messing said, "Let's make it 'Abby' and 'Roberta,' okay? Can I see Elizabeth tonight? She needs to know I'm with her, supporting her."

"Like I said on the phone, she's in a coma, so I don't think—"

"Never underestimate the unconscious mind, Abby. She'll know I'm there, coma or not."

"I think it would be wise to wait. I was only allowed in her room to see if I could identify her. The staff is pretty stingy about any time with visitors. They want to keep her calm."

"Okay, I get that. But why would *you* be able to identify her? Did you know Elizabeth?"

"It's kind of a long story. But I promise you, when she's able to have people in, I'll call you myself."

Roberta glanced at her watch. "I have to examine a litter of kittens someone abandoned at our back door and you can come with me." She looked down at Buttons. "You, too, baby. I know how you love kittens."

"Wait a sec, okay?" I said. "Let's make sure we're talking about the same person. The Web site photo wasn't the best." I pulled Richter's family picture from my purse and handed it to her. "Do you see your friend?"

She pointed immediately to JoLynn. "That's Elizabeth right there. My God, she—she looks so . . . scared and small."

For some reason I'd hoped she'd say that JoLynn wasn't her lost friend, that this was all a big mistake. On top of that, I felt immediate sympathy for Elliott Richter. The fact that JoLynn apparently had another name and a past she'd failed to share wouldn't be news he wanted to hear. "You're sure that's her?" I said.

Roberta took the photo and examined it more closely. "Of course I'm sure, but who are these other people?"

"The family she's been with," I said, thinking I didn't want to tell her much before I heard what she had to say. "I know you're busy and I'm hoping you can tell me everything you know about your friend so I can continue my investigation."

"Certainly, but those kittens can't wait. Come on." She passed the picture back to me, turned and left the room.

I took my cue from Buttons and followed. He was pretty spry for a snaggletoothed old dog. We didn't go far and I heard the kittens mewing before we even reached the treatment room. Buttons was on Roberta's heels, his wiggling nose in the air.

A heavyset woman who had the sense to wear plain green rather than animal-print scrubs was holding up one squalling kitten and rubbing its belly with a cloth.

"Someone had to pee really bad," said the woman. Then she put the tiny tabby to her nose and smiled. The cloth she now held in her free hand bore a telltale yellow stain.

"Good. That means they're probably not dehydrated yet," said Messing. "We'll take over here, Mary. I need a fecal on the dog in room five. Can you handle that?"

The woman nodded and left the room like she'd been asked to count the day's receipts and take half the money home. Note to self: No matter how much you love animals, your next job will *not* be at a vet clinic.

Roberta was already busy examining the kittens, Buttons resting at her feet, when she said, "Did Kent hire you to find Elizabeth? If he did, I might have to revisit my opinion of that bastard."

"I assume Kent is the jerk of a husband?" I said.

"Yes. Pretty-boy Kent Dugan, not even concerned enough to file a missing-person report when Elizabeth disappeared. And brother, did he get pissed off when *I* called the cops." She picked up the kitten squealing the loudest and rested a finger near the tiny calico's heart.

Diva was a calico like this little baby and immediately I wanted to take her home. I should have known this would happen once I walked into this place. "You said her husband got upset when you called HPD?" I asked, trying to stay focused.

"He said it was none of my business." The doc reached behind her to a cabinet and removed several small packaged syringes. "When the policeman called me, I figured Kent must have shown him his charming side because he convinced the cop she left on her own. When I checked with the police a week later, I was told an officer had gone out to the house and found no evidence of foul play, but that they'd keep Elizabeth's information on file."

"Sounds like you did what you could," I said.

"I suppose, but I'm certain something went very wrong to make her disappear without a word. That's why I put her picture up on that Web site. Excuse me a second." She took a phone from her lab jacket and used the intercom feature. "I need someone to feed kittens in treatment one." Then Messing closed the phone and looked at me. "I really want to see Elizabeth for myself. I don't care if—"

"As I said, she's heavily sedated and—"

"Where is she?"

"In the neuro ICU at Ben Taub," I said.

"Thank you. I'll be there tonight and I don't give a damn what they say about visitors." Messing continued examining the other kittens.

"The best way to help her is by talking to me. I need to know how long you knew her, where she came from, things like that."

A teenage boy charged into the room holding a measuring cup filled with creamy liquid. He was a taller, masculine version of the dark-haired Dr. Messing. She was too young to have a son this age. Brother, maybe?

"You heated that to ninety degrees, right?" she asked, nodding at the measuring cup.

"Yes," he answered.

"Cute litter, huh?" she said to him.

The doc held up another blind kitten and he grinned, revealing a mouthful of braces. Then he stroked the tiny head with one long, thin finger. Roberta put the animal back in the box and instructed the teenager to feed—but not *over*feed—the litter using the needle-free syringes she provided. He carefully left with the box of kittens and the milk.

Messing looked at her watch. "You were asking how I knew her. I owned a condo next door to theirs. Elizabeth and I met when we were both getting our mail one day, about a year before she disappeared. I was drawn to her at once. She reminded me of those kittens, of the hundreds of kittens and puppies people abandon at our clinic door. She looked like she needed to be rescued."

"She was sad? Scared? Worried?"

"All of the above. I invited her into my home and

from then on we had coffee together on my days off. She was the sweetest thing. Polite, quiet, always asking about the animals."

"Did she ever say anything about extended family or other friends?"

"She said her parents were dead, but that's the most I ever got out of her. She never went into detail about her past—avoided answering me when I asked. The only clue I ever got was when she said she'd had a difficult childhood and Kent promised to fix all that and take care of her."

"But she regretted her decision?"

Roberta hesitated. "I think so, but she never uttered a bad word about him. I could see what he was like, though. Controlling, demanding, calling her cell phone every five minutes. I swear the only time she ever left the house was when she came to see me."

This fits the pattern of someone being abused, I thought. "Was she afraid to leave home?"

"That was my guess. My practice has brought me in touch with every kind of human behavior—it's not only animals we deal with here, but their owners. I've come to know Kent Dugan's type."

"And you're absolutely positive she didn't leave on her own?" I said.

"Not *absolutely* sure. Maybe she got brave one day and made a break for it. Maybe I was wrong to think she'd confide in me if she planned on running off. Or at least say good-bye. God knows I would have helped her get away."

Time to ask the obvious. "Any sign of physical abuse?"

"No. I think his abuse was all emotional or mental or whatever the right word is. I dubbed him 'the snake'— to myself, of course. I usually pick an animal counterpart for everyone I get to know. And Elizabeth was no mongoose, unfortunately. More like a pet mouse whose days were limited."

I wondered what my animal counterpart was—and immediately decided not to ask. "Has Dugan said anything about his wife since Elizabeth disappeared?"

"I wouldn't know. I moved out of the neighborhood

after I adopted two Dobermans. They needed a bigger yard."

"Can you give me the Dugan address?" I reached in my bag for my BlackBerry.

Roberta's dark eyes grew concerned. "You won't tell him where she is, will you? He doesn't need to know. He doesn't *care* about her."

"But if they're still married, he has a *right* to know. He's her next of kin."

Now her eyes flashed with anger. "I don't give a damn about his rights. He certainly never cared about hers."

I took a deep breath and decided to tell her the rest. Roberta cared about Elizabeth or JoLynn or whatever her real name was, cared a lot. "I *really* need that address. See, the wreck was no accident. Someone tried to kill your friend."

Buttons suddenly sat up, his old eyes focused on Roberta's face. Her beautiful, dark skin lightened a shade, especially around her lips. When she finally spoke, it was a whisper. "It was *him*. I know it was him." Then Roberta knelt and stroked Buttons, trying to hide the tears welling in her eyes.

"I promise you that a policeman will probably inform Dugan, not me," I said quietly. "The husband will know the authorities are on alert. And if it helps, Elizabeth has security and private-duty nurses."

Roberta looked up at me. "Don't let Kent Dugan fool you or the cops." Then she stood and finally gave me the address. I thanked Roberta and gave her my card, then started to leave the way I came in. But before I was out the door to the waiting room, I heard her call, "I don't know what animal you are yet, Abby. I think you're part bloodhound, though, and that's good."

16

After I walked out of Oakdale Veterinary Hospital and into the ninety-degree heat, I took out my phone and called Cooper. Apparently he was dealing with a drunk or a druggie, because I could hear curse-laden shouting in the background. He told me he'd call back after he "straightened out a situation." His attitude—calm and in control—reminded me of Jeff. *Jeff,* I thought as I slid behind the wheel, *I'll see you soon, thank goodness.*

I pulled out into traffic, the air-conditioning blasting away the sweat on my forehead created by the thirty-second trip to my car. I headed for home, even though I wanted very much to go straight to Dugan's address or at least find his phone number and call him. But that wasn't my place. Once I gave Cooper the information, he would decide how to proceed.

Cooper didn't call back until after I'd made it home around five o'clock. I'd stopped at Central Market to pick up dinner—a Mediterranean salad, roast beef for sandwiches and a container of Kalamata olives. I was craving salt and since Jeff will eat any olive on the planet, even if it just fell off a tree, I went with the kind that made my mouth water. Diva checked out what was on the menu once I placed the grocery bags on the counter. Smelling no salmon, she left with an angry swish of her tail.

When the phone rang, I'd been hitting the olives hard and was filling a tall glass with ice water.

"What's going on, Abby?" Cooper asked.

"I found out where JoLynn Richter was right before she showed up at the ranch last year."

"Wow. I'm impressed. Tell me."

I did, then said, "But she might still be JoLynn Richter, not Elizabeth Dugan, right?"

"I don't know, Abby." His ragged voice was filled with skepticism. "Cops tend to go straight to the less-than-pleasant aspect of human nature—that tendency people have to lie through their teeth. But tell me what you're thinking."

"I keep going back to the letter she wrote me. Katarina Richter could have given her up for adoption, JoLynn found out and for some reason, she felt like she had to provide proof to Elliott Richter when she arrived at the Richter home. She gave him that missing birth certificate with Katarina's name on it to back up her other ID. As added proof, maybe she even showed Richter the tip sheets I sent her, the ones that help adoptees find their biological parents."

"But if she really is JoLynn Richter, why fake a birth certificate?" Cooper asked.

"Sorry. Guess I should explain. Adoptees have to petition the court for their original birth certificates. That costs money. Maybe all she had was the birth certificate issued after she was adopted with the first name Elizabeth and a last name we don't know."

"Couldn't she have explained this to Elliott Richter?" Cooper sounded exasperated.

"You're right. What she did is way too contrived. There's more we don't know." Disappointment washed over me. I so wanted some part of JoLynn's story to be true—and why, I didn't know.

"What did you pick up on last night?" Cooper asked. "Do any of those Richter folks know something?"

"Oh, for sure. But even Elliott Richter hasn't been all that forthcoming."

"Why do you say that?" Cooper said.

"He knew JoLynn's driver's license was fake before you did. Matthew told me last night. Richter's holding back for some reason—and I can't figure out why. The only thing I know is that he wants JoLynn to be the real deal and hopes I can prove it."

Cooper sighed heavily. "Are all your cases this complicated?"

"Not all, but the tough ones are like trying to dig a ditch in the ocean. Right now I'm grateful I can bring in the heavy equipment like you, Jeff and my sister to make the job easier."

He laughed. "I've never been referred to as heavy equipment. Anyway, tell me about the family."

I took a generous gulp of water and gave him a more complete rundown on last night's interviews, ending with Matthew's confession about using a private eye. "For all we know, the birth certificate might not have even existed."

"True. All we have is Richter's word. But his word has been good in the county for a long time, so I'm still ready to give the man the benefit of the doubt. I've been asking around, and no one in town much likes that family—except for the main man, Elliott Richter. He's well respected. I checked into the financial situation. He's worth megamillions, a lot more than I realized. The relatives have a lot to lose if Elliott rewrote his will in favor of JoLynn. Maybe we should ask Richter if that's what he's done."

"That's your next step, then?" I asked.

"Nope. First I get Kent Dugan down to the hospital for an ID—tonight if possible."

I wanted to be there in the worst way, wanted to meet the guy, but I also wanted my alone time with Jeff. "Okay if I bring my HPD investigator friend?"

"Sure. I'd love to meet him."

Though Jeff was tired after his long day at the courthouse—he says court is more tiring than fieldwork—he agreed a trip to the hospital might be interesting. First we'd shared our quiet dinner and engaged in other activities not so quiet before heading to Ben Taub to meet up with Cooper Boyd.

Jeff held my hand a whole lot tighter the minute we walked through the hospital doors. He'd been shot in the chest by a bad guy last year. I understood his reaction without his saying a word. He didn't like being reminded of the day he nearly died and neither did I. It was a very silent elevator ride.

We found Cooper in the neuro ICU waiting room—

he'd sent the private security on a break—and since he and Jeff seemed to hit it off immediately, Jeff reverted to his old self. Law-enforcement types seem to quickly discover they know some of the same people. But they both put on their game faces when Kent Dugan arrived.

As Roberta had mentioned, Dugan was a pretty boy—reminded me of a Calvin Klein underwear model, as a matter of fact. He wore jeans with small tears and frayed seams along with a rock group T-shirt—at least I assumed Wilting Wilma was a rock group and not a euphemism for something I didn't want to know about this guy.

"Where is she?" He sounded downright panicked and seemed to be addressing anyone and everyone in the waiting room.

Cooper introduced himself and said, "She's in very capable hands. Let me show you a picture first—see if you recognize the young woman we're talking about."

When we'd first arrived, I gave Cooper the article I'd found under the clock, as well as a copy of the picture I'd scanned and Photoshopped. I'd enlarged JoLynn's face and cropped out the family. I wanted to avoid having anyone ask the questions Roberta had, about who all the other people in the picture were.

Dugan grabbed the photo and stared. "That's her, but where did you get this?"

"Never mind," Cooper said. "We need to talk, Mr. Dugan."

"I have to see her." He started for the ICU doors, but Jeff did a quick side step and blocked his path.

"Who are *you*?" Dugan asked.

"Sergeant Kline, HPD Homicide." He took out his pack of Big Red and offered a stick to Dugan. "Let's sit over there and chill for a minute."

Dugan didn't even seem to notice the gum. "Is Elizabeth dead? Is that why you're here?" The man couldn't be more than five-nine and had to look up at Jeff, who's six feet tall.

"Not dead—though someone *did* try to kill her." Cooper gestured at the cluster of waiting-room furniture. "She's not going anywhere and we need to discuss what happened."

Being double-teamed had the desired effect and Dugan walked over and sat on one of the sofas, his eyes focused on the ICU entrance.

We all followed and I held out my hand. "I'm Abby Rose, by the way. I helped identify your wife."

Dugan squeezed my hand briefly and squinted up at me. "I don't know you. How could you identify Elizabeth?"

"That's a long story." I sat on the edge of a faux-leather and chrome chair opposite him, and Cooper sat next to me. Jeff went over to a counter where an industrial-size coffeemaker sat. He started checking cupboards for cups, since none were visible.

"As I told you on the phone," Cooper said, "we pulled your wife from the wreckage of her car. Her brake line had been cut. I understand she's been missing for more than a year."

"Um, yes." Kent Dugan's expression told me he was surprised we knew that piece of information, but he quickly recovered. "Who would want to kill Elizabeth? She'd never hurt a fly."

"Good question. We're hoping you can help, Mr. Dugan," Cooper said. "What about her disappearance?"

"She *has* been gone, left on her own. She said she needed time away from the relationship. She's ten years younger than me and wasn't as ready to settle down as she thought."

"How young is she?" Cooper asked.

"You don't know?" Dugan said.

Cooper leaned forward, his gravel voice low. "What's her age, Mr. Dugan? Where is the rest of her family?"

Dugan stiffened. "She's twenty and Elizabeth has no family except for me."

"Interesting." Cooper sat back. "When people disappear voluntarily, it's been my experience they head straight for Mom or Dad—or maybe another relative. What you're saying is that she had nowhere to go."

"I—I never looked at it that way." Dugan seemed a little flustered by this assessment.

"What's the story with this nonexistent family?" Cooper asked, taking a Styrofoam cup of coffee from Jeff.

Jeff handed another cup to Dugan and tossed packages of creamers, sugars and stirring sticks onto a table beside the sofa. Jeff raised his eyebrows questioningly at me and I nodded. I was ready to settle in with some much-needed caffeine and watch Cooper work. I was certain I'd learn a lot.

"I don't know what happened to her parents," Dugan said. "I don't believe she knew, either."

I blinked at this answer. What the heck did that mean? "Where did she grow up?" I asked.

Dugan's tongue traveled over his lips and he took a sip of coffee. He then stared into the steaming cup he held with both hands. No wedding ring, I noted. "Elizabeth and I . . . we didn't know each other that good when it came to our pasts. We agreed it wasn't important. We loved each other and that's all that mattered."

Cooper leaned in again. "What kind of bullshit answer is that?"

From the corner of my eye I caught Jeff's expression as he filled cups for the two of us. Small grin. He liked Cooper's style.

Meanwhile, Dugan's magazine-ad face tensed. He avoided Cooper's hard stare by stirring sugar into his coffee. "She wouldn't want me telling you, but I guess you won't let me see her until I do. Elizabeth was adopted and it wasn't a good situation. She wanted to forget. That's all I know."

Cooper smiled. "Thank you. Where'd you meet her?"

"What does that have to do with anything?" Dugan looked at me, perhaps to avoid Cooper's unblinking attention.

But Cooper wasn't letting him off the hook. "I ask, you answer. Then it's your turn, okay?" Pleasantly spoken, but no question. Cooper wasn't fooling around.

"At community college. San Jacinto." Dugan's reply was clipped. He was getting impatient now.

Cooper reminded me of a sculptor chipping away at stone. I could recognize the personality now emerging, the one Roberta had described. Dugan had no control here and he hated it.

"Any children?" Cooper asked.

"No." More edginess in his tone now.

"She never contacted you after she left? Not once?"
Cooper pressed.

Dugan shook his head, and I decided he was trying to
recapture the concern he'd displayed when he arrived.
"I would have notified the police if she had. But I always
knew she'd come back. And in her own way, she has."

"Not exactly her own way," I said, holding the coffee
Jeff had given me. He was settled in the chair next to
me now. I was afraid Cooper might be pissed off by me
voicing my opinion, but his passive face gave nothing
away.

"Can I ask why you're questioning me like this? What
have I done wrong?" Dugan said.

"What do you do for a living?" Cooper said, ignoring
this request to get off the hot seat.

"I'm a consultant," he replied.

Cooper leaned back, sipped his black coffee. "Really?
Sounds important. You have a business card I could
have?"

"I didn't bring any with me. I didn't think I'd *need*
one." Testy again. There was a real struggle going on in
this guy's head.

I glanced at Jeff because the tension seemed like a
balloon around us ready to burst and I wondered if he
felt it, too. But he was as calm as a plate of oysters,
probably loving every minute of watching someone else
interrogate a man whose emotions were all over the
map.

"What kind of *consultant*? Suit-and-tie kind with one
of those big firms?" Cooper asked.

"I'm freelance. I work from home."

Cooper smiled again, cocked his head. "Doing what?"

Dugan stood. "That's enough. I want to see my wife
right now."

Cooper and Jeff slowly rose in unison, like they'd
been a team for years. I stayed in my chair, amazed at
how intimidating Cooper could be without ever raising
his voice.

"I'm sure you do want to see her. Sorry about the
delay, but this is a very *active* investigation. Attempted
murder gets a police officer's attention. Let me see

whether her nurse thinks this is a good time for a visit."
Cooper took his time walking over to the double doors.

"You must have been surprised to get a call about
your wife after all this time," Jeff said. He'd finished his
coffee in no time and didn't bother offering Dugan a
stick when he pulled the Big Red pack from his jeans
pocket.

"I was more upset than anything. She's hurt and she
needs me. I wish I could have been here the minute they
brought her in." Dugan had regrouped. He was about
to get his way and that apparently made a huge differ-
ence in his demeanor.

"Oh, I'm sure you do wish you could have been
around." Jeff's tiny dose of sarcasm was lost on Dugan
but not on me.

I've learned from Jeff that relatives are usually the
first suspects in a murder or assault and I was guessing
he and Cooper quickly pegged Dugan for the not-so-
nice guy Roberta had described.

Cooper gestured for Kent Dugan to come to the ICU
doors and he strode quickly in that direction.

Jeff and I stayed back. As soon as the door closed
behind them, Jeff pulled out his phone. I looked at him,
puzzled, but he just chewed his gum.

He speed-dialed, waited a second, then said, "This is
Sergeant Jeff Kline from Homicide Division. Can you
run a name for priors?" A short silence, then Jeff said,
"Thanks. See if we have a sheet on a Kent Dugan." He
spelled the last name. "I'll wait."

"You think he's been arrested?" I said.

"Hang on, Abby. This won't take long." And he was
right—a moment later he said, "Appreciate it." Jeff
snapped his phone closed. "Hot checks, petty theft and
a fraud charge Dugan pleaded out. Guy's done no time,
though. Probably talked his way out of everything."

"How'd you know to make that call?" I sipped my
coffee, but it had gone nearly cold in the frigid waiting
room. I set it on the table.

Jeff fixed a strand of my hair behind my ear. "Honest
people don't get vague with the police about simple stuff
like family history. They usually talk *too* much. Believe
me, I've learned some dirt during interviews that I didn't

need or want to know. Dugan was evasive about his wife and himself. To me, that says he knows a lot more than he's saying. Something's definitely hinky."

I nodded in agreement.

"Your friend Cooper made him right off the bat," Jeff said.

I said, "But at times, Dugan seemed genuinely concerned about JoLynn or Elizabeth or whatever her real name is."

"Concerned, yes, but maybe not for her welfare. Continuing to dig around for that girl's story is a good idea." He drew me to him and whispered, "Now, here's my good idea. Why don't you and I—"

Cooper had sneaked up on us and now cleared his throat. Jeff and I stepped away from each other.

"What happened in there?" I asked.

"He picked up her hand, seemed shaken by her appearance. Could have been an act. The staff has questions for him—name, address, phone number, and of course they told him he's got a date with the billing department. He'll be out in a second."

I said, "You look puzzled. What are you thinking?"

"There's something else going on here," Cooper said.

"That's what I thought." Jeff told him about Dugan's rap sheet.

"Thanks for running the background. He's a damn paper hanger?"

I must have looked confused because Jeff said, "That's what we call the hot-check writers."

"And petty theft? Fraud? Those are little-girl crimes, all of them," Cooper said with disgust.

Just then, Kent Dugan and a woman in scrubs emerged from the neuro ICU and the two of them came over to us.

"Shelly Young," the woman said. "I'm Miss Richter's private-duty nurse tonight. Mr. Dugan is unable to help me concerning his wife's medical history and says there's no other family to give us what we need. Do any of you have information about her previous heart surgery? Or know someone who does? The physician can't disturb her medical coma to figure out what kind of repair she had, but she might require medication, even though her EKG shows a strong, healthy heart."

"I *told* you she wasn't taking any medicine and like you said, her heart is fine." Dugan seemed downright hostile now.

Heart surgery? Whoa. I thought about Elliott Richter, wondered if he knew. I opened my mouth, deciding Jo-Lynn's welfare was more important than keeping secrets about Richter from Dugan, but before I could speak, true to her word, Roberta arrived as quietly as a snowflake falling on a feather.

"I can tell you about her heart surgery," she said.

Everyone focused on the newcomer. "I'm a vet and I recognized the anomaly when she told me."

Dugan stepped back, trying to hide his surprise. He was all pleasant when he said, "Roberta. Hi. This is awful, isn't it?"

She gave him the stink eye and addressed the nurse. "I may not be a medical doctor, but I know plenty about heart problems, since dogs suffer from similar health issues. Considering what Elizabeth knew about her condition, I'm guessing she underwent an aortic repair."

Shelly Young smiled. "Thank you so much. You don't happen to know when she had the surgery?"

"Sorry, no," Roberta said.

"She may have been quite young by the size and condition of her scar," the nurse replied. "I'll add this information to her history for her cardiology consult—the one her neurologist has already ordered." Shelly Young turned and left.

Roberta's gaze returned to Kent Dugan. "Are you trying to make these people believe you didn't know about Elizabeth's surgery? That you never bothered to ask how she got that scar down the middle of her chest?"

I was sure she wanted to add "you asshole" to the end of her sentence, but she kept her cool.

"It's Dr. Messing, right?" Cooper said. "I'm Chief Boyd from Pineview PD and I'm investigating this accident."

"Accident? Abby said *someone* tried to kill her." Roberta was staring straight at Dugan. She stepped toward him, no doubt because she considered him a lying sack of dirt.

Jeff ran interference again by blocking *her* path this time. He said, "I know she's your friend, but this is a hospital waiting room. Let's keep it low-key. I'm Jeff Kline, by the way. HPD."

Roberta said, "HPD? You guys are a little late to the party. I told you people last year this . . . this *man*, if that's what you want to call him, was capable of harming her."

"That doesn't mean he did," Jeff said. "Why don't we ask if you can see your friend, okay?"

Roberta took a deep breath and let it out slowly. "Sorry. This isn't your fault. And thank you. I *do* want to see her."

Jeff took her elbow and they walked toward the ICU doors.

"Don't you have business downstairs in billing, Mr. Dugan?" Cooper said.

"Not exactly. For one thing, they only want my information for notification purposes. Apparently someone else is picking up the tab. But that doesn't matter because Elizabeth and I never made our relationship legal." He smiled at Cooper and said, "Think I'll be going now. It's getting late and I'll need to be here to see her early tomorrow. The nurse said her favorite music might help. People can sometimes still hear when they're in a coma."

As we watched him leave, I said, "If he comes back for something in the next few seconds, please keep me from harming him."

Cooper's gaze followed Dugan as he headed down the hall. "If it helps, he won't get anywhere near her tomorrow. I'll make sure of that. Won't be a hard sell to the staff, since apparently the two haven't cohabited for a year." Then he turned to me. "And now, I have a job for you, if you're willing."

But before I could ask him what he needed, Elliott Richter and Ian McFarland came walking from the elevators toward us. Jeez, they must have passed Kent Dugan on the way.

I took a deep breath, feeling like I'd just received an audit notice from the IRS. "He doesn't know about Dugan yet," I whispered.

"He will in a few seconds," Cooper said.

Richter quickened his pace when he saw Cooper and me and said, "Is something wrong?"

"No. JoLynn's condition is about the same," I said.

"But *something's* not right. I can tell by your faces," he said.

Ian gripped Richter's shoulder and squeezed. "Abby said she's no worse, Elliott. She *will* be all right, you know." He then stuck his hand out to Cooper. "Ian McFarland. Elliott and I had a meeting in Houston today. Ran rather late, but Elliott wanted to stop by to check on his granddaughter."

While the two shook hands, Richter honed in on me. "What's going on? Why are you here?"

"I—I planned on calling you as soon as I could. I learned that JoLynn was living in Houston right before she arrived at your ranch," I said.

"Okay . . . she had to be somewhere," he said. "What else did you learn?"

"She was living with a man named Kent Dugan and using the name Elizabeth," I said.

"So this man must know something about her past," Richter said. "Have you spoken with him?"

"Yes. He claims she told him she was adopted and not much else," Cooper said.

Richter looked back and forth between us. "But I can tell that you don't believe him. Where can I find him? I want to talk to this man."

Ian said, "Elliott, calm down, old friend. These fine, professional people are conducting their business and making progress. Whatever they learn, whatever is important, they'll inform you in due time. Officer Boyd would tell you that you shouldn't put yourself in the middle of the inquiry. Isn't that correct, Officer?"

Cooper nodded his agreement. "We've only learned within the last twenty-four hours about JoLynn's life before she came to the ranch, but there's eighteen other years we know nothing about. Mr. Dugan hasn't been as forthcoming as I'd like, but I'll deal with him."

"You think he's a liar?" Richter's throat had reddened. This was the most emotion I'd seen from him and now that I was taking his inventory, the man looked exhausted, not to mention stressed to the max.

"Please, Elliott. You're becoming overwrought. Despite your cloak-and-dagger attempts at hiding things from me, I know you've seen your physician and that can't be good." Ian looked at me. "He wouldn't want me telling you people this, but he's already had a triple bypass. This whole affair has been a little much for his ticker, I'd say."

"JoLynn had heart problems, too," I said half to myself, never thinking Richter might have no idea.

But he apparently didn't because he said, "What?" like I'd just told him Earth, like Pluto, was no longer considered a planet.

Ian shot me a glance that I interpreted to mean I was a complete and utter idiot. And he was probably right.

Cooper quickly said, "We understand her heart is fine, that she probably had surgery as a child. I take it she never mentioned this?"

"No. Never. Christ, I need to get a specialist in, I need—"

"Her neurologist already took care of that," I said. "She's in good hands, and well protected. I am so sorry I didn't phone you before we came here tonight to meet up with Dugan. My mistake."

"He's here? Right now?" Richter focused on the ICU doors.

Could I screw this up any more if I tried? This man literally needed breathing room, not more surprises.

"Dugan's gone already," Cooper said. "And I will be excluding him from the visitor list until I learn more about him. He does have an arrest record for petty crimes. Nothing serious. But the security you've hired is a good idea."

Ian said, "You've hired security, have you?"

Richter ran a hand through his hair. "Of course."

"Good thinking, but then no one could ever accuse you of anything but." Ian smiled at Richter, probably hoping to ease his friend's mind.

This seemed to work, because Richter was more composed when he said, "Is there anything else I don't know?"

Should I tell him Dugan did not report JoLynn missing? Tell him about Roberta Messing, the friend who might come walking out through those ICU doors any second? I had to. And I did. Good thing, too, because Roberta and Jeff reappeared just as I finished. She and Jeff were arm in arm and Roberta had obviously been crying.

After introductions, Richter said to Roberta, "I understand you tried to help JoLynn while that man she lived with did nothing. I cannot thank you enough for your concern."

But this whole exchange was making me nervous, making me think about what might happen if I was to tell Richter that JoLynn's name really was Elizabeth Something and that she and Richter were not related. That would be a much tougher message to deliver than what I'd told him tonight.

17

Jeff left my place early Thursday morning. He wanted to eat breakfast with Doris before he went on to the Travis Center police headquarters. After we'd left Ian and Richter at the hospital last night, Cooper reminded me that he needed my help. His request? That I tail Kent Dugan, find out where he went and what he did all day.

I'd eagerly agreed, thinking this was a good idea. Jeff shrugged and offered no opinion, but I could tell he wasn't exactly enthused. On the way back to my place I asked him if he was concerned and he said, "You can handle yourself fine. I just got a bad vibe from that guy." He'd then added his third stick of gum to the wad already in his mouth and promptly changed the subject.

Since Diva didn't like getting up before seven a.m., she stayed curled in bed while I showered, then dressed in lightweight khakis and a sleeveless blouse. This could be a long day and I might have to spend time in the ninety-five-degree heat if forced to tail Dugan outside the air-conditioned comfort of my car.

I grabbed a couple of bottles of caramel Starbucks from the fridge, along with several bottles of water. I also took a box of cookies from the pantry. *Cookies,* I told myself, *are wonderfully portable.*

I'd bought a pair of camera binoculars last year and fit them into my shoulder bag along with my two phones—the computer phone and my small mobile—and the BlackBerry. I planned on getting a new all-in-one techie gadget because I love new techie stuff, but right then there was no time to even think about transferring all my files from three gadgets to one.

The condos where Dugan lived were north and west of my place and I had to fight morning rush hour. Cookies are excellent for enduring a slow ride, and half the box of chocolate-covered shortbread was gone by the time I reached the right neighborhood. It was only eight a.m.

I parked across the street and a block away from the row of white brick condos, which looked more like one-story patio homes. I always thought of condos as having two floors, but apparently I was way behind in my real estate knowledge. I made sure the Camry faced the direction of the nearest main thoroughfare. I didn't want to be doing any U-turns if he drove past me toward the freeway. I repositioned my mirrors now that his house was behind and to my left, and sat for thirty minutes. Then his front door opened.

Dugan wasn't alone. A young woman dressed in skin-tight cropped pants and an off-the-shoulder green shirt came out with him. She was holding a cup of coffee and followed him to the silver compact car in the driveway. She kissed him good-bye and started back to the condo.

Damn. Follow him or wait for him to drive away and catch *her* if she was about to leave, too? I knew what I was supposed to do, what Cooper had asked me to do, but my gut said I might not get another chance to catch this woman alone. I turned my head toward the passenger side as Kent Dugan whizzed by, then made that U-turn I thought I wouldn't have to make.

The young woman still held her cup when she answered the door, but she'd put on a thin Oriental-print silk robe over her clothes and clipped up her strawberry blond hair. Guess Dugan preferred blondes.

"Can I help you?" the woman asked.

I smiled, trying for something cordial, the kind of smile that is neither happy nor sad. "Is Mr. Dugan home?" I asked. "I'm a detective assisting the Pineview Police Department concerning the accident. Mr. Dugan and I spoke at the hospital last night, but—"

"You just missed him. He's gone to see his sister. He is so upset about what happened."

Sister, huh? I held out my hand and said, "I'm Louise Morrell, by the way. I'm working with Police Chief Cooper Boyd. He doesn't have the manpower to leave Pineview for Houston every day to work this case, so he's asked me to help with interviews."

She switched her coffee cup to her other hand to take mine. "Kent mentioned Chief Boyd. Said Elizabeth's case was in good hands with him. But I don't recall him mentioning your name. Of course he was nearly in tears when he got home last night, so he probably forgot."

"He sure seemed upset." I nodded solemnly. "Since he's not here, mind if I ask you a few questions?"

She furrowed her very lovely forehead. Even without makeup, she was stunning. In fact, she looked a lot like JoLynn. "I don't know anything about the accident. Even Kent is confused about exactly what happened."

"We're simply searching for background information. I take it you knew his sister went missing last year?"

"I didn't even know Kent *had* a sister until Chief Boyd called Kent yesterday. Kent told me he didn't want me to have to share his . . . what's the word he used?" She looked up at the ceiling.

"His pain? His burden? His problems?" I suggested, working hard to eliminate any trace of sarcasm.

She smiled and pointed at me. "Burden. That's it."

"Even if you've only recently learned about her, you'd be surprised what morsels of information can lead to a break in a case. Can we talk for a few minutes?"

"O-kay," she said, sounding wary. "But maybe I should call Kent first. Won't take a minute."

"Don't bother him. He was very distraught last night and it sounds like he still is. Besides, I plan to catch up with him at the hospital anyway. I'll tell him I was here."

She seemed to be using every brain cell to decide whether this sounded like something Kent would approve of. Finally she said, "Can you ask your questions while I put on my makeup? Otherwise I'll be late for work." She opened the door wider and then turned and walked through the foyer. "Follow me."

I scanned the living area as I trailed after her. Modern furniture, black-and-white motif. Everything in its place. Not even a stray magazine. The master bedroom was no different except for the color scheme. Red in here, the paisley burgundy and gold pillows neatly arranged on a queen-size bed. This was nothing like my place, where I was always tripping over shoes or ending up with a pair of panties clinging to my sandal as I tried to leave my bedroom. Nope, this was *House Beautiful* perfect.

"You have a lovely home," I said, halting in the entry to the master bath.

"Thanks," she said. "You said your name is Louise?"

"That's right. But I didn't get yours."

"Georgeanne. What do you want to know?" She'd begun using a foam wedge to apply glittery bronze foundation to her tanned face.

"After you found out about Kent's sister, did he tell you anything about her disappearance?"

She discarded the wedge in a wastebasket beneath the faux-marble sink. "He said she's done this before. He felt sad, you know, that he couldn't help her."

Help her disappear permanently? I thought. "She disappeared before?"

"That's right, but like I said, the subject made him very, very upset. If my sister—I mean if I *had* a sister, which I don't—fell off the side of the earth, well, you know I'd be upset, too. Guess I can't really help you much, can I?"

"He didn't have a clue why she went away?" I asked.

Georgeanne kept on with her careful makeup application, focusing on her eyes now. "If you ask me, from the way he talked, I think she had a screw loose." She pointed her mascara wand at her temple and rotated it, making the "crazy" sign.

"She was mentally ill?" Not even the Richters hinted at this possibility.

Georgeanne turned and looked at me, one brown eye shadowed and shaped, the other plain and far prettier, in my opinion. She said, "Please don't say anything like that to Kent. Gosh, I probably shouldn't even be talking to you."

"Then this will be our secret," I said—a promise I intended to keep.

"That's good. He might get royally pissed if he thought I bad-mouthed his sister." She continued on with her makeover. Reminded me of Richter's house-keeper Estelle.

"He gets angry?" I said. "I know my boyfriend has a real temper. Calls me names, throws things." Did I just tell the biggest lie of my life? Oh yes.

"He doesn't get mad much, but boy, when he does, look out. If my mee-maw knew I was with a man who used those words—you know, the really bad cuss words? Anyway, she'd yank me by the hair all the way back to Lufkin. That's where I'm from. I was Miss Lufkin in the Miss Texas USA pageant and Kent saw me on TV. Said he wanted to meet me."

"He went to Lufkin to find you?" I asked.

"Well, not exactly. I work for Ace Printing. I'm the receptionist—actually my boss calls me his right-hand girl." She smiled, looking as proud as punch. "Anyway, Kent found me somehow and came calling at the office. We hit it off right away."

She was almost done with her makeup and I needed a little time to check the place out, so I said, "Do you have another bathroom besides this one? I had one too many cups of coffee."

"Sure. Out the bedroom and at the end of the hall."

I walked back into the hallway and saw the open powder room door. But there were two other closed doors on the way there, one on each side. I opened the one on the right. A guest room, this one all brown and tan and as orderly as the other rooms. There was nothing homey about this place. It just seemed so cold.

I carefully shut the door and tried the one on the left. But seeing that the traditional bedroom doorknob had been replaced with a keyed one, I knew it would be locked—and it was. Was this where they threw their junk mail, magazines, orphan slippers, empty boxes, Christmas decorations and all the other stuff that cluttered my place? I didn't think so. No, there was something else in there, something maybe even Georgeanne didn't know about.

I heard Georgeanne in the bedroom then and rushed down to the blue and white powder room, closed the door and quickly flushed the toilet. I ran the water a few seconds and then came out. She was waiting for me at the living room entry.

"I really have to get to work," she said.

"Sorry if I've kept you," I answered. I glanced into the kitchen on my left as I walked toward her. Black appliances, mottled gray granite countertops, all of it blending with the living room visible through a pass-through bar. Nothing unusual, just more neat-freak ambience. "I promise I won't tell Mr. Dugan I dropped by. He has enough on his mind right now."

Georgeanne smiled. God, she looked like a clown now and smelled like a bottle of cheap perfume. "Thanks. Maybe we can have lunch one day and you can tell me what it's like to be a detective because, you know, I think that is so very, very cool."

"Sounds like a plan," I said as we left the condo together.

Her car was in the garage and mine was parked at the curb. I left first and headed toward the freeway, but then took a turn down a street to my right when I saw the garage door open in my rearview mirror. I waited for a few minutes and then drove back to the condo, went past it about a block and parked. I wanted to know what was in that room.

18

I figured there had to be windows in both extra bedrooms of Dugan's place and I jogged back down the sidewalk—the jogging for the benefit of the man and woman walking toward me with their twin Scotties. I figured I needed an excuse for being in the neighborhood, since I sure wasn't dressed for delivering religious literature. The Scotties started lunging and barking their heads off as I approached, so I made a detour for the street to avoid losing a chunk of my leg. The man mouthed "Sorry" as they pulled their pets quickly past me.

After I returned to the walkway, I glanced back to make sure they weren't looking before I made a hard left into Kent Dugan's driveway. I hurried past the garage to the locked-room side of the house. The window's vertical shades were shut, but fortunately even a blind hog stumbles over an acorn every once in a while. One slat was twisted enough that I could see into the room— make that see into *part* of the room. A copy machine stood against the left wall, and not your standard Hewlett-Packard ink-jet, either. Laser and color, maybe? And there was a laminator, the type I recognized from my high school days when I'd help the librarian laminate posters for the teachers. It was almost as big as the copier. What kind of consultant needed office equipment like this? Did he publish manuals or something?

I turned my head and pressed the other side of my face against the window, trying to get a glimpse of anything else in the room while I considered the laminator thing.

But then I noticed I had a problem.

Kent Dugan was standing next to the garage, head cocked. "What the hell do you think you're doing?"

Uh-oh. Think fast, Abby. "I—I was, well, you didn't answer the door, and I thought maybe you saw me through the peephole and decided you didn't want to talk to me—which I perfectly understand. I wanted to ask you a few questions."

"Really? Well, you know what? I could have you arrested for trespassing." His anger was probably being broadcast all over the quiet neighborhood. "What's your interest in Elizabeth, anyway? How did you know her?"

"I—I—" My gaze wandered beyond Kent to the sidewalk.

The Scottie walkers were back and they had slowed to take in this unpleasant confrontation.

Dugan followed my stare. He sounded perfectly nice and in control when he said, "It's nothing, Mr. and Mrs. Lewis. I'm just a little upset because they found Elizabeth and she's hurt and now I have an unexpected visitor."

"They *found* your wife?" Mrs. Lewis said. "That's wonderful news. Will she be okay?"

"That's not clear yet. I'll let you know." He turned back to me and quietly said, "How's about we go inside and discuss this problem privately, *Abby*."

The couple took this as a cue to be on their way. Besides, those Scotties might rip the couple's arms from their sockets if they didn't get on with their walk.

Dugan, meanwhile, marched around the garage toward the front of the condo and I followed.

He opened the door, his anger almost palpable. Did I really want to go in there with him? Not exactly, but since I'd been accompanied by two police officers last night, and Dugan certainly didn't fall off the stupid truck, I figured he'd mind his manners.

Once we were both inside, he gestured to the living room. "Sit down. And then I want you to tell me why they won't let me in to see my wife. See, I was turned away at the hospital."

"She's not your wife, so maybe that has something to do with the hospital's decision." I wasn't taking any attitude from this guy without giving some back.

Dugan's lips pressed together. He seemed to be collecting his thoughts. As his expression relaxed, my guess was he was considering it might be wise to keep his enemies closer than his friends—that is, if he had any friends besides Georgeanne.

He walked over and sat down, pushed his hair off his forehead and leaned back. He looked tired . . . and frustrated. "Sorry I went off on you. I'm worried about her, that's all."

But I wasn't about to sympathize with a man I trusted about as much as I trusted my ability to hoist a baby elephant. I remained standing. "Apology accepted. Maybe you're ready to share more of what I'm sure you know about Elizabeth. Does she have a last name, by the way?"

He raised one eyebrow, offered his best photo-shoot shy smile. "You won't believe this, but she never told me. We hooked up instantly. The attraction didn't last for her, but I still care. Anyway, after she moved in, she would introduce herself as Elizabeth Dugan to people we met."

"You're right. I don't believe you. In fact," I said, "I don't like you, I don't trust you and I'm leaving."

I started to go, but he stopped me with his next words. "I thought you wanted to ask me questions, Abby Rose—adoption PI. You're *that* Abby, right?"

I tried to will down the flush creeping up my neck and attacking my cheeks. Didn't work.

He went on, saying, "Yellow Rose Investigations, right?"

I hate nothing more than smugness and he was full of himself now. But I smiled when I said, "As my daddy would have said, you're sharper than a pocketful of toothpicks, Kent. You have a computer and actually know how to get on the Internet. I'm so impressed."

"Not hard to find out stuff about a superstar like you," he said.

Since I'd seen no computer in my pass-through with Georgeanne, I was guessing it wasn't visible from the angle I'd had into the locked room. "I'm sure you've learned plenty more about me. What does that have to do with your wife . . . excuse me, your un-wife?"

"Do they teach that in detective school, Abby? How to never answer questions?"

"Did you try to kill Elizabeth, Kent?" Maybe the direct approach was best, especially since I felt so uncomfortable. I didn't like the way he kept using my name. Maybe familiarity does breed contempt and it's an immediate birth.

"You've been talking to Roberta too much, Abby. To answer your question, I didn't have a clue where Elizabeth went, so I sure as hell couldn't have tried to kill her. Now it's your turn. Did you find out about Elizabeth's past? Is that your connection to her?"

"I'm not telling you anything." But despite how much I disliked Kent, maybe I *had* let Roberta's assessment color my thinking. He could be telling the truth, at least about the murder attempt.

He stood, came closer. "I've got you wondering—and that says a lot about you, Abby. You're thinking about giving me the benefit of the doubt and I appreciate that. Your eyes are intelligent. No secrets there. Very nice eyes."

Was this how he charmed people? With his acting skills? Or was he being sincere? The fact that he was a check forger and a thief was enough to tip the scales. Jeff was right. I needed to be careful around this guy. "I'll be going now. Sorry about our little set-to outside." I could keep my enemies close, too.

As I left, he called after me, "Don't be following me around after this, brown eyes. It would be a waste of time."

I walked to my car, making an effort not to sprint, because hell, I wanted to. I started the ignition, mentally running through a list of unkind words directed mostly at myself—ones like *dufus* and *damn fool*. I should have researched this guy before I ever got in the Camry this morning for the ride over here. Man, did I screw up today.

I waited until I returned home to call Cooper and tell him the whole story, including how I'd messed up and alerted Dugan about a tail.

"Don't beat yourself up, Abby. You learned some

important information. We figured Dugan for a liar and we were right. How far the lies go is the question," he said.

Pacing in the kitchen, Diva winding between my legs, I said, "Do you believe he knew where JoLynn was and, like stalkers sometimes do, decided to kill her—maybe simply because she left him?"

"It's a thought. Or maybe he was afraid of what she knew about his 'consulting' business, what she might spit out one day that could bring him down. That guy is smart and the smart ones worry me. No more tails. Keep your distance."

"No problem there. Besides, he'll be looking for me now and I'm sorry about that."

"You followed your gut and no detective should apologize for that. With this guy's background, I'm guessing the laminator and high-end printer are part of an ID shop. HPD forgery division might be interested in following up on what you saw through that window."

"ID shop? Could that be where JoLynn's fake ID came from?" Thank God I could still put two and two together.

"You got it. But a crook like Dugan wouldn't have expensive equipment for a small operation. He could be raking in lots of money supplying documents for illegals or identity thieves. That fake driver's license of JoLynn's was top-notch. The hologram was nearly perfect."

"But that might mean she was in on this ID shop. Maybe Richter's relatives are right—she *did* come to the ranch to scam Elliott Richter out of his money." *And if Richter found out*, I thought, *maybe he had that car fixed up to get rid of JoLynn.*

"I know what you're thinking, Abby. But Richter had plenty more options than to kill a scammer. Like coming straight to me. Or sending JoLynn packing."

"True," I said, still trying to make sense of this. "We don't know enough, do we?"

"No," he said. "Let me bug the forensics people about any more evidence from that smashed-up car, alert HPD to Kent Dugan's so-called job, and then we'll see where we stand."

We said good-bye and I hung up. But I kept pacing,

trying to think this through until the phone still in my hand jangled and startled me. It was Kate.

"Sorry, Abby, but I need your help—and I know you won't like the request."

"Have I ever turned down a request from you?"

"It's Aunt Caroline. I made arrangements for her to join the diabetic support group on a trip through the grocery store today. The dietitian will be teaching her and a few other newly diagnosed diabetics about their food choices and how to shop for the right foods."

I instantly regretted my eagerness to help. "And you want me to go with her?"

"I planned to take her during a break in my schedule, but two patients called for emergency appointments. I had to fit them in. Can you pick her up about twelve forty-five?"

I tried to sound cheerful when I said, "Sure. No problem. Where do I take her?"

Kate told me and when I hung up, I looked down at Diva and said, "This day is unraveling faster than that sweater I tried to knit for my seventh-grade boyfriend."

19

On the drive to the grocery store, Aunt Caroline was as edgy as a hungry coyote, fidgeting, snapping at me, telling me my driving was atrocious—which it was *not*. Just getting her out of her house and into my Camry took plenty of persuading and when we pulled into the Kroger parking lot, I was afraid she might balk again.

But with a "Let's get this silly exercise over with," she ignored my extended hand to help her out of the car, got out and strode ahead of me, her Prada handbag swinging on her arm. Maybe they'd give out a "best-dressed-diabetic-on-tour award" after this meeting ended and make her happy.

A checker directed us to the in-store coffee shop. We were running late thanks to Aunt Caroline's earlier stalling, so if she'd hoped to be the center of attention here, she got her wish.

A lean, dark-haired woman smiled broadly when we took our places at one of the small round tables. The woman was the only one standing and I assumed she was in charge.

"You must be Caroline. And who have we brought with us to help today?" she asked.

"*I* have brought my niece Abigail, and perhaps you are woefully misinformed, young woman, but a plural pronoun to describe a solitary person is *very* condescending. Exactly who are you, anyway?" Aunt Caroline said.

I cringed, wanting to crawl under the table. No one did imperious better than my aunt.

The woman didn't even blink. "I'm Judith, the dietitian. You spoke with my assistant on the phone. Can we all introduce ourselves to Caroline? Remember, first names only, unless you prefer to waive anonymity."

"That wasn't me on the phone," Aunt Caroline called out, interrupting the first person who tried to give her name. "It was my other well-intentioned but overprotective niece. This better be worth my time."

Now I wanted to slither under the floor tiles. Or shake some sense into you-know-who.

But Judith, bless her heart, didn't miss a beat. "You may not be happy about coming here today, but we're happy to have you. At some point I hope you will appreciate what you learn. Now, introductions, please?"

There were seven other people, and all but Aunt Caroline and a woman named Esther were carrying around way too many pounds. I'm bad with names, especially when they're dumped on me all at once, and I didn't remember anybody but Esther. One of the men was sitting in a store electric cart and checked his blood sugar at least twice since we'd arrived. I guessed his weight had to be more than three hundred pounds. *This must be so hard for him,* I thought. Harder than for Aunt Caroline. I'm very familiar with the comfort that food can offer and felt fortunate to be blessed with an overactive metabolism. My guess was that this man and I probably shared the same love of white bread and junk food.

Judith said, "We'll begin in the bakery to our right. We'll be reading a lot of labels today, so I hope you've all brought your bifocals."

Hmmm. Actually Judith *was* pretty condescending, but I decided to let Aunt Caroline bring that up again. Once the group started moving toward the bakery, that left only a lone man sitting and reading a newspaper near the deli display case. As the group moved out, he looked over the top of his paper at their retreating backsides. I hadn't noticed him when we first sat down and since I could see nothing but his eyes, I wondered if he was amused or interested or just plain confused by this meeting.

The diabetic group's first task involved searching for whole-grain and low-fat breads. Anything white and with a butter split top was apparently a no-no. Sorry, but a

PBJ on nine-grain bread wasn't the same, but maybe I could learn, set an example for my aunt and for Doris, who was still trying to understand her new diet—the healthy one Loreen was teaching her about.

Judith led us up one aisle and down the other, stopping at the pickles and olives to remind everyone that most diabetics are at higher risk for heart attacks and should watch their salt intake. I felt myself blush, recalling my recent olive binge. Aunt Caroline, meanwhile, was offering dramatic sighs and, when those were ignored, kept interrupting Judith's spiel to ask how much longer this would take.

We were headed to frozen foods, where I was sure I'd hear about a ban on pizza, when we passed the wine and beer aisle. "Wait a moment, young woman," Aunt Caroline commanded.

Sheesh. Could I pretend I wasn't with her?

"What about the diabetic wine?" she asked. "They do make that, right?"

While everyone giggled, I turned my back on my aunt, probably an unconscious attempt to find a hiding place. That's when I noticed the man who'd been reading the paper. He'd been watching me . . . or us, but quickly grabbed for the nearest end-of-the-aisle object when our eyes met. It happened to be toilet paper.

Something about him made my antennae go up. Maybe the fact that the only thing in his basket was a travel-size bottle of shampoo. He kept staring at the toilet paper as if it bore one of those healthy-lifestyle bread labels that were about as long as *War and Peace*.

What the hell was this? Could he be related to or be a friend of one of the diabetics? Was he following me? Or was he just a plain old creepy shopper? His blond-mixed-with-gray hair was chin-length and stringy; his pale eyes were frosty. The three-day growth of beard and less-than-clean clothes pushed me toward creepy shopper rather than follower. Maybe he wanted to hit on one of the diabetic ladies for a handout.

I refocused on Judith, who was lecturing on the danger of alcohol consumption for diabetics. "Alcohol translates to pure sugar, ladies and gentlemen. It can use up all your medication. See, your medication doesn't differentiate between the alcohol sugar and the rest of the digested food feeding your cells. Your medicine will attack that alcohol and eat up everything with it, and perhaps leave you dangerously hypoglycemic. We do all remember what *hypoglycemic* means, right?"

Aunt Caroline rolled her eyes and waved her hand in the air. "Oh, for crying out loud, let's get this over with. Move on, young woman."

I heard murmurs of agreement and thought, *Oh my God. If Judith doesn't wrap this up soon, Aunt Caroline might just lead a diabetic rebellion.*

Kate owed me. Owed me big-time.

After we left the store, the torture continued in the car and ended only when I dropped Aunt Caroline off. I breathed a sigh of relief as I headed for home. My aunt had told me in no uncertain terms never to arrange anything like that grocery tour again without her approval—an approval that would never come, of course. I didn't even bother to remind her that Kate set this up. Aunt Caroline wanted a scapegoat and I allowed her the privilege just to cut her diatribe short. I was lucky I didn't get pulled over for speeding in a residential neighborhood, but I couldn't get away from her fast enough.

My paranoia about the strange shopper hadn't gone away and I watched my rearview and side mirrors plenty during the drive. Houston traffic, unfortunately, makes it very difficult to pick up a tail. But in West University Place, where I live, it would be a lot harder for someone following me to remain anonymous. But I never saw any suspicious-looking vehicles and pulled into my driveway extremely glad to be home.

I called Kate as soon as I got in the door, and her receptionist, April, said she was in session, but she'd give her the message to call me. After sampling cheese, nectarines and chips and salsa at the store, I wasn't hungry. I decided to check my e-mail while I waited for Kate's call. I was hoping she and I could do dinner and I could bring her up to speed on my interesting, if flawed, day, maybe get her take on Kent Dugan's behavior.

Diva appeared from some hiding place as I went to

my office. She stretched, blinked away sleep and then followed me to the computer. When I connected to my server and my e-mail box came up, I saw Penny's message with the attachments. The foster-kid pictures. Damn, I'd forgotten all about them.

After I downloaded the photos, I viewed them in a slide show. I examined face after beautiful face, black, brown, white in equal numbers, the kids' first names and case numbers beneath their pictures and alongside little biographies. Sometimes brothers and sisters appeared together and their bio stated they wanted to be adopted to the same home. I felt so sad, even though most of these kids were smiling for the camera. What had they gone through? What had they seen or experienced that children shouldn't have to endure? Did these kids ever find permanent homes or had they aged out of foster care?

And then, when I got to the 2003 pictures, there she was. Elizabeth. Case number 48932.

I stopped the slide show and stared at a teenage JoLynn . . . or rather Elizabeth. No smile on her young face. Her bio was brief. She was fifteen, loved books and wanted to be a librarian. She liked Brad Pitt and the beach and wouldn't mind a home where there were small children. She was a good babysitter.

I sat back in my chair. Another piece of the puzzle? Or another mystery to solve? I picked up the phone and called Penny.

Lucky for me, she was in her office. "Hi, Abby. Did the pictures help?"

"Yes indeed." I gave Penny the name and case number. "Is there any way you can get me a last name? If she was adopted, that means she has a family who would want to know about her medical condition."

"Hmmm. What year was that file from?"

"It was 2003," I answered.

"She could sign a release—but that won't work, will it? She's in a damn coma, poor thing."

"Isn't this a special circumstance?" My tone was pleading, a little pathetic sounding, to be honest. "We need to know everything we can about this girl. Her past might have something to do with how she ended up nearly dead. Maybe she had a parent or guardian who abused her and that person didn't want her to ever talk about it to anyone."

"Or didn't want her revealing why she ended up in the system," Penny said. "Okay, I've now *made* this a special circumstance. I'll get back to you as soon as I can."

I thanked her and hung up, then returned to reading other e-mail so I wouldn't have to look at that heartbreaking picture of the girl we knew as JoLynn.

When the phone rang a half hour later, Kate was on the other end, not Penny.

I said, "I wanted to fill you in on the case and my absolutely wonderful experience with Aunt Caroline today. Are you free for dinner?"

"I do have a break from seven to eight—I know that's late, but everyone in Houston seems to be having meltdowns today. Then I have group therapy from eight to nine. We can order in something, maybe from the vegetarian place I love?"

"Can we compromise on the comfort of pizza? It's been that kind of a day." She agreed and I hung up, already thinking about parking in the Medical Center again. Might as well end the day on another frustrating note.

We compromised on two medium pizzas, since Kate didn't want pepperoni "leaking" over to her vegetarian side of the pie. I enjoyed every slice and talked as we sat on one of the couches in Kate's family therapy room.

"So you've figured out that Kent Dugan is not a nice man." Kate closed her pizza box and wiped her mouth with a napkin. I noticed she'd eaten only one small slice. "I hope you'll take the chief's advice and steer clear, Abby. Let Boyd handle him."

"Even though Dugan knows more about JoLynn than he's telling, I'm definitely keeping my distance. I've already screwed up enough trying to investigate him."

"You found out about the copy machine and laminator," Kate said. "That's important."

"True. I'll bet he made the fake inspection and registration stickers as well as the driver's license for JoLynn."

"Why would he make her a fake ID?" she asked.

"That's what we need to find out," I said. "I only know it can't be a coincidence that she lived with someone who could have made those forgeries for her."

"What if she really is Dugan's sister?" Kate checked her watch. We had only an hour together and our time was almost up.

"Then why introduce herself as his wife?" I said. "And I'm not only taking Dugan's word on that. Roberta Messing believed they were married."

"Could all this be part of some bigger fraud?" she said.

I considered this. "You mean Dugan has known all along where she was, that *he* sent her to bilk Richter out of his money?"

"I hadn't thought it through that far, but yes, that could be the answer," she said.

I sighed. "Why do I *not* want to believe the girl in that hospital bed would move into a stranger's house so she could take him for as much as possible?"

"You saw a comatose young woman, a helpless, battered girl. Our only knowledge of her before her car wreck comes from the Richter relatives and the veterinarian. Some of those folks thought she was a sweet, gentle book lover. Some thought she was a manipulator. If we conclude who she is and what she's like without firsthand information, that's not really fair to her, is it?"

I smiled. That was it. "Thank you, Doc. You're absolutely right. I always trust my instincts on whether a new client is sincere, but JoLynn and I have never actually met. I only know her through everyone else's perception."

Kate stood. "People are never one-dimensional and they do love to keep secrets. JoLynn is probably no different. It's a fascinating aspect of human nature, one that has kept me very busy today. Now, could you help me clean up before my clients start arriving for therapy?"

"Sure. But you didn't eat much." I picked up my empty pizza box and Diet Coke can.

"I wasn't all that hungry." She walked over to the

open kitchenette door and dumped her box in the garbage can. Then she held out a sponge in exchange for my trash. "Wipe the crumbs off the table, would you?"

In this tiny interaction, I could see her physically withdrawing from me—this after I mentioned her appetite.

I gripped her arm. "Look at me, Kate."

"What?" She tried for a clueless expression and failed miserably.

"It's time you let me in."

"What are you talking about?"

"You're thinner than ever, you say you have no appetite and you don't share your feelings anymore. I want you to talk about how that man shattered your belief in yourself."

She blinked away the sheen of tears. "Okay, but not tonight. I have work to do."

The walk to where I'd parked in a garage several blocks from Kate's office did nothing to rid me of the worry I felt seeing my sister still hurting after so long. She'd been duped into believing a man cared for her, fell hard and then was forced to face the truth.

And then it dawned on me. Why should I be surprised she went straight to the con angle with JoLynn? Duh. Sometimes I think I'm about three-fourths of a half-wit.

It was eight o'clock and the sun was about to give up for the day, but the heat and the traffic left the air thick with exhaust and humidity. Just breathing made me tired, but then this had been a long, difficult day.

I reached the garage, took the elevator up—way, way up—then walked toward my car. The Camry looked lonely in its far-off corner. I'd had to crowd into that spot when I arrived, but now most people had left. My hollow footsteps on the concrete were joined by another sound.

I looked back, saw no one.

But I was certain I wasn't alone.

I picked up my pace, fumbling in my bag for my remote and car keys.

Too late. When I turned this time, I saw him coming at me fast. The man was quick and efficient. He restrained me from behind with a damp, gloved hand over my mouth and a muscular arm around my chest and shoulders. He pulled me against him and whispered, "You need to quit digging around in her past. You don't know what you're getting into. *Stay away*."

Over the noise of blood pounding in my temples, I thought, *Dugan?* But then the man's hand pressed harder against my nose and mouth. *Sweet and wet. So sweet* . . . and then . . . nothing.

20

My alarm was going off, and I thought, *I sure as hell need a new mattress. This one is as hard as bricks.* But then I realized I wasn't in bed and the muffled alarm was my ringing phone.

I managed to sit and press my back against something as equally hard as the floor. Either I was as drunk as a waltzing pissant or something bad had happened. My vision was so blurred I couldn't see much but blended gray and black. I blinked several times, trying to focus.

The smell of mildew, car fumes and garbage surrounded me. The parking garage. *That's it. Kate and I had dinner, I walked here and then . . . what?*

Since the world remained fuzzy and dim, I felt around to my right like the blind woman I'd become, and touched a car bumper.

That's when the real alarm started up—the extra-fancy and very loud car alarm I just *had* to have. *You're a little late in the help department, dear Camry,* I thought. I reached in the direction of where my phone had been ringing . . . wasn't ringing now, thank goodness, because I couldn't handle any more noise. I found my bag and pulled my remote and car keys out. I jabbed at what I thought was the alarm silencer. Nothing. Bad aim.

Damn it, I was about to become deaf as well as blind if I didn't shut that stupid thing off. Another button poke and this time I got it. Blessed silence.

I sat there, and thank God, my sight slowly returned. I realized through the haze of my thoughts that I was near the passenger side of my car up against the parking garage wall. How in hell had I ended up here?

I didn't remember being hit on the head—but then, would I remember? I reached up and felt around for bumps or cuts. Nothing hurt . . . no swelling or blood. *Same head you've had for years, Abby,* I thought. *Yup. Same old head.* Then I laughed—the sound echoing around me like I was in a carnival fun house. I felt groggy as all get-out, but laughing felt good.

"Maybe you should get your little old self out of here, Abby Rose," I said out loud. But the words didn't come out right. They slid together and I laughed again. *You need a nice long nap,* I thought. *Then everything will be fine.*

But when I tried to stand, I discovered that even if you haven't been bashed senseless, your brain can be as screwed up as if someone had removed it and put it in backward. My legs reacted like I'd tried to stand on teddy bear legs. *Well, hell's bells, I sure can't drive, at least not yet.* My phone rang again. "Why can't I have some peace and quiet?" I said as I dug around in my bag. Again, the words came out like one big slurred word.

"Hi there," I said after I opened it and put it to my ear. Yup. I even *sounded* as drunk as that pissant. *What is a pissant anyway?*

"Where are you, hon?" he said. "I've called, like, six times."

I smiled. Jeff. God, how I love Jeff. I took a deep breath and tried to pronounce each word carefully. "I am sitting on the very nasty parking garage floor in the Medical Center and I have no clue how I got here. But you're a fabulous investigator, so I'm sure if I—"

"Abby? Where are you *exactly*?" He was using his best cop voice now. Jeff has the best cop voice in the world.

"Next to my car, you best cop ever. You *are* the best cop ever, you know that? Anyway, my new alarm is sure loud when you're sitting on the ground right next to it. I tested it tonight and—"

"I mean what parking garage? What level?"

I pulled the phone away for a second and looked at it, confused, then said, "You sound upset. You're not mad at me, are you?" Suddenly I felt like crying. What in God's name was wrong with me?

"I am *not* mad. I want to come and get you, okay? So tell me where to find you, Abby."

I squinted at the number on a beam several feet away. "Level ten."

"Which garage, hon?"

"You're asking me? I'm a waltzing pissant. Did I tell you that?"

"You probably have a ticket in your car. It will tell me which garage. Can you get to that?"

"Sure, Best Cop Ever." I fumbled again for the car remote and this time I could see well enough to hit the little lock symbol for the doors. I heard them click open and I slid on my bottom, then opened the passenger side. There was the ticket. I took it and held it close, using the light from the open door. I read him the garage number and he said he was on his way.

Jeff's trusty Nissan with the hundred million miles on the odometer pulled up behind my Camry what seemed like many, many minutes later. I'd stayed in the same, smelly spot even though I now recognized I'd parked close to a discarded bag of fast-food leftovers. Jeff had told me several times to stay put as he talked to me on the phone on his way to get me. He sounded all worried, probably because I still sounded drunk enough that he thought he might need to take me straight to rehab.

Jeff was out of his car quick as a rabbit on a skateboard and Doris hurried right behind him.

"She's here, Jeffy!" Doris stopped near the Camry's trunk.

Jeff knelt next to me, lifted my chin and looked in my eyes. "You look sleepy. Does anything hurt?" His cheek was fat with probably a Guinness World Record wad of gum.

"No. I just feel . . . drugged. Was I drugged?"

"I've never seen you like this, so my guess is yes. I'm gonna pick you up and put you in my car, okay?"

"I think my legs will work now." I used Jeff's shoulder to brace myself as I started to stand.

"I could carry you, Abby—like I carry Diva." Doris was imitating Jeff's studious examination of me.

"No one needs to carry me," I said. "I'm fine. I want to go home."

"Why don't I take you to one of the half-dozen hospitals within two blocks of here?" Jeff said.

Doris stood and started backing up toward Jeff's car. Then she screamed, "Nooooo!" her shriek louder than any car alarm. We hadn't heard her make that much noise in about six months and up here it echoed and echoed and gave my burgeoning headache wings.

"It's the hospital thing," I whispered to Jeff. He was in over his head with two needy women.

Jeff was torn between Doris, who was now crouched down by Jeff's car, and *moi*, who probably couldn't stand up without help. "Doris, it's okay," I said. "We're going to my house, not to the hospital."

"I don't believe you!" she cried. And then she took off toward the elevator.

Jeff whispered, "Shit," but seemed frozen next to me. I grabbed hold of the Camry's back passenger handle and said, "Go. Hurry."

Jeff corralled Doris near the elevator bank. He held her face with both his hands and talked to her. Then he took her hand and led her back to the Nissan. She was crying when he opened the back door and she climbed in.

Then Jeff said to me, "I need to call this in before we leave. Get a uniform and print unit over here so you can tell them what you know."

"You mean so I can tell them what I don't remember? I want to go home, Jeff. I have a headache."

Doris's window was rolled down and she was pouting, her eyes still wet with tears. "Abby wants to sit in the lie-down chair so she can feel better."

I pointed at her and smiled. "Elegantly put."

Jeff said, "Then at least let me ask you a few questions before we leave."

I sighed. "Go ahead."

He took out a fresh pack of Big Red and as he opened the gum, he said, "You walked toward your car from the elevator, right?"

"I'm sure I didn't walk up a mile of stairs, so yes."

"Let me check out the path you were taking. There's probably no collectible evidence, but I can't leave without looking." He helped me over to the Nissan and eased me down into the front seat. Then he took a flashlight from the Nissan's glove box.

I watched him through the windshield and he called, "Your trunk's open." Using the edge of the flashlight, he lifted the trunk door higher.

I stuck my head out the open car door. "I probably opened it when I was trying to find the damn alarm button on my remote."

He nodded, but that didn't stop him from shining the light inside the trunk. As the pounding in my head increased exponentially with each passing minute, Jeff examined the concrete, every support beam and the elevator. Doris, meanwhile, asked me what he was doing and why and if she could stay with me tonight, since she was already wearing her pajamas. That's when I checked my phone and realized it was almost eleven o'clock. I'd been lights-out for more than two hours.

Jeff finally finished, saying he'd found nothing, not even a thread or any marks indicating I'd been dragged to the side of my car. "Turd must have carried you," he mumbled so Doris wouldn't hear him. She picked up words like crazy and cop talk wasn't something she needed to add to her vocabulary.

We finally left and when we reached the attendant, Jeff flashed his badge and quizzed the kid about security and tapes. He said he knew nothing about it, but gave Jeff a card with a number to call in the morning. Then we drove to my house in a record ten minutes.

But Jeff wasn't about to wait until morning. He got on the phone immediately to see if he could get a look at those tapes, saying he'd seen a camera near where I was jumped and another by the elevator.

Meanwhile, I headed straight for the aspirin bottle and the shower. When I came downstairs a little while later, Doris was asleep on the living room couch. Jeff had been sitting in the recliner drinking a Shiner Bock, but stood when I entered the room.

I whispered, "Why didn't she go upstairs?"

He put a finger to his lips and gestured toward the kitchen. I followed him, took a Dr Pepper from the fridge, and then we both sat at the table.

"Doris said she wanted to make sure I didn't sneak you out to a hospital," Jeff said. "I hope I haven't gone ten giant steps backward with her."

"You did a great job calming her down. She'll be fine. But I sure hope she never needs to visit an emergency room or have surgery. Maybe we should come up with a code word for hospital."

"Good idea." Jeff rested his palm on my cheek. "I am so glad you're okay. Whoever did this will be damn sorry when I catch up to him. No tapes until tomorrow, but at least I got the garage manager's attention."

I pulled up the sleeve of my T-shirt. "Look what I found when I was in the shower. I believe this little mark in my arm muscle says I was injected with some drug I definitely never want to take again."

"Damn. I should take you for a tox screen at—" He glanced toward the living room. "Or maybe not."

"I don't *need* a tox screen," I said. "Whatever he gave me has pretty much cleared out—or I feel like it has. Answer me this, Sergeant Kline. How many bad guys aside from serial killers bring drugs to their assaults?"

"None that I know about. A gun or a knife does the job most times. But this turd didn't sexually assault you or rob you or do what serial killers—never mind." He took out his gum pack. Only one stick left after tonight's gum fest. After starting up his newest stick, he said, "Do you remember crawling to your car?"

"If I'd crawled to my car, my knees would have been filthy and maybe even raw. Not so."

"This guy—you're sure it was a male?"

"Yup."

"This guy drugs you and then puts you next to your car. How did he know which one was yours? Had you gotten that close already?"

My stomach sank. "No. He'd probably been following me and then waited until I came back from Kate's office. *Damnation*, Jeff. I need serious remedial work in picking up a tail. Why is that the one thing I cannot seem to do?"

"Knowing you, you probably spend a lot of time

thinking about your case, working things through, and meanwhile you're driving on autopilot. It takes a conscious effort to catch on to a tail. In the future, don't focus on the car makes and models. Look for decals or license plates or rosary beads hanging in windows—anything distinctive—and if you see that little something again, you might want to circle a block, see if they come after you."

I sighed. "Thanks. I will now shelve the bruised detective ego and refocus. I thought Dugan might be the guy who jumped me, but now I'm not so sure. Dugan's shorter than average. This man had to be more like your height, because my head ended up under his chin when he grabbed me. And the voice was different."

"The voice? He talked to you?"

I blinked. "Yeah. Jeez, I remember a little more now."

Jeff nodded, trying to keep his expression impassive. "Good. What else?"

I squinted, trying to recapture that pretty darn scary moment. "Gloved hand—like a winter glove. Whoa. It's been hot enough to toast marshmallows on the dashboard, so that's pretty weird."

"Protection. In case you bit him."

"But the glove smelled . . . no, it *tasted* sweet. But if someone injected me with another drug, that means the stuff on the glove wasn't strong enough to knock me out."

Jeff said, "The sweet taste makes me think chloroform. We had a serial rapist once who tried using the stuff. It worked for the first two women, but he ended up killing a girl because he didn't really know how much to use. Sad to say the stuff's readily available these days as an industrial solvent."

"Yeah. Chloroform. I researched poisons after that awful cyanide murder when I lived in River Oaks. Chloroform doesn't put you out in a few seconds like you see on TV. But it *can* make you kinda stupid."

Jeff grinned. "Remember, I *never* described you that way tonight."

I punched his arm. "Will I hear about this for the next decade?"

"Only if you keep me around that long. But back to business. I know you say Dugan wasn't tall enough, but why would he go after you anyway—especially since he knows you're very cop-connected?"

"He and I had a little . . . *discussion* this morning. I kind of pissed him off. And he might be in a whole lot of trouble thanks to me—or actually thanks to him and what I discovered at his house."

"Tell me. 'Cause I didn't like that SOB from the minute I met him." He started chewing his gum like crazy.

I told him about this morning's visit to Dugan's house, about the laminator and the copy machine and about Georgeanne.

"Dugan's a busy man. You said Boyd planned to call Financial Crimes Division?"

"Is that what it's called?"

"Yeah, but maybe I can speed up that process, get him investigated faster. Then he and I will have a very long talk about how he behaved this morning when you two talked."

"Thanks, but you don't need to—hell, yes, you do, because I like the whole idea. Now, can we call it a night?"

And so we did. Lying in Jeff's arms turned out to be the best therapy for any posttraumatic stress I might have suffered after my visit to the Little Shop of Garage Horrors. It felt good to be absolutely safe, even for a gun-toting tom girl like me.

21

Doris and Jeff left my house early the following morning. Jeff wanted to get to Travis Center early and start harassing the parking garage management again—but only after I'd reassured him a dozen times that I felt fine. I went back to sleep until eight, then got up and took another shower. I still felt grimy from lying around on that concrete petri dish last night. I planned on calling Cooper and Mr. Richter to fill them in on what had happened last night, but Cooper called me before I could pick up the phone.

After we exchanged hellos, he said, "JoLynn is being brought out of her coma, so today and on the weekend I'm working her case and nothing else. I'll be staying in Houston and wondered if you know a decent hotel near the hospital."

"The best place to stay is my house, in my guest room," I said.

"Abby, I couldn't—"

"Yeah, you could. End of story. When will you be in town?"

"I'm on the north side of Houston right now," he said.

I gave him directions, deciding not to tell him over the phone what I'd learned about JoLynn's foster care and last night's nasty little incident. Besides, if I had another chance to talk with someone about what happened, maybe I'd remember more details.

Cooper arrived forty-five minutes later and by the look on his face, I guessed he'd been a victim of Houston morning rush hour.

"Fun ride?" I asked.

"Folks are about as friendly as fire ants on those freeways this morning," he said. "Reminds me of when I worked in DC. Now, *there's* an ugly commute."

I had him drop his overnight bag by the stairs and then we went to the kitchen. I remembered how he'd chosen healthy food for lunch the first day we met at the hospital. I said, "I raided my sister's stash of green tea if you'd like some. She loves the stuff, so I keep it on hand."

"That would be great," he said.

"She does hers with this special little teapot." I held up the heavy cast-iron number she'd bought for me. I loved the way it looked, so I kept it on the stove, but had never actually used the thing.

"Just stick a cup of water in the microwave and I'll do the rest," he answered with a smile.

"Now, *that* I can handle."

I opted for coffee—my third cup, but who was counting? Then we sat across from each other at the kitchen table and I filled him in on everything that had happened yesterday.

When I'd finished, Cooper leaned back in his chair and shook his head. "I'm sorry you went through that. Maybe you shouldn't be involved in this."

I pointed at him, saying, "Don't you say that, Cooper Boyd. I can take care of myself, thank you very much. I have to adjust my strategy, maybe keep the Lady Smith with me—well, maybe not when I go into the hospital, but you know what I'm saying."

He looked surprised. "You carry?"

"Don't look so shocked. There's plenty of girls in the FBI who can shoot, right?"

"Yes, but—"

"Jeff and I were at the range about three weeks ago. I'm in practice and hit plenty of targets smack in the middle."

"I'll bet you did." He smiled. "Does Jeff plan to call you about those security tapes? I'd sure like a look myself."

"I don't know. He was first team today and will probably draw a case. We might not see or hear from him until later in the day."

"This man who attacked you, did he—"

"He did *not* attack me. He grabbed me, that's all."

"And drugged you. I'd call that an attack. Anyway, why go to all that trouble to warn you off? The chloroform, the injection? That's work."

"I never thought of it that way. But you know what? This little incident only makes me more determined than ever to help a client I've never really met."

"I never doubted your commitment, Abby. Talk me through last night one more time."

"Give me a second to picture everything." I took several deep breaths and closed my eyes. "Okay, I leave the elevator. My bag is over my left shoulder, like always. I take about ten paces, maybe. . . . Then . . . I hear something. Or just know someone is there. Okay . . . here's where it gets hazy. Did I look back?" I opened my eyes. "That's what I'd do, right? I'd look back."

"Seems logical."

I felt my heart speed up a little, just like when I realized I wasn't alone last night. "I *did* look back and I caught a glimpse. Hooded sweatshirt . . . bandanna over his mouth and nose. It's coming back. . . . I can see him." I squeezed my eyes shut again. "Oh my God. It was *him*."

Cooper sat straighter. "Him? Who is *him*?"

"The stringy-haired guy from the grocery store, the man with the frosty eyes." I banged my fist on the table. "I knew that creep was following us around in the store."

Cooper shook his head. "You've totally lost me."

"That's because I didn't tell you about parading through Kroger with newly diagnosed diabetic Aunt Caroline—an event that was rather like getting a root canal from a plumber, by the way. I'm sure the guy who jumped me was hanging around us in the store."

He smiled. "You know what he looks like, then. Maybe Jeff can get a sketch worked up. Anything else?"

"Oh yeah. It's all there now. He said, 'Stop digging around in her past. You don't know what you're getting into.' Since the only past I'm digging around in is Jo-Lynn's, he certainly meant her . . . but what *are* we getting into?"

Cooper cocked his head and said, "Beats the hell out

of me. Then he lays you by your car, where I'm guessing no one could see you and maybe take advantage of your altered state of consciousness. Very strange."

"I like that. Altered state of consciousness. Sounds like the name of an intellectually challenging piece of artwork. Anyway, I was in the shadow of the wall and the sun had gone down. Garage lights were dim, too. No one could have seen me where he left me."

We went over the scenario one more time, but nothing else came back to me. Then Cooper made a call to the hospital and of course had trouble getting anyone to answer his questions about JoLynn and what was planned for her today.

"Guess I have to go over there and wait them out," he said. "Wanna come?"

But before I could answer, the kitchen landline rang. It was Penny. "I have details about your comatose client, Abby. You may want to take notes."

"Really? Can you hang on a sec?"

"Sure."

I placed my hand over the receiver. "Cooper, it's the friend at CPS I told you about. She has information. I need a ride to the hospital to pick up my car, so don't leave me. Give me a minute to talk to Penny first."

"Information is what we need. I want to hear everything, but I'll make myself scarce while you talk, make another cup of that green tea, if that's okay?"

"Go for it." I went to my end table drawer and took out the pad and pencil.

"Okay, Penny. I'm ready," I said.

She had everything on JoLynn and I was glad she'd told me to take notes because there was plenty. I thanked her profusely once she'd finished, and silently vowed to get another donation check in the mail for the foster-care program.

"We can go, Cooper," I called from the foyer. I grabbed my shoulder bag from the hook on the hall tree and he met me at the front door.

He'd found the Starbucks car cup I'd put in the sink to dry. "Thought I'd take this to go. Green tea unclogs your arteries, or so I'm told. Maybe it's effective on brain cells, too."

After we climbed into Cooper's truck, I gave him directions to the scene of last night's ugliness and started telling him what Penny had told me, my notes in my lap to help me along.

"JoLynn, or Elizabeth, as she was called when she was in the foster-care system, came late to CPS, when she was nine years old."

"That means she should remember who her parents were. Who adopted her."

"Here's the thing," I said. "No one adopted her. Apparently she was abandoned at the Houston bus station—not a nice place, if you've ever been there. When CPS got ahold of her, she said she didn't remember anything. Not her name, not her parents, not where she came from. Nothing. She picked the name Elizabeth for herself and aged out of the system at sixteen."

"Is that unusual—her aging out and not being adopted?" Cooper asked.

"She was an older child and I've heard that's a more difficult placement, but I'm not an expert in foster care. I've had a few dealings with them, that's all. Penny said JoLynn ran away from every foster home she was placed in—sometimes more than once. They'd find her at Covenant House almost every time."

"The teen shelter?" Cooper said.

"Yeah, anyway, there was also a medical report about her having had heart surgery, probably no more than six months before she was found. She was followed by a cardiologist through her entire stay in foster care. That may have been a factor in her never being adopted—even though she didn't require medicine and had no activity restrictions."

"Did they pursue where she might have had this surgery?"

I sighed, remembering my last big case and what I had learned about Children's Protective Services—the overextended, overworked, overpopulated system. "Let me tell you what I know about CPS. They're not an investigative agency and neither is family court. They don't have the time or the people power to hunt down leads. Apparently the police checked Houston-area hospitals looking for anyone with her condition who might have had recent surgery, but came up with nothing. The investigation probably went no further than that."

Cooper's jaw tightened. "But local law enforcement should have done something more."

"Like the FBI would have?" I cast him a cynical glance.

"Touché. We wouldn't have touched her case, especially if she wasn't a kidnap victim or the media wasn't involved." He did cynical better than I did.

"Penny said the kid's picture appeared in the newspaper once and that was it. No one claimed her. They put her in foster care, where she apparently caused enough problems to be reassigned about ten times. JoLynn sounds like a girl who was lost—even to herself. She had no identity, Cooper. So she made one up." Sadness welled and stuck in my throat. I'd been damn lucky. Kate and I struck it rich when it came to our adoption—and not literally, even though we ended up with money. Daddy loved us . . . cherished us. And JoLynn never had that. There are probably so many kids who never get a chance to be truly loved.

"Her family abandoned her in a bus station?" Cooper said. "That's pretty cold if you ask me. But hold on. She could have been snatched, abused, then abandoned. Maybe she didn't remember anything because she blocked things out. We saw that all the time in the bureau with kidnap victims—even the adults."

I considered this. "Yes . . . and with the missing-persons system as overwhelmed as it seems to be, she might have been lost in that labyrinth, too. Someone could have been looking for her since she was nine—not only since Roberta reported her missing last year. Kate needs to talk to JoLynn—if she comes out of this coma okay, that is. She could help her, Cooper."

"She's a shrink, right?"

"A good one, too. She's helped me deal with families over and over and taught me so much about how to get people to open up."

"If she's anything like you, she has to be good. You've got an investigator's brain," he said. "If JoLynn was kidnapped, I might be able to find out something. Child abduction is always taken seriously. If some local law-enforcement agency called us—listen to me? *Us.* Jeez, I'm out of there. Anyway, the FBI does have to be asked in before they can act on local kidnappings, which are usually parental abductions."

"I learned that unfortunate fact from my Web surfing," I said. We'd pulled into the parking garage and after we wound up and around and up and around, Cooper found a spot near my Camry.

As we got out of the truck, I said, "Penny tells me they have photos of JoLynn for every year she was in the system. She'll be sending them to me."

"Good. Then maybe we can match her up with any unsolved kidnappings. There'd be photographs, flyers, reports, if a local law-enforcement agency was involved in a possible abduction."

We started toward the elevator and perhaps because I was already emotional about JoLynn's situation, last night's events came roaring back in 3-D Technicolor.

I felt like I'd been grabbed again, had that hand over my nose, was tasting the sweetness of chloroform.

"Abby? You okay?" Cooper's raspy voice jerked me out of that little fugue quickly, thank God.

"I'm fine." But I was a good five feet behind him and didn't even recall stopping.

"Fine, huh? I'd say that suntan of yours has faded away in less than thirty seconds." He held out his hand to me. "You thinking about last night?"

I walked to him and grabbed his warm, big hand. "Yeah. Tough girl melts under pressure. Let's get out of here and into that meat locker known as a hospital before we really do melt."

Finding JoLynn's neurologist in person was far less challenging than reaching him by phone. He was in the neuro ICU when we arrived, and told us that JoLynn was responding well to the reduction in sedation— apparently she was still JoLynn Richter to them, probably because Elliott was paying the bill. She was far from lucid, but beginning to respond. Before he ran off to save someone else's brain, he told us her private nurse would be out shortly to take us in.

The security guard was sitting nearby and we walked

over to him. Cooper extended his hand. "Cooper Boyd, Pineview PD. And this is Abby Rose. We're working on Miss Richter's case. You new?"

Cooper and the fair-skinned, balding guard shook hands. The man seemed ageless, probably due to his chiseled, hard-body physique. "Joe Johnson. I'm day shift now."

"Pretty boring gig, huh?" Cooper said. I'd been around Cooper long enough to sense a certain wariness in his expression.

And my radar was up, too. Hadn't we been here in the daytime before? Damned if I could remember. Last night's incident might have affected my memory more than I realized.

"I'm a people watcher," Joe Johnson said. "I like private jobs like this one." He smiled.

I noticed a book under Johnson's chair, *An American Tragedy* by Dreiser. Heavy stuff for hospital reading.

"That book is a favorite of mine." I nodded at the floor, remembering my college days when I read literary things like that—books I'd never pick up at Barnes & Noble today. Back then, I'd been questioning my own lifestyle and wondering if I'd end up a materialistic, status-seeking American like those that Dreiser derided.

"Yeah. Good story." Joe Johnson then picked up a *USA Today* on the table next to him and opened it.

Nice manners, I thought, rolling my eyes at Cooper.

Then a woman in olive green scrubs came through the ICU double doors and introduced herself as JoLynn's nurse. Another new face, not Shelly Young, whom we'd talked to before.

"I'm Maxine Norman," she said. "What do you want?" She addressed only Cooper. Maybe I had "Everyone please ignore me" written on my forehead.

"Didn't the doc tell you we came to visit JoLynn Richter?" Cooper said.

"He did," she replied. "I disagree with him, however. You should come back in a few days. She's in no condition to be interrogated."

"Isn't the doctor in charge?" I tried to sound polite.

Forced to acknowledge my presence, the woman had

a stare that made me think she could make an ice cube feel feverish.

"Five minutes." Norman turned on her heel, saying, "Follow me."

"By the way, I found out a little more about the heart surgery." Maybe if I said something medically profound, she'd warm up a little.

"I don't know what you're talking about," Norman said.

"JoLynn had heart surgery, right?" I said.

She put her index finger to her lips. "Keep your voice down. This is an ICU."

I squelched what I wanted to say, which was "Then why are you talking loud enough to be heard in the next zip code?" Instead, I whispered, "The other nurse wanted to know when she had the surgery, and I found out."

"And why is that important?"

So much for making nice with a woman who probably shaved her underarms with a chain saw. "Let's drop the subject. I wouldn't want you deducting minutes from our visit while we go around in circles."

She didn't respond as she directed us into JoLynn's cramped, equipment-filled room and planted herself by the door, arms crossed.

Cooper went directly to JoLynn and I went to the other side of the bed opposite him. Her bruised face was no longer swollen except along her right jaw. Her eyes were closed and thin wires of various colors seemed to sprout from her blond hair and lead to a machine against the wall near where Cooper stood. JoLynn's IV dripped from a bag above my shoulder.

"May I touch her arm?" Cooper asked Norman.

She nodded, but even that small gesture seemed hostile.

He gently placed a hand on JoLynn's forearm and whispered, "JoLynn. My name is Chief Cooper Boyd from the Pineview police. Abby is here, too. You don't know us, but we want to help you."

She raised her eyebrows, but this seemed to hurt, because she grimaced. She didn't open her eyes but said, "Abby?"

"Abby Rose. Your grandfather asked me to help you," I said.

A smile played on her lips. "Grandfather. Yes." *Grandfather* came out as *granfather* and her *yes* went on like a snake's hiss.

Cooper said, "Someone tampered with your car and you crashed into a tree. We want to find out who did that. Do you understand?"

Now a wrinkle of confusion on her forehead cut through the bruises. "Tamper . . . tamper . . . what's that?" Every word seemed like an enormous effort.

"Who might want to hurt you, JoLynn?" I said.

Slowly she opened her eyes. Her irises were as blue as forever, but oddly unbalanced. And then I realized her left pupil was larger than the other. She turned her head ever so slightly my way and her hand reached through the side rail and found mine. She squeezed hard, those crystal eyes alive with fear. "Stop. Please stop."

Then she looked at Cooper. "Stop. Stop. I can't stop."

She was clearly becoming agitated and the nurse came over and told me to step aside. But before that could happen, Nurse Norman had to carefully pry JoLynn's cold, reluctant fingers from my hand.

Meanwhile, the terrified girl kept repeating "Stop," her gaze traveling from Cooper to me and back to Cooper.

Norman said, "This is not helping." She then brushed a few strands of hair off JoLynn's forehead with a tenderness I thought she was incapable of, then soothed her patient with a nearly inaudible "Hush."

The cell in my pocket vibrated against my pelvic bone. Uh-oh. I tried to pretend I didn't hear the buzzing, but clearly everyone did, including JoLynn, who had closed her eyes and in her calmer, sedated slur said, "Is that my phone?"

I almost smiled until the wrath of Nurse Norman was fully visited on me. *"Turn that thing off,"* she whispered.

Having been busted for illegal use of a cell phone in the hospital—not intentional, just a product of what I rationalized had to be memory loss again—I pulled the phone from my pocket. It had already gone over to voice mail and stopped quivering, but I dutifully powered it down.

"Sorry," I said.

"I think it's time you both left anyway," Norman said.

JoLynn again reached for my hand and I put my fingers in hers, saying, "Do you want us to stay?"

"Don't . . . don't go." But she was already drifting off, her hand going limp, her head lolling to the left.

Cooper said, "She obviously needs her rest. We'll be back later."

I didn't want to leave, since we'd gotten next to nothing, but he was right. JoLynn was only beginning to come around. She *had* smiled when I mentioned her grandfather, though, and seemed happy simply saying the word.

When we emerged from the ICU, Elliott Richter was standing in the waiting area, while Simone was slumped in a chair fiddling with a small camera. A tense-looking Adele stood by her brother. Simone was dressed like she'd just come from a rock concert in her wide-legged cropped cargo pants and black T-shirt, whereas Adele had the Ann Taylor thing going.

Richter greeted us, introduced Simone and Adele to Cooper, then said, "How is she?"

"A lot better," Cooper said.

Richter's face relaxed into a genuine smile. "Good. That's very good. Did she say anything?"

"A few words. She seems a little frightened, but then, waking up in a hospital has to be scary." Cooper scanned the waiting area. "Security is more important than ever now that she's coming around, so where's your man? You send him on break?"

Gosh. Joe Johnson *had* disappeared. Guess I'd been too distracted by Simone taking pictures of the waiting room, the double ICU doors and all of us, the repeated snicking and flashing of her camera finally irritating Adele enough that she'd mouthed "Stop it."

Richter said, "A staff member told us you were with JoLynn. I assumed you sent the guard on a break."

"I didn't send him anywhere," Cooper said. "Can you call his agency and have him paged to get back up here? Or I could stay until he shows up."

"I appreciate the offer, Chief Boyd, but I'm paying him damn good money to be here. And he's *not* where he's supposed to be." Richter took out his cell phone. "Excuse me while I find somewhere to make a call." He strode off down the hall, anger evident in every step.

"Guess we'll wait." Cooper smiled politely at Adele.

Her expression didn't change. "My brother has been very stressed by this . . . *incident.* What time frame do you have for bringing the culprit to justice?"

Yup, same snobbish Adele I'd met earlier this week. But I wondered if she was the one stressed-out. She looked a little haggard, despite the perfect makeup and expensive clothes.

"Culprit, huh? Sounds way too nice for a wannabe murderer." Cooper wore a tight smile. He wasn't taking to Adele, but then who would, besides husband Leopold? He said, "The more information I get, Mrs. Hunt, the quicker I can find this *culprit.* You have anything to offer?" He walked over to where Joe Johnson had been sitting.

Adele blinked and said, "Why would you think I—"

"Do that again, Mom." Simone's camera was fixed on her mother's face.

"What in hell are you doing, Simone?" Adele was way out of her comfort zone now, even though I recalled Leopold saying she could handle anything.

Simone took her mother's picture, then said, "I thought *I'd* be the nervous one coming here. But you are definitely off your game, Mom. I love it. Makes me think you might be human."

I could tell Adele wanted to offer a comeback in the worst way, but her mouth stayed half open, apparently no words readily available. Meanwhile, Simone turned her smile on Cooper.

"Do you think they'd mind if I photographed the staff working inside the ICU—that is, if they let me in? This place is so different than anywhere I've been and I'm working on facial expressions, trying to improve my work, move beyond your average sunrise. Everyone moves so fast here, looks so serious, seems so full of purpose. That would be an awesome capture."

"I don't know, Simone." He carefully folded the newspaper Joe Johnson had left behind. "Ask the staff. They might not mind. I think the patients would be off-limits, though."

"I'm cool with that." Simone held up the camera for a second. "I wouldn't bother JoLynn with this thing, that's for sure."

"Then why are you bothering me?" Adele said.

"Because it's fun, Mom." Simone left us and approached the only other visitor, a lone man sitting in a far-off corner, who was staring at his clenched hands hanging between his knees.

"Can we please sit down?" Adele said in a clipped tone.

"Sure. Maybe you should take a few deep breaths, relax a little." Despite Adele's attitude, Cooper sounded plain nice. He saw what I saw—a woman obviously very uncomfortable. Simone was right—Adele was off her game.

Adele and Cooper sat next to each other on the black vinyl chairs, but I remained standing. I'd discovered those seats were like a block of ice.

Cooper said, "Your daughter's serious about her picture taking, huh?"

I glanced over and saw that Simone was sitting near the visitor, talking to him.

Adele sighed. "I suppose. Elliott encourages her, buys her cameras and lenses practically every other week, sends her to amateur-photographer camps and workshops. It all makes me very . . . wait a minute. Why the hell are we talking about this?"

"Because you seem uneasy and I wondered if the issue was your daughter," Cooper said.

"What if I am uneasy?" Adele snapped. "Simone could fail. I mean, what kind of career is photography anyway? She'd work for newspapers or magazines? Travel all over creation. I don't like the idea one bit."

"This *is* about your daughter, then, and not about visiting JoLynn?" Cooper said softly.

I almost smiled. Cooper was smooth. He could get beneath a person's top layer as quickly as a car salesman.

Adele closed her eyes briefly, then looked Cooper in

the eye. "If my coming here can make things easier for my brother, then so be it. I haven't seen him this devastated since he lost Katarina."

I said, "You're here for your brother, then? Not Simone and not JoLynn?"

Cooper shot me a reproachful glance that asked the question I was asking myself. Why couldn't I keep my mouth shut?

But apparently I didn't do as much damage to his gentle probing as I thought, because Adele didn't seem upset by the question. In fact, Cooper had obviously settled her down nicely, because her tone was even when she said, "I'm trying to understand Elliott's . . . attachment to this young woman, Ms. Rose. I truly am."

"It's Abby." I offered a small smile.

Cooper was about to ask her something else, but Richter was back, his neck reddened by anger. And he had that look of fear in his eyes again, the one I'd seen at his ranch when he began to understand that JoLynn might have many more secrets than he'd ever expected.

Richter said, "Someone called up the agency pretending to be me and canceled my twenty-four-hour security."

"*That* explains why the guy left," I said. "Someone called and sent him home."

"Not exactly," Richter said through clenched teeth. "Apparently the people I hired have been off this job for two days."

"Th-then who was that guy we talked to not a half hour ago?" I said.

Cooper's expression hardened. "Damn good question."

22

Though Richter was mad enough to chew nails and spit rivets about the fake security guard, he was more concerned about JoLynn and was anxious to see her. He'd given that message to a staff member heading inside the ICU.

So Adele stepped up and said she would make sure real security would be on the job as soon as possible. After calling to Simone—who was still talking to the morose visitor—that she'd be back as soon as she could, Adele left to make phone calls.

"I could head over to this agency you used, talk to them about how this happened," Cooper told Richter.

"Waste of time," Richter said. "The cancellation was done over the phone, so they don't know a damn thing. I've used these people before, but they specialize in protecting my ship-channel sites here in Houston and my offices in south Texas. They've never done an assignment like this and the impostor was smart enough to call in the termination of services during the evening, when people who know my voice weren't around."

"At least we know what the guy looks like," I said. "We can alert the staff in case he shows up again. But why did he leave? We didn't know you were coming, so how could he? And why wouldn't he believe you'd accept his presence here just like we did?"

"I don't know . . . unless . . . ." Richter's eyes traveled across the waiting room to where his niece was now on one knee, photographing the visitor. "Simone took the stairs while Adele and I rode the elevator. She got here first and as you can see, she's never known a stranger."

"You think she told the guy who she was, that you were on the way, and that's why he decided to split?" I said.

"Maybe," Cooper said. "Let's ask." He caught Simone's eye and gestured for her to come over.

She stood and put a comforting hand on the man's shoulder and he looked up at her gratefully before she left him.

Richter spoke before Cooper could open his mouth and asked Simone about the guard. "Yeah, he was here. I talked to him. He didn't do much talking back, though. Just got up and left."

"Did you never mention your uncle or give him names?" Cooper said.

"No." Simone's tone indicated this was, *like, the stupidest question ever*. "I asked if I could take his picture, that's all. He said 'Not today' or something like that, picked up his stuff and headed for the stairs. I did get one shot off, though, because he turned around to see if I was following him. Then you and Mom came and I forgot all about him."

"Didn't you think that was odd? Did I not tell you I hired security for JoLynn?" Richter's anger was now focused on his niece.

She stepped closer and lifted her chin, stared him in the eye. "You didn't tell me a damn thing, Uncle Elliott. But I guess I'm to blame for whatever's got you pissed off now."

Richter closed his eyes, pinched the bridge of his nose with thumb and index finger. Quietly he said, "I'm sorry. None of this is your fault." He then explained about the fake-security-guard snafu.

"Oh crap. So . . . you're okay, then?" Simone asked.

Richter offered her a puzzled look. "Yes . . . but I don't understand—"

"You said you were sorry. You and Mom never say you're sorry about *anything*," Simone said.

Richter stared down at Simone like he was seeing her for the first time. "I truly am sorry."

Cooper cleared his throat, then asked Simone to show the picture to her uncle to see if Richter might know the man. Simone held the display out and clicked back about twenty times before she found Joe Johnson's photo.

Richter shook his head no, but before he could say anything, Chuckles the Private-Duty Nurse came through the double doors.

"Mr. Richter? Maxine Norman, your day-shift nurse." She extended her hand to him, ignoring the rest of us.

Brightly I said, "Ms. Norman is new, too."

Simone said, "Oh boy" under her breath.

But Richter said, "I recognize you from your résumé photo, Ms. Norman." He looked at Cooper. "The nursing agency faxed me several applications to consider. I chose Ms. Norman myself, as she has outstanding recommendations, has dealt with head-injury patients often, but she couldn't start until yesterday."

"I appreciate your confidence, Mr. Richter," Norman said. "Your granddaughter is sleeping, but responding nicely to the reduction in sedation. Movement in all extremities, pupils reactive though unequal. Vital signs good."

Relieved Norman hadn't mentioned JoLynn's agitation during our earlier visit, I said, "She smiled when I mentioned you, Mr. Richter."

"Really?" he said.

"Let's go in, but only for a few minutes. She needs her rest more than anything." Norman turned and started walking.

"Can my niece come, too?" he asked.

"Certainly," Norman said over her shoulder.

Simone followed and I heard her say, "May I take your picture?"

Richter hung back for a second and said, "If you can get a lead on that man, I'd appreciate it. He made the cancellation call to Brace Security about ten p.m. Wednesday night. Meanwhile I'll have Simone show his photo to the staff."

Richter started after his niece and the nurse.

Cooper called after him. "Have her e-mail me that picture—and send it to Abby, too. You still have our addresses?"

He nodded and disappeared behind the double doors.

Cooper sat down again, looking puzzled and worried. "Guess we wait until protection arrives."

"You think that guy planned another attempt on Jo-Lynn's life right here? Doesn't that only happen on television?"

"He was probably here to gather as much information as possible, maybe get a handle on her condition, follow Richter when they took JoLynn out of here," Cooper said. "Killing her in this place would be way too tough. But how did he find her?"

"There was a small article in the *Houston Chronicle* the day after the accident," I said.

"That explains it. If he tried to kill her, he'd be looking for proof she was dead. What bothers me is how easily he planted himself here. He must have scoped out the original guards, caught the logo on the uniform and knew who to call. He was careful and he was smart."

"Could Kent Dugan have sent him? The switcheroo occurred after *he* knew where JoLynn was."

"Very possible, but what's his motive to kill her?" he said.

"You got me. Maybe she ran from him because he threatened her, he found her and . . . hell, I don't know. But like Jeff said, the guy gives off bad vibes."

Before he could respond, Adele came clickety-clacking back into the waiting room. "Mission accomplished, and this time, I have a picture on my BlackBerry of the man who should be arriving shortly. Where's my brother?"

"In there." I nodded at the ICU.

"Would you like to visit, too?" Cooper asked.

She glanced at the doors, hesitated. "Oh, no. I have to wait for the new security person."

Her whole facade had fallen away, leaving her looking vulnerable and afraid. Too much emotion had been spilled since JoLynn's accident. No one in the Richter family seemed equipped to deal with it all.

"If you're staying here," Cooper said, "then Abby and I can get busy finding out who this Joe Johnson really is. If you'd e-mail us both pictures of any employees—nurses, aides, security—anyone you and your brother have authorized to be here, I'd appreciate it. Mr. Richter knows how to get in touch."

"I will do that," Adele said with a distracted nod. She held her BlackBerry with two hands, her gaze far-off.

We said good-bye and left the waiting area. I had my arms clutched around me to protect against what was becoming the very familiar chill. After we exited the elevator into the lobby, Cooper, who'd seemed lost in thought for the last minute or two, finally spoke.

"The security guard thing is important, but let's step back a minute. Help me process our visit to JoLynn. She seemed pretty mellow until I told her the car was rigged, so she understood what I meant. That piece of information would sure as hell upset me, too."

We paused near the hospital exit and I said, "You think she knows who fiddled with her car?"

"Maybe. Can we pick up lunch and go back to your place? I need to think things through."

"I don't have much appetite, but we can stop at Becks if you want. Black bean burger okay?"

He smiled. "Sounds great."

"Kate loves them, but then, she's a fan of tofu, organic grains and anything else you can take away from the Whole Paycheck Market."

He laughed. "Will I get to meet the shrink this weekend? We could sure use her expertise when we visit Jo-Lynn tomorrow," he said.

"She'd be more than willing. I could leave her a message, since she's probably with a client."

"Do it," he said.

"Hope you're up for *Shrek* and *Happy Feet* tonight, by the way. Jeff's sister has Down syndrome and we watch whatever she picks on Friday pizza night."

"This is a guy who misses Saturday cartoons, so you don't have to sell me on animated anything—but please let me buy the pizza," he said.

"You've got a deal." Then I turned on my cell to phone Kate and saw MISSED CALL on the screen. Jeff's caller ID. "Jeff phoned. Maybe he got the security tapes from the garage."

"I'd like a lead on that bastard who knocked you out, myself."

"Better call Jeff first." Then I said, "Hey there" when he answered.

"Listen, we got a problem," he said.

"You need help with Doris before you come over tonight? We've already made the hospital visit to JoLynn, but guess what happened?"

"You need—"

"Cooper and I have a lot to tell you," I went on. "He's staying at my place over the weekend and—"

"Abby, listen to me. They just pulled Kent Dugan's body out of Brays Bayou."

23

I was too stunned to speak for a second and must have looked it because Cooper put a supportive hand on my elbow and mouthed, "Are you okay?"

My stomach felt like I'd eaten a batch of Texas kumquats right off the tree, but I gave him a thumbs-up to let him know I was fine. Then I said to Jeff, "Dugan was murdered?" so Cooper would understand what we were discussing.

Cooper reacted with raised eyebrows to my words while Jeff went on, saying, "When's the last time you remember anyone swimming in that bayou? Yes, he was murdered."

"Sorry I asked." This terrible development had apparently made us both testy.

"You're obviously in the middle of something uglier than we thought, what with this murder and last night's incident in that garage." He didn't add "so I worry," but I knew that's why he still sounded pretty tense. "Anyway," he continued, "Bart and I caught a drive-by shooting first thing this morning and when we got back to the sixth floor at Travis, DeShay and Chavez were heading out on the bayou call."

DeShay Peters and Jeff were once partners but had been split up because they were both day-shift sergeants. Now all the murder squads—God, how I hated that title—had a sergeant and an officer working together. DeShay was with Chavez and Jeff's new partner was Bart Pulanski.

"DeShay drew the case?" I said. "That's good."

"Luck of the draw. I filled him in on the tampered

car, the coma victim's relationship to the complainant. I told DeShay I'd met Dugan and that you knew him, too, so expect a visit or a call."

I could never get used to Jeff or the rest of his homicide buddies calling victims *complainants*. It sounded like the dead person might rise from the grave for a court appearance. "Sorry, I'm a little blown away by this. What did you say?"

"DeShay will call you."

"I could phone him right now or—"

"He'll get to you when he can, Abby."

"But this is huge. This is, well, *awful*." I was sure glad Cooper was standing next to me because I was feeling a little sick to my stomach. Nerves? Or leftover side effects from the drugs?

I swallowed, heard Jeff sigh.

He said, "I guess because you're Abby, you have to be doing something, not wait around. Did you say Boyd's with you?"

"Yes."

"Can I talk to him?"

"Sure." I handed the phone over.

Cooper said, "What's going on, Jeff?" Lots of *uh-huh*s and *okay*s followed before Cooper closed the phone and handed it back. "Jeff said you'll know where to go when I give you the body location, but I'm driving."

"He doesn't think I can drive? I'm perfectly capable of—"

"My decision. You may think you're fine, but I saw your face in that parking garage a little while ago and just now when you got this news. You're shook up. We do this together or I'll find my way there alone."

I sighed in frustration. "I need my car, Cooper. We can both drive."

"We'll pick yours up later," he said decisively. "We need to get to that scene now."

"Okay, let's rodeo." I said this calmly though I felt anything but calm. A suspect was dead and added to that, either Cooper or Jeff decided not to allow me behind the wheel. So why did I feel a little relieved that Cooper was driving? Probably because that guy screwed with my head last night. I preferred control, not having to deal with rubber legs and feeling like I was drunk.

Turned out we didn't have far to go. Since Cooper was in plain clothes and had come to Houston in his truck, he had to show his badge and ID to the officer standing on the Brays Bayou embankment. We were waved on when the officer told us that Sergeant Peters was expecting us. Guess Jeff called DeShay.

Patrol cars and officers from the Harris County Sheriff's Department and HPD were waving along the rubberneckers who were delaying traffic on the overpass. No one on foot had stopped to look—maybe because this was not a walker-friendly part of town.

I saw the familiar black baseball caps that the medical examiner's investigators wear, as well as the navy-clad Crime Scene Unit officers. The body had been dragged up to a spot where the concrete met the grass. Because of the steep embankment, DeShay had to sit by the corpse—his position such that I couldn't see Dugan's face, thank God. No matter how ugly the guy had been on the inside, his face and body *had* been beautiful. If he'd been tossed from the top of the embankment and rolled down fifty feet of sunbaked ground and concrete to the water, I was betting his outside matched his inside now.

I pointed out DeShay to Cooper and he eased down the bank to join him by the body. I stayed where I was, arms crossed, keeping my focus on the two men as they greeted each other. That way, I saw nothing more than Dugan's wet, muddy pants. A few minutes later they came back to where I stood. DeShay shed his gloves and held out his arms. "How's my girl?"

We hugged and I said, "I miss you, DeShay. You can still come over, you know."

"Yeah, but then I'd start thinking about the best partnership HPD ever had. My man and I got it done, Abby. You know that."

His "man" was Jeff and they had been a good team. "What happened to Kent Dugan?" I said.

"Wish I knew. Not shot or knifed, far as I can tell. The body was definitely moved to this location if I'm reading the lividity right. Someone probably rolled him up in the carpet remnant CSU has already picked up. And that's about all I can tell you for now. What can you tell me?"

"He was a player," Cooper said. "Should have gone to jail more than once but never did."

DeShay turned to me. "Abby, you met the complainant more than once, from what Jeff told me. Got any clue about next of kin? 'Cause we sure can't find anyone. His cell phone got wet, so we don't have that to help us right now. I'm hoping the tech guys can recover something, anything."

"He has a live-in girlfriend named Georgeanne, but I don't know her last name. She works at some printer place—she might have told me where—it sure wasn't Kinkos—but I can't remember."

Cooper said, "Someone tried to kill his *last* live-in girlfriend. Jeff said he filled you in on that. Maybe we need to find out if this Georgeanne is okay . . . or might have had a little struggle with our friend Dugan."

"A warrant to search Dugan's place is on the way. But this other girlfriend—the one before Georgeanne—she had a wreck and is in a coma, right?"

"They're gradually bringing her out and she's at least able to talk. Pretty groggy, though, as of an hour ago."

The medical examiner's body movers, wearing their "don't get a hernia" back braces, took a stretcher down to pick up the body, and the CSU officers backed off to allow them room. My stomach knotted up again. I did not want to see Dugan when they brought him up, not even in a body bag. No matter how much I disliked him, I sure as hell hadn't wanted him dead. I turned my back enough that I couldn't see what they were doing.

DeShay's dark forehead was beaded with moisture and the waistband of my capris was soaked with sweat. Cooper looked cool and calm and I wondered how he managed that in ninety-degree heat.

"Since it's hot enough to evaporate dirt, can we discuss this in the comfort of air-conditioning?" I said.

"I don't have the unmarked. I sent Maria for a search warrant of the Dugan residence." DeShay checked his watch. "She should be back pretty soon."

"Who's Maria?" I asked.

"Officer Maria Chavez. My new partner." He smiled as wide as a small dog with a large bone.

So the "Chavez" Jeff had told me about was female. As the three of us walked up to the street, I said, "By the look on your face, I'd say she's hot."

"Oh, yes. Like my granny always said, when God shuts a door, He opens a window. Jeff may have been forced to close a door, but there stood Maria waiting behind the curtains. Smart woman, my Maria. Very smart."

I pulled my purse-size SPF 30 cream from my bag and squeezed a dollop on my palm. "Can we please find shade somewhere to talk while we wait for her?"

"No need," DeShay said, looking past me. "She's making the turn onto South Main now."

I rubbed sunscreen on the back of my neck, which would make the hair back there greasy, not to mention wet from sweat. I reminded myself we were headed to a dead man's house, not my aunt Caroline's. No one would even notice.

Officer Chavez pulled up to where we stood.

"Get in," DeShay told us, opening the back door.

Cooper and I climbed into the Taurus. Then DeShay took the front passenger seat. The car was blessedly cool and smelled like a pine tree. I noticed an air freshener hanging on the rearview.

Maria Chavez turned. "Who are you two?" She wore an orange cotton shirt and her shiny dark hair was French-braided, her olive skin beautiful despite little or no makeup. I could tell why DeShay had taken a shine to this one.

"Chief Cooper Boyd, Pineview PD. And you're Officer Chavez?"

"That's me. And you?" She lifted her chin in my direction.

"I'm Abby Rose."

"Wow. The famous Abby my partner talks about all the time? Did you know DeShay Peters is the president of your fan club?"

"Maria, get moving," DeShay said. "That is, if you know where we're going."

"Oh, I know—probably better than you, amigo." With that, she put the car in drive and made a screeching U-turn that practically landed me in Cooper's lap. I hitched on my seat belt and gave Cooper a wide-eyed "Holy crap" look.

We filled them in on what we knew about Dugan as Chavez drove to the condo—drove like she'd *stolen* this cop car. DeShay took notes, barking at Chavez several times to slow down so he might have a chance of reading what he wrote later on. Then Chavez asked us a few questions. She was certainly abrupt, but after a few exchanges I realized this seemed to be her way, maybe because she'd decided a female in Homicide Division needed to come across as tough and in control.

When we arrived at our destination, we were all surprised to see another Taurus sitting in the driveway. A man wearing a tie and short-sleeved dress shirt was walking away from the front door. The badge and gun on his belt indicated he wasn't a Jehovah's Witness out on a mission.

"Hamlin, what the hell are you doing here?" DeShay called.

Meanwhile Chavez said, "What'd you do, Peters? Alert everyone in HPD?"

"I didn't talk to anyone besides Jeff," he said. "Hamlin works in the financial crimes division, so Jeff wouldn't have sent him." DeShay met this new officer halfway up the front walkway, Chavez tailing behind muttering about how this was their case and they didn't need any damn help—and she was probably including us.

While the three of them greeted one another, Cooper looked at me. "I called HPD last night, left a message for the forgery unit." He started toward them and I followed.

Cooper cleared his throat. "I'm Cooper Boyd, Pineview PD. I made a call last night—"

"Got your message, Chief Boyd. You think this residence is a possible ID shop?" Hamlin asked.

"Yes," he answered with a nod. "Seems it's more than that now, though."

My turn to clear my throat. "Um, hi. I'm Abby Rose, a PI connected to this case."

Hamlin grinned. "*The* Abby Rose? Jeff Kline's best friend? Russ Hamlin." He extended his hand and then took mine in both of his, squeezing hard. "We know how you helped him after he was shot. We owe you."

I felt uncomfortable being praised by HPD for helping Jeff, praised by the men and women who put their lives on the line every day. I wanted to move past this. "Are there two warrants for this house, then?" I asked.

"I didn't have enough for a warrant, but since Dugan's dead, I suppose you do," Hamlin said to DeShay.

Chavez smiled and held up the paperwork. "Exigent circumstances, too. We can go in without an invitation, since the complainant's condition indicates another crime scene. I am learning fast how to ask for these warrants and get exactly what we need."

"Anyone home?" DeShay asked Hamlin.

"No one answered," he said. "But that doesn't mean much."

"Not good." DeShay rested a hand on his SIG Sauer. "I hope we don't find a dead girlfriend. Take the back, Chavez."

Hamlin's expression went serious. "You want me to back her up?"

"I don't need any help," Chavez said over her shoulder as she started around the garage.

"Excuse me for carrying a weapon, Miss Homicide," Hamlin shot back.

"Sorry about that, my man," DeShay said. "She's new in homicide. Got a lot to prove. Can you stay with Abby and Cooper until we find out what we got inside?" DeShay looked at me. "Tell him what you know about Dugan, Abby."

Hamlin said, "You're gonna need the Moby, unless you got the keys. Heavy door, dead bolt, too."

"The ME investigator took the keys, so Moby, here I come." DeShay hurried to the unmarked and opened the trunk.

"What's a Moby?" I asked. "A whale with an attitude? A rock star who suddenly grew muscles?"

Hamlin smiled. "Lady has a sense of humor. You need that in our business."

DeShay started for the front door carrying a two-handled battering ram. I'd seen those things on *Cops* a hundred times. Now I knew what they were called.

"Let us know when we can go in, Sergeant Peters," Cooper said as DeShay rushed by.

"You got it," DeShay said over his shoulder.

A few seconds later I heard DeShay shout, "Houston Police Department. We're entering the residence," before the earsplitting crunching and cracking of the door drowned out anything else he might have said. From the sound of things, I was betting that door had been reduced to sawdust.

Hamlin said, "What's your connection to Dugan?"

"Cooper and I knew him. Sort of." I didn't add that I knew him far better after our little conflict—was it only yesterday? I licked my lips, the heat fueling my sick stomach and the headache that I'd thought was completely gone.

"So you got my message about the guy?" Cooper said.

Hamlin nodded. "Got a message from Jeff Kline, too. I decided to come out right away. I arrested Dugan for being a paper hanger back when he used to live in an apartment across town. Very downscale place compared to this. Looks like he bought himself a piece of the American dream—probably with someone else's money."

Cooper and I filled Hamlin in on the possible forged IDs we knew JoLynn had in her possession at the Richter place.

"You think Dugan made her those IDs, huh?" he said.

"Seems logical." I was about to come clean about peeking in windows and seeing the copier and laminator that backed up my theory, but DeShay appeared on the front path and waved at us with a gloved hand, saying the house was clear.

We all went inside the well-air-conditioned condo and I felt better almost immediately. Ninety percent humidity can't be good for anyone's health.

The home's pristine appearance remained unchanged from my last visit.

"No one's here," DeShay said. "Some kinda neat freak, our friend Dugan. Hamlin, you'll be interested in the room down the hall to the left. I had to force that one open, too."

"He had a shop? Did I die and go to heaven?" Hamlin pulled gloves from his pocket, his eyes wide and bright, just like his smile.

"Hey, that's your territory, man, but tell CSU when they get here what you want carried to the crime lab 'cause I don't know anything about financial shit, not even my own."

"I will be more than clear about what I need. Can't wait to get in there." Hamlin snapped on his gloves and started toward the hall.

DeShay looked at me. "Maria found the girlfriend's last name on a credit card bill. She's on the phone in the kitchen trying to locate Georgeanne Wilson now."

"And then we'll question her?" I said.

"Maria will. I don't want to intimidate this woman. At least not yet. You get what I'm saying?"

Yet he was sending the less-than-shrinking-violet Maria Chavez to question her? Maybe she had interpersonal skills I'd somehow missed in the little time since we'd met.

Cooper said, "Can we stay and observe?"

"You both know what you're doing, so sure," DeShay said. "But I gotta say, nothing's jumping out at me aside from the ID shop. I'll do a little more hunting. See if I can get a lead on this guy's least-best friends."

"Just so you know," I said, "Georgeanne and I hit it off when I paid her that visit. I can help out with her."

"I might take you up on that later, Abster. But we have to do this my way for now."

"Abster?" I said. "I'm not an *SNL* joke, DeShay."

He smiled. "Touchy, aren't we? Anyway, I can't rule this out as the primary crime scene until CSU tells me so, but even the damn garage is cleaner than my front room. I'll be checking out the master bedroom closet if you need me. Lots of shoe boxes on the top shelves in there."

Touchy? I was *not* touchy. "I'd like to see the ID shop." I nodded in the direction Hamlin had gone.

DeShay smiled. "Cooper, my man, make sure Abby keeps her hands in her pockets—if she can get her hands in those pockets. Nice threads, Abster. Glad you're showing off what you got today."

I gave him a playful punch in the arm as Cooper and

I walked by. Maybe my capris were a tad tight, but my T-shirt was clingy only thanks to the weather.

We found Hamlin busy looking in one of two tall filing cabinets when we got to the now-unlocked room.

He said, "Check this place out. Dugan went totally high-end. Shoulda kept track of the bastard. Probably raking in cash left and right with this stuff. Excellent-quality IDs, that's for sure."

I glanced around the room, realizing DeShay had been right. I wanted to search through everything . . . open cabinets and drawers, lift the lid on the color laser printer, see what was in those filing cabinets for myself. But I stayed put just inside the door and said, "That printer probably cost, what? Twenty grand?"

"More than that," Cooper said. "We had one similar at the bureau. I heard it cost forty."

Hamlin nodded. "That's in the ballpark."

I kept exploring with my eyes. "Big old laminator, too. Nice desktop computer. So this is what you need to create the driver's license JoLynn had?"

"If the folder labeled 'holograms' and the one marked 'licenses' contain what they say they do, then yes. Dugan has every weight and color of paper and card stock in here. Probably has blank passports and Social Security cards, too." Hamlin's gloved fists rested on his hips as he glanced around the room like this was his best Christmas ever.

"But you don't know exactly what he's got in those filing cabinets?" I said.

"Have to wait on CSU to photograph everything before I start making my list for evidence collection. That hard drive is definitely going to the property room—that and who knows what else."

"We *have* to wait? Don't you have a camera?" I was beginning to sound as anxious as the third monkey on the Ark's gangplank.

Cooper rested a hand on my back. "If the guy wasn't dead, Hamlin could take his own pictures, but now we *have* to wait on CSU."

Hamlin added, "We know Dugan created and sold fake IDs, probably bribed someone to sell him the blank Social Security cards, but I want client and seller names.

Dugan may be dead, but whoever he did business with is going down and that's why I have to dot all the t's and cross my eyes." He did cross his eyes then, probably hoping I'd chill out.

I had to smile, because this made him look like he had the mental capacity of a windshield wiper. "How long until CSU gets here?" I said, once he'd grinned back at me.

"They're part of Homicide Division," Hamlin said. "Homicide needs to come first and they have the Dugan crime scene to work. But come on over here. There's something a little strange that I can show you."

My hands still in my pockets, I walked over to the filing cabinet with Cooper alongside me. I'd left my bag in the unmarked and wished I had my phone so I could snap off a few of my own pictures.

Hamlin carefully bent over the open filing-cabinet drawer and pointed a gloved finger inside. "See what's under those files?"

"Looks like newspaper," I said.

"That's right. Wondered at first if the guy was lining the bottom of the drawer for some reason," Hamlin said. "But he didn't do that in any of the other drawers."

Being careful not to rest my stomach against the side of the drawer, I tilted my head and tried for a better look. "Looks like about an inch-thick stack of newspaper. Why no file? Dugan seems to have filed everything else."

Hamlin looked at me. "You sure you're not a cop?"

"She's not, but I'd sign her up," Cooper said. "Anything else unusual?"

"Nothing obvious," Hamlin said. "We have to wait."

An agonizingly long thirty minutes later a female CSU officer arrived and began photographing everything. Hamlin then removed the files to get at the newspapers beneath. From my vantage point in the doorway, I decided they were clippings, not entire newspapers. Lots of clippings. Hamlin set them on the spic-and-span desktop and the CSU officer took more pictures after Hamlin removed the letter-size manila folder that sat on top of them.

An unfiled folder? That was strange, too.

Hamlin glanced our way after opening the folder for the officer to photograph its contents. "We can take these to the kitchen counter while she finishes up in here." He turned to her. "The hard drive goes to Tech, the newspaper and folder to Latents when I'm done, okay?"

She nodded and went back to work.

Carrying the newspapers and folder away from his body like a tray of coffee, Hamlin joined us in the hall. "Let's see what we got here." He gestured with his head toward the front of the house.

We walked to the kitchen and Hamlin placed the stack on the immaculate granite counter. I caught the *Houston Chronicle* date header beneath the folder—looked like from two years ago.

Hamlin said, "I have my digital camera in the car. Be right back." He left before I could say anything.

I said, "But they already took pictures, and I thought he said—"

"He's taking his own photos," Cooper said. "If they send these for latent prints, none of us will know the importance or lack of importance of the newspapers. With his own set of pictures he can read what he wants whenever he wants and hopefully will share that info with us. That is, if it's anything related to JoLynn. Might be nothing, Abby. Just mementos."

"This doesn't feel like *nothing*, Cooper. Dugan concealed these things—though, I'll admit, not very well. But he had a locked door and probably left Georgeanne, and maybe JoLynn before her, with strict instructions to stay out of his office. From what we've learned, both women were under his thumb."

Cooper was about to respond, but Hamlin returned with his camera, breathing hard, rivulets of sweat running from his scalp.

He fiddled with his equipment for a second and then moved the folder aside to photograph the top article.

I took in a sharp breath and must have gasped, because Cooper and Hamlin said, "What?" in unison.

"Th-that article on top," I said. "That's the same one I found online about the Richters. And there was a copy under a clock in the Richter library."

Cooper said, "Maybe this is proof Dugan knew about the family, perhaps knew where JoLynn had gone."

Hamlin was squinting at the article. "And you know this how?"

"Long story," Cooper said. "But JoLynn definitely had a fake ID that I'm betting was made right here."

Hamlin fanned out the articles, then started taking pictures. This gave me time to look over the clippings. I began to understand their connection to the first one. These all seemed to be personal-interest stories from cities and towns all over Texas and beyond. Gosh, how I wanted to scoop them up and take them home rather than hunt them down one by one on the Internet, see how they were connected to the article about Katarina—that is, if they were connected.

"Do you mind if I get the newspaper names and dates on these?" I could look up the articles online and print them—at least the ones that *were* online.

"No problem." Meanwhile Hamlin picked up the folder he'd set aside and opened it.

I was glancing around the kitchen looking for something to write on, but the magnetic whiteboard on the fridge, the one that had the words "Georgeanne—milk today!" printed on it in black marker, probably wouldn't do.

Cooper took out his little notebook. "I'll help."

"Thanks." I read off the newspaper names and dates while Cooper wrote them in his notebook.

A minute later we were interrupted by Hamlin, who now held out a stack of photographs in his palm. "These were in the folder. They mean anything to you?" He placed them on the counter one by one, touching only a corner with his gloved hand.

The first one was a grainy shot of a petite blonde placing flowers on a grave. "That's JoLynn at Glenwood Cemetery. The caretaker told me a girl fitting her description brought flowers every week to Elliott Richter's family plot."

Hamlin looked confused. "So she *is* related to the Richters?"

"Since we know her mother abandoned her at a bus

station when she was nine and Katarina was already dead by then, I doubt it," I said.

"Then why go to the cemetery?" Cooper asked. But he seemed to be asking himself this question, not us. "Unless she had someone take these pictures to show Elliott how devoted she was to Katarina, her long-lost mother . . . who was *not* really her mother."

"That doesn't make sense. How would she present these photos to Richter?" I said. "By saying, 'Oh, by the way, here's proof of what a loving family member I am.' I don't think so, Cooper. Maybe we should consider the possibility that Katarina placed JoLynn with someone and that's the person who abandoned her."

He scratched his head. "Maybe. Big maybe, in my book. No matter what, Dugan took these pictures for a reason. You see a camera in that ID shop, Hamlin?" Cooper asked.

"Yup. A nice Canon. A forger needs good resolution from an expensive digital so he can magnify whatever he wants to copy—get a nice, up-close picture of what he hopes to re-create. That's an excellent way to capture every nuance and color blend on the target document. I'll print out any pictures that he had on the memory stick and if it looks like it's related to your case, I'll e-mail them to you."

I rattled off my e-mail, telling Hamlin that Cooper was staying with me. Then I said, "These are pretty poor-quality photos. Like something I'd take with my cell phone. Since I know next to nothing about photography, can either of you explain how an expensive digital camera would give us these?" I waved my hand at the pictures.

"Maybe they *were* taken with a cell phone," Cooper said.

"More likely a telephoto lens." Hamlin was staring hard at one of the cemetery pictures.

"But why?" I said. "Unless . . ."

"Unless Dugan was stalking her, getting a handle on her routine so he could kill her," Cooper said.

"Okay . . . but then, who murdered him?"

24

We left Dugan's condo not long after, since there was really nothing more to see. I'd hoped Georgeanne would show up because I wanted to ask her a few questions—like exactly when her boyfriend, Kent, disappeared—but I had a feeling she'd be spending a long time with Maria Chavez. Having met Georgeanne, I couldn't see her killing her boyfriend, rolling him up in a piece of carpet and tossing him into the bayou, but Jeff would argue that anyone is capable of murder under the right circumstances. Yes, I could be wrong. I often am.

As promised, Cooper took me back to the garage to pick up my car, and I paid both his fees and mine, which turned out to be enough money to feed a third world nation. They *are* proud of their parking garages in the Medical Center.

We went back to my house, and while Cooper called Pineview PD to find out—as he put it—"how many people pissed in the street or let their dog run wild" in his absence, I took Cooper's notebook and got busy on my computer. I printed out all the newspaper articles I could find. Most of them were from Texas, a few from Oklahoma and Arkansas. I gathered the pages and took them out to the kitchen, where Cooper was *still* on the phone. Maybe in his absence Pineview had been reduced to three truckloads of bean pickers without a foreman.

But when I saw his expression after he hung up, I regretted making light of his job, even in my head.

"The Montgomery County crime lab pulled Dugan's prints off JoLynn's wrecked car—where the air bags had been removed. He was in AFIS—that's the Automated Fingerprint Identification System."

"Duh. I know what AFIS is. He's the one who tried to kill her, then?" I said.

"Ordinarily that wouldn't be enough evidence. The air bags could have been removed at any time, even when they lived together. Did you know there's a black market for air bags? But get this. They found his prints on the brake line," he said. "That's far better evidence that he tried to get rid of her."

"Which leads us back to my earlier question at the condo. Who killed him?"

But my brain was spinning with possibilities this time, and one of the scenarios made me a little sick. Could Elliott Richter have learned about JoLynn and Dugan's relationship before I ever told him? Learned about them before he even plopped down that ten grand and hired me?

"Talk to me, Abby," Cooper said.

I sat in one of the kitchen chairs, placed the printouts on the table in front of me.

He took the spot to my right. "Come on. What are you thinking?"

"That Elliott Richter hasn't been straight with us. Maybe true to character, he *did* investigate JoLynn when she came knocking on his door a year ago."

"You're saying Richter knew about Dugan?" he said.

"Maybe. But that makes me wonder why he'd hire me—unless he needed more answers other than her relationship with Dugan."

Cooper cocked his head, smiled a little. This case sure had changed him from the glum man I'd met little more than a week ago. He said, "And how does all that address the question of who killed Dugan? Because the prints say he's the one who fiddled with that car."

"What if Richter found Dugan and questioned him about JoLynn?" I said.

"Are you thinking he told Richter things about Jo-Lynn, filled in her past with not-so-nice information, gave Richter information he failed to give us the other night at the hospital?"

"I don't want to think that, but what if Dugan con-

vinced Richter that JoLynn had betrayed both of them?"
I said. "Told him she wasn't his long-lost granddaughter,
that she heard about Katarina by reading the *Houston
Chronicle*?"

"You could be right, because I also learned they
found JoLynn's prints on that paper you found under
the clock. But if she was a scammer, why didn't Richter
simply kick JoLynn to the curb? And like you said, why
in hell would he hire you and ask me to do everything I
could to help find whoever did this to her?" Cooper said.

I considered this and came up with nothing. "I don't
know, Cooper. You got any ideas?"

"I prefer simple explanations until I see evidence to
the contrary. For now, we assume Richter told you the
truth—that he wanted you to find out about JoLynn's
past and help me figure out why someone might want
her dead. We have absolutely no evidence he knew anything about Kent Dugan."

I relaxed some then, let out the breath I'd been holding in. "Keeping it simple like you said, maybe Dugan
tried to kill JoLynn because first of all"—I held up one
finger—"she had the nerve to leave him." I added my
middle finger. "And second of all, she'd settled into a
very nice lifestyle by pretending to be someone she
wasn't—pretending by using the tools Dugan had given
her to accomplish that feat. I'm thinking that would en-
rage someone as controlling as Dugan."

Cooper nodded. "My first thought when I saw JoLynn
being life-flighted away from that wreck was that someone wanted her to suffer, to be terrified before she died.
Fits Dugan, wouldn't you say?"

"Absolutely. I want to believe Elliott Richter, Cooper.
I need to believe someone cares about that girl."

"You care," he said softly.

Before I could reply "And so do you," I heard my
cell phone ring. I hurried to the counter where I'd
dropped my bag earlier and had to dig deep to find
the thing.

It was Kate. "Mind if I join you guys for movie night?
My last client is at four today and—"

"Do I mind? I wish you could be here this minute.
We have lots to talk about." I told her about Kent Du-

gan's death but decided to save the rest for when she got here. She said to expect her around six, after she went home and picked up Webster. The poor dog needed a night out, too.

"My sister," I said to Cooper after I folded the phone shut and sat back down next to him. "She's joining us tonight."

He'd been reading the printouts and still held one in his hand. "Glad I'll finally get to meet her. About these articles. This one details a story similar to Katarina Richter's. And so does the other one I've read so far."

"I skimmed a few back at the condo and got the same feeling. How similar?" I asked.

"Very. Well-off people with missing relatives. Disappearances long enough ago that someone Kent or JoLynn's age could walk into their lives and say they're the grown child of that missing relative. And they would arrive with documents—fakes of course—to prove it. A lot of homework involved, though. I sure hope that hard drive HPD hauled off will tell us something more."

"You're describing what JoLynn did," I said half to myself. I looked at Cooper. "We're back to that."

"Yup, we are. Let's read through everything before we act on our assumption that JoLynn was a con artist. She's sure not fleeing to Mexico in the near future, so we have time to figure this out."

"There's something about her, Cooper. I mean, I haven't had a real conversation with her, but from what I saw on her face in the hospital, from what Roberta said, from what the relatives told Kate and me, this girl was vulnerable and sweet and—"

"Abby, we need to shelve the emotions and search for the facts. Do you have a highlighter handy? There's plenty of names in these stories, people we can check on to see if they ever met Jolynn or Dugan and lost money to either of them. I want to make the names stand out and then make a list."

I got up and scrounged in the built-in kitchen-desk drawer until I found a couple of highlighters—both bright pink.

Cooper held his up for inspection. "My favorite color."

"I promise never to mention you touched something *pink*."

He grinned as we divided the printout pile.

I soon lost track of time reading the stories, many of them, like Cooper had said, strikingly similar to what happened to Katarina Richter. Every family with some-one missing. *The missing.* I'd never considered them be-fore this case, never thought what it meant to lose touch so completely with someone you loved, to be left without answers. True, my biological parents had been missing from my life and I'd learned my mother was dead. But I had never known her. These accounts of personal loss were far different from my own.

Since Cooper hadn't said a word, either, just moved his marker across name after name, we were both a little startled when Jeff came in through the back door.

Cooper stood and they shook hands.

"Good to see you again," Jeff said. He went to the counter, grabbed a paper towel, spit out his gum and tossed it in the trash. "It's Miller time. Join me?"

"Sounds good."

Jeff looked at me. "Chardonnay or beer?"

"Wine mellows me far better than beer and after the stuff I've been reading, I could use mellowing."

The beer was Corona, not Miller, and the wine came from World Market—a discounted bottle from Napa Valley. We all sat at the kitchen table, and Cooper and I told Jeff everything we'd learned today.

When we were finished, Jeff looked at Cooper. "You think Dugan's killer jumped Abby last night?"

I hadn't even considered that possibility and a chill raced up my arms.

"I've given it some thought," Cooper said, "but I didn't want to bring it up yet. Abby's looked a little green around the gills several times today." Cooper eyed me with concern. "Sort of like you look now."

"I am perfectly *fine*." I slugged down what remained in my wineglass like a cowboy who'd bellied up to the bar and ordered a shot of tequila. Hell, maybe I could use a shot of tequila. The thought of Aunt Caroline and me being followed around in a grocery store by a murderer . . . *damn.* "Aunt Caroline was with me in that grocery store when I saw the guy. Maybe he followed me to her house when I drove her home. Maybe he—"

Jeff placed his hand over mine. "He wasn't interested in your aunt, hon. He wanted to scare *you*. I've already made arrangements for you to give his description to our sketch artist tomorrow. Turns out those surveillance cameras in the garage weren't operative."

"They're broken?" I said.

Cooper snickered. "Seventy percent of the time, surveillance cameras are a joke. Either they're shut off, out of tape or produce such poor-quality pictures that they're useless."

"Did I *really* want to know that?" I closed my eyes, but decided I was done being afraid. Past experience— like being followed, being held hostage, little things like that—had planted seeds of fear, but I was pulling those weeds out of my brain this minute. Amazing what the mind can do, because I grinned, feeling the anxiety recede almost at once. "A sketch artist. Good. I can't wait to see my garage man again, if only on paper."

"What I still don't get," Cooper said, "is why your assailant clearly protected you from further harm after he warned you off the case."

"That's got me buffaloed, too," Jeff said.

"Okay, let's backtrack so I can get this straight," I said. "You two believe that the parking garage guy knew about Dugan, too? I mean, we know Dugan and JoLynn were connected. But maybe this guy didn't. Maybe his warning was all about *her*."

Jeff nodded. "I agree. That's why I've asked DeShay to mention chloroform to the ME. If garage guy used chloroform on both you and Dugan, that answers your question. The evidence would still be circumstantial— bad guy warns you off your investigation into JoLynn's past and uses chloroform. Then chloroform is used on Kent Dugan to subdue him before he gets tossed in the bayou. But how many turds are using chloroform these days?"

"Okay. Now I understand," I said.

"Being Friday, bodies have been piling up at the ME's office, so DeShay has to wait for Dugan's turn. But his first question to whoever performs the autopsy will be about chloroform."

I shook my head, feeling a little overwhelmed by all this information. "There are still so many unanswered questions."

"You're good at pulling things together, hon. Between you, Cooper and DeShay, you've got a dream team."

Jeff was definitely getting lucky tonight, and obviously understood my smile because he winked at me.

Then I heard Kate at the back door—I knew it was her because Webster was barking his excited head off. When they came in, she released him from his leash. First he sniffed Cooper, then slobbered a few kisses on Jeff and me. Greetings accomplished, he bounded off to find his best friend, Diva. A little hide-and-seek was in order.

"Kate," I said, "this is Chief Cooper Boyd, the police officer I've been working with from Pineview PD."

Their mutual smiles as he took her hand warmed my heart a little. At least she wasn't looking all sad and wary. Maybe she was coming out of her funk.

He said, "Please, no *Officer* or *Chief* anything. It's Cooper."

"Abby says you're former FBI," she said. "I have this secret wish to be a profiler, but I'm not sure I could take dealing with so much evil day in and day out."

Jeff and I exchanged confused glances and I wanted to say, "She wants to be a profiler? When did that happen?" But then I thought about the guy who'd sent her into her tailspin, how she'd never seen through him, despite all her training and experience as a psychologist. Maybe she'd decided profiling skills might save her from falling for idiots in the future.

Kate went to the fridge and took out the bottle of chardonnay. "I need to catch up with the three of you. I see Cooper needs a refill." She nodded at his empty beer bottle.

Not long after, Loreen dropped Doris off and we ordered our pizzas. Jeff nixed the double pepperoni Doris begged for and we went veggie all the way to support his effort to keep her diet as healthy as possible. Kate and Cooper, of course, loved this idea.

The movie Doris chose was *Happy Feet*, but I was glad to see that Cooper and Kate weren't the least bit interested in the DVD. They remained in quiet conversation through both run-throughs, Webster and Diva cuddled together nearby.

What a nice ending to an awful week, I thought, as Doris asked Jeff and me for a third replay.

25

I met with the police sketch artist Saturday morning, and we worked together re-creating the man I'd seen in the supermarket and again in the parking garage. The eyes were his most striking feature and she did such an accurate drawing I actually got goose bumps when I studied her final product. She said Jeff would be picking up the sketch later today, and my guess was she'd done this as a favor, since I doubted she worked on Saturdays. Jeff had many friends in the department who'd do anything for him. But then, so would I.

I walked to my car and slid behind the wheel, leaving the windows open as I turned the ignition and blasted the air-conditioning. Once most of the heat had left my car, I rolled up the windows and started home. I'd left Cooper in my office around ten a.m. and I assumed he was still searching for information on the names culled from the newspaper clippings.

Jeff promised Doris they'd see the latest Disney feature at the "big TV," as she always called the movie theater. He was taking her to a first showing followed by a trip to shop for new jigsaw puzzles, so those two probably weren't at the house.

Kate would be waiting for my call once I returned home so we could all head to the hospital and visit Jo-Lynn. We wondered if she and Kent Dugan might have spoken right before her wreck—perhaps a call where he asked her to get money from Richter and hand it over to him. Since she apparently didn't have a cell phone and Dugan's was damaged, we couldn't check on any recent contact between those two except by asking.

Then, thinking about the job Richter wanted me to do—keep hunting for clues to JoLynn's past—I pulled my phone from my bag and called Penny.

"Hi, Abby," she said when she answered. "Have you solved your Elizabeth case yet?"

"No, and I hate to bother you on the weekend, but I could use a teeny bit more help. I know you can't give me the names of any of the girl's foster parents, but I remember that a police officer picked her up at that bus station. I could talk to him, right?"

"Talk to *her*. Officer Shauna Anthony. She worked with us on plenty of child abuse cases—but she retired because of health issues . . . maybe two years ago, if I remember right."

"Do you know how I can get in touch with her?"

"Sorry, no, but I think there's a retired officers' group. They might be able to help."

"Thanks so much, Penny." I disconnected, then punched my speed dial number for DeShay.

He answered on the first ring. "My Abby girl is calling. If you want Dugan's cause of death, I can't help you. The autopsy should be completed later today."

"It's not that. I need to find a retired HPD officer and since Jeff is with Doris at a movie, he can't help me right now." I explained who the officer was and why I wanted to talk to her.

"I'll see what I can do."

"Thanks, DeShay," I said.

"They'll be calling me for the autopsy soon, so I might be late getting back to you."

"I understand," I said. By the time I disconnected, I was nearly home.

Cooper was indeed still in my office when I came in, a cup of steaming green tea on the desk. Boiling-hot tea in August? Was he immune to a heat index of about two hundred?

He leaned back in the leather chair, fingers laced behind his neck. "It is so nice to have friends in high places. If I'd been forced to rely on Pineview PD's resources rather than the FBI to track down all these folks in those newspaper clippings, we'd be waiting for weeks."

"What did you find out?"

"I have phone numbers and addresses, should we need them. But I won't go that route first. I'm hoping JoLynn is alert enough to answer questions. Kate called, by the way. She said she'd drive us to the hospital so we can use her parking spot."

"That's the best news I've had all day. She say anything else?"

"No, why?" He was hedging, looked embarrassed, actually.

"Come on. What did you two talk about?"

"I mentioned how you'd noticed a copy of *An American Tragedy* under our faker Joe Johnson's chair. I asked her what her take on that was."

Huh? I thought. He and I and anyone with half a brain would know what a book like that told us about Joe Johnson. He wasn't your average stupid criminal. "What else did you talk about?" I gave him a knowing grin.

"Okay, smart-ass. We got to talking about the book. Then we went on to other things we like to read. She's a Sinclair Lewis fan like I am."

"Really?"

"Yeah, really. You happy now? I like your sister. She's brilliant and gorgeous and I want to get to know her better, okay?"

I smiled. "Take it slow, okay? She had a bad experience not long ago. When she's ready, maybe she'll tell you about it."

"Hope I get the chance. Want to give your sister that call so we can get to the hospital? Maybe we can ask JoLynn about using that fake ID."

I wanted to say, "Why don't you call Kate? I have to brush my teeth or try to make my hair look like it only needs conditioner and not a therapist." I mean, Sinclair Lewis and green tea? Could there possibly be two other people on the planet with that peculiar bond? I thought not.

But I did make the call and Kate pulled into my driveway in less than fifteen minutes. Obviously she'd been ready and waiting. Good sign.

I took the backseat and Cooper sat up front with Kate. She'd traded in her 4Runner for a Scion and they started talking about the importance of hybrid cars almost immediately. I just enjoyed the ride. When Kate dropped me off at Ben Taub so I wouldn't have to walk in the heat, Cooper insisted he'd accompany Kate from her parking spot. I didn't argue.

Elliott Richter and nephew Scott were standing in the tiny, stark lobby when I walked in. Guess the relatives were on a rotating hospital assignment to accompany Richter here.

After we exchanged hellos, I said, "Why are you down here?" I nodded at the windows. "Unless you wanted a look at a log cabin smack-dab in the center of a hospital complex."

Richter glanced through the floor-to-ceiling window at the very old log cabin just across the Ben Taub Loop as if he'd just noticed it for the first time.

Scott, preppy as usual in a red polo and bone-colored khakis, said, "What the heck is that building for, anyway?"

"I think it's one of those strong statements Texas landowners are famous for. *This house is mine and I ain't movin' no matter what you want to build here.* The cabin dates way back, probably has as rich a history as Glenwood Cemetery. I've been there to your family plot, by the way."

Richter looked at me sharply. "Why?"

"I did a little research before I met you. Did you know JoLynn went up there every week to visit Katarina's grave?" I glanced back and forth between Richter and Scott.

Richter's eyes showed his surprise. And Scott decided the floor was suddenly fascinating.

I said, "Scott, I'm getting the feeling you knew."

He looked up, and when he spoke, he addressed his uncle, not me. "I went with her a couple times. She was—how can I say this? She was . . . *obsessed* with Katarina. I couldn't answer her questions, Uncle Elliott. I remember when Katarina came back, how sick she was, but that's all. I told JoLynn to talk to *you* about her mother."

"What kind of questions did JoLynn ask, Scott?" I said before Richter could respond.

"She wanted to know what Katarina liked to read, the

places she liked to go, what she liked to do. That's natural . . . normal, I guess. When I had no answers, she'd sit there and cry and I—I'm not so hot with crying women. I couldn't help her."

Richter stared out at the log cabin. "She and I never talked much about Katarina. I only told JoLynn that she was very much like her mother. I wish now I would have told her that I recognized that same kindness, that JoLynn's eyes always showed how much she cared, how she seemed to want to absorb every word I said. But it was uncomfortable after all these years to have someone care that much." He looked at me. "I don't have an ounce of insight, Abby, and yet JoLynn wanted to know what made me tick."

An awkward silence followed, one I couldn't stand for more than a few seconds. I said, "Back to my original question. Why are you down here in the lobby? It's not very people-friendly."

"JoLynn is being moved out of the ICU," Richter said. "The new security guard is keeping watch during the transfer. We almost went to the cafeteria, but since it's in the basement, I was afraid I wouldn't get the call once JoLynn has been settled in her new room."

"She must be better," I said. "That's great news."

Scott grinned. "She is. She recognized me, held my hand."

"Great." I looked at Richter. "You didn't bring up the accident or tell her about Dugan's death, I hope."

"Chief Boyd has made himself very clear," Richter said. "That's not my place. Besides, she's frightened and in quite a bit of pain now that the sedation has been decreased. My focus is on her comfort. I want her moved to Methodist as soon as possible."

I couldn't wrap my brain around the fact that he knew she had fake ID, that she could be a fraud, and this still didn't matter. Maybe Kate could get inside his head.

"Cooper and my sister are on the way from the parking garage," I said.

"Ah, Kate. Very pleasant young woman," Richter said. "She'll be good for JoLynn. The trauma she's suffered is beginning to sink in."

I looked at Scott. "How are you doing with all this?"

"I'm relieved JoLynn is recovering, that she could move out of ICU. But she was pretty upset when she found out they drilled a hole in her skull to drain a blood clot."

"They did?" I glanced back and forth between him and Richter.

Scott said, "Yeah. You can't see where they shaved her hair, because the bandage covering the hole is back here." He pointed to a spot behind and above his ear.

"I thought you knew," Richter said. "Her clot was small, not life threatening, thank goodness."

But I was imagining the tools necessary to do this procedure. I thought about my shop class in high school—the one I took because of the pleasant boy-to-girl ratio—and remembered drill bits of all sizes. No wonder she was scared and in pain. She'd lived through the equivalent of a horror movie.

"How long will the move take?" I said.

Richter checked his watch. "I don't know why it's even taken this long. This hospital may be excellent for trauma, but my God, the rest of the place is . . . never mind. They saved her life and I can't complain."

Kate and Cooper arrived then and I explained why we were waiting around in the cramped lobby.

Then Cooper surprised me, probably surprised everyone, by saying, "Mr. Richter, I'd like to chat with you in private—maybe in the cafeteria?"

Richter stiffened, glanced at the cell phone he was gripping like a lifeline. "And why is that?"

"I'll explain downstairs. A few questions, that's all."

"The rest of us can wait here," Kate the Accommodator said quickly.

"Sorry." Cooper's eyes offered her a bigger apology than I thought necessary. "This shouldn't take long."

"Wait." Richter seemed about as happy as an ex-smoker who'd forgotten his Nicorette. "I want Abby to accompany us. She works for me, Boyd. She's aware of everything that's gone on."

Cooper hesitated, then said, "Sure. Kate, you okay hanging out with Scott?"

"I'd like to get to know him better," she answered

with a smile. "We didn't get much of a chance to talk at the ranch the other night."

So Cooper, Richter and I went downstairs, got coffee and sat at a table as far from the food stations as possible. The lunch crowd had dissipated and the place was nearly deserted.

"I have some serious questions, Mr. Richter," Cooper said. "Consider this talk an informal interview. If I learn I need to take this discussion further, we'll talk again at the Pineview police station, where I will get your answers on tape."

"On tape? Do you suspect me of something?" Richter said.

"Like I said, this is informal. No tape, no notes, no lawyer required," Cooper said. "We simply need to get to the truth."

Uh-oh. Cooper was ready to ask about things we'd speculated on in the last few days. I knew this because I was sitting across from Cooper and the hardness I'd seen in his stare when he'd brought out the worst in Dugan the other night was back with a vengeance.

"You think *I* don't want the truth as well? Get on with your questions," Richter said.

"Are you aware that Elizabeth 'JoLynn' Dugan is most likely *not* your granddaughter?" Cooper said.

Gosh, don't beat around the bush or anything, I thought.

Richter's expression went from irritated to *jumbo-size irritated* in an instant. "What are you talking about?"

"Aside from the fake ID, the missing birth certificate and credible evidence she was scamming you, I suppose I *don't* know what I'm talking about."

"What are you implying, Chief Boyd?" Richter said. Man, his stinger was out now. This was not a guy used to being challenged.

"From what I've learned about you," Cooper said, "I'm guessing you knew all about her misrepresentation not long after she arrived at your place a year ago."

I was certain Cooper was being tactical, using speculation, not facts, but his delivery seemed especially harsh.

Richter picked up the plastic stir stick he'd used for

his coffee, not looking at either of us. Finally, he raised his head and stared at the man who now seemed like an accuser. "What are you after, Boyd?"

Cooper said, "There've been some ugly developments in this case."

How I wished Cooper had asked Kate to come with us. No sending out a distress signal now, though. "Maybe we should tell you the most dramatic development first," I said. "Unless you already know."

"Dramatic? Would you two just get to it?" Richter said.

Cooper was sitting back, arms crossed, and he glanced over at me with raised eyebrows. "Go ahead. Tell him."

"Kent Dugan was murdered yesterday," I said.

Richter's skin immediately washed out to pasty gray. "I—I didn't know."

Anyone can lie with words, but the skin *never* lies. He looked like he could use a bed in the cardiac-care unit about now. Why was he so upset? I had no idea.

"We don't know how he was killed yet, but they pulled his body from Brays Bayou. You know anything about that, Mr. Richter?" Cooper asked.

Oh boy. This little *interview* was making me so tense my nerves might poke through my skin.

"You think I had something to do with his death?" Richter shot back. "I didn't even know the man existed until a few days ago."

Wanting to calm Richter down before I had to recall the ever-changing CPR steps, I said, "But that's one of the reasons you hired me, right? To find out who tried to kill JoLynn? That person was probably Dugan." I hoped my voice conveyed the genuine care I felt for this very odd man. Maybe Cooper thought I was playing good cop to his bad, but I was being sincere.

"*Dugan* tried to kill her?" Richter had quickly regained his stride, not to mention his color, and his interest in this trumped his anger.

"Evidence is strong in that direction," Cooper said. "But I still need you to clear up a few things. If I start gathering phone records and talking to potential witnesses in Pineview, will I find out you knew about Kent Dugan long before JoLynn's accident?"

Richter said, "Let me jump from A to D. You believe

I found out about Dugan and asked him to get rid of
JoLynn because she was lying to me about who she
was?"

Impressive leap, I thought. Was he smart or was this
the truth?

"That's one theory, but then I have to ask, why hire
Abby?" Cooper said. "Who'd want someone snooping
around when they might just uncover that you conspired
with Dugan to kill JoLynn. Unless hiring a PI was all
for show and you figured she couldn't investigate her
way out of a paper bag."

I didn't have time to be offended by the paper-bag
remark because Richter quickly said, "I do my homework, Chief. I'm very aware how good Abby is at her
job and that's why I asked for her help. I knew absolutely nothing about Kent Dugan until the other night
and if I'd wanted to get rid of JoLynn, I would have
sent her packing, not have her killed."

"But you wanted me to make sure JoLynn is who she
says she is, right?" I said. "You were worried about the
fake license and fraudulent inspection stickers."

"No," he said. "You don't—"

But I kept going. "If you wanted the truth about Jo-
Lynn, why didn't you hunt for that truth when she first
arrived at Magnolia Ranch? Why *didn't* you know about
Kent Dugan?"

"I just didn't." Richter's mouth tightened into a stubborn line.

Cooper said, "You want us to believe that a successful
businessman, known to check facts scrupulously, didn't
look into this young woman's story? Because I plan on
finding out, if that is the case."

Richter studied the swizzle stick again for what
seemed a long time. "You'd be wasting your time. I'm
certain you won't understand—I'm not certain even *I*
understand—but before the attempt on JoLynn's life, I
didn't want to know *anything* about her past."

"You never suspected she was a fraud?" I said.

Despite my attempt to say this in a gentle way, he
turned to me and his steely eyes bored into mine. "She
is not a *fraud.*"

Delusion alert. Oh my gosh, Kate. I need you. But I

kept my tone even when I said, "Okay, here's what I've learned. She was never adopted, Mr. Richter. She was abandoned in a bus station when she was nine and aged out of foster care. Did you know any of this before I found out?"

"Abandoned?" He closed his eyes briefly, seemed to be gathering himself. "Who could be that cruel to her?"

"I don't know yet," I said, "but it's possible JoLynn—who has also used the name Elizabeth—and her boyfriend Dugan planned to set you up by playing on your weakness: Katarina."

Cooper said, "But JoLynn may have betrayed Dugan by coming to you without Dugan's knowledge and—"

Richter held up his hand like a traffic cop. "Wait. I need to clarify something. JoLynn wasn't a *fraud* in the way you two are thinking, no matter what her background. She asked for nothing from me. Not a red cent. I doubt she conspired with Dugan. Aside from Katarina, she is the most genuine person I've ever met."

Cooper looked surprised. "Doesn't her behavior sound less than *genuine*, sir?"

Richter sighed heavily. "This is very difficult for me, but let me tell you how this all came about . . . hopefully explain my behavior without sounding like a fool. Katarina's cancer? Ovarian. She fled the ranch when she found out, went away without telling me where she was going or why. She was running from me, knowing I'd be calling every doctor in the country and be breathing down her neck trying to save her. She was so young, so strong-willed, she thought she could run, not only from me, but from the cancer, too."

I closed my eyes, taking this in. "Ovarian cancer? Then when did she have a baby—wait, are you saying Katarina couldn't have children?"

"Exactly. She came home to die once she knew it would be useless for me to interfere with her decisions. She'd been through treatment on her own, treatment that didn't work. She wanted to deal with her cancer without me taking charge of her life."

"B-but why?" I asked.

"Because of who I was. We'd been at odds since she was small. I started trying to control her the minute I lost my wife and thus alienated her. I can only thank God she came back to me so I could offer her comfort in the end. *Offer comfort*—not impose my will." His eyes filled and he took a deep breath. "She never had a child. She couldn't."

Cooper's attitude, his tough-guy interrogator persona softened a little. "I'm sorry for your loss. Very sorry. But this still doesn't explain—at least to this dumbass—why you brought JoLynn into your home and treated her as if she was your granddaughter."

Richter looked so fatigued, as if revealing all this had left him completely empty. "You ask why I took JoLynn in? Because I could tell she'd been running. For a long time. It's in the eyes, you know. Katarina had the same look when she came home—frightened, knowing she needed someone to be there for her—even her bastard of a father. She didn't want to be alone anymore."

"Okay . . . I understand what you're saying," I said slowly. "You couldn't have cared less about JoLynn's background. You needed her as much as she needed you."

"Ah, Abby, I see you took notes when you met my family. I'll bet you found them to be a very cold bunch. Funny thing, since this attempt on JoLynn's life? I'm seeing my family in a different light. Despite their contempt for JoLynn, despite their jealousy when I invited her into my home, they've all gone 'bloody soft,' as Ian would say." Richter smiled sadly.

Cooper looked plain bewildered. This was all too touchy-feely for him. Jeff would have reacted the same way.

Richter recognized this because he said, "Maybe I'm not getting through, Chief Boyd. You mentioned I run a successful company. Well, I've learned that unfinished business always catches up with you. And the loss of Katarina caught up with me the day JoLynn appeared on my doorstep. Only someone very desperate would do what JoLynn was trying to do."

"You should have told us all this. Told us both. Why didn't you?" I said.

"I was in denial, that's why. I hoped by some miracle you'd discover JoLynn *was* my granddaughter. That Ka-

tarina's cancer came after she gave birth." He paused.
"But I was lying to myself. There was no child. But
when I nearly lost JoLynn, I realized I don't give a god-
damn whether or not we're blood relatives. Right now,
all I care about is finding out if she's still in danger. I
couldn't protect my daughter, but I can protect this girl.
Whoever killed Kent Dugan could be after JoLynn,
too."

Now I understood why he'd gone white when he
learned of Dugan's murder. A killer was still out there
with JoLynn in his or her sights. I said, "You believe
the way to protect JoLynn is to uncover her past rela-
tionships, the ones that might have led to the attempt
on her life?"

"Yes," Richter said. "And please listen carefully, both
of you. I hope to learn that truth without my family
finding out she is not my granddaughter. They need to
believe she's the real thing."

"Because . . . ?" Cooper prompted.

"Money, of course. To make her seem like the real
deal, so they wouldn't contest my will. I researched the
adoption registry—hoping they would accept her when
I spouted off a few facts. You see, some of them might
skewer her—figuratively, I mean—if they thought she'd
cost them even a fraction of their inheritance."

"Like your son?" I said.

He didn't answer. Maybe that was too much to admit
to. He said, "Since I have changed my will to include
JoLynn, I don't want anyone making trouble for her
when I'm gone. That's why I destroyed the birth certificate she gave me right before I hired you, Abby. Having
dispensed with denial, I knew it was a forgery and I
didn't want anyone throwing it at a judge."

"This is probably an impossible secret to keep," Cooper said. "And not my biggest concern right now. Someone killed Kent Dugan. I can't believe that his murder
attempt on JoLynn followed by his own violent death is
a coincidence."

"Understood," Richter said. "That bothers me. Bothers me very much."

Cooper nodded. "I won't give out any more information than I think is necessary and I know HPD operates the same way."

Richter looked at me. "I still want to know JoLynn's story, want to know what she's running from. That's why I hired you and that's why I want you to continue on."

I started to remind him that he was repeating the same controlling behavior that had sent his daughter away, but Cooper interrupted me. "One more thing. Dugan *never* contacted you and never promised to keep your family from knowing JoLynn wasn't related to you? For a price, of course?"

"No. If he had come to me, I would have paid him whatever he asked. Every aspect of my life is open to you for your private examination if that's what you need to uncover the truth. But I *didn't* kill him because he tried to blackmail me and I would have never conspired with him or anyone to harm JoLynn."

Cooper's features relaxed and he almost smiled. The tension that had been strung like a tightrope between the two of them suddenly slackened.

"I believe you, Mr. Richter," Cooper said. "But I *will* examine your life if necessary. Right now I need to find out about that stranger who parked himself outside the ICU, not to mention the man who warned Abby off the case and then drugged her."

"Could Dugan have hired those two men?" I asked.

Cooper considered this for a second or two. "I don't know. Since his attempt on JoLynn failed, Dugan might have been concerned we'd find evidence to nail him for the wreck, or he was worried any future blackmail plans involving Mr. Richter would be ruined if certain facts about JoLynn came to light."

"But he would have to get rid you, too, because you know everything I know," I said. "And then he'd face the wrath of your officers, maybe the FBI, and of course Jeff's large network of friends—also known as HPD. Dugan couldn't have been that stupid."

"Your garage assailant was very careful not to seriously harm you. Maybe you've figured out why," Cooper said.

"You think?" I said.

Cooper didn't answer.

But Richter's concern was evident. He said, "With Jo-Lynn out of ICU and with at least two men connected to these . . . these *crimes*, JoLynn's still in danger. And you are, too, Abby. I'm the one who put you in that position and—"

"Don't even think about firing me, Mr. Richter. I can take care of myself. That man caught me off guard once, but I guarantee you, he won't get the jump on me again."

<u>26</u>

"I won't fire you, Abby. But please be careful," Richter said. Then he got the call he'd been waiting for. Guess his cell worked down here after all. Scott gave him Jo-Lynn's new room number and we were off.

On the elevator ride, I thought about the cop Penny had told me about and wondered if Shauna Anthony could give me any leads that might provide Elliott Richter with the information he still wanted about JoLynn. Then my brain skipped to the evidence at the condo. We assumed those newspaper clippings belonged to Dugan, but what if they'd belonged to JoLynn?

"The newspaper clippings," I said as we got off the elevator.

"What about them?" Cooper said.

Richter wasn't listening. He was off like a cat with its tail on fire, heading for JoLynn's room.

As we trailed behind, I said, "Maybe those articles belonged to JoLynn and not Dugan."

We stopped to allow an orderly pushing a gurney to pass and ended up with our backs against a wall.

"I see where you're going with this," Cooper said. "*JoLynn* created JoLynn Richter—not Dugan. After all, she had learned at the foot of the master—and I hate saying Dugan was masterful about anything, but Jo-Lynn's driver's license was the best fake I've ever seen."

"She could have split after using Dugan's ID shop to make herself over," I said. "Which would have pissed off Dugan in a major way. The ultimate betrayal—conning the con man. Maybe it took him an entire year to research all the people in those articles, figure out exactly who she'd chosen as her new family. But we do know he found her. I mean, his prints were all over that wreck."

We started down the hall again.

"And that explains the attempt on JoLynn's life, but again, it doesn't explain why someone wanted Dugan dead. We're missing something, Abby."

"Right," I said. "And maybe we missed whatever that something is during the condo search. What about the pictures of JoLynn taken at the cemetery? I don't understand why he took them, aside from him being a twisted, angry stalker."

Cooper and I halted outside JoLynn's room and looked at each other and he whispered what I was thinking. "Maybe Dugan didn't take those pictures."

I would have loved to think this through more, but Cooper opened the door.

The security guard, a large black man, stood and blocked our path the minute we tried to enter.

I liked him already.

"They're okay, Henry," we heard Richter say—only heard because we couldn't see around the mass of humanity that was Henry.

The guard stepped aside and we squeezed into a room where the bed alone would have made the room crowded. Add six people and a patient with equipment, and I was thinking we all might have to grease our hips to turn around.

Scott said, "Henry and I will wait in the hall."

Once they were gone, I could actually see JoLynn and my sister. Kate was on the window side of the bed, helping JoLynn drink water through a straw.

Richter stepped back into the far corner and gestured for us to come closer. "JoLynn's doing much better today."

Cooper went to the bedside and looked down on her. He gently said, "Do you remember me?"

Her eyes moved in his direction and Kate carefully took the straw from between JoLynn's dry lips.

"Police?" JoLynn said.

"That's right." Cooper glanced at me. I'd taken the

only available floor space, near the foot of the bed. "And her?" Cooper said.

JoLynn said, "Abby, right?" Then she glanced at Kate. "Your sister?"

Kate smiled and nodded. "These are the people helping you. They have questions."

JoLynn closed her eyes. "I remember what you said, Chief Boyd."

"What's that?" Cooper asked.

"You said someone tampered with my car." Then tears escaped from the corners of both eyes. "I lied. I deserved to die."

Richter stood taller and took a step forward, ready to jump in and rescue the girl he'd taken in as his own. But Kate set down the water glass and held up her hand to stop him. Softly she said, "We all tell lies sometimes. Especially when we're afraid."

When JoLynn opened her eyes, she found Richter. "I am so sorry."

Cooper took over this time. "He knows, Elizabeth. We all know. And it doesn't matter."

JoLynn was still focused on the man she'd called Grandfather. "Elizabeth should have died."

The small space between Kate's eyes furrowed with concern. "But that's you. JoLynn is Elizabeth. And you don't deserve to die."

JoLynn's glance flicked briefly toward Kate, then returned to Richter. "Can you forgive me?"

Richter seemed all *verklempt* again, as he had been downstairs. I wasn't sure he could respond, but he managed to say, "There is nothing to forgive. But please talk to Chief Boyd and Abby. They have questions. I'll leave you with them."

Then he walked to JoLynn's side and Kate scooted her chair away so he could get close to his once and perhaps future granddaughter.

Richter bent, kissed JoLynn's forehead and said, "I love you, Elizabeth . . . or JoLynn. Whatever name you like best. I'll be back when they're done talking to you."

I had to lean forward so Richter could get by me, and

then he was gone. Mr. Man of Stone had cracked. He needed time to repair.

"Which name do you like?" Kate asked.

"JoLynn. I've always liked JoLynn." She repositioned her shoulders and pain brightened her eyes.

"Are you okay?" Kate said.

JoLynn nodded, lips tight.

"Before the chief and Abby talk to you, I need to ask one important question. Did you try to take your own life? Are you the one who tampered with your car?"

I could understand why Kate might have concluded this, seeing as how these last few minutes had revealed JoLynn's rather guilty conscience.

"I'm not that brave," JoLynn said. "I don't know who was that angry with me. Maybe one of them."

"Them?" I said.

"The family. No one but Scott and Grandfather liked me. The family probably knew I was lying. That's why they hated me."

"The truth is, we have credible evidence that Kent Dugan tampered with your car," Cooper said.

Kate shot him a look—one I knew. It's the "Why can't you be more sensitive?" look. She probably didn't think JoLynn could deal with this information on the heels of the suicide query.

Indeed, JoLynn seemed too stunned to speak, but Cooper had obviously gotten Kate's message, because he said, "I didn't mean to upset you. But we found his fingerprints. . . . Well, we know he had his hands on your car."

Then fear overwhelmed her shock. "Where is he? Did you tell him I was in the hospital? Did—"

"Shhh," Kate said, taking JoLynn's hand. "He can't get to you. You're completely safe."

But JoLynn's eyes were darting everywhere. "You don't know him. He found me once and he'll find me again."

This time Cooper's tone was gentle when he said, "He's dead, JoLynn. He can never hurt you again. But we need your help finding out who killed him."

"Dead?" She looked at Kate. "Is that true?"

Kate nodded.

"We know all about his illegal business," Cooper said. "A man like that had to have some serious enemies. Can you give us any names?"

JoLynn lifted her free hand to her forehead, a hand still swollen and scraped raw along the pinkie side. "Enemies? I thought *I* was his enemy."

Cooper looked disappointed, but egad, the kid probably still had major brain fog after her near-death experience.

Maybe we should test her more-recent memory. I said, "We know Kent was on the Richter property recently, since he managed to mess with your car. You never had a hint he was lurking around? No hang-up calls, no sense you were being watched or followed?"

"Hang-up calls? No . . . oh my God." Her hand went to her lips. "I remember now. He called me that night. That's why I left the house. That's why I was in the car. Oh my God."

Kate squeezed her hand. "You remember. That's good. And now you need to remember he can never do that again."

Cooper looked down at JoLynn. "I've already got permission from Mr. Richter to get the ranch phone records. Now that we know Dugan called you and you left in a panic, he could have called other times. Maybe he even asked for Elizabeth."

And if so, I thought, that would bring the family into play, perhaps provide a connection between someone at the Richter ranch—someone other than JoLynn—and Kent Dugan.

Cooper was about to say something else, but Super Nurse Maxine Norman busted into the room like a rhinoceros, pulling Henry along by the hand. "Mr. Richter told me how many people were in here. You may have his consent to torture this poor young woman with your questions, but you don't have mine. Henry, get them all out."

Henry stood behind her and rolled his eyes.

"No problem. We're leaving," I said.

"They can stay, Maxine. Really, it's okay," JoLynn said.

But JoLynn was obviously exhausted and in pain.

Kate stood. "I agree with—" She squinted at the name tag pinned to Norman's olive-colored scrub top. "I agree with Nurse Norman. We can come back another time."

Norman said, "I know these other two clowns, but who are you?"

She smiled sweetly. "Dr. Kate Rose, a clinical psychologist consulting on this case at Mr. Richter's request. Can we call you about when might be a good time to visit JoLynn again?"

Kate's manner, which included her willingness to consult with Norman first, had an amazing effect.

Norman actually cracked a smile. "Our baby doll is doing much better. Just let my patient get more pain medicine in her system and a little rest and she'll be fine. Y'all can come back tomorrow."

Kate, you're a damn genius, I thought as we filed out of the room.

Back at my house after the hospital visit, Cooper and Kate huddled together and worked on some kind of to-do list concerning the case—which probably included pressuring the phone company to release the requested information on the landline at Magnolia Ranch. I knew this because Cooper grumbled all the way to my place about how slow they'd been to cooperate.

I hadn't heard from DeShay about getting in touch with Officer Shauna Anthony and was about to search for her on Switchboard.com when Jeff called. He said he e-mailed me the completed police sketch, since he and Doris wouldn't be by the house until later tonight. Doris had her Saturday chores to do—things like laundry and cleaning her room. Jeff always spent time alone with Doris on his weekends off, and not out of guilt, like when he'd first brought her to live with him. He loved her, wanted to care for her. And that made me think of Elliott Richter. Same story, different version.

I hung up and hurried to my computer. I opened the e-mail attachment and printed out a few copies of the police-artist sketch, once again amazed at the picture. Unfortunately, this man's face was seared into my brain now and something else was going on in my head. This face bothered me and not only because of what he'd done. What was it?

I heard the *ding* indicating another e-mail message was coming through—a brief one from DeShay. "Going into autopsy, here's what you need."

It was Officer Anthony's phone number and address. I phoned her right away and told her who I was and what I needed. She preferred we meet in person to discuss an old case. She told me, "People want to e-mail and yak on their cell phones all day long, but I never liked that when I was working. Face-to-face is my way. Besides, I can speak to you much more coherently that way. I have some concentration problems. You'll understand when you get here."

She gave me directions and I left my office. In the living room, Kate and Cooper were deep in conversation.

I cleared my throat and they both looked my way. "Officer Anthony wants to meet in person. Cooper, you want to come along?"

"Not a good time, Abby. I finally found someone who could make things happen at the phone company. She promised to e-mail the Richter phone records to your computer. Take good notes, though."

Did the man not notice in the last week that I'm not the one walking around with a notebook in my pocket? But maybe he wasn't noticing anything but Kate right now, and waiting on those phone records was a great excuse to hang around her. No problem there. Not at all. I was happy to leave them alone.

After the events of this past week, I sure didn't want to be tailed. Staying away from the freeways made rear-view paranoia far less stressful—far fewer cars to deal with. The drive to Anthony's retirement community—a gated neighborhood west of the 610 Loop, with well-tended lawns and small brick homes—took a good thirty minutes longer than it might have.

I navigated the treelined road that wound around a golf course and passed the community pool. Since it was close to six p.m., and the hottest part of the day was over, the chaise lounges and umbrella tables were filled with men and women who'd probably saved their pennies to live here among the pines. No one looked under sixty.

That's why I was surprised when Shauna Anthony answered the door, supported by a cane. This woman couldn't be older than late forties, early fifties.

"Abby Rose," I said. "Thank you so much for seeing me right away."

The woman's skin told me she was black and yet her beautiful dark eyes indicated she might have Asian blood, too. And then I noticed a golden retriever sitting like a statue behind her.

"Aren't you a pretty young thing?" Shauna said. "I would have come to you, but I don't drive much anymore. Come in and meet Oliver."

But Oliver's concern was for his mistress, not meeting a stranger. Shauna hobbled around to face the other direction and the dog was close by her side as she slowly made her way through the tile foyer to a living room beyond. I passed a riding scooter, much nicer than what I was used to seeing in the supermarkets. I remembered Penny mentioning health issues. Looked like they were pretty big ones.

Two brocade wing chairs flanked a low, round oak table. A tray with a pitcher of iced tea and two glasses sat there along with a floral china dish of shortbread cookies. Slices of lemon gleamed in the sweating pitcher, and a bowl of sugar and spoons completed this welcome.

The dog hovered near Shauna, eyes on her face. She said, "I'm fine, Oliver. Would you mind pouring the tea, Abby? My hands aren't obeying my commands today. Damn MS steals your life inch by inch."

Shauna—she'd insisted on the phone that's what I should call her—settled onto the leather sofa facing the wing chairs and Oliver pressed close to her legs. After I fixed us both tea and eyed the cookies hungrily without taking one, I sat across from her.

"I'm not always like this," Shauna said. "I'm in a flare-up right now."

"I—I didn't know. We could meet another time or—"

"No. It's rare for me to be on the giving end of anything these past two years. Seems all I can do is take from others now. My friend next door fixed the tea and

if you don't eat her cookies, she'll be offended."
Shauna smiled.

"I'll have a couple to go," I said with a smile.

Shauna said, "That's a promise." She then pointed my
way. "Visit Abby, Oliver."

The dog came over and sat in front of me, head
cocked, liquid brown eyes on my face.

I petted his silky soft head. "What a beautiful animal."

"Oliver has been a godsend," she said. "He's always
close. Even knows how to bring me my cell or the other
phone if I fall down."

My gaze fell on a photograph on the end table to
Shauna's right. I was guessing the black man and the
Asian woman in the picture were her parents. The man
wore an HPD uniform.

Shauna caught me staring and said, "He was shot by
a crackhead on the east side ten years ago. Died at the
scene. My mother took her own life six months later."

I swallowed hard and managed to utter those inade-
quate words, "I'm so sorry."

"Don't be. They both made choices, choices they left
me to live with. I'm okay with it all now. MS is good
for something. It's taught me that most bad things that
happen are not my fault. My father's murder and my
mother's suicide? Those horrible events were out of my
control. And getting MS? Not my choice, either."

Choice, control and loss. That's what this case had
been all about and still was. And here was someone who
knew a great deal about those things. "If you get tired,"
I said, "let me know. I can come back."

"Your line of work is adoption inquiries, right?" Oliver returned to her side and rested his head in her lap.

"Yes," I said with a smile. "Did you check me out
after I called?"

"You don't think I'd let any old stranger walk into
my house and ask me about my job?"

I should have known. Once a cop, always a cop. "You
worked with CPS on several cases?" I said.

"True. Funny how a woman who never married and
who never had kids would be suited to that job. Guess
I didn't feel obligated to take them all home like some
other officers I knew. Is this about an adoption that took

place after we removed an abused child from a home?"
She looked at Oliver and patted the sofa beside her. The
dog jumped up beside her and lay down.

"No, this is about something else. Do you recall picking up a nine-year-old girl from the bus station over a
decade ago? Apparently she'd been abandoned there."

Shauna's features changed from warm and welcoming
to troubled. "How could I forget?"

Oliver raised his head, looked at Shauna and whined.

"What can you tell me about her?" I said.

Shauna licked her lips and reached for her tea with a
shaky hand. "Medicine makes my mouth so dry." After
she took a sip by holding the glass with both hands, she
said, "God, that was an awful night—raining like hell.
The child was soaked and I wondered if those blue lips
came from being cold or from being sick."

"You thought she was sick?" I said.

"I did. And after I took her to medical and we
stripped off those wet clothes, we saw that big scar down
her chest, so I thought I was right. She sure didn't like
getting a physical—cried through the whole thing, which
sure brought her color back. The doc said all the crying
was probably because she'd seen the inside of one too
many hospitals. She'd had recent heart surgery."

"Did she talk about being sick?" I said.

"That girl wouldn't talk about anything. Someone left
her alone, chilled to the bone, in that hellhole bus station, so I couldn't really blame her. At first, anyway."

"She *wouldn't* talk? Are you saying she had a
choice?" *Back to that choice thing again,* I thought.

Oliver relaxed, again resting his head in Shauna's lap.
"I remember thinking when I went home after that night
shift, after spending hours with the child and getting
nothing but a wide-eyed stare, that she knew her name,
knew her parents, knew it all—and she'd been told to
keep her mouth shut."

"Really?" I said. "That didn't come through in the
report."

"Because I had nothing to support my conclusion. I'd
questioned hundreds of kids by that point in my career
and they always gave *something* away, but not her." She

shook her head. "Not her. I heard later some shrink said she had amnesia. Bullshit, if you ask me."

"I understand no local hospital had treated her heart condition," I said.

"True. I went to every Houston-area hospital myself, carried her picture with me. Questioned doctors and nurses. That child became my mission. No one had reported her missing. No one cared that she'd be going into the system. Made me sick, to be honest."

"Did you ever get any leads?" I asked, realizing I was glad I came here. Shauna was right about face-to-face interviews. She cared about JoLynn. No police report or foster-care file could have conveyed this woman's concern.

"Leads?" Shauna said. "Well, her clothes and shoes were from Kmart, could have been bought anywhere. We sent her picture and description to every major law-enforcement agency including the FBI, and I personally checked databases for more than a year after we found her. Nothing came up. She wasn't wanted. She'd been . . . discarded. That makes me angry to this day."

"And this little girl helped erase her own past by keeping quiet," I said. "Why? Was she afraid?"

"Probably. It was so frustrating. Even the necklace was a dead end," Shauna said. "I had this gut feeling it would lead me somewhere, but I never caught a break."

"The necklace?" I said.

"I'm not sure I even mentioned it in my report. I was afraid a superior might accuse me of wasting time on an investigation that was going nowhere. She was already safe in foster care. But I did some digging around on my own, knowing how important the necklace seemed to the girl. The night I picked her up at the bus station? She wouldn't let go, kept twirling her finger in the chain. Cheap chain, but attached was a beautiful silver piece—a tiny owl sitting on an open book. I'd never seen anything like that owl. I sent the picture with her wearing it all over the place."

"Where did you send it?" I asked.

"Faxed it with the information I sent to the FBI, sent a copy to all the missing-children organizations. We're talking eleven years back, so we weren't quite as connected to the Internet then. Especially patrol officers like me."

"What about local jewelers?" I asked.

"I didn't have the time or authorization to pursue something like that, but every time I went to the mall, or to a Sam's Club or even Target, I checked the jewelry cases. I haven't looked in several years, though. I don't get to those places much anymore."

Oliver whined, rolled his head so Shauna could stroke under his chin.

"This picture of the necklace? I didn't see it in her file."

Shauna smiled. "Not the necklace alone. Her wearing the necklace. If you have any of her foster-care pictures, you've seen it. I enlarged several photos and circled the necklace when I sent off info about her."

A clue had been right there all the time and I hadn't even noticed. "Would you like to see a picture of the girl you worked so hard for? She's twenty now, uses the name JoLynn." I reached into my bag for that photo Roberta Messing placed on a missing-persons Web site a year ago.

Shauna's dark eyes brightened and Oliver's head popped up. "Are you kidding? I'd love to see what she looks like."

I brought her the picture.

She stared for several seconds and her eyes filled. "She's a beauty, isn't she?" Then Shauna met my gaze. "You never said why you're asking about her after all this time. Two years ago, the cop in me would have asked that question right up front. But now? I suppose I'm simply grateful someone cares."

"A man tried to kill her . . . and now he's been murdered. And don't worry—JoLynn has a solid alibi, so she didn't retaliate. But both the police chief I'm working with and I believe the answers to this case—why that man wanted her dead and why he in turn was killed— may lie in JoLynn's past, the same past she refused to share with you."

"Oh my God. After all these years, she's in danger again? Because I got the sense her fear was more complicated than being lost." Shauna rested back against the cushions. "I should have tried harder. I should have—"

"Choices, remember?" I said. "Even children have the right to make them. She shut you out."

Oliver was on alert now, sitting on the sofa with his total focus on Shauna. God, what a wonderful dog.

She looked up at me, her eyes brilliant with emotion. "Promise you'll finish this job, Abby? The one that I couldn't?"

"I give you my word. And you and Oliver will get a full report."

Oliver barked when I said his name, and before I left with a Ziploc full of cookies, I hugged Shauna and shook his paw.

27

I returned home after dark to a house that smelled like teriyaki. Jeff, Doris, Cooper, Kate and even Aunt Caroline were sitting around the kitchen table. If Cooper Boyd didn't have my aunt's complete attention, I might have heard what a terrible niece I was, how I never gave her a first thought, much less a second. After all, I'd failed to call and check up on her.

But Aunt Caroline was all smiles, as flirty as any seventy-five-year-old woman can be—in other words, a seventy-five-year-old in complete denial. Did she think she had a chance in hell with Cooper?

A new jigsaw puzzle was laid out on the table and Jeff was sitting close to Doris to help her look for pieces to fit into the barnyard scene. Doris fell in love with cows after coming to Texas, so I was guessing that's why she chose this particular puzzle.

Cooper smiled at me sheepishly—sheep, cows . . . it was a regular farm in here—and I got the feeling he was guilty about not accompanying me to visit Shauna.

"Did Officer Anthony help?" he asked.

"Maybe." I hung my bag on its hook by the utility room door. "She gave me a small lead, as well as some insight into JoLynn. Don't know if I can get any further than she did with the lead—which went nowhere for Shauna."

"Give Cooper a chance to figure it out," Aunt Caroline said. "He's former FBI. They know how to solve everything."

Jeff looked at Aunt Caroline with a knowing smile and said, "You are so right, Caroline."

His sarcasm was lost on her because she said, "You are most certainly correct, Jeffrey."

"Jeffy knows how to solve, too," Doris said. "He says that's his job. But I don't know what *solve* means. Can we look on the Internet, Abby?"

Aunt Caroline actually had a momentary lapse in narcissism and said, "I never meant to imply that Jeffrey is not a very excellent police officer."

Doris certainly gets right to it, I thought.

Jeff grinned. "Don't worry about it, Caroline."

"Did you eat, Abby?" Kate, true to her family role, deflected attention from another awkward moment courtesy of Aunt Caroline.

"I ate a few cookies." I held up the now half-empty bag of shortbread.

I don't know who eyed that bag more hungrily, Doris or Aunt Caroline. Kate noticed, because she took the bag from me and handed it to Doris. "You ate all your stir-fry, so here's dessert."

Aunt Caroline watched as Doris opened the bag and dug in. She wanted those cookies, but knew she couldn't steal one with Kate watching. Cookies and diabetes don't exactly go together and Aunt Caroline needed to learn that lesson.

"Did you say stir-fry?" I was hungry, despite the recent high intake of butter and sugar.

Kate stood and so did Cooper. He said, "Kate and I cooked—she said you'd be fine with me bumbling around in your kitchen. We saved some for you."

"Vegetarian?" I said warily. Tofu is not my idea of a happy protein.

"We made a batch with chicken and one without," Kate said.

"While we heat it up, tell us about this lead," Cooper said.

I glanced at Jeff and asked if he wanted to be in on this conversation.

"We can hear what you're saying from here," he said. "Doris might beat me to the punch and finish this puzzle."

"Is there punch?" Doris said. "With ginger ale and orange juice?"

"Not that kind of punch," Jeff said. He began to explain.

Meanwhile, Aunt Caroline sat on one of the barstools at the counter separating the kitchen prep area from the dining area. Seems she was keeping as close to Cooper as possible. "What's this clue?"

I said, "JoLynn had a piece of jewelry with her the night Shauna Anthony picked her up from the bus station. I guess it was pretty unusual."

"Unusual how?" Cooper held out a plate and Kate spooned on a mound of chicken teriyaki and brown rice. She knows I'm a *white*-food fan, but I was famished and not about to complain.

"We'll find out after I eat," I said. "We've had a photo of this necklace since I got the foster-care file."

The teriyaki turned out to be better than any takeout and I silently credited this to Cooper's touch. He probably added enough of another white food on Kate's banned list—salt.

After I put my plate in the dishwasher, I went to my office and pulled up JoLynn's foster-care photo file. I enlarged a few shots of the necklace that appeared around her neck in not one but every single picture.

Some of the photos couldn't be sharpened, but I finally ended up with a pretty decent close-up of the owl jewelry. Shauna never mentioned the owl eyes were tiny jewels and that rhinestones outlined the pages of the open book the owl perched on.

When I emerged from my office, Doris's attention was now on a DVD playing—*The Little Mermaid.* Everyone else was still in the kitchen and Aunt Caroline's small cream leather bag was slung on her arm. She was getting ready to leave. I hoped this picture didn't renew her interest in the case and make her hang around. I was tired and might say something I'd regret should she stick her nose in my business.

"Here's what Shauna described." I handed the picture to Cooper.

Aunt Caroline set her bag on a barstool and peered around his shoulder. Kate flanked him on the other side.

"Was she wearing that necklace when she was pulled from the wreck?" I asked Cooper.

"No way. I went through all the belongings the paramedics bagged, hoping to ID her. I would have remembered this," he said.

Cooper handed the photo to Jeff. As he looked at it, Jeff said, "Why didn't she have any ID, Coop? Seems strange to take off without anything. You found her license later at the ranch, right?"

"Yeah . . . in her purse," he said. "We found out this afternoon that Dugan called her the night of the crash, scared her. She drove off in a panic and I'm guessing that's exactly what he wanted."

"I don't doubt it for a minute," I said.

"The phone company finally sent me the records this afternoon and I have a stack to go through. Since we now know he called, we can see if the phone number on the incoming call right before the crash appears on the records earlier. JoLynn claims she never talked to him before that night, but maybe someone else in the family did."

"The family members all have their own phones, Cooper," I said.

"True, but guess who pays the bills? Elliott Richter. I've got everyone's records."

Just then Aunt Caroline tapped the printout of the necklace. "I can tell you what this necklace means to me."

"Yes, Aunt Caroline?" I said politely. But I was wondering why she always had to be the center of attention.

"This is probably custom-made. Very intricate, very detailed. If your JoLynn was some street urchin, where did she get something like this?"

We were all stone silent for a second. If anyone knew about jewelry, it was Aunt Caroline. I finally said those words she always loved to hear. "Good question."

"I know," she said with a smug smile. She then held out her right hand to show off her ruby and diamond ring. "This was designed for me. In fact most of my important pieces are custom-made. I once had a good friend who showed me how jewelry like this is created. Believe me, this precious little owl didn't come from any store."

"You are a fountain of knowledge," Cooper said.

Don't encourage her, I wanted to say. But she was off and running and she did hold everyone's attention. She said, "Since these owl eyes have to be canary diamonds— I can tell by the color—I'm certain the other stones are diamonds as well. Too bad they're small because they'd sparkle so much more with added facets."

Aunt Caroline went on, but finally tired after a fifteen-minute lecture on handcrafted jewelry. I could see the fatigue in her eyes.

Once again she was ready to leave, but Kate stopped her, saying, "Please check your blood sugar first? For Abby and me? We don't want you driving into any trees."

But she complied only after Cooper nodded and said, "Kate, that's a great idea."

Kate, Cooper and I arrived at the hospital on Sunday morning around noon. Last night we'd all agreed JoLynn needed to come clean abut her past. It seemed like the only way to protect her while we continued to follow leads like the necklace and the phone records.

We discovered most of the Richter family at Ben Taub. Matthew and Piper were hanging around near the elevators and offered snooty hellos when we passed them. Adele and Leopold were waiting outside JoLynn's room along with strongman Henry. Their greetings were warmer, but not by much. We found Ian and Richter visiting JoLynn and they actually seemed happy to see us. No Scott or Simone. There wouldn't have been room for them anyway. I was betting Ben Taub wanted this family out of here as much as Elliott Richter wanted JoLynn transferred out. Probably a very demanding clan.

The picture of the necklace was folded in my bag and I'd also brought along the sketch artist's work as well as Simone's photo of the fake security guard, which Adele had sent to my computer. JoLynn's bed was rolled up to a sitting position and though she looked tired, her features weren't drawn with pain like yesterday. She wore a cotton nightgown with tiny peach flowers and a ribbon woven through the neckline. My guess was this came from Adele.

Cooper said, "Would you mind if we talked with Jo-

Lynn for a few minutes? It's pretty crowded with more than three visitors."

Ian was leaning against the window, but he straightened and said, "Certainly, Officer" in his pleasant British accent.

Richter seemed more reluctant to leave, but Ian managed to steer him into the hall. Cooper closed the door after them.

Kate gestured to the lone chair by JoLynn's bed and said, "Abby. Your turn to sit today."

JoLynn smiled and said, "Cramped, isn't it?"

"Can't stir us with a stick." I sat and looked at Cooper, who stood beside Kate at the end of the bed.

I started off, saying, "Has your grandfather told you that he wants to find out about your past?"

JoLynn's eyes gave her away. She was suddenly on high alert. "Not really. But he knows I lied. I told him all about being in foster care and I mentioned that I got in trouble a few times, but—"

"I'm not talking about foster care," I said quietly. "I'm talking about *before* foster care."

She licked her lips. "I don't understand."

"We need to know about your early childhood, before someone left you in a bus station one rainy night. You were nine. You knew who left you there, but you never told anyone. Now's the time, JoLynn."

Kate slowly made her way around to the other side of the bed and picked up JoLynn's hand, held it tightly. "This is important. A man died Friday. *You* nearly died."

She stared straight ahead, her face vacant, her voice toneless when she said, "I don't remember."

This was the face Shauna Anthony probably saw when she'd questioned JoLynn. And I was certain she'd repeated those three words many times from age nine until today.

I reached into my bag and took out the picture of the necklace and held it up in front of her so she couldn't avoid looking at it. Working hard to be as patient as Kate managed to be, I said, "Do you remember this?"

I saw her eyes widen a little; then the blank stare returned. "Never saw it before."

Now she was outright lying. "Funny thing, because you wore this necklace in every picture they took of you while you were in the CPS system. You had it with you the night Officer Shauna Anthony picked you up, the night you were soggy and scared and alone in the bus station."

"Okay, it was mine. So what?" JoLynn's less-than-sweet side was coming out. But there was more than anger. The fear in her eyes was back.

"We want to help you," I said. "Your grandfather wants to protect you. We can't do that unless we know the truth."

"He's not my grandfather. He was a mark. I conned him and he can press charges if he wants." She pulled free of Kate and crossed her arms over her chest, raising her chin in defiance.

Cooper said, "Nice act, JoLynn. But you're not fooling anyone. You're scared shitless."

She blinked rapidly, fighting to maintain her composure, fighting the hurt and the anger. "What more do you need to know? I was a worthless bag of dirt and my parents dumped me."

I thought Kate might cry the tears JoLynn seemed incapable of shedding. But she didn't. "Who were your parents, JoLynn?" she said. "What's your real name?"

"I don't remember," came the robotic reply.

I took out the sketch-artist copy and laid it on her lap. "Do you know this man?"

She cocked her head one way and then the other as she stared down at the face. "I—I . . . no," she said, finally making eye contact with me again. "But that's a police sketch. Did he kill Kent?"

This time, she wasn't acting. Unlike when she first saw the necklace photo, there wasn't even a hint of recognition in her expression now.

"We don't know if he's the killer," Cooper said.

I added the picture of the security guard. "What about this guy?"

She blinked. Did I see a flicker of recognition before she closed her eyes?

But she said, "I don't know him, either."

I placed the jeweled-owl picture on top of the police

sketch. "Let's get back to this, then. Who gave this to you?"

"I *don't* remember," she said.

I've been called stubborn as a two-headed mule all my life, but this girl had me beat. At least today.

Kate looked at me and said, "Abby, why don't we give JoLynn time to think about all this?"

But, no surprise, Cooper wasn't ready to give up. "We found pictures of you bringing flowers to the Richter plot at Glenwood Cemetery. You know anything about that?"

"What?" JoLynn seemed downright confused now.

"And guess where we found them? At your old boyfriend's place," Cooper said. "Did you know he had those?"

"Are you saying he was following me before he tried to kill me? And he followed me *there*?" Patches of color had appeared on her pale cheeks. She seemed embarrassed and upset that her private moments had been captured.

Now I was the one who was confused.

"We aren't sure he took those pictures," Cooper said. "But they were in a folder in his office. We need your help, JoLynn. Please?"

I only vaguely heard her say, "But I don't remember anything," because I was considering who, besides Kent Dugan, might have taken those pictures.

All I could think about was a girl with a camera—a camera she loved to use.

28

We left JoLynn with her doting surrogate grandfather a few minutes later. The less-than-doting family members bombarded us with questions outside JoLynn's room. They wanted to know what we learned and if we were ready to close the case. We didn't inform them JoLynn was not related to the Richters as per Elliott Richter's request. That left little for us to talk about to folks who would have been overjoyed to learn she was an even bigger liar than they thought. I hated to think of JoLynn that way, but it was true.

While I was left bursting to tell Cooper and Kate my idea that Simone might have taken those pictures, Cooper fielded their questions with expert efficiency. He managed to tell them absolutely nothing—a technique I vowed to get better at. This left Matthew and Piper sulking and Adele, Leopold and Ian wondering what the hell was going on. Then we beat a hasty retreat.

I mentioned Simone and my picture theory on the walk to Kate's car.

"You're saying this teenager took the pictures and then somehow Dugan got ahold of them?"

"It's possible," I said. "What we don't know is *how* he got them."

Cooper said, "We have nothing except her possession of a camera to support your theory. Pretty thin, Abby."

"Don't you think we should investigate the possibility?" I said. "Simone could have followed JoLynn around. I saw her in action and believe me, she's capable of doing that."

"Even followed JoLynn to that cemetery? Can the girl drive?" he said.

Kate laughed. "How old do you think Simone is? Twelve?"

"But why would Simone follow her there?" he said.

"Seems like the kind of thing she does," I said.

"Okay. I give. But I'll let you handle this one. I've got a pile of phone records to examine. That seems like a less-theoretical way to make a connection between family members and Dugan."

Bet the phone company loved his constant nagging, I thought. Plus now he had to wait on whatever HPD could recover from Dugan's soggy cell phone. Obviously Cooper wanted to rely on hard evidence, not my theory about a girl and a camera. But my bet was on Simone.

So when we got to my place and Cooper said he needed to head back to Pineview, I said I'd follow him. Besides talking to Simone, I wanted to search JoLynn's room once more—but now I knew what I was looking for. That necklace.

Cooper shrugged and said to come along. But after he came downstairs with his bag, and Kate and I met him in the foyer, he said, "You heading to Pineview with Abby, Kate? Or do you have plans for this hot Sunday afternoon?"

"No plans," she said.

"Want to ride with me?" he asked.

She gave him a warm smile. "I would love to, Cooper."

The drive took far longer than I anticipated thanks to lots of Sunday traffic heading to The Woodlands Mall and Lake Conroe. On the way, I called Richter and told him I wanted to search JoLynn's room again. He told me he was coming back to Pineview as well, but was probably behind us. Then he abruptly hung up.

Huh? And then I realized he wasn't alone in the car and didn't want whoever was with him to know I was calling. I turned my full attention to Cooper's truck up ahead.

When we reached the ranch and stopped on the curving drive in front of the house, Cooper got out while Kate stayed put.

I rolled down my window.

He said, "Kate asked to see the police station. I'll drop her off back here in, say, an hour? Is that long enough to talk to Simone?"

I smiled. "Sure. You might even take Kate out to dinner. I'm sure you know all the healthy places in Pineview."

He grinned back. "Great idea."

Then the two of them took off, the dust of our dry summer in their wake.

I got out of the Camry, went to the door and knocked. The younger housekeeper, Estelle, answered. She looked surprised.

"Hello, Ms. Rose. Mr. Richter isn't home at this time."

"We've spoken. He's on his way back from the hospital but gave me permission to reexamine JoLynn's room. But first," I said, "if you could direct me to where Simone lives, that would be great. I understand she and her mother and stepfather live on the property?"

Estelle pointed left, where the drive wound behind the barn. "You take that road. It travels around the edge of the property. Mr. and Mrs. Hunt live in the very first house you'll come to, a stone house set back in the woods."

"Thanks. Mr. Richter might be home by the time I return." I started for my car.

Estelle called, "Would you like me to call, see if Simone is there? She could be out."

"No. I'd like to drive around the property anyway. Beautiful place, Magnolia Ranch. If she's not home, I'll come right back here." Showing up unannounced might give me an advantage, especially if Simone was hiding the fact that she'd followed JoLynn around, taken pictures and then somehow hooked up with the charming, good-looking Kent Dugan—a man who liked young, naive women.

Cement gave way to gravel as soon as I reached the barn and the Camry crunched along for about a half mile. To my left, I saw horses in a rolling pasture that was growing brown from lack of rain. On my right, woods filled with pines, maples and oaks shaded the bumpy road. I came upon a fieldstone two-story house with a green slate roof, though I nearly missed the place, since it was set back so far from the road.

I thought about parking in the narrow driveway, but a red Corvette already occupied the spot closest to the door. And if Adele and Leopold came home, they might be annoyed if they had nowhere to park. I pulled over onto the small stone shoulder.

I wanted to surprise Simone and got my wish.

When she opened the door, she said, "What are *you* doing here?" Her crazy hair was bound into a ponytail on top of her head. She wore a Coldplay T-shirt nearly hiding her cutoff jean shorts.

"You mind if I come in?" I said.

She shrugged and opened the door wider. "Whatever. But I'm pretty busy. And the parents aren't home."

"I came to see you," I said.

She sprinted up the stairs before I was even inside, and yelled over rock music coming from above for me to follow her. As I went after her, I caught a glimpse of an elegant formal living room off the marble foyer. It was filled with the kind of furniture Aunt Caroline likes. Nothing comfortable, everything pretty.

Seconds later, standing in the doorway of Simone's bedroom, I was thinking this could have been declared a state disaster area. Besides pictures clipped to a thin clothesline strung from one end of the room to the other, and larger photographs covering every available space on the walls, there were clothes, books and shoes piled on the bed and heaped on the floor. CDs and DVDs spilled out of several laundry baskets. *Lots* of CDs. The music was blaring from the entertainment center opposite the cluttered bed.

The walk-in closet behind Simone appeared to have empty shelves and racks, so I assumed all this came from in there.

Simone pointed a remote at the entertainment center and the music stopped abruptly. She dropped the remote, then stood with her hands on her hips in a small clearing in the center of the room. "I'm leaving for school in a few weeks and as you can see, I have *way* too much stuff. This is a disgusting example of my past materialistic life. I'm giving most of it away."

I nodded. "Good idea. You couldn't fit half of this in a dorm room anyway."

"My mother wants me to live in an apartment. She networked with future Longhorn moms and had my roommates all picked out. But I'm living in the dorm. Period." She sounded a little defiant, like I might actually argue with her.

"Sounds like you know what you want," I said.

She seemed to relax then and said, "Why are you here?"

"I'm hoping you can help me. Did you know that the man JoLynn used to live with is the person who tried to kill her?"

"Are you kidding me? So they caught him?" Simone pulled a giant black garbage bag from a box near her bare feet and shook it open.

"They didn't *catch* him. He was murdered."

She stopped shoving clothes into the bag and stared at me. "Really? That's a giant coincidence."

"Which probably means it's *not* a coincidence. Mind if I sit down?" I nodded at a chair by the computer desk stacked with what looked like yearbooks.

"Go ahead." Simone sat cross-legged on the floor, her eyes never leaving me as I stepped carefully over to the chair, placed the yearbooks on the floor and sat.

I noticed her camera bag on the desk before I swiveled the chair to face her. "This is serious business, Simone."

"You don't think I know that?" Her defiance was back, but this time it was tainted by fear. Why?

"I know your photography is very important." I glanced around. "Did you take all these pictures?"

"Yeah. So?"

"You're good. I was wondering if you took any pictures of JoLynn, because I don't see any in here."

"Why would I take her picture?" Simone started peeling blue polish off her ragged fingernails.

"Because from what I saw in the hospital and what I'm seeing here"—I pointed at one wall where there were photos of Scott sitting at a computer, her uncle riding a horse, her mother wearing a ridiculous hat and Matthew kissing Piper at their wedding—"you take pictures of everything."

Beneath her pale makeup, the redness of a flush began to break through. "Maybe I did take a few pictures of JoLynn. So what?"

"No problem. Except for the ones she didn't *know* you were taking. That's kind of invasive, wouldn't you say?"

She took a deep breath and rubbed thumb against index finger so hard I thought she might take off a layer of skin. "She was an interesting subject. She was like this . . . enigma."

"You followed her?"

Simone nodded.

"Where did you follow her?" I said.

"Not many places. She didn't leave the property much. Usually Scott drove whenever she wanted to go somewhere."

"Tell me where she went."

Simone let out a huge breath and shifted her gaze from her hands to my face. "She went to that old cemetery, okay?"

"And you took her picture there?"

"Bad pictures. I couldn't get close and I'm not good with the telephoto lens yet."

I noticed that my heart had sped up, that I could feel my throat pulsing. "What did you do with those pictures, Simone?" I didn't add, *Sell them to your new friend with the six-pack abs and the pretty-boy face?*

"I think I threw them away," she said. "They were awful. After I printed a few straight from the camera and saw them, I didn't even load them on my computer—they were that bad."

"You *think* you threw them away? Come on, Simone. You're a very smart girl. You can do better than that."

She held up her hands. "Okay, okay."

Ah, here it comes, I thought. The Dugan connection to this family. A very bad connection for Dugan, though. One that led to his death.

But Simone said, "I lost them. Lost my camera, too.

That's why I don't even have any copies to look at and learn from my mistakes."

"*What?* I saw you with a camera at the hospital the other day."

"That's my *new* camera. I replaced the one I lost with the exact same model, got the money from Uncle Elliott. And you *can't* tell my mother. She doesn't think I can make it as a photojournalist—which is what I want to do. If she found out I was stupid enough to lose my camera, she'd say, 'Simone wants to be a photographer and she can't even keep track of her equipment.'"

"Were any other photos missing?" I asked.

Simone thought for a moment. "Just the ones on the camera. There were more of JoLynn I hadn't downloaded or printed out. No matter how spoiled rotten my relatives all are, they make for some great shots, and I had a few pics of them, too. I'm always catching little arguments, Scott and Matthew getting into it over a poker game, Uncle Elliott's face getting dark as night when someone doesn't hop when he says hop, my mother being, well, my *mother*. She's the only one who doesn't understand that I have to do this."

"And none of these photos ended up on a disc or on your computer?"

"No," she said.

How I wished I had a photo of Dugan with me. Maybe Simone saw him hanging around. Could be that when he tampered with JoLynn's car, he somehow found the camera and the pictures and took them. "Did you lose the camera and printed-out photos of JoLynn at the same time?"

"I'm not sure. Since they were all fuzzy and terrible, I never wanted to see them again. As for the camera, well, my parents and I went to U.T. for a visit and when I was unpacking once we came home, I realized I didn't have my camera case. I called the hotel, but nothing from our suite had been turned in by the maid service. It's an expensive camera, so I'm sure someone in Austin is learning how to use it as we speak."

"I hate to ask, but could your mother have taken that camera without you knowing? She had access. And she doesn't like the idea of you becoming a photographer, right?"

Simone's jaw nearly dropped. "Oh man, I never thought of that. I was a 'real pisser,' as my dad said, on that trip. Oh my God. Maybe she was trying to teach me a lesson."

"Did she seem surprised when you were using a camera again as if nothing had happened? I mean, if she took it away and then you show up with the same—"

"I get what you're saying. No. She wasn't surprised. She seemed as annoyed as ever, but she knew Uncle Elliott would be the person I'd go to, and she wouldn't argue with anything he bought me."

My mind was racing now. But I couldn't share my suspicions about Simone's mother possibly being in on the murder attempt. Still, I was wondering if Adele did a little detective work of her own, found Dugan and showed him the pictures of JoLynn, maybe asked him how he felt about his ex-girlfriend living with rich folks. Maybe she merely wanted Dugan to take JoLynn far, far away. Or maybe she asked him or paid him to tamper with the car. That would be a very bad deal for this kid if her mother did something like that.

"What are you thinking, Abby?" Simone asked.

"I'm trying to make sense of this," I said. "When was the trip to U.T.?"

"About a month ago. Why?"

"Just considering other scenarios of how your camera disappeared. Maybe a student saw it and stole it. Anyway, thank you for coming clean. You've been a huge help." I didn't even want to look her in the eye now. What if her mother *did* hire Dugan to kill JoLynn? And maybe, when he asked for more money, she felt she had to get rid of him.

"You won't talk to my mother about this camera thing?" Simone said. "Maybe one day she'll show up and hand me the one she took and we'll laugh about it. At least that's my dream if I live that long."

"Not to worry. I don't think she and I run in the same circles." I hated not being straight with her, hated what might lie ahead if her mother was arrested. I'd seen firsthand how quickly Adele had taken charge when the security guard disappeared. Now I wondered if she'd hired the impostor herself and covered it up by helping her irate brother, Elliott, find a new man for the job. After all, the impostor was at the hospital for a reason, perhaps hired to finish the job Adele first gave to Kent Dugan.

"You'll keep this between us?" Simone was saying.

"That's what I want to do," I said with a smile. Now I was resorting to semantics.

Simone hugged me and then thanked me profusely. And I felt like a rat. I told her I could find my way out.

I left the house, wondering if I should leave Simone with the house unlocked. *Who could find this place?* I thought, heading for my Camry. *No one but the family probably knows it's even here.*

Boy, was I wrong.

Pine needles must have muffled the footsteps of the man who grabbed me and again I found myself in an oppressive and painful bear hug. But unlike before, I'd never heard him coming.

Then I smelled chloroform and thought, *Not this again.*

29

The man didn't put chloroform over my mouth and nose, just stifled me with a big, strong hand. I was dragged away from the driveway into the trees and out of sight. Surely Adele and Leopold were coming home soon. . . . Or maybe Simone was watching from her window. Right. The window on the other side of the house.

The man said, "I can use the drug again or you can come with us willingly. But no calling for help."

I was being given an option? Gee, how accommodating. "No chloroform," I mumbled through his fingers.

And then another guy appeared from the woods, he, too, as silent as a snake. I recognized him right away. Joe Johnson. Mr. Fake Security Guard. First thing he did was stuff a wad of something in my mouth and secure it with a bandanna tied around my mouth and head. Then assailant number one—I was betting I'd recognize him, too, when I got a look—gripped my elbows and put my hands in front of me so the faker could apply a pair of lovely little plastic cuffs. I hadn't had this much fun since Aunt Caroline's last dinner party. What did these people want?

I didn't see a weapon of any kind. They used brute force and the threat of chloroform. Very *weird*.

"Your keys?" Joe Johnson said.

I nodded at my right pocket. I'd left my bag in the car, not to mention the gun I swore I would carry with me. And didn't. I don't like carrying the .38 around and now I was paying the price.

Joe took my keys and tossed them to another person

who silently joined us from a different direction: Estelle. The only person besides Simone who knew where I went after leaving Richter's house. *Estelle?*

Joe said, "Bring her car."

Estelle nodded and pointed the remote at my Camry, disengaging the alarm.

Bring my car where? I thought. My worry meter shot farther to the danger side of the scale. They were taking me somewhere else. Not good.

The guy who grabbed me took my elbow again and we started walking. I glanced to my left and saw the stringy-haired man's face. Yup, same guy from the supermarket and the parking garage. Only his hair was clean now and tied back in a ponytail that hung down his neck.

Turned out their Jeep was hidden on a hard dirt road that wound through the woods. I didn't remember seeing an entrance to this path, but then again, Magnolia Ranch was huge. I could have missed it, or the entry could have been farther down the larger gravel road that skirted the woods.

Ponytail sat beside me in the backseat. Joe Johnson drove. Whatever was in my mouth was absorbing every bit of saliva and becoming a soggy, disgusting lump of whatever. Gauze, maybe?

Though I didn't turn around, I heard what was probably my car bumping along behind us. For some reason I worried about my tires. Sheesh. I'm being kidnapped and I'm thinking about my car? Was this how my mind was choosing to calm me down? By making me think about something as stupid and mundane as tires? If so, it was working. Then I got even more silly, thinking, *Three against one? No problem, Abby. You can take them.*

Five minutes later we came to a shack that sat off the road among the trees. The small structure was built with wood now gray with age. Planks slanted precariously or were missing altogether. *Not a great place to hide a kidnap victim while you ask for the ransom,* I thought. Too close to the ranch. Maybe this wasn't about ransom. Maybe this was all about JoLynn. Yes. Estelle was the watchdog inside the ranch—a new employee, if I remembered right. Joe Johnson replaced the security guard to get close to JoLynn, and the other guy? I was guessing *I'd* been his assignment.

Ponytail helped me out of the backseat and we all went inside the shack through a squeaky half door. The place was completely empty—no furniture, no old appliances or stoves. Nothing. But it was cool and smelled of the surrounding pines.

Johnson carried in a blanket from the Jeep and laid it out on the filthy wood floor. "Time to talk," he said.

Talk? I love to talk. Beats getting killed every time. And talking required that they remove this miserable gag. Tethered hands held out in front of me, I squatted, then sort of fell back on my bottom. That's when I realized *they* might be the ones doing all the talking.

"You have been a thorn in my side, Abby Rose," Johnson said as he joined me on the floor. "No pun intended."

A funny guy. Great.

Estelle and Ponytail sat on either side of me, and that's when I realized Estelle held my bag. Now I was getting pissed off. First my car and now my purse?

She opened the bag and took out my gun. "I found this in the glove compartment."

Joe held out his hand and Estelle handed him the Lady Smith. He looked at the .38 with disgust and set it down behind him. Then he said, "My brother will remove the gag. Trust me, no one can hear you cry out from this spot in the woods. But the cuffs have to stay on. I know about your exploits, what a capable young woman you are. You might run."

Ponytail removed the gag and didn't seem bothered by handling the slimy ball of whatever from my mouth. He tossed it in a corner and stuffed the bandanna in his jeans pocket. I wished I were wearing jeans rather than capris, because the mosquitoes were already on the attack.

"Thank you," I said. I am not usually polite to my abductors, but I'd learned from experience not to make them unnecessarily angry. They can usually get worked up without my help.

Estelle removed the necklace picture and the drawing of Ponytail from my bag now.

"The Altoids are way at the bottom, if that's what you're looking for," I said. "Ponytail here could use one."

She smiled as she smoothed the papers in the middle of our little circle.

Johnson looked at his brother. "Way too good of a likeness, Nick. This worries me."

"Why?" I said. "Is he in some database? Are you worried the police will find him? Because they will, you know."

Johnson said, "Unfortunately, that's not the kind of database he's in." He pointed at his temple. "He's in this kind of database, in someone's memory. Now, can you keep quiet so I can tell you something important?"

Me? Keep quiet? Guess he didn't know me as well as he thought. "Answer this first. Why did you do it? Had she conned you out of money?"

Johnson looked completely confused.

"That's her thing," I said. "You know, that girl in the coma? The one you wanted to sneak in and finish off? She's a con artist."

Johnson's neck reddened. Didn't I just tell myself not to piss off my kidnappers? And yet I'd gone and done it anyway.

"You don't know the first thing about her," Johnson said. "You listen to me or I'll put the gag back on. I am being forced to trust you, something I did not wish to do. But circumstances and your persistence have forced me to take these measures."

He talks funny, I thought. Stilted . . . with a trace of an accent. Nick, too, now that I'd heard him say more than a sentence.

Estelle said, "I followed you when you said you wanted to meet with Simone. I listened at the door. The girl is clueless. You should have left her out of this business."

"I'm feeling pretty clueless myself right now," I said.

"Then let me clear things up for you. I am JoLynn's father," Joe Johnson said.

I blinked, too stunned to speak. Her *father*?

"And," he went on, "if this investigation of yours goes

any further, you will be putting her in serious danger. I might not be able to protect her again."

"Protect her?" I said, trying to figure this out.

Johnson said, "This is her uncle—you heard me call him Nick, but that is not his real name. Estelle is Nick's daughter."

"Let me guess? Not her real name, either." Three mosquitoes were feasting on my calf and I slapped at them awkwardly with my tethered hands. "So you're all JoLynn's biological family?" I took a look at the three of them and saw a hint of resemblance to JoLynn—especially in Estelle, who I was betting wore all that makeup and changed her hair color for that very reason. What the hell was this about?

"Yes, we are her family," Johnson said.

"The family that abandoned her in a bus station eleven years ago?" The anger that rose in my throat surprised me. "What kind of people are you?"

I could tell my words stung Johnson, and Nick bent his head.

Estelle was the one who spoke. "JoLynn knows she wasn't abandoned. She knew her parents were protecting her."

"How's that *protecting* her? She's been through hell." Yup, I was eating fire and spitting smoke now.

"If you promise never to speak of this conversation again, speak of it to *anyone*, then I will tell you her story. But I must have your word." Perspiration dampened the front and underarms of Johnson's T-shirt, and thin rivers of sweat wound down from his head to his neck.

"What will you do if I *don't* promise? Kill me?" Maybe defiance wasn't the right approach, but I couldn't understand why they'd done this to a child. No explanation could possibly be acceptable.

"If you won't promise us this, then we will disappear. We must go soon anyway, get away from JoLynn. Sadly, if you speak of us to others, JoLynn's blood may be on your hands." Johnson's eyes held mine, waiting for my answer.

"On my hands?" I said. "Let me get this straight. You want me to give up on this case, let a killer go free?"

"You mean Kent Dugan's killer?" Johnson said.

"Yes," I said. "Which one of you got rid of him after he harmed JoLynn?"

"We don't kill people, Ms. Rose. We do not know who was responsible for his death. And if you promise to remain silent, you will understand why we have no interest in harming you."

He could be lying, but I didn't think so. No matter what, I'd do what was right, promise or not. "I promise. Now tell me the truth."

"I see the skepticism in your eyes, but once you hear what we have to say, I believe you will keep this secret," Johnson said. "You are a good person."

"You get a kick out of drugging and kidnapping good people?" I raised my eyebrows in inquiry.

"That was unfortunate, but we thought a warning might make you give up," Nick said. "We were wrong."

"Tell me this big secret," I said. "Because people are probably already looking for me. I'm supposed to be at the ranch."

"Estelle left a note for Mr. Richter before she went to see what was happening between you and Simone. She wrote that you wanted to see the town and since Estelle's work was done, she agreed to show you, and then perhaps the two of you would get something to eat."

"You think they'll buy that? Pretty lame, but go ahead. Talk." I no longer felt afraid. Maybe this was another form of denial, a way to feel safe while I was wearing plastic handcuffs and sitting in a shack in the woods. At least Nick left the chloroform in the car.

"First let me tell you that my brother and I came from Europe when we were young men, brought to the country by a man in Chicago who wanted us to work for him. We were jewelers by trade, like our father and his father before."

I glanced at the picture of the little jeweled owl.

Estelle noticed this and said, "JoLynn's father made that for her. He didn't want her to forget she was a wise and special girl." She looked at Johnson. "Can I show her?"

He nodded and Estelle pulled the necklace from her

skirt pocket and put it in my palm. "The picture doesn't do it justice."

I stared down, bent my fingers and touched the canary eyes and the rows of tiny diamonds. "It's really . . . very beautiful," I said.

"I will continue," Johnson said. "My wife and I had only one child, our daughter, who now calls herself Jo-Lynn. We made very little money working for this jeweler—both my brother and I in the same place. Our boss was not a nice man. Not an honest man. I was designing at night—sketching rings, pendants, bracelets—and waiting for the day when we could save enough to leave his employ, to get citizenship and go out on our own." He swallowed, seemed to be welling with emotion now.

Nick took over. "But the poor child was sick. Very sick. Her heart." He patted his chest with his palm. "She needed an operation. But when my brother told this man who brought us to America, he said we could not take her to the charity hospital for the operation. He said our visas weren't real. We were *illegal*. We would be deported and that meant JoLynn would never get the help she needed. Not in our country."

"Where is your country?" I asked. They sounded Russian, maybe.

"Some things are unimportant to this story," Johnson said. "You do not need to know—that way you cannot tell anyone."

"She got her operation, though," I said. "That much is certain."

"She did," Johnson said, "in another city. Not Chicago. We had to leave there."

"Because . . . ?" I said.

"Because we stole, stole for JoLynn. To save her." Johnson hung his head. "This was a bad thing done for a good reason. *An American Tragedy*." He looked up and met my eyes, smiled a little.

"You stole from this jeweler?" I said.

"No. We thought we could not steal from him. He would know who did this crime and why. He would send us back to our country. We would be disgraced. But we knew he bought and sold diamonds on the black market. Diamonds are very easy to smuggle. So easily hidden."

Johnson paused, took a deep breath and wiped his sweaty forehead with his forearm. "We would have been better off taking the diamonds right from him. But we learned this lesson too late."

"You took them from one of his customers, someone who knew they'd been smuggled into the country?" I said.

"Yes, Abby. This is the mistake we made." I was looking at a nearly broken man and yet there was still strength in his eyes when I got past the sadness.

"What happened?" I said quietly. "Did this person you stole from come after you?"

"You have no idea. He is *still* after us. And he killed my wife . . . left a note on her body that JoLynn was next. He would find us and he would slit her throat for what we had done."

I felt the hairs rise on my arms. "This man was a criminal, then?"

"Yes. A *career* criminal," he said.

"In other words, the mob," Estelle whispered. "He didn't care about the diamonds. It was about revenge. You do not steal from the Chicago mob."

I sighed heavily. "You gave up your daughter to hide her, make sure she was away from you?"

"Yes. We learned Texas has the closed files. She would be adopted—she would have a good home, a new name. A safe place to grow up."

Oh my God, I thought. *We failed her miserably.*

Johnson said, "But the pull of your only child is like an ocean current, Abby. Before we left her, we told her we had someone to help us. The diamonds weren't all spent, you see. This person we paid agreed to send us messages about her."

"Someone in the CPS system knew about her? Knew about her situation?" I couldn't believe it.

"This is a country where money is more important than blood. More important than a sick child. I will not tell you his name, but only that he died from a heart attack a year ago."

I could find out who he was through Penny, but what good would that do now? "Let me guess. By the time

JoLynn aged out of foster care, you began watching over her yourself."

He nodded. "She was so lost. My heart was breaking as I watched her struggle—but I couldn't watch her all the time. I asked my brother and his daughter to help me."

Nick spoke up again. "We didn't want this evil man in Chicago to find her. We had to keep our distance. We travel, take odd jobs. And keep coming back to make sure she's all right."

"Do you know what her first job was?" Johnson said. "A clerk in a jewelry store in the mall. Maybe this was her way of saying, 'Come and get me. I'm right where you think I might be.' I worry about that part of her, the part that wants to come back to us."

I closed my eyes, no longer feeling the insect stings or the tight plastic on my wrists. This information was so overwhelming, I needed time to take it all in. Could I help these people somehow? Bring their fractured family back together? I didn't know. And I also didn't know how any of this pertained to Kent Dugan's murder. I said, "Did you know that JoLynn moved in with a criminal? I'm talking about Kent Dugan, of course."

Estelle said, "We knew. One of us is always close. My uncle was very worried after he watched Dugan and surmised he was a criminal."

"Did you know he tried to kill her?"

"We knew he found her and this was a worry," Johnson said.

"How did you know?" I asked.

"Because I saw him," Estelle said. "I followed JoLynn when she left Kent Dugan, took the job with the Richters to keep tabs on her. Like Mr. Dugan, we have become quite good at creating names and backgrounds. She was pretending to be someone she wasn't and we didn't understand, but JoLynn was safe here. Or so we thought."

"When did you see Dugan?" I asked.

"Right before her crash," Estelle said. "But I didn't know he did something to her car. I learned from listening to you and the chief, to Mr. Richter's conversations with others. And when Mr. Richter said he wanted to find out about JoLynn's past to help protect her, we knew we had to stop you."

"But you are very good at what you do, Abby," Johnson said. "Your e-mails from this Penny person at CPS. I was very, very worried."

"Are you saying you hacked into my system?" I felt my face heat up. How? I'm no novice when it comes to computers and thought my system was as safe as possible. But I also know it's not impossible to hack into home computers, just like it's not impossible to get into government sites.

"I see this makes you angry," Johnson said. "But I had no choice. I have learned many skills in the last eleven years, some of them from people you do not want to know about."

"You and your family drugged me, scared me, invaded my privacy and . . . and"—I held up my hands—"tied me up. That's wrong. You don't have the right to do that."

"It is wrong, yes. We do not deserve your forgiveness for these things. Our job is to keep JoLynn safe."

"But you haven't succeeded," I said, not bothering to keep my voice down. "Did it dawn on you that someone in the Richter family talked to Kent Dugan when he came around here? That Dugan offered this person information about JoLynn's recent stint as an identity thief, probably for cash?"

From the look on Joe Johnson's face, I was betting he had no idea. "What are you saying? How does this mean we haven't succeeded? Mr. Dugan died."

I said, "Mr. Dugan was *murdered*, probably because he failed to kill JoLynn and would probably be caught for that attempt on her life. And then he might just spill his guts to the first cop he talked to about how someone here, on this ranch, asked him to get rid of her."

Silence followed. Their turn to absorb information.

Finally Estelle said, "I saw Dugan, but never saw him talk to anyone. He hung around in the woods, watched JoLynn when she was riding. My uncle was preparing to deal with him, make sure he left her alone, but he was too late. She was injured and we were so frightened for her."

Johnson said, "The newspaper said nothing about a murder. They said Mr. Dugan was found in a bayou." He thumped his head. "I should have known we couldn't be so lucky as to have him simply die."

I realized I was hanging on to the necklace for dear life. "Why did you have this, Estelle?"

"Because you searched her room and missed this. We worried you'd come back, or the policeman would do his own search. JoLynn had hidden it in a pocket near the head of the bed."

I looked at Johnson. "You thought that somehow I or Chief Boyd could trace this necklace back to you?"

"As I said, you are a very good investigator. We didn't know what you might be able to learn from it. I have foolishly sold similar pieces when we needed money. Like a painting, some jewelry tells much about the creator. I didn't want you to track me through my work."

"This is important to JoLynn," I said. "Why not put it back where you found it, Estelle?"

Johnson said, "I see you care very much about my daughter. It's in your eyes. Please help us protect her. Please keep our secrets."

"For now, I will. But if you've lied to me and I find out you had anything to do with Kent Dugan's death, all bets are off. He wasn't a good man, but he didn't deserve to be murdered."

Johnson said, "Then all bets are *on*. Thank you for helping my daughter. Thank you a million times." He took out a pocketknife and cut off the cuffs.

Then he handed me my gun.

30

A gun is a threat and there was no reason to threaten these people any more than they had already been threatened—by the murder of Johnson's wife, by the note left on her body, by having to live in the shadows, maybe forever. Their secrets felt heavy, their trust in me a burden. I didn't know what I would do with this information and that thought alone started eating away at my very empty stomach immediately.

By the time Estelle and I got in my car to drive back to the ranch, it was already dark. I was thirsty and hungry, but because we were supposed to be out seeing the sights and having dinner, I didn't think I'd be eating anytime soon.

"Are you sure you never saw Dugan talk to anyone in the family?" I said.

"I am certain. Since I get around to all the houses on the ranch—I'm Eva's slave and get to clean all of them—I'd be the one to see something."

"All the houses?" I said. "Who does that include?"

"You've been to Simone's place—well, her stepfather and her mother's place. Scott lives about a half mile away. He's easy to clean for, since he spends most of his time at the big house. Matthew and Piper have just torn down his old home and are rebuilding, so I don't have to clean for those snobs, thank God. Ian's on the far side of the property. He and Adele don't get along, so it's probably a good thing he's a couple miles away."

"This ranch covers two miles?" I said.

"At least," she said.

"Wow. And they make you clean all those houses by yourself?"

"Yup. But Mr. Richter pays me better than anyone I've ever worked for and Eva takes care of the big house aside from making the beds and cleaning the bathrooms. She thinks someone might break one of his crystal vases or steal him blind, I guess."

"You live in the house?"

"Yes. But not for long. I'll have to leave now. I loved being so close to my cousin, even if I couldn't tell her who I was. Mr. Richter will take good care of her—that is, if you let him. He truly loves her."

I shifted my gaze to her profile as we bumped along on the gravel road toward the ranch house. "I hope that's how this all turns out. She deserves a family." And this made me wonder why my sister hadn't called. She'd be anxious to leave for Houston. After all, clients would be at her door early tomorrow and she tried to be in bed by ten if she had to work the next day.

"My cell's in my bag," I said. "Could you check the battery?"

"Your battery is fine. I turned your phone off before we talked. Do you want me to turn it back on?"

"Um, yes, *please*," I said, once again annoyed at how they had completely invaded my personal space. Even though I understood their reasons, I was still irritated.

"We have to walk into the house like we've become friends," Estelle said. "Can you do that?" I heard the sound of my phone powering up.

"I don't know a damn thing about Pineview, so you better give me details. And I need to know about our imaginary dinner. Where did we eat?"

On the short drive, she told me a little about the town and we agreed that we'd stopped at the Sonic drive-in and binged on fast food and shakes. God, how I wished this were true. Then I took my cell from her. I had three messages. They were all from Kate asking me to call her. By the third one, she sounded worried, saying she didn't know where I was.

I parked the Camry alongside Cooper's truck—three other vehicles sat in the driveway, too—and as we walked toward the house, I said, "If you left a note, then why is my sister calling me and sounding so worried?"

"I don't know," whispered Estelle.

We'd reached the door and it opened before Estelle could use her key.

Cooper and Kate greeted us, relief written on my sister's face. She said, "Where have you been? Cooper has a patrol car out looking for you."

"You didn't get the note?" I forced myself not to glance Estelle's way.

They backed up so we could enter and we walked into the foyer.

"What note?" Elliott Richter called. He was in the formal living area to the left and seemed out of place in his jeans and Western shirt. Adele looked right at home, though, as did Leopold, Scott and Matthew.

Estelle spoke up, thank God. "I left a note, sir. When no one was home yet, Miss Rose mentioned she'd never seen the town. I told her I could show her around. I knew Otto and Eva would be here to fix dinner."

Richter's glance traveled around the room. "Anyone see a note?"

Lots of negative headshakes and I wondered if Estelle was lying. Maybe Johnson told her to leave a note and she forgot.

Cooper was on his cell calling off the search party and Kate was looking me up and down. "You're all sweaty, Abby . . . and look at all those mosquito bites on your legs."

"Those skeetos are out in droves. We checked out the property, too. Walked into the woods. The ranch goes on for miles," I said.

"May I go now?" Estelle said to Richter.

"You've eaten?" he said. "Otto prepared a delicious pork roast with oven potatoes."

Estelle started to speak, but I beat her to it. "No, we haven't eaten. Guess we lost track of time." No note meant no written evidence about dinner together. And my mouth was watering at the mere mention of pork roast.

"Then follow me. You both should fix a plate." He started down the hall to the kitchen with Estelle, and I grabbed Kate's hand and told her to come, too.

"Cooper and I ate in town. Isn't it a darling little place?" she said.

"I love the town square." I kept my eyes straight ahead. No one could read my lies better than Kate.

Then I heard Cooper call, "The posse has gone back to the police station. Where y'all going?"

Kate waited for him to catch up and I was hoping his presence would distract her from asking me more questions. I sure hadn't heard a word from her yet about heading for home.

The huge professional-style kitchen had a large preparation island in the center with stools lined on one side.

Richter said, "Otto's worked hard enough today. I can probably feed you two without his help. Chief? Kate? Can I offer you anything?"

"Just water for me," Kate said. "I can get it myself if you point me to the glasses."

Soon Kate, Estelle and I had tumblers of ice water, and Cooper was helping Richter pull leftovers from the stainless steel refrigerator.

Then I noticed that Estelle, who'd taken the stool next to me, was fidgeting. I looked down and saw why. The note was on the floor. She dragged it with her shoe, then bent quickly and picked it up and slipped it into her pocket; the pocket with the necklace.

I didn't like this one bit. Lies can catch up with you in not-so-pleasant ways, but my guilty conscience was put to sleep when Elliott Richter removed my dinner from the microwave and set the plate in front of me. Herbed pork, red cabbage and golden potatoes made everything wonderful.

Richter excused himself to return to his family. "I'm hoping they'll all go home now that you two are safe and sound."

After a few minutes, Estelle said, "I'll head to my room if you don't mind?" She carried her plate of half-eaten food to the sink, cleaned it and put the dish and silverware in the dishwasher.

Cooper watched her retreat, then said, "I thought you came to talk to Simone. To check out JoLynn's room for that necklace? What happened?"

Simone. With what I'd just been through, I'd forgotten

about her. "I did talk to her, as a matter of fact. Before I decided to invite Estelle for a drive. I mean, Estelle's probably seen and heard plenty, yet we never questioned her."

"I questioned her as soon as I found out JoLynn lived here," Cooper said.

"Okay, you questioned her, but I didn't. Anyway, that's not what's important." I lowered my voice. "Get this. Simone admitted she took the pictures of JoLynn at the cemetery."

Cooper said, "That's one question answered. How did they get in Dugan's hands?"

"She doesn't know," I said. "She said she threw them away because they were such poor quality. She also lost her camera."

"That's certainly true." Richter was back and he'd heard us. "I bought Simone a new one. What does this have to do with the investigation?"

He obviously hadn't heard the first part of what I'd said about the cemetery pictures. So I told him.

"Are you considering the possibility that Simone somehow met this Dugan man?" Richter said. "Gave him the photos?"

"I don't think so. Her biggest concern was her lost camera and how to replace it. She thought she may have left it behind on a trip to U.T."

"Yes. She went with Adele and Ian. Those two in the same room is bad enough, but in the same car? No wonder Simone was distracted enough to lose something as important to her as her camera."

Ian? I'd assumed Simone meant Leopold when she said she took the trip with her parents. "Can you excuse me a minute for a restroom break?" I said. If Estelle was still around, I needed to ask her something.

I stood quickly and started for the big hall.

"There's a powder room right off the utility room this way," Richter called.

"I noticed you have a bathroom with cherubs last time I was here. I love cherubs," I said over my shoulder.

As I hurried down the hall, I noticed the living areas were both empty, so the rest of the family had taken off. I made the left turn and saw all those closed doors.

Which one belonged to Estelle? I had to talk to her. Now.

But when I saw JoLynn's door ajar, I knew where she was. Replacing the necklace. Sure enough, she was in the room. Her back was to me and she was fluffing pillows at the head of the bed.

She gasped and turned when I whispered her name.

"You scared me," Estelle said. "You can't act like we're suddenly *best* friends, Abby. You'll make Mr. Richter suspicious."

"I know. But I have to ask you something important. You've cleaned all those houses. Did you notice if Adele Hunt or Ian McFarland had a camera similar to Simone's?"

"Actually, I thought Simone lent hers out. Which was odd because she was in love with her camera. Hardly ever let it out of her sight. Then I decided Mr. McFarland must have bought one just like hers. Simone probably convinced him—so she could have a spare handy in an emergency."

"Thank you, Estelle. Thank you so much."

I paid a visit to the bathroom then, the one that reminded me of Glenwood Cemetery. I sat on a little bench against the wall and thought for a minute. Ian found the pictures, maybe in the trash here at the ranch or maybe in Simone's camera case on the trip to U.T. He got worried. What else did his daughter have on her camera? If Ian somehow met up with Kent Dugan, and Simone saw them together, she might have taken their picture with her new telephoto lens, just like she'd taken pictures of JoLynn. He couldn't know unless he looked at *all* her pictures. And he had to be concerned that others might see any or all of what she'd shot. So he stole the whole friggin' camera.

I stood, put my hands under the cold water and then rested my palms against my warm cheeks. *I don't want to bring Estelle into this if I don't have to.* I walked slowly back to the kitchen. Maybe I didn't have to reveal how I learned where the other camera might be.

I found Richter and Cooper holding beer glasses when I returned, while Kate was cleaning up after me.

"I realize now that I didn't see Ian here tonight," I said. "He came back from Houston with you, right?"

"Yes. He called Simone right after dinner—which didn't make Adele too happy," Richter said. "He took off right after he spoke with Simone and I assumed she said something that bothered him. She gets to him. Gets to all of us at times."

Cooper said, "Why the interest in Ian?" He knew I wasn't simply making polite conversation.

"I have this gut feeling. Can we act on it without every single piece of evidence in place for once?" I said.

"You suspect Ian of something? That's ridiculous," Richter said.

"Can't hurt to ask him a few questions," Cooper said. "Is this about the camera?"

Richter looked back and forth between us. "Simone's camera? The one I bought for her?"

"Actually, this is about the one she *lost*." I walked over and picked up the cordless phone from its spot on the kitchen desk. "Do me a favor, Mr. Richter. Call Simone. Tell her mother or whoever answers that you didn't get to see Simone today and want to say good night."

"What's this about, Abby?" But he took the phone and dialed.

"I'll explain later."

I breathed a sigh of relief when Simone apparently answered and she and her uncle talked briefly before he wished her that good night.

When he disconnected, he said, "I've never done that before. She seemed . . . glad to hear from me. Now, please, what's going on?"

"I wanted to make sure she was safe—and she is," I said.

Cooper was already headed for the door and I grabbed my bag and was on his tail. "Kate, we'll call the two of you when we get this figured out."

"Um, okay . . . sure," I heard her say.

We took Cooper's truck and I gave him the general direction of McFarland's house. I was sure glad he didn't ask me how I knew.

Cooper said, "Is there evidence on the camera Ian took from his daughter?"

"I don't know. But he believed there might be. I'm

guessing he thought Simone caught him meeting with Dugan," I said.

"*That's* what you asked Simone about today—her pictures, about what she saw." Cooper was driving so fast I was holding on to the handle above the passenger door for dear life.

I said, "When Ian called his daughter after dinner, I'm betting she mentioned my visit to her earlier today."

Cooper steered with one hand and unclipped his cell phone from his belt. "And that's why McFarland took off in such a hurry." He flipped open the phone and pressed a speed dial number. "This is Boyd. I need you and the patrol car at Ian McFarland's house. And I need you *now*." He paused to listen, then said, "It's on the Richter property. Look it up on a damn map if you have to, Marshall." He closed the phone and looked at me. "I don't know how much more I can take of this job."

Those were probably the longest two miles I've ever gone. What had Ian done? What did he plan to do now? Finally we saw the house lights up ahead. Cooper killed the headlights and slowed his truck to a crawl. "I prefer surprises," he said.

"I'm not sure you could surprise anyone. This road is too noisy."

"Worth a try," he said.

The wide rectangle of light coming from McFarland's open garage door made the last few feet of our trip easy. We stopped right before a giant oleander bush—there was one on either side of the driveway. "Stay in the truck, Abby. Let me ask this guy a few serious questions first."

He reached across me, opened the glove compartment and took out his weapon. Something semiautomatic, but it was impossible to tell the make in the dark.

After he quietly left the truck, not bothering to fully close his door, I took my Lady Smith from my bag and slid across and out the driver's side.

I stayed hidden behind the oleander and saw Cooper with his weapon trained on the door inside the garage that led into the house. The Lexus in the garage had all the doors as well as the trunk open. From the looks of things, someone was taking a trip. And I was betting that someone wasn't coming back anytime soon. Cooper positioned himself beside the front passenger door, maybe eight feet from the entrance to the house.

When Ian McFarland came out into the garage with a box in both hands and saw who was there to greet him, he froze.

"Put down the box and place your hands on your head," Cooper said.

"What's this?" Ian said. "We're playing cops and robbers, are we?"

"Put down the box, Mr. McFarland," Cooper repeated.

"Or what? You'll shoot me?" And then suddenly, McFarland threw the box Cooper's way and whipped a pistol from his waistband. "Why don't I simply take care of this little problem myself?" He raised the gun to his temple.

I felt my stomach drop. I didn't want to witness a man murdering himself. I was sure Cooper didn't, either. I set my Lady Smith on the gravel and stepped out from behind the tall bush.

"Please don't do that," I said.

"Look who's joined the party. How many times have you seen a man make a bloody mess of his head? And I'm using the word *bloody* in the literal sense, by the way."

"Never saw anyone commit suicide. And I don't want to now," I said.

"Abby," Cooper said slowly, his eyes fixed on McFarland. "Get back in the truck."

No, he didn't know me very well, either.

"Brits aren't big on guns, are they, Ian?" I started walking toward him, my elbows bent, hands so he could see I held no weapon.

"Please, let me handle this," Cooper said in a strained whisper.

I kept my eyes on Ian. "I talked to Simone a long time today. Saw the photos all over her walls, the ones she'd taken. She's talented, Ian. And I'd say half of them were of you."

"That's why I hoped to leave without a word," he

said. "She doesn't need this disaster of a father in her life. Now I have to depart another way."

"And what's your thought process on that?" I said. "You kill yourself and leave us with unanswered questions—leave her devastated. You think she'll want to go off to school then? You think she'll want to pick up a camera when she finds out she might have driven you to this?"

From the corner of my eye, I saw Cooper inching closer to Ian.

"That's ridiculous. It's not her fault," McFarland said. "I was a fool. I had no idea Dugan would try to kill Jo-Lynn when I told him she was trying to con Elliott out of every penny she could get her hands on. Money that belongs to *my* daughter. Then Dugan comes round looking for her. The idiot. The stupid, stupid *idiot.*" The gun was wobbling in his hand now, not pressed against his skull.

"How did you find Kent Dugan?" I asked.

"Through JoLynn's cell phone, the one I nicked not long ago. She kept it hidden with a bag of old makeup under her sink. I charged it up and voilà—I had her history."

"If you do something stupid, Simone will blame herself for taking those pictures," Cooper said. "Kids always find a way to blame themselves."

Cooper and I were on the same page now. Meanwhile, he was getting closer by the second without Ian seeming to notice.

But the desperation I saw in Ian's eyes made my hands shake, made my mouth grow dry. But then he started to lower the pistol and I almost let out an audible sigh of relief.

And that's when we heard the siren of the approaching police car.

All hell broke loose.

Cooper dived at Ian and someone's gun went off—I didn't know whose because I ducked at the sound, my hands over my head.

Then I heard them scuffling and opened my eyes. They were rolling on the concrete as Cooper tried to restrain Ian.

I stood and hurried back to where I'd left the Lady Smith, cursing all the way. By then, the patrol car came to a screeching halt in front of the driveway. But I made it to Cooper and Ian first. Neither of them now held a gun—both weapons were swept aside during the struggle and lay five feet away.

I raised my .38 and shot into the garage ceiling.

The two men stopped moving. Nothing like a gunshot to get everyone's attention.

Then Marshall came rushing in, weapon drawn. "Drop your weapon, ma'am," he shouted.

Cooper, meanwhile, used my distraction to his advantage. Ian was pinned and very much under his control. "Not her, you dumbass," Cooper said to Marshall. "Cuff this one."

If I didn't laugh, I probably would have cried. So I laughed.

31

The police station in Pineview reminded me of JoLynn's latest hospital room. Small and smelly. Cooper and Kate didn't seem to mind sitting elbow to elbow behind his desk as we waited for DeShay and Chavez to drive from Houston and pick up Kent Dugan's killer. I sat in a corner on a molded plastic chair drinking a Diet Coke. Ian McFarland was in one of the two holding cells, being watched by Marshall. After all, he did threaten to kill himself an hour ago. Cooper decided to keep him here, rather than in the basement jail of the old courthouse near that town square, the courthouse I was *supposed* to have seen today.

Cooper complied with Ian's wish that his daughter not be called right away. Ian wanted to give his official confession to HPD first. But that didn't mean he wouldn't give us his *unofficial* confession, despite Cooper reading him his Miranda rights twice. No, Ian simply wouldn't shut up—that is, until Elliott Richter and the nerdiest lawyer on the planet arrived. If the attorney cinched his pants any higher, he'd strangle himself. Ian suddenly stopped giving us his version of events.

The nerd was the company lawyer—a stand-in until Richter could find his friend "the best defense attorney in Harris County." Richter actually shouted this out to Ian through the open door separating the office area from the holding-cell area. A suicide watch, Marshall had pointed out to Cooper, meant that the door must remain open.

I wondered if Richter's offer to get another lawyer would stand when he learned how his friend Ian uncovered JoLynn's past by stealing her phone and tracking Dugan down. I'm sure he had an easier search than Cooper and I. The Internet can find anyone with a number attached to their identity and Ian found out where Dugan lived thanks to that number. Then he researched Dugan thoroughly before talking to him, learned he ran an ID shop and put two and two together. That's how JoLynn inserted herself into their lives—by making fake documents.

At first, he thought Dugan was in on the scam, but Dugan apparently didn't believe a word Ian said—until Ian showed him the photos his daughter discarded in the trash when she'd been visiting over at Ian's place.

"All I wanted was for Dugan to come and get his girlfriend, blackmail her into leaving by threatening to expose her to Elliott," Ian had said while Marshall used the first-aid kit to clean abrasions on Ian's face. Ian was sitting on the cot in the cell and we were all in the small area right outside. "That way," Ian went on, "Elliott would never know what I'd done, that I was the instigator. At least, that's the deal I made with Dugan. Paid him a pretty penny, too."

Instigator? I thought. *Has anyone ever used that word in a confession before?*

"What real harm was she doing at Magnolia Ranch?" Cooper asked—which I found a surprisingly sympathetic question for him. "I mean, there's plenty of money to go around. I believe JoLynn made your friend Elliott happy."

"Don't you agree that would have changed over time?" Ian said. "Money aside, I didn't want Elliott to get his heart broken. He's got a lousy ticker as it is."

I said, "She needed a home and he needed a granddaughter. She was a threat to your own daughter's inheritance. Maybe your own. Isn't that what worried you the most?"

"Absolutely not. I was protecting Elliott as well as Simone's inheritance. How was I to know Mr. Dugan would corrupt her automobile—I don't even quite understand what he did to the car, by the way. I suppose he was a psychopath bent on revenge and I had no way of knowing he was capable of murder."

"Actually," Kate said from her spot against the farthest wall from his cell, "the correct term is antisocial personality disorder."

"Thank you for correcting me, Dr. Rose. I will store that information to impress my future cell mates."

I said, "Maybe you didn't realize what a bad dude he was, but like our daddy would have said, 'You roll around with the hogs, you better expect to get muddy.'"

"I am certainly ashamed of what I did behind Elliott's back. But I never intended to kill that man. I met with him late Thursday evening hoping to terminate our relationship. I wanted nothing more to do with him after what he'd done—that murder attempt he was so proud of. But he grew hostile, wanted money to keep quiet, and when I drove off, he got in the way of my automobile."

That's when I started to wonder what the autopsy showed. Somehow, I doubted Dugan's death was an accident. Ian wanted us to believe that, though, wanted to sound noble and concerned, if only for his daughter and his friend. I also began to consider the possibility he never intended to harm himself. He'd been caught like a minnow in a bucket in that garage tonight. Maybe his repeated pronouncements of remorse along with his confessions were all for show.

I finished my Coke just as I heard the sound of a car. DeShay and Chavez must be here. I saw that Cooper rested his hand on Kate's back when the two of them stood, and smiled to myself. They probably had a very nice drive on the way up here and maybe an even nicer dinner. I wanted all the details on our ride home.

DeShay held the door for Chavez and said, "I hear you have someone who needs a ride back to the city." He looked at me. "You never stop working, do you, Abby girl?"

"Take him," Cooper said, "because I'm tired of listening to him yak."

Richter and the nerd backed up to give the new arrivals room, and Richter shot Cooper a look.

Cooper saw it and said, "Sorry if that bothers you, Mr. Richter. You're a very smart man, but you made a mistake with McFarland. Your friend is bad news."

Richter's face reddened, but he didn't argue.

"Can we go home now?" I asked DeShay.

Maria Chavez went in to get their prisoner and De-
Shay walked by, ready to help her.

"Sure. And we can give you a fast escort. We drove
up in a marked car and will go back to Houston with
lights, no siren."

I smiled. "Sounds good to me."

On the wonderfully fast ride home behind Chavez, the
speed demon, Kate wanted to talk about how I'd figured
things out. But I was afraid I'd let something slip about
JoLynn's biological family. I told her she knew everything I did, that maybe I'd gotten lucky on this one using
a little guesswork. She didn't need to hear the details
of what happened in McFarland's garage, either. So I
questioned her about her time spent with Cooper and
she was happy to share. This was the old Kate and I
couldn't be happier to see her revived.

Jeff was waiting for me after I dropped off Kate at
her house. I'd called him from Pineview PD and though
I didn't share everything then because I wasn't exactly
in a private place, DeShay apparently filled him in during his drive to Pineview to pick up McFarland.

"Doris upstairs?" I said, after he gave me a wonderful
hug—a hug far different from the one I'd experienced
in the arms of Ponytail Nick. And again, I was reminded
of my promise. I hadn't realized that promise might
mean giving up a small part of myself—a portion of the
complete openness Jeff and I shared. This was information I could never share with a cop, not one as dedicated
as Jeff was to bringing in criminals. And JoLynn's family
had broken the law.

"Doris is spending the night with Loreen," he said. "I
thought you could use a massage after the day you've
had. Come on."

He took me by the hand and led me up the stairs.
When he opened the bedroom door, my hand went to
my mouth. "What have you done?"

The room was lit with candles, and vases of yellow
roses sat on the tables, the dressers and my small vanity.

"I know I'm not the big romantic type, but you were
gone all day and when I found out what went down,

how you stared down that turd without your weapon, I got a sick feeling right here." He touched his belt. "If I ever lost you . . ."

I put a finger to his lips. "That's not happening."

Then he asked me a question I didn't want to answer, because I didn't want to lie. "Did Dugan hire that jerk to tackle you in the parking garage?"

"Probably, but with Dugan dead, we may never know. The fake security guard might have been Dugan's pal, too."

"That makes sense, but I—"

"No more talking. I heard someone up here was giving away massages."

32

Turned out, JoLynn Richter went home to Magnolia
Ranch without even making the transfer to Methodist
Hospital. She was transported by ambulance with Maxine
by her side on Tuesday, two days after Ian McFarland's
arrest. Just hours later, Ian was out on bail after being
indicted for second-degree murder. Seems the preliminary
autopsy results indicated Kent Dugan had been run over
by a car at least twice, probably more. Some *accident*.

I was busy writing up my case report for Elliott Richter late that afternoon when he called me. "I was wrong,
Abby, and I've apologized to Chief Boyd as well. I
wanted you to know I've decided not to assist Ian in his
defense. I simply cannot support him, not after what he
did. In some twisted way, I suppose he thought he was
protecting me. At any rate, I shouldn't have behaved
the way I did in that police station."

"You believed in your friend. That's not a bad thing.
But he has money of his own, right?" I stroked Diva,
who was purring on my lap as I sat in my office chair.

"Plenty. Simone doesn't know I've refused to help
him and I've convinced Adele not to tell her. At least
not now. I understand he's hired a high-priced attorney."
Richter sighed. "You know what that means."

"Bad-guy victim and high-priced defense attorney? I
smell acquittal. But that won't happen for at least a
year," I said. "How *is* Simone handling this?"

"She doesn't know he found her pictures and stole
her camera. That may come out in the trial. Maybe he'll
tell her himself now that he's free. I've instructed him

to clear off my property, though. I don't want him any-where near JoLynn."

"I don't think he meant for her to get hurt," I said. "He was . . . jealous on several levels. Wanted her gone. At least that's my take."

Richter was silent for several seconds. "Jealous? I never thought of it that way."

"He was your friend, closer to you than any of your family. Until JoLynn showed up."

"You are a very smart young woman. And another smart young woman in my family will be headed for school, despite being devastated by her father's arrest. I've convinced Adele to soften her approach with Si-mone, support the girl's dream rather than beat her down," he said.

"Good for you. Simone is very special. And how's JoLynn?"

"Making amazing progress. The young are so resilient. We have the physical therapists coming every day. But Ms. Norman's days are numbered. I'm working on pa-tience and acceptance, but she's trying me, Abby. And she's chased Estelle off. That young woman was the hardest worker I think I've ever had."

You have no idea, I thought. He then gave me an open invitation to the ranch and I told him to expect me often, especially when Otto was cooking pork roast.

Not long after I hung up, my doorbell rang and to my surprise, I saw Cooper Boyd on my security monitor. He was wearing street clothes, which seemed odd if he was in town to talk over the case with DeShay and Chavez.

After I let him in, I opened my arms for a hug. "I don't think I got to thank you for being such a great partner."

"I'm the one who should be thanking you. You fig-ured out Ian stole his daughter's camera, not to mention that he confiscated those pictures and told Kent Dugan JoLynn was at Magnolia Ranch."

"You ever need someone to interview eighteen-year-old girls, I guess I'm your woman. I feel bad for Simone, though. Her father was the typical good-guy parent as opposed to her bad-guy mom. She adores Ian."

"Maybe she'll adore him less when she realizes exactly what he did."

"You mean when she has all the facts? Facts are important to you, Cooper Boyd," I said with a wry grin.

"Cut me some slack, Abby. I'm newly unemployed."

"What are you talking about?" I said.

"I quit. I'll go back to help my successor, but today I'm in town to hunt for an apartment. I've had no luck with the classifieds and decided I needed your help again. Got any ideas where I should start looking?"

"I have a former client who's a Realtor. Her name is Emma Lopez and I'd love to see her again. But you're skipping past the important part. Why did you quit?"

"I gave small-town police work my best shot, but this case? I realized I'm not done working the bigger crimes. I've been offered reinstatement in the Houston FBI office. They didn't want me to leave DC in the first place, but . . . never mind. Let's save my history for another time."

"Sure. Come into my office and I'll look up Emma's number," I said.

He took out his cell phone and flipped it open. "While you're at it, I'd like to add Kate's number to my address book. I sort of forgot to get that important piece of information."

I rattled it off, thinking that this day had gone very well.

Epilogue

Kate and I visited JoLynn several times in the months following her return to Magnolia Ranch as did her good friend Roberta Messing. Maxine was gone after a few weeks and so were the therapists that her surrogate grandfather had hired. Knowing what Ian McFarland might say in court when his day came, Elliott Richter explained to his family that JoLynn was mistaken about Katarina, though she sincerely believed she was related to the Richters when she made the false ID. I was guessing they'd been reassured their piece of the pie wouldn't be affected by her mistake, because they all seemed a lot more friendly to her. And I also got the feeling Scott Morton was absolutely tickled the two of them weren't blood relations.

Once JoLynn was nearly recovered—a few memory problems lingered, but that's all—I called and asked her if she'd do me a favor and take a little trip into the city with me. There was someone I wanted her to meet. She agreed and when I arrived at Magnolia Ranch, she looked better than ever. There was only a faint scar on her forehead and she seemed truly happy.

I didn't tell her where we were going, just said it was a surprise. JoLynn felt very connected to Kate and so that's where our conversation turned on the two-hour drive.

JoLynn stretched out her legs and settled back. "Kate's got a new guy, doesn't she?"

"What makes you say that?" I said.

"Every time we talk, even though she's all about helping me heal emotionally and all that stuff, she seems, well, happier than when we first met."

"I have to agree," I said, setting the cruise control.

"And it's a guy, right?"

"Being twenty, you'd think like that. But you're right, it is a guy."

"I'm twenty-one now," she said. "Come on. Tell me, Abby."

"You remember Chief Boyd?"

"Of course. He quit right after I got home from the hospital. I thought having to find out all my secrets, all about Kent and Ian and the wreck, made him tired. I mean, he's old."

I laughed out loud. "He's in his forties, JoLynn."

"That's old. Are you saying Kate's with him?"

"They're dating," I said.

"See? You said *dating*. That's an old word."

"Then I'm old, too," I said.

"I hope Cooper's cool. I made a huge mistake hooking up with Kent and won't be that stupid again. Kate deserves a great guy. She's beautiful and so, so smart. One thing she told me has really stuck. She said, 'When we know better, we do better.' "

"Sounds like Kate," I said.

The rest of the drive I quizzed her about the Richters and how she was getting along. I was surprised to learn she felt sad when Simone went off to school. They'd become friends. Then JoLynn said she was looking forward to getting her GED so she could go on to college, too.

When we pulled in front of Shauna Anthony's house, JoLynn still had no idea why we were here. Like Cooper once said, there is something to be said for the element of surprise.

The visit was no surprise to Shauna, however, and the iced tea and shortbread cookies were again laid out.

Once we were all sitting down with our tea and our cookies, Oliver close to his mistress as usual, I said, "Do you remember this lady, JoLynn?"

"I—I don't think so." She squinted at Shauna.

"Well, I remember you," Shauna said. "You were about this high." She held her hand three feet off the ground. "And you were scared to death."

JoLynn covered her mouth, eyes wide. "Oh my God. You're the police lady."

"I am so thrilled to see you all grown-up, young lady. I'm sorry no one ever adopted you. I should have taken you in myself."

JoLynn smiled. "Someone's adopting me now. Mr. Richter's started the legal process to make me his daughter."

"That's the best news I've had since I woke up and found out I was still alive this morning," Shauna said.

JoLynn didn't seem to know whether to laugh at this joke, so I took the lead and said, "I'm stealing that line, Shauna."

"Tell me this. Do you remember what happened that night?" Shauna said. "It sure has troubled me all these years."

JoLynn didn't even blink. "The shrinks in foster care said I blocked it all out. I don't remember—though the longer I sit here, the more I remember how nice you were to me. You bought me a candy bar—a 3 Musketeers."

Shauna's tired eyes brightened. "That's exactly right. Isn't that odd you remember something so small and yet you blocked out the big things—like who left you there at the bus station."

"Let me tell you, that candy bar was the best thing that happened to me in a long time, Officer Anthony. I never forgot how good it tasted and no candy bar has ever tasted that good since."

I watched them interact, feeling good, but I was looking for something else, some kind of recollection on Jo-Lynn's part. Did she recall why she'd been left there that night? Or was she telling the truth, that she'd blocked it all out?

A half hour later we left, both of us with cookie-filled Baggies. We were spending the night in Houston and I planned on taking her out to dinner with Jeff, Kate and Cooper so we could celebrate JoLynn's return to good health.

But on the way to my house I couldn't keep quiet another minute.

I said, "Your father loves you very much. I hope you'll always remember that."

JoLynn's head turned sharply in my direction. "Are you talking about my new father?"

"No. You could fool Shauna and everyone else with your faulty-memory story, but not me."

I looked at her from the corner of my eye. She seemed terrified.

"Your secret is safe," I said. "You need to know there are angels on your shoulder. Tiny, invisible versions of the angels at Glenwood Cemetery."

"What do you know about me, Abby? Who have you talked to?"

I regretted saying anything now. I couldn't tell her I'd spoken with her biological family. "Let's just say I have this feeling you remember what happened before you were dropped off at that bus station."

"I can't talk about that. Not even to you," she said.

"I understand. Answer me this, though. Why did you go to the cemetery every week?"

"Because after I learned the Richter story, I wanted to be loved as much as Katarina was. If I was close to her every week, maybe I could become what she was—someone's beloved child."

"You are that, JoLynn. You are that."

I saw a tear slip down her cheek and I reached over and squeezed her hand. "I'm not a big believer in secrets. Mostly because my job is to uncover them. But don't be afraid. I've been trusted with one secret I'll take to my grave."

My cat is allergic to people. When I heard Chablis sneeze as I came in the back door, I stopped and held my breath. Something wasn't right. Since I use special shampoo, she does not react to me.

I'd been on an overnight business trip to Greenville-Spartanburg and felt guilty about leaving my three kitties. The sneezing sounds only made the guilt worse. What had gone on while I was away? How did human dander—I mean *dandruff*—find its way up poor Chablis's nose?

But there could be a simple and logical explanation other than allergies for a sneezing cat. Like an illness. Oh gosh, she's sick. That's it.

I released my grip on the rolling suitcase, the thought of Chablis being ill pushing logic down to the hippocampus or wherever common sense goes when you have more important matters to attend to.

I dropped my tote bag on the counter and started toward the dining room—my kitchen, dining area and living room all blend together—but before I'd taken five steps, I stopped. Something else besides a sneezing cat now had my attention.

No background noise. No *Animal Planet* playing on the television. I always leave the TV tuned to that station when I go away. If the cats are entertained by *The Jeff Corwin*

Experience or *Heroes* or *E-Vet*, I believe my absences are far more tolerable. Okay, I'm neurotic when it comes to my cats. Not cat-lady neurotic. I'm about forty years too young for that, but still a little crazy when it comes to them. They have been, after all, my best friends since my husband's death.

Think, Jillian. What could no TV mean?

Though Chablis, Syrah and Merlot are brilliant, could any of them turn off the television?

Don't be ridiculous. Even you *have trouble figuring out how to use the remote.*

Okay. Maybe there was a power failure.

I glanced behind me at the microwave. The clock showed the correct time: one p.m. Did the new high-def plasma TV blow up in a cloud of electronic bits and pieces? Maybe. Didn't matter, though. Not now. None of my cats had shown their faces and that's all I could think about.

"Merlot, I'm home," I called as I passed the dining room table and went into the living area. "Syrah, where are you? Chablis, I missed you."

I let out a sigh of relief when I saw Chablis sitting on the chenille sofa, her blue eyes trained on my face. But her seal-point champagne fur seemed awfully puffed out, even for a Himalayan. Was she totally swollen up by an allergen other than dandruff? Something like fish? Oh my gosh! Wouldn't that be a bummer for a cat?

I knelt near her and stroked the side of her cheek with the back of my fingers. Then I ran my hands over her body, looking for the mass of giant hives I was sure I'd find.

Nothing. She was all bloated hair and giant purrs—nothing more. "I am truly sorry for leaving you alone overnight, Chablis. Is this a case of feline nerves?"

Chablis blinked slowly, opened her mouth and squeaked. How pitiful. She'd lost her voice. Yes, she was sick all right. A virus? Maybe leukemia? Cats do get leukemia.

Stop it, Jillian. Call the vet. That's what you should do.

Then I heard Merlot's deep, loud meow. He sat on window-seat cushions that offered him a spectacular view. This was his favorite spot, a place where he spent hours imagining exactly what sort of fish resided beneath the blue waters of his very own South Carolina lake. Yes, he knows the entire lake belongs to him, despite never being closer than the window.

But he wasn't gazing out on the lake; he was looking right at me and his fur was all wild and big, too.

Oh my gosh. They're both scared. That's it. Very, very scared.

And then I saw why. Broken glass glittered near Merlot's paws—paws that could each substitute for a Swiffer duster.

My heart skipped. Broken glass . . . yes, a broken *window.* "Merlot! Be careful." Panic escaped with my words and I ran over to him. I petted his broad, beautiful head, then made sure none of his paws was bleeding. He seemed fine other than his electric-socket hairdo. He reminded me of those huge shaggy stuffed animals at a carnival.

I hefted him off the cushions—he weighs in at twenty pounds—hoping to keep him clear of the glass, but he was having none of that. He jumped right back up and was amazingly nimble at staying away from any shards. While I examined the damage, he intently examined me as if to ask, "What are you going to do about this, my overnight traveler?"

The jagged hole was in the lowest pane—a hole only large enough for a hand to reach in and unlatch the window. And it *was* unlatched.

"Someone was here, weren't they, Merlot? That's what you're trying to tell me." God, how I wished he could talk.

The thought of a stranger breaking in to my house and frightening my cats made me angry. I felt heat in my earlobes, a warmth that promptly spread down my neck to my chest. Irish skin never lies. But before I let my emotions run rampant, I inhaled deeply, let the air out slowly. I'd had plenty of practice taking calming breaths since John died.

Assess the situation, Jillian. That's what John would do if he were here.

I felt soothed just thinking about John and then realized Syrah had not made an appearance. Syrah and John had been very close but that didn't mean John's favorite cat wouldn't come running at the sound of my voice. Between the silent TV, the scared animals and the absent Syrah, anger gave way to a tinge of fear.

"Where are you, baby?" I called. "Come here, Syrah."

He probably got locked in a bedroom or the basement after someone came in the window and searched the house. Yes. And this thief obviously had dandruff.

I ran for the hallway leading to the bedrooms, Merlot on my heels. Chablis was too busy sneezing to follow. I made a frantic hunt through all three thousand square feet of my house, the house that was supposed to be our dream home, the one John and I had built on Lake Greenwood. But this was no longer a dream come true. John, at fifty-six, had been twenty years older than me, but still far too young to die of a heart attack. How quickly dreams turn to nightmares.

As I ran from room to room, I found no closed doors, no Syrah hiding behind an armoire or dresser or under any beds. He wasn't in the closets or the basement, either.

I went outside to check the trees and the roof for a frightened cat. The intruder might have let him out when he made his escape. But the leaves had been falling for weeks and spotting his deep gold Abyssinian fur against the reds and yellows of the oak, hickory and pecan trees in my yard proved difficult. But Syrah is a vocal cat and I didn't hear any shuffle of leaves or meowing in response to my calls. He wasn't there.

Merlot was sitting by the door waiting when I came back inside. He didn't take his gaze off me. I took my cell from my pocket, ready to report the break-in. Merlot began purring—you can't miss his meows or his purrs—and I wondered if he was trying to comfort himself or me. Maybe both.

"What is your emergency?" a calm woman said after I called 911.

"Um . . . um . . . my cat is missing." I walked back to the living room and picked up the remote.

The dispatcher said, "Ma'am, this line is for true—"

"I've had a break-in. There's a broken window and—"

"Your name, ma'am?"

"Jillian Hart. I live at 301 Harbor Drive in Oakville." I hit the MUTE button before I tried the TV. Having DVR is nice since you can kill the sound before you turn on the TV. Mr. Sony Plasma worked just fine, though—tuned to *Animal Planet* as it should be. I pressed the OFF button.

"Ma'am? Are you there, ma'am?"

"Yes. Sorry."

"I see this is a cellular number, but are you calling from the home?"

"Of course. My cat is gone and—"

"Officers are already on their way. Do you feel safe or do you believe the intruder might still be there?" Her South Carolina drawl was breaking through her calm now.

"I've searched the house. No one's here but me and my two babies."

"Do you fear for your safety?"

"I fear for my *cat's* safety and—" Tears sprung unexpectedly and I bit my lip.

"Ma'am, is something wrong?"

"Yes. It's just that . . . I don't know where he is. I can't find him." I sounded absolutely pathetic. Syrah was a cat, not a gone-forever husband whom I'd loved with all my heart. But still, that cat was my friend. I was worried sick.

"I understand your concern. May I call you Jillian?"

"Yes, of course."

"How old are your babies, Jillian?"

"Chablis is five and Merlot is eight. They're fine. Well, not exactly fine because Chablis is having an allergic reaction and—"

"Should we send an ambulance?" Her sweet composed tone was now laced with concern.

I heard a distant siren. "I have medicine. She'll be okay in an hour or two. I just haven't had time to give her an antihistamine."

"Where are your children, Jillian? I don't hear them but I assume they're with you?"

"Oh. You're confused. Chablis and Merlot are my two other cats."

"I see." Sweetness and concern had now left the building. She couldn't have sounded any colder if she were standing in a blizzard in North Dakota.

I stayed on the line as instructed—I was "ma'am" again—but I no longer felt the love from Ms. Dispatcher. She only offered an occasional, "Are you still there?"

Meanwhile, my panic worsened as I waited for the police. Possibilities ran through my head. The person who broke in obviously let Syrah out. My beautiful, wonderful cat could be lying dead by the road after being hit by a car. He could have fallen off the dock into the lake and drowned. He could have— *No. Stop this.*

I decided to do something constructive rather than conjure up worst-case scenarios. To make sure my other two cats wouldn't run out the door if they got the chance, I put my cell on speaker and set it on the coffee table, then dragged their travel carriers from the foyer closet. For once, crating them wasn't like trying to bag smoke. They were compliant. Yes, they were still scared.

I left them in the living room, not wanting them out of my sight. I dreaded the arrival of sirens and uniformed strangers. This would only add to their fear.

It didn't take long for the cops to show up. Five minutes later, I heard the cruiser's engine and the dispatcher quickly disconnected when I told her they were here. Oakville is a small town—teensy compared to Houston, where I'd lived with John prior to moving here. No problem getting anywhere in five or ten minutes in Oakville. I ran to the foyer and answered before they could even knock.

I was sure glad I'd put Merlot and Chablis in their carriers because, as expected, they freaked out and started up with a cat duet suited best for an opera: loud, mournful and tragic.

Two officers stood on the porch and one of them said, "Deputy Morris Ebeling. Are you Jillian Hart?"

"Yes. Come in." I stepped back to give them room.

"Deputy Candace Carson," the other one said as they came inside.

She looked to be in her twenties and Morris had to be about sixty, his face puffy and pasty. His stomach hung over his equipment-laden uniform belt, his gut reminding me of a sack of potatoes under his brown shirt.

I led them into the living room and Candace immediately went to the carriers, knelt and murmured to Merlot and Chablis in a comforting voice. They quieted at once. She was an animal lover, thank goodness.

"What exactly happened here, ma'am?" Morris said.

"I don't know," I answered. "I was on an overnight business trip and came home to find a broken window. And my other cat is missing."

"Anything else gone?" Morris said.

"Nothing that I could tell. But who cares?"

"Um . . . sure. Right," Morris said. "Who cares?"

The sarcasm wasn't lost on me, but his attitude didn't bother me. I wanted my cat back and if he could help, even unwillingly help, I was grateful.

Candace rose after one last "It'll be okay, baby" to Chablis. She said, "May I search the premises, Ms. Hart?"

Shiny French-braided blond hair was coiled at the nape of Candace's neck. It made me wish I had long hair again. Her eyes were as blue and intense as Chablis's, which I found comforting in a way.

"You might want to start there." I pointed out the broken glass on the window-seat cushion.

"I'd like to search from the bottom up if you don't mind. The basement stairs?"

"I've already looked everywhere," I said. "If Syrah were here, I would have found him."

"You looked everywhere? Then we've got a contaminated crime scene." Candace looked like a kid on the playground who'd had her lunch money grabbed by a bully.

Morris raised his eyes to the ceiling. "Not this again. A damn cat is missing, Candy. Did you hear the lady say anything about missing valuables? Her TV and stereo are right here."

"But—" Candace started.

"Bet this was just some kid workin' on a dare." Morris took a tin of Skoal from his pocket.

"My name is *Candace*," she answered through clenched teeth. "You ever consider that this lady is so distressed about her missing cat that she might not realize valuables are gone?"

"Oh, for criminy sake. Then puh-leese, go find every piece of lint you can, *Candy*." Morris pinched some tobacco and mashed it between his lower teeth and gums.

Candace's cheeks colored, but she took a pair of latex gloves from her pocket and put them on. "That's exactly what I intend to do, Morris. Or is it 'Snookems'? That's what your wife calls you, right?"

Morris colored but said nothing.

"The basement, Ms. Hart?" Candace said.

I pointed to the kitchen. "Through there. You'll see the door to the stairs."

Morris was shifting his weight from one foot to the other. Seemed to me like he wanted back in his police cruiser as quickly as he could manage it.

He said, "I need to start the paperwork, Ms. Hart. Excuse me for a moment." He went out the front door and took his sweet time before coming back with a clipboard. In the meantime, I'd filled a dropper with Benadryl, unzipped the top of Chablis's carrier and given her a dose. Poor baby's nose was running like a faucet.

Morris sat on the reclining wing chair adjacent to the sofa, and I was surprised how his sitting in that spot jolted me. The leather chair had belonged to John, and no one had touched it since his death.

It's okay, Jillian. It's only a chair.

But anxiety mixed with grief made my stomach knot up. I would have preferred to pace off this unwelcome emotion, but instead I sat on the edge of the sofa. Merlot and Chablis were already worried about their friend Syrah. They needed me to at least act like I was in control.

"You live alone, ma'am?" Morris said.

"No, sir. I live with my three cats." Maybe I could make him understand through some sarcasm of my own that cats are as important as people.

But he didn't bother to write their names down, though he did stare at me, one bushy gray eyebrow raised. "No gentleman residing here with you? Because I heard tell you was married."

"You *heard tell*?"

"No secrets in Oakville, Ms. Hart."

"Apparently there is, because my husband died unexpectedly not long after we moved here."

His forehead wrinkled in confusion, as if to say, "Why didn't I know this?" Then he said, "Sorry to hear that. Sorry indeed." He sounded like he actually meant it. Maybe he wasn't a mean old coot after all.

Candace returned to the living room, and without saying a word, focused first on the window and then on the glass still lying undisturbed on the cushions. At least I'd done something right.

She took out her phone and snapped a few pictures before removing a folded brown paper bag from her uniform pocket.

"Candy, what the hell you think you're doing, girl?" Morris said.

"It's *Candace*. I am collecting evidence." She carefully picked up the pieces of glass and put them in her bag.

" 'Cause a cat ran off? Now I know you take your job real serious, and I try my best to respect that, but I'm thinking the county crime lab won't be happy about this particular evidence."

Candace said, "Someone invaded this kind lady's precious home, so I disagree."

Morris sighed heavily. "For my report, exactly when did this happen, Ms. Hart?"

"I got in at one o'clock. Did I mention this . . . this *person* turned off my TV?"

"You left it on while you were gone?" Morris said.

"Yes . . . um, I like people to think I'm home when the cats are alone." For some reason I felt a little embarrassed about the true explanation. I added, "Obviously that tactic didn't work."

"Can I offer a piece of advice, Ms. Hart?" Morris said. "Get yourself a nice state-of-the-art alarm system. We got a guy in town who does that stuff. Name's Howard. Howard Stewart. Nice fella and—"

"Did you *touch* the television when you came in, Ms. Hart?" Candace interrupted. She was on her knees by the window seat, staring intently at the cushions, her tweezers poised and ready to collect more evidence.

"I touched the remote," I said. "I thought maybe the TV wasn't working."

"Damn," Candace muttered, getting to her feet. "More of the crime scene compromised. Okay, we might still get prints off the remote and maybe even off the TV. Yeah. Maybe the perp shut off the television using the monitor buttons."

"The *perp*?" Both of Morris's eyebrows were working now. "We don't have 'perps' in Oakville. We got stupid-ass drunks and outta-control kids who should eat dinner with their mama and their daddy more often. This is about a broken window, Candy."

"And you have no idea when this break-in occurred?" Candace continued, seemingly unflustered by her partner's lack of interest in what had gone on in my house.

But I sure appreciated her interest. "I left yesterday afternoon for a quilt show in Spartanburg. I make and sell fancy quilts for cats."

"Figures," Morris said under his breath.

I shot him a look. "I also make quilts that I donate for the children of men and women killed in Iraq. I had a meeting with a charitable group in Greenville this morning, gave them pictures of my designs and took their order for a hundred children's quilts. Anyway, I left here yesterday around eight in the morning and I've told you when I returned."

"You mind if I dust your TV and remote?" Candace said. "I'd also like to see if I could lift prints off the window latch and the outside molding."

Morris rose, his face no longer pasty. Florid seemed an apt description. "I don't think so, Candy. I still have seniority, and we'll be leaving." He gave me what was obviously a forced smile. "You catch sight of any teenage boys lurkin' around or peekin' in your windows, you give us a call. And Billy Cranor can fix that window for you. He owns the hardware store."

Morris turned and marched toward the foyer, waving a hand for Candace to follow.

But before she left, she took my elbow, leaned close and whispered, "I'll be back when my shift is over. See, I've got my own fingerprint kit. This bad guy's not getting away with this. Not on my watch."

They left and I didn't know whether to laugh or cry. *What a pair,* I thought as I let Chablis and Merlot out of their carriers. They both started to run for the hallway, but then stopped and looked back at me.

"Come on, you two. We have flyers to make about our lost Syrah."

As soon as I said the word "lost," tears began streaming down my cheeks. I walked to my office, Merlot and a wobbly, sleepy Chablis right with me.

It was only after I'd printed out a hundred pages with Syrah's best picture prominent in the center, only after I'd stopped feeling sorry for myself, that I realized I'd never told Candace about Chablis's human allergy.

Our perp suffered from dandruff. And he or she obviously had never heard of Head & Shoulders.